The Dim Sum of All Things

The Dim Sum of All Things

Kim Wong Keltner

AVON
TRADE

An Imprint of HarperCollins*Publishers*

HarperCollins books may be purchased for education, business, or sales promotional use. For information please write: Special Markets Department, HarperCollins Publishers Inc., 10 East 53rd Street, New York, NY 10022.

FIRST EDITION

Designed by Elizabeth M. Glover

Library of Congress Cataloging-in-Publication Data

Keltner, Kim Wong.
   The dim sum of all things : a novel/by Kim Wong Keltner.
      p. cm.
ISBN 0-06-056075-4
1. Chinese American women—Fiction. 2. San Francisco (Calif.)—Fiction.
3. Interracial dating—Fiction. I. Title.

PS3611.E48D56 2003
813'.6—dc22   2003057892

08   JTC/RRD   10   9   8   7

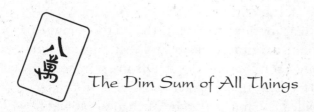

The Dim Sum of All Things

Many strange tales have been told about sassy receptionists and their antics in the urban wild, but none so strange as the story of Miss Lindsey Owyang, a Chinese-American wage-slave who turned twenty-five last summer.

Lindsey was a fairly clever receptionist, but she was more than just a worker bee who had mastered the intricacies of voice mail and fax dialing. She was a third-generation San Franciscan of Chinese descent who could not quote a single Han Dynasty proverb, but she could recite entire dialogues from numerous *Brady Bunch* episodes. She knew nothing of Confucius and did not speak any Cantonese or Mandarin, but she had spent years studying the Western Canon and had learned to conjugate irregular French verbs. All that reading of European literature did her a heap of good now. When she graduated from college, prospective employers didn't care about her mastery of iambic pentameter; they just wanted her to answer the telephone and type with robotic efficiency.

She considered herself lucky to have landed her job at

Vegan Warrior magazine. The publication was a style resource for the vegetarian community, and most articles featured organic food, hemp fashions, astrology, and eco-travel. In their mission statement, the editors bragged of their firm commitment to equality and social justice, but their philosophy didn't prevent them from summoning Lindsey to perform all their menial tasks. Each morning, she mopped spilled rice milk from the kitchen floor, and in the afternoons she was dispatched to retrieve soy lattes.

She and a few other closet meat-eaters had infiltrated the staff of smug Limoges-liberals who drank cruelty-free decaf. As the majority of employees stomped through the office in Birkenstocks and Chi Pants, Lindsey was an outcast because she wore makeup and owned one vintage sweater with a modest rabbit fur collar. Coworkers regarded her with suspicion, but she was happy enough to keep to herself.

When the phones weren't busy, she deionized the drinking water and scoured the tofu cheese from the inside of the microwave. While performing her various housekeeping duties she had time to ruminate on the philosophies of the various dead white men she had studied in college. However, as a modern Chinese-American woman, her worldview was quite different from theirs.

One day, as she unclogged a bloated gardenburger from the sink drain, she was pondering the existence of certain white males who were obsessed with Asian women. She called these men the Hoarders of All Things Asian, or just Hoarders, for short. These shy, Caucasian beta-males, with dirty blond hair and sallow complexions, moseyed through the world, blending effortlessly into the general population. But Lindsey had learned to spot them. Over the past few months she had been noticing that she attracted numerous stares from these nerdy white guys wearing tan jeans and vanilla-hued cardigans, and she deduced that their clothes were meant as some kind of urban camouflage. Their gray pallor, mixed with beige wardrobes, combined to create an overall "greige" appearance. And when they tried to pick up on her, saying garbled things like "Konichiwa, Chinese princess," she assumed they had bland, taupe personalities to match.

She had a theory that these neat'n'tidy nerds were disguised as "good guys" but were actually stealthy predators who feigned interest in Asian cuisine, history, and customs in hopes of attracting an exotic porcelain doll like those portrayed so fetchingly in pop culture movies and advertisements. These Hoarders of All Things Asian sought the erotic, hassle-free companionship they believed to be the specialty of lily-footed celestials, geishas, fan-tan dancers, and singsong girlies. They were unable to distinguish these fantasy ideals from modern women, and, like fishermen in sampans, tended to cast their nets toward any vaguely Asian-looking female, expecting to be lavished with the mysterious, untold delights of the Orient.

These creepy men frequently approached Lindsey at coffeehouses, on park benches, and in bookstores. She sometimes spotted one cruising Clement Street, or dining alone in a Chinese restaurant, or clinging to a ticket stub from the Pacific Rim film festival with clammy, froglike fingers. They trawled the land in search of Asian flesh, and she was sickened by the idea of being targeted as some kind of exotic sex toy.

She felt like she had discovered a new comet, and she monitored the night sky for potential dating dangers. She was convinced that, if Dante had been Chinese, he would have designated a specific circle of hell for the worst of these loathsome trolls. She liked to think of these fetishists cast into the Underworld, confined in a criblike pen where they could not escape to molest her. She wanted them corralled into a muddy pit, where they would remain, wallowing in miserable, Woodstock-like conditions for all eternity.

Although Lindsey was admittedly attracted to white boys, she shrewdly eliminated romantic candidates who exhibited any Hoarder tendencies. She hated the idea of some pervert zoning in on her because of her black hair, almond-shaped eyes, or any of the submissive, back-scrubbing fantasies her physical features might suggest to a large, clumsy mammal in tube socks.

Her wariness stemmed from the fact that she had convinced herself that her Chinese heritage was not one of the main components of her identity but was simply a superfluous detail. As far as she was concerned, her *Chinese-ness* was not the first thing someone should notice about her.

Walking home from work one day, she stopped at the video store to browse. As she perused the biography section with tapes about Mark Twain, Ernest Hemingway and Virginia Woolf, her mind drifted. She had always had romantic notions about becoming a famous author, but she often wondered if writers all had big fat butts and sat around in sweatpants all day. They all died depressed, crazy, and poverty-stricken. And that certainly wasn't what she wanted. Also, the writers who called her office were always so irritable and condescending, as if they ruled the world from stylish and lofty "home offices." She figured they were just sitting in studio apartments, wearing coffee-stained pajamas and smelling of buttered toast.

Her daydreaming was interrupted by a gruff voice. "What do you mean, you don't have *Hackers*?"

She instinctively crouched down behind the nearest partition. Behind a row of suntanned butts with "wild" airbrushed across the fleshy cracks, she knelt and hid. She hid because she recognized the man's voice, and his name. When he grumbled, "I'm Miles Olin. Call me when *Hackers* gets returned," she was certain he called her office at least twice a day. He was one of the magazine's writers, and yes, she was right about the coffee stains. Instead of pajamas, he wore a crummy brown jogging suit.

If ever there was a name that had Hoarder written all over it, it was Miles. There was no method to her determinations, but at some point, she had included it in her mental pantheon of all-time popular Hoarder names, which also included Gordon, Dennis, Doug, Jim, Don, and finally, Steve. (The last one, she admitted, was perhaps a contender only as a fluke, seeing as how so many guys were named Steve nowadays.)

After the writer left the store and lumbered from sight, Lindsey popped a stick of gum in her mouth and decided against getting a video.

"That guy's an asshole," the clerk said as she passed the front counter.

"Yeah," she replied, "some people are."

Resuming her walk home, she passed the stationery store that sold Hello Kitty stuff. She was mortified by her secret love for Kitty, Mimmy, Chococat, and Keroppi. It was all so stereotypical, so tragically Asian of her to adore the fuzzy, mouthless, big-eyed baby animals.

In grade school, she had once descended on this very store for a brief shoplifting pick-me-up. As her white friends loaded up their jumpers with Little Twin Star erasers, Snoopy mini colored pencils, and Hello Kitty key-chains, Lindsey walked out with a gluestick, fearing that any Sanrio product would associate her with the immigrant outcasts who snacked on Pocky sticks at recess. She never let her grandmother, Pau Pau, put anything Chinese in her Bugs Bunny lunchbox. No rice, no *cha-siu baus*. She felt that only sandwiches with Safeway cold cuts were accept-able lunchtime fare.

At one point, she even told people she didn't like Chi-nese food. Nope, didn't like it at all. Would rather have pizza. Of course, it was all some kind of preteen sham. She always ate Chinese food with Pau Pau, and not just chow mein or sweet-and-sour pork. No, Pau Pau prepared the hardcore *what-the-hell-is-that* kind of Chinese food: organ meats and unrecognizable fish parts that had been sliced to bits with a cleaver as long as a human arm earlier that morning in Chinatown. "Fresh," her grandmother insisted.

For Lindsey, the description and details of real Chinese food—real Chinese *anything*—were too complicated to begin explaining to white people. Of course, not that any-one ever asked. Maybe they didn't want to seem too curi-ous or too objectifying. White guilt was like smog in the Bay Area, like filthy puffs of charcoal gray exhaust blasting out of Muni buses and impregnating the city air, hanging around the horizon like a ring of oven grease, but perhaps, at times, contributing to prettier sunsets.

As she walked, thoughts of grammar school and her younger self still lingered in her head. She recalled how much she hated her name back then. She felt her first name made her sound like a British missionary's neglected child dying of consumption, and her last name made her sound so, uh, Chinese. She wanted an ordinary name, and not just a plain one like Wong or Chan, although those might be a slight improvement over *Owyang*, which sounded so ugly in the mouth—loud and clanging, like something you'd scream after getting your finger smashed against a giant brass gong. She wanted an anonymous name, preferably one that wouldn't declare her ethnicity so blatantly. Kids at school would pretend to trip or get hurt and they'd shout, "Ow! Yang!" Then they'd erupt in howls as they cast their pale faces her way. Kids used their index fingers to stretch their eyelids into slants and they'd sing, "Chinese, Japanese, knobby knees, look at these!" Sticking out their flat chests, they'd shimmy around the playground like seductive Suzie Wongs.

Over the years Lindsey eventually accepted her name. Having met Chinese kids who'd been teased much more relentlessly, she realized her name could have been much worse. Beethoven Sing was ridiculed for his utter lack of musical talent, Dorcas Foo was routinely called both a dork and a fool, Ima Ho had to constantly deny being a prostitute, and poor Gina Fang never escaped her schoolyard nickname, Vagina Fangs.

As Lindsey hiked from downtown toward Russian Hill, she passed several boutiques filled chockablock with fabulous orientalia: wide-legged pants with floriental designs, pillows made from antique kimono remnants, paper lanterns, cloisonné dishes, and jewelry made from those coins with the square in the middle. She loved the brocaded fabrics, sandalwood scents, and gorgeous junkiness of it all, but she was disturbed by the confused disregard for each culture: Mandarin jackets stacked with Japanese obi, and Ganesha postcards jumbled with Mao Tse-tung coasters. She especially hated the plastic Buddha-on-a-cellphone toys.

She trudged up Leavenworth toward the apartment she shared with her grandmother. Her family owned the building, and her mother and aunties had all grown up in the spacious top-floor unit. As a child, Lindsey had passed most afterschool hours and some nights there, usually waiting until after dinner for her parents to pick her up and take her to their own home in the Sunset District. Living in her grandmother's apartment now was a good arrangement. She had moved in after college graduation, which allowed her to gingerly dip her toes into adult life while keeping one foot planted in safety. She enjoyed free meals and non-existent rent payments.

As she crossed Hyde she barely missed getting creamed by a Ford Explorer as its driver jabbered obliviously into a cell phone. She wanted to spit her gum at the Eddie Bauer Limited Edition, but she refrained. She was very conscientious about not littering.

Another block away, Lindsey passed the bookstore where, in a rare moment of self-motivation, she once purchased a writing how-to book that advised her to tackle whatever subject she knew best. But Lindsey didn't think she knew anything. Not really.

She knew about growing up in San Francisco. But books

about her hometown never described the city as she knew it. She understood why people gushed poetic about the fog and the hills, but she wondered why no one ever mentioned homeless people crapping in otherwise fine parking spaces, or the authentic smells of polluted baywater and rotting garbage that wafted down Columbus Avenue. She had never gotten around to visiting any of the city's main attractions, had only sped by them in the backseat of her parents' car a thousand times to and from school. She had ridden a cable car only once, back in the second grade when it had cost a nickel and she'd had to board while holding her grandmother's hand.

Oh, she also knew about living with Pau Pau. But neither San Francisco nor her granny seemed like exciting topics to write about. And, besides, becoming a working writer wasn't a real-life possibility. She just kept the idea swirling inside her dreamy head, along with notions like becoming a famous Abstract Expressionist painter, winning the California lottery, or finding True Love.

Lindsey bounded up the stairs to the third-floor apartment and kicked off her Kenneth Coles. Flopping onto her bed, she put her head down for a moment. She sensed that her grandmother wasn't home, because the odor of tiger balm wasn't overpowering, just simply there.

Unzipping her jeans, she exhaled a sigh of sudden sexual frustration. Sadly, the screwing of boys was not something that was going to happen in her grandmother's apartment. Aside from the boner-wilting old lady stuff—the sexy dentures stewing in the bathroom cup, the medicinal un-aromatherapy of arthritis plasters, the eye-watering fumes of tiger balm caressing the air—any form of dating white boys was just not mentioned in this household. Perhaps someday a well-mannered boy, fresh off the boat from China, would bring over a roasted pig and a bag of money in exchange for the simple honor of asking her to the movies. But she was well aware that no hottie would be unlocking the chink in her chastity belt anytime soon. Even if she got Pau Pau out of the house, there would be no way to respectfully get it on with a white devil on the same mattress where her grandpa, Gung Gung, had died. Especially not under the all-seeing portrait of him shaking hands with Jimmy Carter. Wasn't gonna happen.

Pau Pau was still in Chinatown playing mahjong. Every day, even on the weekends, she scrambled her 110-pound, 4-foot, 10-inch self onto the bus, and rode nine blocks down Clay Street to a quiet alley where she happily gambled away the hours. If she was on a winning streak, she might not come home for dinner.

Lindsey zipped up her pants, deciding that a stroll down to the mahjong parlor would be good for some fresh air. She gathered up her keys and a sweater, and quickly fluffed her bangs and teased her straight, shoulder-length hair in the mirror. As was her habit, she pinched the half-inch of extra weight at her waist and surveyed her 5-foot, 2-inch frame for any newfound blubber. Content enough with her appearance, she ran down the stairs with a sudden burst of energy.

The air on the shaded sidewalk smelled faintly of honeysuckle as she walked up and over Clay Street. The light of the afternoon dimmed, and she entered a narrow alley, which was quiet except for the sound of elderly residents meandering by or tending to the potted plants on their balconies. She heard tinkling Chinese music playing from a window overhead, and as she walked, she wondered if this alley looked the same a hundred years ago, when it was the site of gang wars over slave girls.

Approaching the door of the mahjong parlor, she half-imagined she'd need a secret knock or password. Maybe a peephole or rectangular slit would open to reveal the bloodshot eyeball of a wary guard. She listened for the sound of a whirring, rushing waterfall created by the swirling motion of a thousand clicking mahjong tiles under golden hands. Hearing only silence, she rang the bell.

A Chinese man in a ribbed undershirt and slippers answered the door. He spoke to her in Cantonese and she panicked. Eight years of skipping afternoons at St. Mary's Chinese School had left her with only a limited Cantonese vocabulary of obscenities, racial slurs, and food names. She dared not speak any Chinese for fear of accidentally saying, "Piss your mother's fried noodles up the ass."

She blurted out Pau Pau's American name, "Lucy Lee," and the man yelled it back over his shoulder and shuffled away.

Her grandmother appeared and escorted her into the gambling clubhouse. With a tattered sofa, an old televison that broadcast Beijing news, and a card table loaded with tea and hot water thermoses, the room was homey. Low lamps, like those in paintings of dogs playing poker, dangled above the mahjong tables. Fluorescent panels and the glow from a red-and-gold altar gave the place the ambience of an old auntie's tenement kitchenette, complete with the bracing scent of Pine-Sol. There was no opium, and no doped-up nubile Chinese beauties.

Pau Pau patted Lindsey's arm and brushed her palm against her cheek affectionately, "What you doing here?"

She introduced the old men and women in the room, and they all nodded and smiled with various amounts of teeth, some missing, some gold.

"They all happy because now they see my tiles!" Pau Pau whispered loudly. Then she added, "Let's get something to eat."

After quick good-byes, they stepped out into the cool, damp alley. Pau Pau fished a Salem cigarette from her saggy knit pants and lit it with detached satisfaction.

Merging into foot traffic, Lindsey was reminded of the hundreds of times she and Pau Pau had walked these narrow Chinatown paths. When she was little, she had refused to go to preschool and had screamed at every baby-sitter, so her parents had eventually decided to park her at Pau Pau and Gung Gung's travel agency office. Walking now, she gazed at the purple glass circles embedded in the pavement and remembered how much they'd delighted her when she was a child. For a moment she stopped and stared at a tank of lethargic Dungeness crabs.

"Fai-dee!" her grandmother yelled, pushing her way through the crowd. Pau Pau always walked purposefully and fast, not thinking twice about throwing an elbow or shoulder to get other pedestrians out of her way. Lindsey lagged behind, mumbling many "excuse me's" and "pardon me's" as she tried to navigate the walkway.

A few blocks away, they arrived at a restaurant decorated with rosy pink wallpaper in a Versailles-meets-Hong Kong pattern. Crystal chandeliers drooped with stringy clumps of oil-saturated dust that coated the brass chains like coconut sprinkles. At the small tables, English- and German-speaking tourists, along with locals speaking different Chinese dialects, chewed on piping-hot dumplings and fried taro root squares.

Pau Pau used her thin, machete-like arm to hack through a swarm of bewildered Midwesterners who waited patiently in the cramped doorway stacked with a high, swaying tower of cardboard boxes. She walked briskly toward four decrepit Chinese men hunched around a small table, and she chided them loudly in Cantonese, shooing them away. They unbent their skeletons, stood shakily on weary legs, and shuffled out the door clutching their plastic decks of playing cards. Pau Pau smiled and waved for Lindsey to come sit down.

"They already finish eat," she explained, pushing aside the dirty plates. They sat for a few seconds, but when no server came immediately to the table, Pau Pau became impatient and walked decisively into the kitchen. Lindsey heard muffled shouts, and a few exclamations later, her grandmother returned carrying teacups, napkins and chopsticks. She was followed closely by two waitresses balancing small heaping dishes of greasy, meaty morsels.

Lindsey removed a moist towelette from her backpack and sanitized her hands before eating. She picked at the wide noodles folded with shrimp and green onions as Pau Pau urged her to eat faster before the food cooled and congealed. After gnawing on a soft and frightening chicken's foot, Pau Pau picked her teeth behind one cupped hand and lit a cigarette under the No Smoking sign. Lindsey drank tea to wash down the lard that was coating her esophagus.

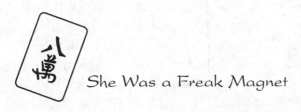

She Was a Freak Magnet

Although Lindsey didn't realize it, living with her grandmother had begun to change her in small ways. She was gradually becoming more thrifty, and also more germ-phobic. Now in the habit of washing and saving disposable utensils, she reused plastic bread bags to carry her lunch to work, and she checked out magazines from branch libraries instead of buying them. In public places she never touched a handrail, doorknob, or toilet seat without first covering the inside of her hand with a napkin, and she trained herself to inhale with only shallow breaths when she stood in crowds. She now kept wads of Kleenex in every pocket, with a few tissues stuffed up her sleeve for good measure. Her purse was equipped with a small sewing kit, a plastic hair bonnet in case of rain, and a small bottle of Purell antibacterial gel for any germ-related emergencies.

Her paranoia about germs wasn't completely unfounded. After all, she did take the bus to work every day. Nothing was as repulsive as the combined odors on a Muni bus. Although she smelled weird things daily in her grand-mother's apartment, like rubbing alcohol and salted fish, hairspray and vinegar, or menthol and suet, none of these odors could compare to public transportation's urine-based fragrance. On a good day, the only additional smells were diesel exhaust and Eau de Nursing Home, but this morn-ing Lindsey was experiencing a particularly complex bou-quet of whiskey-infused sweat, an overdousing of a Chanel #5 knockoff, peanut butter with an after-whiff of Egg Mc-Muffin, and lastly, a lingering human-produced gas that wafted somewhere from her right.

As she lifted the inside of her sweater collar over her face like a surgical mask, the last assault to her nostrils was a scent akin to wet dog mixed with stale bologna. Settling into her *Jane* magazine, she recalled the time her friend Mimi complained that white people in bad weather reeked like poodle hair.

Flipping through the pages of the magazine, Lindsey suddenly heard a soft-spoken, priestlike voice somewhere within her personal space.

She steeled herself for the inevitable. Years ago she had accepted the fact that weird people on the bus somehow al-ways found her and sat either right next to her, or at least within touching distance. The voice came closer.

"Ni ho ma?"

She hadn't had coffee yet, her Advil hadn't kicked in, and wherever that voice was coming from, she knew that someone was about to get in her face.

She looked up from a mouthwash advertisement and saw a pasty lead-singer-of-Chicago-look-alike approaching. He sat down beside her, slowly inching forward as if she were a lamb at the petting zoo. With a pained voice, he asked, "Where are we going this morning, China Doll?"

In this type of situation Mimi swore by the deadpan staredown technique, but Lindsey didn't want to risk eye contact. The guy nudged a bit nearer.

"Speak Eng-lish?" he asked, his own speech becoming broken. She glanced around at the other Muni passengers, but they all looked away. Staring at the man's sand-colored, shapeless shoes, she cringed as he inched even closer. She felt his eyes laser-cutting small holes like cigarette burns into the boob region of her white Banana Republic sweater.

Imperceptible to those surrounding her, she checked the grip of her rubber soles against the bus floor and quickly, in one maneuver, lurched up. She strode to the front of the bus, feeling Chicago guy's eyes still pinned to her cardigan.

Thankfully, the bus was pulling into the next stop at Fifth and Market. She was still four blocks away from work, but she was willing to walk. She'd do anything to escape the greige guy.

Lindsey leaped to the sidewalk and swung at some hovering pigeons with her Gap bag, yanking the drawstring back like a yo-yo just in time to avoid accidentally swatting the guy who sat in front of Walgreens combing his calico cat. She had a certain affection for that furry feline, with its purple sunglasses, even if she did think it too unsanitary to touch. She considered petting the cat and then disinfecting her hands with the Purell gel in her purse, but instead, she just kept walking.

She arrived at her building and rode the elevator to the eighth floor. Once inside the office, she checked on the temporary worker who was taking her shift that day. Grabbing a steno pad, she darted back into the elevator.

She walked to New Montgomery and was a little intimidated as she strode through the Palace Hotel. She was excited to attend her first work-related seminar, even if she was slightly confused as to why her boss was sending her to a conference.

The topic of the seminar was How to Establish a Community of Diversity in the New Millennium Workplace. Just saying that phrase out loud bored her.

At *Vegan Warrior,* establishing a community of diversity was going to be a little tough, seeing as she *was* the community. She was the only non-white employee, and as the receptionist, she was a peon who didn't have the authority to create a more diverse staff, and she was never asked even once to partake in brainstorming meetings of any kind. She didn't know what her boss expected her to bring back from this session. She supposed her Chinese face must have counted for something.

As she grabbed an orange juice and made her way to a seat, she realized that she was not alone in her predicament; a smattering of other non-white participants dotted the room with deer-in-the-headlights expressions.

A permed, middle-aged white woman in a shapeless, teal-and-mauve tunic welcomed the crowd and plugged the names of several corporate sponsors. She then spent ten minutes describing her very own book about melting pots and business plans, *Cash Cow at the End of the Rainbow.*

Lindsey scanned the room, observing that the audience sorely needed diversity in terms of haircuts, fashion, and personal hygiene. Something was definitely wrong with people whose politics blinded them to the benefits of emollient face creams and attractive footwear, she thought.

An LCD-projector with PowerPoint slides flashed the Merriam-Webster dictionary definition of the word "diversity," and the audience was forced to read aloud in unison. Some people clapped weakly. A vegetarian luncheon was mentioned. Lindsey longed for assault weaponry.

"The New Age must be dedicated to establishing a reputation for diversity!" The woman's voice rose to a screech at the last syllable, which jolted open the eyelids of a few snoozers. Lindsey opened her notebook and wrote:

REPUTATION FOR DIVERSITY

Starring Chow Yun Fat as an undercover cop searching for Lindsey Owyang, a karaoke superstar whom he's protecting so she can play the lead role in the upcoming live-action Hello Kitty movie. Chow Yun Fat infiltrates a tedious conference to protect Lindsey O. from the excruciating boredom that might create slight crow's feet on her creamy visage or cause her eye sockets to bleed. The undercover cop becomes enraged that the vegetarian potstickers are served cold and flavorless, so he lifts his machine gun studded with inlaid jade and pumps cloisonné bullets into a crowd of frumpy women without makeup and earnest men in sensible shoes. RATED R.

She continued her notes:

WE ARE ALL DIVERSE

A Gary Coleman comeback vehicle starring Samuel L. Jackson, Jennifer Lopez, B.D. Wong and the guy who plays Mini Me in Austin Powers. *Gary escapes from the plastic surgery clinic where he has been held hostage since the cancellation of* Diff'rent Strokes. *After 10 years of radical surgeries, Gary now looks like Mini Me. Samuel L. Jackson is the clinic gardener who hides Gary/Mini Me under a hydrangea bush as the savage clinic guard (played by an unknown actor who bears an uncanny resemblance to Mr. Drummond) uses a weed whacker to decapitate various exquisite topiaries. B.D. Wong is a social worker from Los Angeles who has come to the clinic for a routine eyelid surgery, and he and Samuel Jackson try to convince Gary to embrace his inner black man. Jennifer Lopez plays the voluptuous anaesthesiologist whose butt Gary/Mini Me falls in love with. RATED PG-13.*

Lindsey looked up for a moment and fixed her eyes on a skinny Chinese man sitting a few tables away. His bad posture and lack of muscles, paired with his camellia-white skin, inspired another vignette:

A fey drone by day, he trades his wire-rim glasses for contact lenses at night. Before he heads to Tranny Shack, he slithers into a stretchy sequined number so tight that it holds together his boneless body with a pleasantly clingy pressure, giving him such confidence that his coworkers at the San Francisco Food Bank would never suspect his secret life as a female impersonator. His version of Madonna's "Live To Tell" is a triumphant affair at the "Man-donna" Midnight Show. RATED R.
SLOUCHING TIGER, HIDDEN DRAGQUEEN.

As she wrote, she could feel a pair of eyes on her. Yep. Hoarder at ten o'clock. His overactive sweat glands made his skin appear coated in Vaseline. He looked like a genetic cross between a sea slug and country singer John Denver. Catching her eye, he wiggled his eyebrows at her. For the rest of the conference Lindsey made sure to avoid him.

A few hours later, when the conference finally ended, Lindsey remembered to walk home via Chinatown so she could pick up the salted chicken Pau Pau wanted for dinner. Although there were numerous stores along Stockton Street that sold takeout and various roasted fowl, Lindsey made sure to go to the one that Pau Pau liked best.

As she waited in line she dreaded her upcoming exchange with the butcher. The man's maniacal expression showed the emotional toll that resulted from chopping carcasses all day. He wore a paper Popeye hat and wielded his cleaver with half-open eyes, like he was asleep standing up, yet he managed to slice and dice with expert precision.

Lindsey practiced in her head what she would say to the man and watched as he slammed down his cleaver before ambling over to a teeming tank to retrieve a live catfish. He netted the writhing, whiskered animal and smacked its head a few times with a stainless steel rod. With each clobbering, the fish just wiggled even more defiantly. Lindsey's jaw dropped. The catfish was like Rasputin. It just refused to die. The butcher eventually threw it in a sack and hoisted it over the counter to an old lady. Lindsey almost passed out.

Her head was reeling when the butcher returned to his block and pointed his cleaver at her. Wide-eyed, she held up a single index finger and stammered, "See, uh, *see yow gai,* please."

She knew *see yow* was soy sauce, and *gai* was chicken, but that was practically the extent of her vocabulary. Immediately, the butcher began to fire questions at her in Chinese: How many? Cut up, or whole? With sauce or plain?

It was her own fault. She knew that uttering one phrase in Chinese made people think she knew more words than she actually did.

Lindsey froze, and the way her eyes got as big as frying pans made the butcher cackle like a madman. He seemed to know she couldn't understand him, and even more worrisome, he stared deep into her eyes like he was looking right through her head clear to the back wall. He kept talking, seeming to enjoy making her uneasy. He began to maneuver the cleaver around like a swordfighter in the movies, and Lindsey guessed he was asking if she wanted the bird halved, quartered, or what. She was so freaked out that she gestured for him to just throw the chicken whole into a bag. He laughed at her squeamishness as he twisted off the shins and wrung off the limp, softened neck, then in one lightning-quick motion he sliced the head clear in half. Lindsey almost fainted at the sight of the cross-sectioned brain.

After she paid for the chicken and exited the store, she started up the hill. Pretty soon she realized that she really needed to pee, and estimated that she wouldn't be able to make it home in time. She had to map out a strategy.

It was really difficult to find a public rest room in Chinatown. Not to mention they were always really filthy. The word "filth" achieved a new superlative in relation to this neighborhood's water closets, and Lindsey was worried.

She thought about sneaking into one of the restaurants, but they all had signs posted Toilet for Customer Only, and she was afraid of getting caught and thrown out. She briefly considered eating a meal at one of the fancier places, just so she could use the bathroom. But she didn't have time for that. She ducked into one of the trinket shops instead.

Lindsey feigned extreme interest in some discounted happicoats, and when the salesgirl wasn't paying attention she made her way to the back of the store and found a door. She peered inside. Nope. Broom closet and extra inventory of fart bombs. She tried an adjacent door, and the foul odor told her she had found the right place.

Lindsey held her breath and secured her parcels in the crook of her forearm. There were no seat covers or tissue, and as she squatted she tried not to think of all the employees, deliverymen, and assorted germbags who might have done their business there. As she peed she noticed the black, gummy soot and shoe dirt that had begun in the corners and seeped across the concrete floor. With the exception of the well-worn path from the door to the sink to the toilet, the sticky layers had built up into an encrusted relief of godknowswhat. The drainage grid in the center of the floor was crooked and corroded, clogged with a few soggy cigarette butts and stanky, greenish water.

As she balanced there, she reached for the paper napkin in her sleeve, but it was trapped under the plastic bag handles weighed down by the heavy chicken. She managed to rip a few shreds of tissue from the fifth pocket of her Levi's that were crunched down at her knees, and soon her task was done.

At the sink, goopy snail trails of pink liquid soap had

long since dried and turned gray. She lifted the faucet lever
and shuddered as she picked up the remains of a slick,
cracked bar of soap whose shape had been influenced by
the countless spinning grips of latherseekers, and now resembled a set of brass knuckles. The soap was deeply scored
with furrows of grime from a hundred previous hands that
had deposited all their ink, scalp scum, sloughed skin, and
various dogday particles onto the soft, wet pellet.

Her hands felt dirtier after washing them, and she used
her last tissue to flush the toilet and turn the doorknob. On
her way out of the store, to appear inconspicuous she asked
the salesgirl for the price of a lucky bamboo sprig, and
when she walked away without buying it the shopgirl called
her a cheapskate tourist.

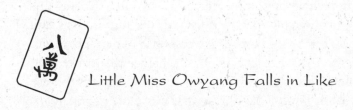

Little Miss Owyang Falls in Like

t all began when he pissed her off at work. Lindsey had sent him a scathing e-mail about his inadequacy at keeping the common areas litter-free. She constantly found detritus from FedEx packages, crumpled Post-it notes, and Twix wrappers around the office, and she suspected they were his. Everything he touched seemed to turn into trash, and he left a trail around the office for her to clean up. And she had had it. And that's what her e-mail said. Three little words: "I've had it." She followed that sentence with a detailed description of his offenses and the usual plea to work as a team, blah blah blah.

Michael Cartier was the magazine's travel editor, and although Lindsey hadn't had much contact with him, she did suspect that he was a closet meat-eater like herself. She had once overheard him getting berated in the lunchroom by Yvonne, the public relations planner, because he had destroyed the sanctity of a microwaved baked potato by sprinkling it with bacon bits.

She tried to picture him now, conjuring basic details

about his appearance, such as brown hair and eyes, perhaps around six feet tall with somewhat squarish shoulders. As she tried to remember any other details about him, she was unprepared for the reply that shot back to her screen. This guy had his own three-word e-mail as a response. When she clicked open the message, there it was. That sentence that packed the sucker punch, the phrase that girls waited for months to hear from their boyfriends, the phrase that was most definitely inappropriate at the moment, yet somehow thrilling:

From: michaelcartier
To: lindseyowyang

I love you.

She sat and stared at the eight letters, which looked so trite on heart-shaped Mylar balloons and Hallmark cards but which now seemed like the most original, refreshing combination of lines and circles she had ever seen. At first she scoffed, reacting with a "don't get fresh with me, young man" attitude. She fumed at her desk for about ten seconds, but then she allowed herself to wonder, What does this mean? One doesn't dash off those words to just anyone. No guy writes that sentence to someone he doesn't like, even a little. For instance, even if it was a joke, she couldn't imagine any guy writing those words to the old hippie accounting secretary with the chin hairs and stained polyester pantsuit.

Could it be true? Could Michael, this non-cleaner of his own coffee mug, actually, you know, love her?

She didn't know it yet, but she totally fell for it.

*   *   *

This was by far the most exciting thing she had experienced within these vegan-chili-splattered halls. This enigmatic e-mail distracted her from the monotonous duties of her workday: cleaning the mailroom with Simple Green, confirming an appointment with the catch-and-release exterminator, and ordering time sheets printed on acid-free paper for allergy-sensitive employees prone to eczema. Between phone calls, she changed the toner cartridge in the printer and restocked the vending machine with turkey-jerky and carob-flavored gluten krispies.

An hour passed, and in that time she convinced herself that there was something about Michael that intrigued her. He reminded her of the days when she'd been annoyed by teasing high school boys but had secretly liked the attention. Ah, her stupid, lost youth.

She told herself that she didn't miss having dates with sexy but self-centered guys. Rather, she had gotten sick of them never being on time or calling her back or picking up the tab every now and then. She had become tired of being disappointed at parties, of always wanting to go home and cry and die, just like in songs by the Smiths. She had given up on her social life early on, and now, as a receptionist extraordinaire, she was hardly interested in spending weekday happy hours with her nine-to-five tormentors who ostracized her for eating chicken and, she suspected, held her personally responsible for the caged animals in Chinatown.

Just because she spent most evenings at home with her grandmother didn't mean she had lost her youth. She had *chosen* to get rid of it. Actually, she had left it in the garage to collect dust. But something about Michael made her want to drag that old youth thing out from behind the Oriental rugs.

So she started flirting with him.

I know you love me, Stud, but don't think you're going to sweet-talk your way out of cleaning up after yourself.

There. That was sassy. She wasn't turning to mush. Yet. Barely a minute passed before he replied:

You're quite cute when you're irritated.

Hmm. What was up with this person? She decided she had no choice but to be cool. She wouldn't fall for it.

I don't understand people who claim to love me but have never even talked to me in the hall.

It was true that Lindsey and Michael had hardly ever spoken in the year she'd been working at the magazine. Maybe once she had said something like, "Here's your mail," or "*Lonely Planet* is on line three."

Michael skulked through the office hallways without saying much. Now that she strained her mind for clues about him, she remembered that once in a staff meeting, she had noticed his voice was tinged with something south of the Mason-Dixon line. She regarded him now as quite a mysterious entity. She left for the day feeling flattered, intrigued, and also a little annoyed. She didn't admit to herself that she felt a little gooey inside, too.

The next day she wore her pink angora sweater to work. It was a subconscious sex message that she would be too embarrassed to admit, even to herself. She wore it for Michael, of course, and not for the accountant who passed her in the hall and accused her of wearing the processed pelt of a murdered rabbit. Lindsey shrugged it off. She was thinking more Playboy bunny than bunny killer.

She scanned the office foyer for Michael but did not see him. When he finally did appear, exactly nine minutes later, she seemed to notice for the first time that he was quite handsome. He had a sullen, brooding kind of masculinity that reminded her of how hopelessly hetero she was. Despite two lesbian friends and some vaguely imagined scenarios that involved kissing girls, seeing Michael Cartier at this very moment made her fallopian tubes vibrate in a warm sort of way. She thought she felt her uterus move.

Her vision zoomed in on his well-groomed hands and his calm, confident walk. As he stared at her with his chocolate brown eyes, she noticed a softness around his cheekbones that hinted at some kind of sensitive wounded puppy thing.

She could tell that her pink sweater was working its furry, fuzzy magic. From experience she knew that pink and angora together cast a magical spell over the heterosexual human male. It was something primal; seeing her fluffiness would give him the Cro-Magnon urge to pounce on her, carry her back to his cave, and impregnate her.

Then perhaps he would barbecue some meat (optional).

"Good morning, Lindsey," he said, enunciating her name slowly, but without stopping or breaking his stride.

"Hello," she replied, feeling a pure ray of energy exit her

eyes and enter directly into his. Sensing the intensity of his gaze, she felt a surge of adrenaline and suddenly wanted to run away and hide.

She watched him move around the corner and disappear into his office.

END OF TAPE 1. PLEASE REWIND, LIKE, A THOUSAND TIMES IN YOUR HEAD.

When Lindsey was nineteen she dated, hated, and berated many boys. She wanted them to love her, not just feel her up and then not pay for the movie. She vowed to stop letting boys get the better of her.

So she became a bronze medalist in the mind-fuck Olympics. She flirted heavily with guys and then pulled back and ignored them. She wore barely-there dresses to class but made sure she could quote Descartes or Sartre more accurately than anyone else in her study group.

She learned to keep guys in a constant state of aroused angst and developed a haughty attitude that she wore like a dainty pantyshield for daily protection against feeling "not so fresh." Her invisible defense told boys, "I know you want me, but I regret that you're just not museum-quality. Oh, and by the way, I've got way better grades than you."

Straight As got her through a lot of heartache. She told herself, "Yeah, he dumped me, but he's gonna take six years to graduate with his crappy mass communications major, and I'm graduating summa cum laude in four years with a double major in English and French Literature."

She trained for hours in the gymnasium of her mind. She became adept at the double entendre, going out to dinner armed with impeccable table manners and a forked tongue. She savored the chase but never actually tasted the food. By the end of the dating marathon, she was always left with hunger pangs. Proficient as she was at mind manipulations, the pursuit of boys soon became like a video game requiring so many quarters to get to level 10 that she eventually ran out of coins. She began to realize that maybe there wasn't any prize at all at the end of the game. Perhaps she would get her initials on a digital scoreboard, but that was it.

Lindsey counted the times Michael walked by her desk that day. While she busied herself answering calls and filling out forms for office supplies, she counted seven times that he happened to breeze past. Even though she was situated near the coffee, watercooler, and mailroom, she convinced herself that her angora sweater was pulsing like a beacon in the night and he couldn't help but be drawn to her. Three times she caught him looking at her, and when their eyes met he smiled, but she held back and didn't smile. She wasn't the type to doodle his last name as if she already dreamed of marriage, but she definitely started thinking about him in a different way. In that kissy kissy love way. How embarrassing.

Bananas, Twinkies, and Eggs

O ccasionally Lindsey's older brother, Kevin, treated her to dinner. He was the top salesman for a company that manufactured and sold microchips to Asian countries, and he pitied his sister's lack of status as a worker drone. The fact that she had no Mercedes-Benz, no Palm Pilot, and no stock options really disturbed him. Her sad-sack salary was evidence that she desperately needed guidance.

"You like quail egg, right?" he asked.

"I guess I'll try it," Lindsey said, sipping her ice water as Kevin poured his Asahi into a frosted glass.

"So what's going on? How is it living with Pau Pau?"

"It's okay. Sometimes she wakes me up with her hacking cough and spitting."

"Well, I guess it's a small price to pay for free rent." He carefully rubbed his chopsticks together to rid them of their tiny balsawood splinters.

She stewed a little over the "free rent" jab.

"Hey, I vacuum and take out the garbage," was all she could think to say in her own defense.

"Well, if you got a job that paid any real money, you could move out." He mixed his low-sodium soy sauce with a big chartreuse marble of wasabi.

Lindsey squirmed. "The worst part is not being able to bring any friends over," she said.

"Why can't you?"

"Well, Pau Pau doesn't really say I can't. It's just that, well, the smell of all those Chinese herbs and medicines is terrible!"

Kevin shrugged. "Just open a window."

"Are you kidding? She'd say, 'I'll catch "ammonia" and die.' It's no use, anyway. As soon as the air in the apartment dips below a level of 75% Chinese odors—like mothballs and soup—she'll boil something stinky so that anyone who's not Chinese will keep their distance."

The sunomono salad and hamachi arrived. Kevin removed the fish from the rice, dunked it in the soy sauce bath, turned it over a few times, and placed it back under a strip of seaweed.

Lindsey crunched on some thin slivers of vinegared cucumber. "I don't want to be disrespectful, either. She'd probably have a heart attack if I brought someone home."

"Well," Kevin said, "you can have your *girl* friends over, but not, like, white guys, for Christ's sake."

He balanced a piece of oshinko onto a mound of ginger. "And besides," he added, "if you gotta date white guys, at least you could go out with an *egg*."

"What's an *egg*?" Lindsey asked.

"You know, like how you're a *Twinkie*—yellow on the outside but a total white girl on the inside—"

"You mean a *banana*?"

"Yeah, that too. People who are white on the outside and yellow on the inside are *eggs*. Some guys are born white but deep down they wish they were Asian. You know, like Jim."

"You mean, like a *Hoarder of All Things Asian?*"

She suddenly realized she had spoken those words too loudly, as a few other diners glanced over at her.

"What's that?" Kevin said, coughing from the strong ponzu marinade.

She straightened up in her seat. "Jim is a typical Hoarder. He hangs around, pretending to be your friend, but all he wants from you guys is access to your sisters and girlfriends."

When Lindsey said "you guys," she was referring to Kevin's group of high school buddies who still formed his core group of friends. They were all various types of Asian, with similar slicked-back or spiky haircuts, clean-shaven faces, and designer golf gear. As teenagers, they all gave Lindsey the cold shoulder for "talking white" and going to that "white school," meaning a college preparatory instead of a public school like Lowell. The fact that she studied French and actually enjoyed it was somehow proof of her having crossed an invisible enemy line.

Kevin chewed and talked with his mouth full. "At least Jim appreciates Chinese culture and is clean-cut."

"You mean, circumcised?"

"Oh, shut up."

Lindsey smirked. "Jim is one of those born-again types who was always trying to entice me to ice cream socials at Berkeley."

A crackle-glazed porcelain tray arrived with more nigiristyle sushi, followed by an order of *natto*. The fermented soybean paste smelled so vulgar that Lindsey covered her nose and mouth and checked the soles of her shoes to see if she had stepped in crap. Kevin jokingly tried to force-feed her a bite, but she refused.

"Get that away from me," she said. "I'm not eating something that smells like ass."

Kevin shrugged, chewed, and swallowed. After a few more bites he said, "Well, couldn't you at least try to like Asian guys? What about one of my friends?"

"Nah, I've known them all for so long. They're practically relatives. Besides, I can't help who I like. One thing's for sure, I'm not going out with a traditional Asian guy who wants a subservient, house-cleaning concubine, and I'm definitely not going out with a nerdy *egg*-boy like Jim."

"Listen," Kevin said, chewing a piece of unagi, "all guys, of any race, want their girlfriends to be subservient, kowtowing concubines—so you might as well marry someone who'll provide a good future for you."

"I'll provide my own good future," Lindsey said.

"Yeah right."

"I could," she insisted.

Her brother paused to eat a few bites. "Why don't you go out with my new housemate, Ted Hamamoto? He's got a great job in financial services."

"Hamamoto?" Lindsey accidentally knocked over a dish, sending a splatter of shoyu sauce across the table. "Pau Pau would crap the biggest brick ever if I went out with a Japanese guy. She'd go more insane than if I had a legion of crackers over."

"Why? What's the big deal?"

"Well, for one thing, the whole reason she came over here with Gung Gung was because the Japanese killed her family, Dummy."

"Oh, right," he nodded, vaguely remembering that that was the story.

She added, "Don't even mention we ate at a Japanese restaurant."

The complimentary green tea ice cream arrived, and Lindsey ate a scoopful, letting the creamy, cold lump dissolve slowly on her tongue.

After Kevin dropped her off at home, Lindsey opened the apartment door to a familiar sight: Pau Pau was half-asleep on the couch, watching *Bonanza*. She awakened drowsily and asked, "You eat yet?"

"Yeah, already ate. I'm full. Go to sleep, okay?"

The elderly woman nodded, then bobbed her head up just briefly enough to squint at Lindsey's black boots.

"I told you no wear this thing," she said crankily. "Look like man shoes." Pau Pau shook her head in exasperation and went back to her half-lidded watching of Lorne Greene.

Lindsey went into the kitchen and found a bitter-smelling concoction bubbling on the stove. She turned off the heat and tiptoed down the hall.

Once inside her bedroom, she slipped her feet out of her boots and looked down at her socks. With legs slightly apart, she scrunched all her toes into the carpet and felt the pressure of nine of them as they matted down the short pile fibers.

You see, she had a midget toe. On her left foot, the

fourth digit was noticeably undersized. A stunted runt. A dwarf. The toe itself was not shriveled or mangled; it was just a miniature nub, fully formed with a teeny nail, yet nonetheless abnormal.

When she was a toddler, the little thing looked right as rain. But as the rest of Lindsey's body grew, the stubborn toe did not progress accordingly. It just remained at rest, as if too tired or petulant to keep up with the others.

Her mother told her the toe would eventually catch up with the other nine little wigglers, and her father explained that it was the little piggie that had no roast beef so it was a bit malnourished. He had no expanation when Lindsey asked why the corresponding toe on her right foot had no such protein deficiencies.

This midget toe made Lindsey very aware of the sandal-wearing population, and made her highly sensitive regarding footwear in general. She always noticed people's shoes and envied girls who walked confidently with their painted toenails peeking from espadrilles, huaraches, or even flip-flops. She never dared to be so brazen with her own feet. She imagined that if she ever ventured to step outside in a pair of fashionable slides, with her midget toe exposed to the fresh air, mayhem was bound to follow. Surely Diane Arbus would leap out from behind a trash can and snap a photo of the deformed toe nub for *Ripley's Believe It or Not!*

As a result, Lindsey always felt safest in her clunky black boots. Even on hot summer days, she always wore socks. And not just anklets. Mostly she wore tight knee highs that threatened to cut off the circulation in her calves. She was reluctant to risk the casual slippage of a flimsy, cotton-acrylic sock. She liked to keep her left foot under tight control, like a kidnapper who keeps a sack over the head of his victim. She often thought of the ingenious burlap hood sported by the Elephant Man.

Lindsey changed into her nightgown and performed her regular bedtime routine of teethbrushing and haircombing. As she scooted under the sheets, she unconsciously paused to rub the little toe, perhaps for good luck, and with the hope that someday it might decide to grow. She lay in bed and quickly fell asleep.

Back in college, while watching Lindsey dilute her latte with extra milk, her friend Mimi had once joked that Lindsey liked her coffee white and weak, just like her men. In Mimi's opinion, all the dudes Lindsey dated were duds, and the particularly pasty-looking ones were called Milk Duds.

But it wasn't like Lindsey never dated Asians. She had recently gone out with a few Chinese guys, but only because Pau Pau liked to play matchmaker. Every few months or so, Pau Pau would announce that a young man, a grandson of a friend, would be picking her up for a date. How humiliating! But what could she do? She was living rent-free, and these arranged "dates" meant so much to Pau Pau, who worried about her granddaughter's marital status.

Lindsey was already twenty-five, no spring chicken. She was no *cherng-gai*, if such a thing could be translated. Pau Pau schemed with her merry band of mahjong ladies, and together they cooked up ways to manipulate each other's grandkids into forced social situations. Who knew how it all came about? Maybe like this:

Pau Pau: *Poong*! I win! Now you all owe me $300 each.
Somebody else's Pau Pau: How about $100 and my
grandson takes your granddaughter to dinner?

Lindsey had gone on quite a few of these fake dates.
Thus far she had met an actuary with a ricebowl haircut and
an aversion to eye contact, an engineering student with an
impressive aquarium, an electronics wizard with a massive
collection of *Star Wars* action figures, and, her least favorite, the pudgy androgynous one. She hadn't clicked
with any of them, and there was no way she was going to
let any of them peel off her jog bra and Hello Kitty undies.
She wondered if she would ever find any guy—Chinese,
white, or otherwise—whom she could even tolerate for a
second date, let alone fall in love with.

Pau Pau arranged for Mrs. Kwok's grandson to take Lindsey out one evening. Kam was what Lindsey could only describe as a Gang Guy. He styled his hair in a gravity-defying
rooster pouf and wore vinyl pants with a switchblade knife
attached to a gold mesh belt.

Lindsey took a deep breath as she climbed into Kam's car,
a custom-painted, bright purple Honda Civic that seemed
lower to the ground than normal. Dangling from the
rearview mirror, a plastic lantern with fake jade beads and
red fringe hit her in the head as he swerved into traffic.

She glanced at all the homemade, racing-inspired decals
on the windows.

"I like your stickers," she said, trying to make conversation.

"Cool, huh. Hey, you like *kar-oke*?" he asked, cracking
his knuckles as he gripped the steering wheel.

She wasn't sure if he'd said "karaoke," but she nodded nervously, afraid she'd get shot if she said no. Did Pau Pau know she was setting up her granddaughter with a mini-mafioso descended from the Pacific shores of ancient and majestic Cathay?

They sped through several intersections and came inches away from sliding under a Peterbilt truck. When she asked why the car rumbled so loudly, Kam proudly straightened his skinny shoulders and explained that he made "special-ized adjustments" to the engine and muffler. For several blocks neither of them spoke until Kam finally said, "Oh, that's hecka sick."

"What?" Lindsey said.

"That car was hecka tight, back there by the *li-berry* . . ."

Lindsey looked over her shoulder just as they passed the Green Street library and spotted a fluorescent Honda race-car not unlike the one she was currently trapped in. To get a better look, she pressed the button to open the automatic window and was relieved by a gust of fresh air that diluted the macho stink that wafted from a bottle of "air freshener" glued to the dashboard.

"*Crose* the *win-dor*! It leaves streaks," Kam said, annoyed. He revved the engine as they waited at a stoplight. After a moment, he gunned the accelerator toward some pedestri-ans while she slid jerkily on the slippery, Armor-Alled seats.

On Post Street, across from the heart of Japantown, Kam parked the car, got out, and walked toward a glassed-in storefront, leaving Lindsey in the passenger seat as if he had forgotten she was there. She unbuckled her seat belt and followed him inside, her nostrils instantly permeated with the smells of spilled beer, stale smoke, and popcorn.

The cramped lobby was crowded with various video game machines and a Neoprint sticker booth. A corkboard listed karaoke room rates like a sleazy hotel, and single sheets of binder paper were tacked to the wall, showing the prices for sodas, snacks, and individual cigarettes. The guy behind the counter looked Lindsey up and down while he and Kam talked in Cantonese for several minutes.

"Come on," Kam ordered, and she followed cautiously, her eyes darting around to locate alternative exits should her situation at any time require an escape route. The hall was strangely quiet, and she imagined sinister happenings somewhere on the premises. Everywhere she looked, Magic Marker signs announced No Smoking or Drinking, but meanwhile, guys with cigarettes dangling from their mouths hoisted cases of beer down the halls, disappearing into private rooms. The doors resembled those of her high school classrooms, and through the small windows Lindsey could see the spinning light from disco balls. She prayed there would be no hot tubs in her evening's future.

They entered a room where a party was already in progress.

"Kam!" a bunch of drunken guys yelled. They were all very H.K. (Hong Kong) with shiny shirts and ostentatious yellow-gold wristwatches. Girls in midriff-baring nylon tops sat and puffed on ultra-thin cigarettes, tapping their feet, all in similar white heels. Lindsey sat on the edge of a sticky, brown banquette and absorbed the fact that no one here cared about her presence. She did not exist. A girl in a sheer, sequined tank top wailed a tuneless song in Chinese. Compared with the silence in the hallway, the volume was deafening. Lindsey wondered if anyone would hear her scream if she tried.

On a low glass coffee table, Styrofoam cups filled with Coke and cheap rum balanced atop thick binders filled with laminated pages of song selections.

"Pick one!" said a girl in size zero spandex jeans who had finally noticed Lindsey. Lindsey flipped through the pages, carefully touching only the edges to avoid the smudges and stains. A group of girls looked on.

"How about this one?" Lindsey asked, pointing to a Depeche Mode song. All the girls frowned, as if she had just revealed herself as someone who was not to be trusted. No one addressed her for the remainder of the evening.

She endured two more hours of off-tune caterwauling, passing the time by counting dots on the acoustic ceiling panels. Kam eventually offered to drive her home so he could return to enjoy the company of his friends without her.

Climbing out of the grape Honda, she politely thanked him.

"I had a good time," she said.

Kam nodded and stubbed out his cigarette in the ashtray. "Hey, you *tink* I can have money for gas?" he asked. "I gotta buy premium, you know."

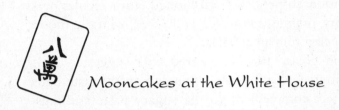

Mooncakes at the White House

Lindsey knew it was time for mooncakes by the pregnant October moon that reflected golden light in the blue-black ocean like spilled milk. Her favorite fattening treats would only be available for the next couple of months, and she looked forward to gorging herself.

"Go buy four boxes, for gift to mahjong ladies," Pau Pau reminded her in the morning, so after work Lindsey walked to Eastern Bakery on Grant Avenue.

Inside, old men nursed Styrofoam cups of tea. A few of them sat and dozed over single servings of coffee-crunch cake or peanut rolls. The well-trafficked linoleum flooring crackled under Lindsey's feet as she stood in line and stared at the different varieties of seasonal confections.

Compared with somewhat healthier baked goods like scones, muffins, or knishes, mooncakes were distant relatives—perhaps squat, Samoan cousins. A compact, oily hockey puck giddy with cholesterol, a mooncake was a hunkered-down, indolent lard-ball of nutty vanilla smoothness, consisting of buttery flesh made of sweetened lotus seed or black bean paste. Both fillings were rich, and tasted precious, like translucent edible amber, or creamy ebony. Floating inside, suspended in cushioned fat molecules, was a dried, salty, orange-yellow egg yolk, sent from the moon goddess to clog human arteries.

Solid and greasy, the fire-colored yolk suggested Halloween, and its tangy chalkiness mingled on the taste buds as the perfect complement to the sugary paste stuffings. The delicacies were covered with a chewy, glistening pastry shell and embossed with Chinese characters and floral shapes. They were packaged in crinkly pink paper with red Chinese letters.

Lindsey ordered two boxes of double-yolked lotus paste mooncakes and two boxes of black bean ones. She steered clear of the fruit and nut varieties, and she got the willies when she spotted the kind with chopped ham. She remembered that, as a child, she had once upset Pau Pau by spitting out a mouthful onto the shag carpet. She shuddered at the memory, then ordered a single, plain lotus cake for herself before heading home.

That evening Lindsey sat at the kitchen table chewing on a fatty cube of pork. She wondered if Michael was still at work, perhaps scattering confetti from the three-hole punch for her to discover in the morning. She wondered if he really liked her or was only messing with her to stave off boredom.

Pau Pau brought heavy porcelain bowls to the table: steamed rainbow trout with a delicate soy and scallion broth with hot peppers, sweet glazed pig's feet, and Lindsey's favorite—a mélange of shrimp, tofu, bean paste, and a smattering of other ingredients with Chinese names she could never remember. The dish, like many of Pau Pau's invented recipes, appeared on no restaurant menu anywhere in the city. She tried to watch and take mental notes as her grandmother worked, wondering if the combinations and flavors could ever be duplicated by another.

Lindsey's mother and aunts never cooked any Chinese food whatsoever. They preferred Shake 'n Bake chicken, pastas with sauces based on Campbell's cream of mushroom soup, and tuna casseroles with cornflake toppings. Lindsey's parents had raised her on SpaghettiOs, fish sticks, Swanson frozen entrées, and the vast assortment of Oscar Mayer luncheon loaves. Now she was the only one who ate her grandmother's food.

"We've been eating that stuff for a lot longer than you, and we're sick of it," one aunt had said.

"If we want Chinese food, we can just go to a restaurant," another added.

When Lindsey asked her mother to come over so the three of them could eat together, Mrs. Owyang always declined, saying, "You go ahead and eat with her, that food is bad for my blood pressure and gallstones."

Her mom hardly ever came to visit. She claimed she was too busy at work, had to clean her house, or just didn't have time to dawdle. Nonetheless, it had been her idea that Lindsey should live with Pau Pau. Gung Gung had purchased the building in the late sixties, and at one time or another several relatives had taken advantage of any available units. By the late nineties, everyone had found their own places to live, and Pau Pau was left alone when Gung Gung passed away.

"Why don't you move into one of the apartments?" Mrs. Owyang had suggested after Lindsey had returned from college to find she could hardly afford a decent San Francisco apartment. It had seemed like a good alternative, but even the discounted rent of the ground-floor studio had eaten up more than half her monthly paycheck.

"*Ai-ya,* you can live upstairs with me!" her grandmother had insisted for weeks. "You don't have to pay! Nice room, and I won't bother you."

Lindsey eventually gave in, which pleased her mother and aunties immensely. They were glad because Lindsey's presence meant they could go about their business, unfettered by guilt or the inconvenience of running errands such as driving Pau Pau to Kaiser for checkups. Lindsey could do all that now.

After dinner, she pulled on a pair of jeans and her lime-green cardigan.

"I'm going out for a while," she hollered as her grandmother wiped down the sink and rinsed the small pink melmac cup that was her dentures' home away from home.

"*Ai-ya!*" Pau Pau gestured to Lindsey's sweater. "*Yook sheern!*" She shook her head and told Lindsey to change out of the offending garment. "This color no good on Chinese!" she explained. "Don't you know? Makes look yellow, sick."

Lindsey went to her room and changed into a black wool V-neck sweater instead. When she reappeared, Pau Pau was even more upset by her color choice. "*Ai-ya!* Someone die? Gee whiz!" She threw back her head, exasperated. "You are so young! Should wear bright color! And so cold . . ." Pau Pau sprang up and retrieved a scarf from her own bedroom and wrapped it tightly around Lindsey's pale neck.

"See? See? *Gow la* . . ." Pau Pau was satisfied that her granddaughter was now protected against the fog rushing over the steeple of St. Brigid's Church, which was visible through the kitchen window.

"Okay, bye." Lindsey yanked on her boots and beat it out of there in a hurry. Once out of sight at the bottom of the three flights of stairs, she loosened the bright blue fabric that reeked of Chinese herbs. She shoved the scarf in her backpack and rubbed her neck with her fingers, sniffing her hands to make sure she didn't smell like an old Chinese lady.

She was stuck in the 1980s and she knew it. She loved a-Ha and Wang Chung, but not because they sounded particularly Chinese. Rummaging around in her car's cassette box, she selected a tape of Malcolm McLaren's *Madame Butterfly* remix and sped off toward Mimi Madlangbayan's house.

Thankfully, her best friend also remained trapped in the eighties. Mimi still wore feather earrings, shoulder-baring *Flashdance* tops, and spandex stirrup pants. When she answered the door, she was wearing a plastic bag on her head, her follicles soaking in Manic Panic hair dye.

Her father, Mr. Madlangbayan, peered down from the top of the stairs. Recognizing his daughter's childhood friend, he beckoned her up to the kitchen.

"Stay for dinner, we're having dog!" He cackled uproariously.

"Uh, he's kidding," Mimi said. She hated her dad's favorite joke, and she rolled her kohled eyes, slamming the door as Lindsey scooted in.

Mimi spent the next hour fussing with her hair as Lindsey helped herself to a complete set of manicuring supplies. She had pampered all her fingers by the time her friend emerged with blond roots at the crown of her long, straight black hair, tipped with fire-red highlights at the ends.

"Wanna do yours?" Mimi asked.

"No, but can I borrow your baby-blue cashmere sweater?"

"Yeah, let me find it." She threw open the door to her overstuffed closet and began to sift around. From under heaps of dresses and racks of shoes, she yelled out, "Hey, I ran into Tracy yesterday, and she said she saw Steve E. with his new girlfriend."

Lindsey digested this factoid, noting that Mimi still said her ex-boyfriend's name with affectionate, slightly tortured propriety.

"What's she look like?" Lindsey asked.

"One guess." Mimi poked her head out and raised an eyebrow that had been plucked to within a sixteenth of an inch of its life.

"I dunno, what?"

"She's Filipina."

"I knew it," Lindsey thought to herself. "I always knew he was a Hoarder." She fell back on the mattress and mentally reconstructed the details of past interactions she had had with Steve E., combing for clues and analyzing how his Hoarderness could have slipped past her radar.

From the closet, Mimi said, "Yeah, I guess because I don't speak Tagalog or have an accent I wasn't Filipina enough for him, but now he's got the real thing. I hear she cooks him homemade *ponsit*. Is that depressingly subservient or admirably Martha Stewartish?" She emerged with the sweater and tossed it on the bed.

Lindsey shrugged. She was surprised to hear Mimi talk regretfully about "not being Filipina enough." Mimi usually downplayed her Asian descent as much as Lindsey avoided talking about her own Chinese background. Although they had been friends for a long time, they hardly ever shared conversations about their experiences as Asian-Americans; they talked mostly about guys, clothes, and pop culture. They each mentally compartmentalized their Asian identities, associating them only with their parents and family. Despite their closeness as friends, they kept their Asian selves separate from each other and had habitually avoided the topic throughout childhood, their teen years, and up to the present.

While Mimi embarked upon an entire reorganization of her hundreds of shoes, Lindsey lay on the bed and thought back to a conversation she had had with Steve E. at a party a few months ago. "Yeah, I should have known," she told herself, recalling their discussion about vacations. "Any white guy who's traveled alone to Manila and can't wait to go back has Hoarder written all over him. Hunh. How did I miss that?"

"Do you think Steve would have liked me more if I had an accent?" Mimi asked, now relacing a high-heeled sneaker at the edge of the bed.

"Um, yeah, but that's twisted," Lindsey said. Mimi looked down at the shoelaces in her hand.

"No, not the laces," Lindsey said. "Steve is twisted. A sick, fetishist puppy from the inner circles of Hell." She looked up and noticed that Mimi was suddenly near tears. Lindsey sat up and patted Mimi's shoulder. She switched to a more sympathetic tone of voice and said, "Baby, you're perfect the way you are."

"Really?"

Lindsey gave her friend a reassuring hug, trying not to inhale the residual toxic fumes from Mimi's chemically singed hair. As Mimi whimpered slightly, Lindsey said, "He'll be sorry. That Hoarder's gonna end up wallowing in the ninth circle of the Underworld with nary a single Asian lady to wipe the sweat from his brow. He'll be begging for St. Joseph to toss him cold, greasy *lumpia*!"

As she shifted her weight, she accidentally squished a gold Via Spiga sandal under her boot and winced. Seeing the metallic straps bend and contort, she thought briefly of her midget toe and how it would never be loosely cradled by such glamorous strips of softened leather. Quickly, she dismissed her sandal-envy and concentrated instead on how she would avoid the wrath of Mimi and her meticulous, shoekeeping ways.

"Oh, don't worry about that," Mimi said. She sniffled a little, loosened an arm from their embrace, and reached for a tissue. Lindsey picked up the sandal and readjusted the straps to their proper form. She smiled sympathetically. "Don't worry, Imelda, he's an idiot."

Driving home with the luxurious sweater resting on the passenger seat, Lindsey cranked up the radio as it played "Turning Japanese" by the Vapors.

"I got plans for you," she said to the sweater as she sang along all the way down Bush Street, making all the green lights.

She pulled her car into the garage and went upstairs, making sure to open the front door quietly so as not to wake her grandmother. After she washed up and changed into her nightgown, from her bedroom window she looked out at the altar that burned at all hours in the Chinese family's duplex across the street. She watched her neighbor place kumquats and sticks of incense on the red lacquer cabinet. Getting into bed, Lindsey gazed into the red glow from the single crimson Christmas light that illuminated the round belly of the ceramic Buddha figurine, and slowly she blinked to sleep.

The following afternoon Lindsey sat on the bedspread-covered sofa and studied the living room decor. In her apartment there was no altar; instead, the walls were covered with many different sizes of framed photographs. She saw snapshots of cousins crunching candy canes beside a blue-and-silver tinsel tree, Pau Pau and her school-age daughters at the airport clutching Pan Am satchels, and a picture of herself when she was five, in front of the Snow White ride at Disneyland. But these mementos were overpowered by the sheer quantity of the other frames that sandwiched them, all photos of Gung Gung in his prime, spanning a period of thirty or so years.

Gung Gung had come to San Francisco in 1915 from a village in southern China called Toisan. He and another boy had immigrated as the "paper sons" of a successful Chinese-American merchant. Although the boys were unrelated and neither had met their so-called "father," they pretended to be brothers and were given new American names. To acquire U.S. citizenship, they became Sam and Bill Gin. Now, so many years later, no one mentioned or even remembered their true names.

That was all that Lindsey knew about Gung Gung's beginning, and as she studied the photographs on the wall it was difficult to imagine her dapper grandpa as an immigrant boy. Somewhere along the way he obviously became a true believer in American superiority and was never one to miss a photo opportunity. In his three-piece suit, he was captured on film with the politicians of his day: Alan Cranston, Dianne Feinstein, George Moscone, Jerry Brown, and a young Ted Kennedy. Lindsey remembered him telling her as a child never to give up on the idea that, in the United States, even a Chinaman travel agent like him could be president . . . and why not him? If he could shake hands with enough influential dignitaries and capture the moments for posterity, maybe he could get that much closer to his goal. He even painted the exterior of their twelve-unit apartment building bright white, topped it with an oversized flagpole waving the stars and stripes, and named the place The White House Apartments. "I live in the White House!" he used to brag. The neon light he had installed above the entryway still buzzed brightly, twenty-four hours strong.

One particular photo caught Lindsey's eye. The black-and-white glossy showed Pau Pau and Gung Gung standing with another couple, and a caption read, "San Francisco Chinatown Lions Club welcomes Mayor Joseph Alioto and Wife, 1967." The men shook hands as the women beamed for the camera. Lindsey was struck by how lovely Pau Pau looked in a Chinese dress with a high Mandarin collar, fitted short sleeves, and diagonal neck opening.

She didn't hear Pau Pau shuffle up behind her.

"What you look at?" Pau Pau asked.

"This picture of you is so . . ." Lindsey did not immediately know the word she sought.

"I was not so young, but not bad!" Pau Pau laughed, her lips parting only slightly as she sucked on a toothpick. "Still, long time ago . . ." she trailed off.

Lindsey examined the photo for a few more seconds.

"Where did you get this dress?"

"I had lots like these! In China too. Had lots, but could not bring here."

"How come?"

Pau Pau pinched Lindsey's cheek, somewhat harder than usual.

"I had to carry *your mommy*. She was only baby. Bring no-thing else," she said. Her voice carried what could only be described as sarcasm, as if she meant to say, "You silly, stupid girl!"

Pau Pau looked up wistfully to the cottage-cheese ceiling, then pointed to the photo of her younger self.

"I had this dress make in Chinatown. Not so expensive make, so had many same style, different color and what is . . . pattern. Different pattern, *hai la* . . ."

"Do you still have them?"

Pau Pau nodded with bright eyes. None of her daughters had ever expressed interest in cheongsams. When they were younger, they reviled any old-fashioned dresses they said would make them look "too Hong Kongie." They preferred blue jeans and white go-go boots, and later, macramé ponchos and shapeless, granny-type frocks. Rebuffed by her own kids, Pau Pau now seemed flattered that her Americanized granddaughter was interested in her old cheongsams.

A few minutes later, digging in the back of her closet, Pau Pau unveiled one Chinese dress after another, all with the same notched collar and hidden side zippers. A variety of rich brocades, slubby-textured silks, and cotton blends were represented in both vivid colors and subdued hues. Intricate spirals, delicate nature motifs, even canary and black op-art diamonds added to the mix.

"Wow! These are great!" Lindsey exclaimed. "Can I try one on?"

"You too fat, not so skinny like me!"

Lindsey sucked in her stomach.

"Okay, you try, you try," Pau Pau said after some reconsideration.

Pau Pau did not think to step outside the bedroom for modesty's sake while Lindsey removed her T-shirt and jeans. She casually observed Lindsey's body, noting with minor curiosity the changes that had occurred since last bathing her more than two decades ago.

As Lindsey hoisted up her left heel, Pau Pau said, *"Siu siu, tschow gerk,"* addressing the midget toe with affectionate honors, just in case it was listening. Pau Pau referred to her granddaughter's special foot as a "small, stinky foot," even though it was not particularly either. Lindsey's foot was a size seven, and even the midget toe never smelled bad. Pau Pau was just in the habit of calling it that.

The elderly woman had her own theories about the midget toe. While Kevin made jokes about having dropped a giant can of concentrated Hawaiian Punch syrup on Lindsey's foot when they were kids, Pau Pau took the whole matter more seriously. She once quietly mentioned her own mother's bound feet, with their broken bones, gray flesh, and putrid smell. She recounted how, as a child back in Shanghai, she had watched her mother unwrap the strips of cloth beneath her embroidered slippers, and saw how the fabric was sometimes soaked with the faintly yellow pus that leaked from the crevices of the collapsed foot. Pau Pau believed that Lindsey's little toe was not an aberration but a genetic reminder of the suffering endured by the generations of women who came before. While Pau Pau herself had escaped the pain of footbinding, she said she was reminded of the old Chinese custom every time she thought of her granddaughter's toe. She was superstitious about it, too. Not knowing if the toe was a blessing or a warning, she said it was important to keep the nub happy, or at least appeased. She suspected that, if treated badly, the toe might retaliate and perhaps grow to gigantic proportions. As a matter of course, she always encouraged Lindsey's sensible sockwearing habit.

Lindsey stepped into a narrow silver dress and got the zipper up most of the way, but the neck opening was impossibly small.

"See, must be slender for these kind! Too much sport as teenage!" Pau Pau swatted at Lindsey. "Sport make big feet, too!"

Back when Lindsey was in high school, Pau Pau used to criticize her for being on the soccer and swim teams, saying that these activities were unladylike and would make her grow "deform," even more deformed than just one little roast beef–deficient toe. Now, noting that Lindsey's body was still more athletic than willowy, she shook her head in dismay, regarding Lindsey's muscles, however small and out of shape, as the unfortunate result of tomboyish defiance.

"If listen to me then, you might fit now," Pau Pau said

with a shrug. "You put back, okay? I brush denture." Pau Pau pulled out her mouthpiece and shuffled away.

Lindsey began to react differently to the bits of trash she suspected were Michael's. Through sidelong glances she deduced that Coca-Cola, Twix, and Reese's peanut butter cups were his vending machine items of choice. She never saw him with the oatmeal-nut clusters that looked like clumps of cat litter, and this apparent snack wisdom made him more attractive to her. Now, whenever she saw an empty Coke can on the conference table, she picked it up and scrutinized it for a lip imprint before tossing it into the recycling bin. She liked to think it was Michael's mouth that had touched it.

To any casual observer, there was nothing going on between Lindsey Owyang and Michael Cartier. But *she* was certain there was. He came in each day around 9:30 A.M. and, timing his arrival, she mastered the art of the casual pose. She was convinced that she could feel his presence before he popped out of the elevator. Sometimes she would flash him a smile as he walked by her desk, or sometimes she would deliberately not look up from her Excel spreadsheets.

Michael played right along. He obviously liked it when she looked up from her work or asked him how his weekend was. When she ignored him (every third day, down to a science), he would pause for a second and look at the *New York Times* headlines, or pick up an imaginary paper clip on the carpet.

Today, as scheduled, she feigned indifference when he walked in. But, God, she could tell without even looking up that he looked gorgeous today, his face a bit flushed from walking in the morning air.

"Hey Lindsey, did I get any calls yet?" he asked. He stopped to casually sort through the incoming faxes.

She continued to itemize the FedEx bill, coding amounts by department and adding them up on her calculator. She did not look up for a while, but when she finally did glance at him, he, in turn, made her wait as he pretended to study a fax.

"No calls yet, but I'm sure you can invent better excuses to talk to me," she said, smiling mischievously as his eyes sprang off the fax to meet her flirtatious gaze. She noted with sporting satisfaction that his face brightened and his demeanor shifted.

He leaned over the raised partition of her desk, and she looked away coyly, suddenly disarmed. She was unable to sustain eye contact, afraid she'd actually kiss him right there or betray that she wanted to.

"Okay then," he said with a smile. "I'll try to be more clever next time." He headed toward his office, looking back once over his shoulder, keeping his eye on her.

She blushed, and a small smile curled around her strawberry-glossed lips. This was fun.

Later that morning, she was replaying the scenario in her lightly Aqua Netted head when the phone rang her out of a fantasy world involving Michael's hand under her linen skirt.

"Good morning, thank you for calling *Vegan Warrior*."

"Hello, is Lindsey Owyang there? This is her dad."

She snapped quickly out of her Spice Channel brain and into her dutiful daughter persona.

"Oh, hi, Dad."

"Hi there. Are you busy?"

"No, not really. What's up?"

"This weekend is the Gin Family Association dinner at Empress of China. Can you make it?"

"Um, yeah, I guess."

"Mom and I will pick up you and Pau Pau around six on Saturday then, okay?"

"All right."

Lindsey hung up the phone and pressed the Replay button on the soft-porn video that was projected on the inside of her eyelids. She had just gotten Michael's hand into her underwear when the phone rang again.

"Vegan Warrior."

"Did you pick up the hypertension medicine for Uncle Bill?"

Her brain was still elsewhere. "What? Who is this, please?" she asked the caller.

"Um, *hello*, this is your *father*."

"Oh, hi. Yeah, sure, Dad."

"Okay, see you Saturday."

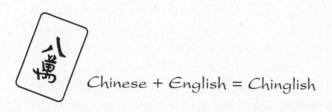

Chinese + English = Chinglish

When Chinese immigrants first came to San Francisco in the mid-1800s, laws excluded them from bringing their wives or families to join them. As a result, the men formed Benevolent and Family Associations that grouped men according to their homeland villages or last names and provided services and a sense of community to the immigrants, who could not count on any city services to guide or protect them.

Chinatown was then, and is now, a very unknown place to those unfamiliar with its day-to-day reality. There's a lot to see beyond its touristy curios and souvenirs. But as with most environments, if you look closely enough and stand quietly, you might unexpectedly catch a glimpse of something small but authentic: an elderly man in an old-style Mao jacket fishing a five-dollar bill out of the gutter, a red-tailed hawk silently circling above a squalid alley searching for a pigeon lunch, or a plump little girl inhaling a sweet *jeen-deui* sesame ball.

Among these sights on an early Saturday evening, you

might have seen Lindsey, holding open the heavy car door for her ancient uncle Bill. Her family was completely blocking the single-lane traffic on Grant Avenue as they tried to maneuver the old guy from the sedan to the curb in front of the Empress of China restaurant. Cars were at a standstill all the way down past California. Drivers within view of the elderly man waited patiently out of respect, and those in minivans further down the line seemed resigned to the fact that Chinatown traffic was always terrible. All refrained from honking their car horns, as if lulled into a calm melancholy by dusk's darkening shadows.

Lindsey's Auntie Vivien was hoisting the wheelchair out of the trunk, while Mr. Owyang shifted the car into park and went around to the passenger's side to lift Uncle Bill out of the seat. Gin family elders with red sashes rushed out to greet Uncle Bill, who stared out blankly from his cataract eyes. A Chinese man fastened a boutonniere across Uncle Bill's lapel, next to his small pin bearing the dignified image of Dr. Sun Yat-sen. Other men crowded around and lifted Uncle Bill's stroke-impaired arm and shook his hand vigorously.

Lindsey felt stupid just standing there holding the car door. She watched the old men fuss over her uncle and wondered what past deeds he had accomplished, and what kind of life this man had led. She felt out of place, as if her ignorance of Chinese grammar might be discovered at any moment. She looked up at the apartment lights blinking on one by one, and the sight reminded her of an Elmer Bischoff painting she'd once seen at the University Art Museum in Berkeley.

"Hey, close the door," her dad called, starting up the engine and lurching the car forward. Lindsey obliged and followed her uncle's entourage into the restaurant foyer and up the elevator.

Once they arrived on the fifth floor, a chubby singer who resembled an Asian Pillsbury Doughboy belted out "melodies" in Cantonese, and the volume from the speakers was as loud as the chandeliers were blinding. The walls were decorated with swaths of embroidered crimson silk and antique canopies stitched with turquoise and gold thread.

Newly arrived guests all wrote their names on a red tablecloth and collected their seat numbers as Mr. Hong Kong Poppin' Fresh continued his set from the stage. Lindsey and her family sat bundled in their coats, cracking salted melon seeds between their teeth. Shortly thereafter, Auntie Vivien sat down with two of her three children, Brandon and Cammie, and Auntie Shirley blustered over to the table, infusing the surrounding air with her signature patchouli fragrance.

They settled in and made small talk as they scanned the other guests, most of whom they only saw once a year, at this banquet. The Gin Family Association continued to invite Lindsey's family every year even though Gung Gung had passed away and two of his daughters had different married surnames now. They were all still considered Gins despite the fact that Gung Gung himself had only become a Gin by means of a false certificate. Looking around, Lindsey wondered which other families were impostors.

She sat next to her mother and looked across the table at her aunties, who were squabbling over whose fake diamonds looked more real. Vivien and Shirley were different from Lindsey's mother, who was the only one born in

China. Although they had all been named for movie stars—Lillian Gish, Vivien Leigh, and Shirley Temple—Vivien and Shirley were as overdramatic and spoiled as film divas compared to their older sister. They said it was tough luck for her that she had had to work as a kid, shelling pounds of shrimp for a local restaurant to help their parents make ends meet. That was back in the early forties, and both Vivien and Shirley weren't born until eight to ten years later. They had benefitted from their parents' following financial success but, unfortunately, had never learned the value or satisfaction of earning one's own money.

Even now, neither had had much of a job history. Vivien dabbled in real estate but mainly lived off the income from rental properties acquired by her ex-husband. Shirley had business cards that touted her as a "painter of auras" and "chakra reader." In reality, she was a part-time file clerk at the corporate office of Whole Foods.

Neither Vivien nor Shirley spoke Chinese very well but conversed with their mother in English or with a hunt-and-peck hybrid of Chinese and English words. They both considered Pau Pau superstitious, judgmental, and somewhat "backward." But they always welcomed her cash handouts. Shirley especially longed for the material possessions and bragging rights afforded by hard work she herself was unwilling to do. Of her unmarried status she often said, "Why should I be made to suffer only because I haven't met my male twin-ray yet? Vivien's ex-husband bought her a BMW but I deserve something, too." She whined to Pau Pau for months about her past life as a dethroned Aztec princess, citing this trauma as another reason why she needed a new car. When Pau Pau asked what kind she needed, Shirley replied, "I'm not materialistic like my sisters. *Bai-gnoh* a brand new VW Beetle."

In contrast, Lindsey's mom was proud of having earned her own way from a young age. Lillian started working in a Chinatown curio shop when she was ten years old, and kept that job all through City College, when she met Lindsey's dad, Earl. He used to say that when they met, Lillian looked like a Chinese Jacqueline Kennedy. Because she always supported herself and her sisters never did, Lillian now considered her sisters lazy spendthrifts who couldn't even discern good quality. It galled her that they wanted QVC jewelry fakes and Volkswagens instead of perfect clarity gems and Mercedes-Benz automobiles. Having watched her sisters grow up as such, she wanted to make sure Kevin and Lindsey were not as spoiled. When they were small, she made sure they were both responsible for weekly chores, and also sent them to Chinese school. She wanted them to be the perfect combination of qualities: well-educated with good manners like upper-class Americans, but with humility and toughness like the Chinese. On principle, she thought all Chinese-Americans needed to know how to speak their mother tongue, and she was disappointed that neither of her kids had absorbed much Cantonese. However, she wasn't too upset, because she knew she would be even more mortified if it turned out that either spoke with even a trace of a Chinese accent. She wanted her children's Chinese and American balance to be just right, and she hardly ever approved of how their ratios were rising or falling at any given moment. But for the most part, she was proud of them. Neither Kevin nor Lindsey was a doctor or a lawyer, but she appreciated that neither of them was drug-addicted or blatantly stupid, which, in this day and age, was a relief.

Lindsey noticed some familiar faces a couple of tables away and waved to a group of people that her parents always referred to as their "Oakland relatives." She had always been unclear about how they were connected to them, and no one ever had a straight explanation. To make things even more confusing, practically all Chinese people they knew were given automatic titles of Uncle or Auntie, even neighbors and the lady who owned the local Laundromat. Lindsey could never figure out who was specifically related by blood, but she wanted to know what linked her to the Oakland folks so she could determine whose names she should bother learning and whose she could just blow off.

As she scooted her chair in a bit, she asked, "Pau Pau, how are we related to those people again?"

"They your aunties, uncles, and cousins," Pau Pau said, pausing to maneuver her tongue around the dark green meat of a melon seed.

"But how, exactly?"

"They from Oakland!" Pau Pau said, seeming exasperated by Lindsey's ignorance.

"I know they *live* in Oakland—"

"Then what you ask for? Waste my time!" Pau Pau was significantly irritated now. Like a great blue heron striking at its prey with a sharp, swordlike beak, Pau Pau's two forefingers, with precision and surprising strength, poked her granddaughter's upper arm, delivering a punishing little jolt that caused Lindsey to immediately cease her questioning. She sat quietly for a moment, embarrassed and contrite.

Kevin snapped open the bottle of whiskey on the table and mixed Seagram's Seven with 7 UP.

"Want one?" he asked, spooning crushed ice into his glass.

Lindsey nodded, but then spied Pau Pau giving her the dirtiest look ever. "Uh, no thanks," she corrected.

"We got here too early," Kevin complained. "The speeches haven't even started yet. And geez, this Chinese music is the worst." Taking a swig from his glass, he leaned back on the legs of his chair, which suddenly slipped out from underneath him, sending him and his drink crashing into a vellum-screened partition.

"*Ai-ya!*" Pau Pau screamed. "*Gum lun jun!*" She scolded him for his clumsiness as he picked himself up. Lindsey and her cousins howled with laughter, but no one else in the huge crowd seemed to notice. Even Pau Pau was chuckling now. Her amused expression reminded Lindsey of the look she had when watching the *Three Stooges*.

The longest speeches by the oldest guys with the biggest ears and lengthiest eyebrows followed next. Lindsey couldn't understand what the patriarchs were saying, but a couple of tables away, a woman was translating for her Caucasian son-in-law, and Lindsey intermittently heard snippets such as "community service," "scholarship," and "earthquake retrofit." Her eavesdropping was interrupted when the elderly man at the microphone said "Dupont *Gie*," and her ears perked up. She knew that *gie* meant "street" and that long ago, Grant Avenue had been called Dupont. She found it remarkable and charming that the old-timer used the former name, and even more shocking to her was the fact that she understood anything at all from the Chinese speech.

She scanned the room, which was a sea of black-haired heads dotted with the occasional dishwater blond of a Hoarder married to a distant relative. The Great White Nerds were sparsely sprinkled through the crowd, looking liked trapped albino mice.

She began to wonder: Why were all the white guys with Asian women always so geeked-out? How come she never saw a fine-ass hottie with one of her Chinese sisters? Buddha knows there are lots of beautiful Asian women. The discrepancy in attractiveness was a greater mystery to her than the identity of the gelatinous, wormlike substance on her appetizer plate.

Lindsey didn't want to be part of one of those interracial couples where the woman was attractive enough but the white guy was inevitably:

a. overweight
b. bald
c. spore-like
d. a and c only
e. all of the above

She saw so many of these aesthetically mismatched couples that she worried people might think Asian girls would settle for any old homely boor as long as he was white. On the contrary, she knew Chinese girls like her were the pickiest of all. And proud of it!

She suddenly remembered her cousin Stephanie and the white husband she had bagged a few years ago. It was a point of some anxiety for Lindsey that her cousin was fourteen months younger than she but had already met and married someone. Over the din of the echoing voice amplified by the microphone, she called across the table, "Hey Brandon, where's your sister?"

Brandon, a post-college do-nothing slacker, was his usual sulking self with his parka hood still fastened around his big pimply head. "I dunno. Maybe she's late because she's pregnant and can't waddle down here. She's lucky she could get out of it. Wish I could. These dinners are always so boring." With arms folded over his chest, he squinted his eyes, then closed them as if willing himself elsewhere.

Finally the speeches were over, and the food came rolling out of the kitchen on stainless steel carts: shark fin soup followed by honey-drizzled prawns and walnuts, sizzling cubed steak and bok choy, snow peas and scallops, salted chicken with a pinkish brown dipping sauce that looked like calamine lotion, and crispy, fatty Peking duck.

The food at these banquets was always the same. Objectively speaking, the food was a delectable twelve-course meal that was expertly prepared; any gourmand would be impressed by the delicate flavors of the various dishes. However, to Lindsey and her cousins, who had all eaten countless feasts such as these, the meal was simply as they expected. They had been spoiled for years by the routine of flawlessly cooked delicacies.

Lindsey spread some *hoisin* sauce on a steamed bun, handed it to her brother, and then prepared one for herself. At a Chinese banquet it was always polite to serve others first. She glanced over at her mom and Pau Pau, who were busy scrutinizing a jade ring that Auntie Vivien had recently purchased from a mail-order catalog. Her mother and Pau Pau seemed to be debating the jade's quality, and they sounded like they were arguing, but Lindsey was never sure with Cantonese. To her it always sounded like shouting and scolding. Alongside Vivien, Auntie Shirley was flicking her fingertips in the air and chanting softly, requesting any negative energy pockets to burst immediately.

A whole steamed fish arrived at the table. The pearly eyeball stared at Lindsey as Pau Pau came over and urged her to try the flesh from the tender cheek area. After the top layer of fish meat had all been eaten, her cousin Brandon wielded a serving spoon in an attempt to flip over the fish and access the filet underneath.

"Stop!" Kevin said. "Don't flip it over—it's bad luck!"

"Why?" Brandon asked.

"It's like flipping over the fishing boat, dummy. Here, go like this." Kevin grabbed the spoon from his cousin's hand and deftly airlifted the lattice of spiky bones away from the flaky meat.

"Hey, want some *jup* from the *yuer*?" Kevin offered a spoonful of fish gravy to his sister.

Lindsey nodded. "I like the way you incorporate any Chinese word you know into your sentences," she commended him.

"Yeah, you like my *Chinglish*? Here, have some *bock fahn*." He scooped white rice into her bowl.

"Why do you want the rice in that small bowl? The plate's bigger," Brandon interjected.

Kevin scoffed at him. "Are you even Chinese? You can't pick up *fahn* on the plate, you need the *woohn*, so you can use your *fai-jee*." He gestured to a pair of chopsticks, then teased, "That is, unless you need a fork . . ."

As Brandon pouted, everyone else giggled, knowing that

Brandon was always clumsy with the traditional Chinese utensils. He often stabbed or skewered his food, unlike everybody else, who had all long ago mastered the art of precisely tweezing slippery mushrooms or stubborn cashews. Even his little sister, Cammie, had absorbed the unspoken knowledge that using a fork at a banquet was only for the smallest children and non-Chinese guests.

As Lindsey glanced around at the smattering of Hoarders, their bumbling way with chopsticks made them all targets for ridicule, as if they all wore training wheels on their heads. She watched some greige guys struggle as they tried to steer food into their mouths. Piping-hot sea cucumber blobs slid through their chopsticks and landed on their Sta-Prest crotches.

"What's with those dudes?" Brandon asked, scrutinizing them.

Lindsey said, "Yeah, I know—like all Asian women can only hook up with computer toads."

"No, I mean, what do you think they're doing here?"

"They've cast our maidens under their white devil spell," Kevin joked.

"Let's go kick their asses," Brandon suggested.

"Some of them might be nice guys. You never know, sometimes those nerds come in handy when your server crashes," Kevin replied.

Lindsey listened and kept her big yap shut at first. But then she blurted, "Why can't they just be cuter?"

After a moment, her brother said, "Well, Mike's not bad."

Obsessed as ever, she first thought of Michael at work, but then Brandon said, "Yeah, Steph's white guy."

He was referring to Stephanie's husband, Mike. Lindsey thought for a second. It was true. Her cousin was married to a surfer type whose personality hinted at evolution beyond the turtle stage. She would have to investigate this aberration, because it created a loose thread in her Hoarder Theory. She scanned the nearby tables, but Stephanie and her husband hadn't shown up.

It was the end of the meal, and a spooky gray tapioca "soup" was served for dessert.

As Lindsey waited for the Chinese exodus to begin, she looked out the floor-to-ceiling windows. Against a backdrop of the moon's glow filtered through shadowy, blue-gray fog, low brick rooftops were silhouetted against neon-lit pagodas and the ominous dark presence of Old St. Mary's Church. Across the way, she stared at an empty balcony with cracked Art Nouveau tiles and black calligraphy strokes painted on a tattered sign. She realized it was the second floor of a crumbling yellow temple that she walked by all the time but hardly ever looked up to see, maybe because the glistening crackle-skinned ducks in the street-level shop windows were too distracting. She reminded herself to look up next time and search for the sooty, lantern-lit overhang, but then she noticed that an ornate wooden awning skirted the building and shielded the temple from the world below. Mesmerized, she was now comforted that only the Empress of China allowed such a peek into the deserted temple. She slid back in her chair, reached out and touched the window's heavy curtain, and she had a vague memory of playing within these same fabric folds with her cousins when she was small. She had been to Empress of China a thousand times before to celebrate weddings, birthdays, her grandparents' golden anniversary, and at least twenty of these very same Association dinners, and now she savored the feeling of being here again. As plain as it was, the gold curtain against her fingertips was a comforting sensation, like napping in the backseat of a car and half-waking to find the thick, bright sheen of her mama's coat draped over her. Gazing at the view now, she felt like a little kid clinging to a coat hem of spring-hued silk shantung, seeing something she wasn't supposed to see. She watched as shopkeepers below rolled aluminum doors over their storefronts and switched off their flickering strobe lights. Chinatown was taking off her makeup and getting ready for a night's slumber. In an hour or so all the restaurant guests would return to their own neighborhoods and the streets would be deserted. All that would remain would be a dark and sleepy Chinatown, wrapped in a flimsy nightgown of moonlight.

Now Back to the Michael We Really Care About

There were signs that this was not just a friend thing. With each day that passed, Lindsey wore less and less to work, having learned over the years that boys were dopes who really responded to seeing skin.

When she saw Michael Friday morning, she let the cashmere cardigan slip off her shoulders as if by accident. She nonchalantly positioned her back to the hallway, knowing that if he wanted to get his caffeine, he'd have to see her butt protruding slightly into his path on the way to the break room. On cue, her satin bra straps made a cameo appearance when her sweater drifted down the smooth skin of her well-exfoliated arms.

"Good morning," he said, stopping in his tracks.

Lindsey smiled even before she turned around.

"Oh, hi," she replied casually. He could have been the one-armed design intern for all she seemed to care. But inside, she was devastatingly pleased.

Today he wore a blue shirt, and she wanted to get close enough to inhale the clean laundry smell of the slightly wrinkled broadcloth. Sometimes when she was away from him for a few days she tried to tell herself that he wasn't really that gorgeous, that she had just built him up in her head and he was only a regular-looking guy. But while he may not have been movie-star handsome, her heart was a melted scoop of ice cream dripping in his hand. She wanted to lick him.

"In case you're wondering, I'm free for lunch today," she piped up unexpectedly, embarrassing herself with this sudden advertisement of availability. She wondered if it showed on her face, all the times she had imagined them together, um, doing it.

A smile quickly overcame his clean-scrubbed face.

"Um, great. Okay." He nodded agreeably and disappeared to retrieve his coffee.

Lunch with her crush! Now she was getting somewhere.

But wait. Was that, "Great, I wanna have lunch with you, too" or was that "Ooo-kay. Great. As if!"

She didn't know. She pondered for a moment, then paced around and misfiled faxes, replaying the conversation in her head a hundred times at high speed until the film reel in her mind got so tangled up that she couldn't focus anymore.

For the next two hours she busied herself with nobrainer tasks, but around midmorning, her boss, Howard, stopped by the front desk to chat.

"Hey, Lindsey! Isn't it time for the Autumn Moon Festival? I want to know all your family's authentic customs. What are you doing to celebrate?" He looked at her a little too intensely.

Lindsey found the role of twenty-four-hour, on-call cultural educator to be exasperating. Plus, he had picked a rotten time to be ethnically sensitive. She had four callers on hold and she was late for the FedEx pickup. Plus, she really needed to go to the bathroom. She wanted to say, "Howard, could you please package up these documents and run them down to the FedEx office? Oh, and put these four calls into voice mail yourself, because my tampon is totally leaking."

But she didn't say that. Instead, she chitchatted about mooncakes, quickly distributed the calls, and quietly bled through the white cotton panel of her undies as Howard yammered on about his love for Sam Woh's.

She was sure her boss was trying to build some kind of cross-cultural bridge, reaching out, as it were. He bragged about eating at this Chinese restaurant that he thought was for locals only, but as far as she was concerned, no actual Chinese person, or real San Franciscan, ate at Sam Woh's. "Only tourists go there!" her mother would say, laughing her ass off at the thought. That is, if her mother ever laughed (or had anything but a really flat ass).

Later, after having darted to the bathroom in the nick of time to avoid a major menstrual meltdown, Lindsey tried to catch glimpses of Michael in the hall, wondering if they would be lunching together or if he thought she was insane. But she didn't see him. A pant leg would saunter by and her heart would do a half-skip. Not him. The elevator doors would spring open with a bing! But he would not be inside. She would hear the hallway door click, but he would not emerge.

At 1:05 P.M. she could no longer stand it. Why had he not come looking for her? She was nervous, yet resourceful as always. She rifled through the UPS bills until she found a receipt for an item Michael had sent. Under the guise of seeking his signature for bill-coding purposes, she planned to enter his office and find out what was going on.

She walked down the hall, ready to thrust the invoice toward him, but she pulled back just in time.

He looked up from his papers.

"I'm starving, how about you?" he said. He reached for his jacket, and she watched him slip a small silver tin of mints into his pocket.

LET'S PRESS PAUSE FOR A MOMENT.

If Lindsey was going to lunch with Mimi, she probably wouldn't bring mints. When Lindsey ate, in general, she did not carry mints. A person carried mints when he wanted to be minty fresh. Minty fresh for, like, kissing.

This mint thing was a small coup for Lindsey. This mint thing was undeniable proof that Michael *like* liked her. He cared about his *breath* around her. Yes. This mint thing was the culmination of her efforts thus far.

PLEASE PRESS PLAY TO RESUME TAPE.

"Let me get my bag and I'll be right back," she said. She spun on her heel and glided back to her desk. Crouching down, she pulled out her Shiseido compact and Bonne Bell lip gloss for a quick touch-up, then checked her teeth to make sure all was fine in the realm of dental hygeine. She smoothed down the back of her skirt and strode back to Michael's office, ready to make a breezy, confident entrance through his door, and into his heart as well.

Unfortunately, when she returned, he was removing his jacket.

"Howard just called an editorial meeting, and I have to go," he said, grabbing an accordion file folder. Fumbling around for a pen, he looked up and placed his hand lightly on her shoulder. He offered a quick "Sorry" and brushed past her.

She stood there numb for a moment. She was light-headed from having not eaten for six hours, and she felt like an idiot as she walked by the glass-enclosed conference room and watched the whole edit staff follow her with their collective eyes. She wondered if it was obvious to everyone that her fragile romantic hope, like a bisque Hello Kitty figurine, had just been smashed to the ground and pulverized into dust.

She took the elevator and went down to the corner cafe. She listlessly consumed a wilted spinach salad. Twenty minutes later, she was back at the front desk, pretty much wanting to die. She turned off the lunchtime voice-mail recording, and the phone immediately rang.

"*Vegan Warrior.* How may I direct your call?" she said, speaking slightly less merrily than usual.

"Oh, thank God," a flustered man replied on the line. "I just got off the phone with that Chinese Merchants' Association about their disgusting animal treatment. They just don't get it, do they? It's nice to finally be talking to an American." He snickered, seeming certain she would sympathize with his experience.

She took a deep breath and released some of the tension that was threatening to snap a vein in her forehead. "How may I direct your call?" she repeated. There was a slight pause as it seemed to dawn on the man that she did not want to engage in anything but the most basic conversation with him.

"Oh, well, yes. Yes, I am calling for Miles Cartier."

What a dip this guy was. He couldn't even get the name right.

"Sir, do you mean Michael Cartier?" she asked.

"Yes, Miles Michael Cartier." He spoke quickly, with contrived urgency, like he was a VIP with mere seconds to talk before hopping on the next Concorde.

But wait, did she hear him right? Was her crush's real name the *Mark of the Hoarder*? How could this tragic flaw have evaded her?

She managed to remain calm. She instructed herself to stay professional, finish the call, and then investigate later.

She cleared her throat before speaking.

"Michael Cartier is in a meeting right now. Would you like to leave a message?"

He said, "Um, yeah, tell him that Miles Olin called. He knows my number."

Great. They were both named Miles. Had the world gone mad?

The next day was a bright, sunny Saturday, so naturally Lindsey wanted to sulk in bed. But she had spent last night doing just that, and Pau Pau was worried. Without knocking, she burst into Lindsey's stuffy room.

"What's wrong? Sick?"

Pau Pau's panicked shriek pierced Lindsey's eardrums

like a searing acupuncture needle perforating the inner coils of her brain.

"Don't yell at me!" Lindsey hollered out from beneath the covers.

"Not yelling!" Pau Pau said. "Is normal speaking voice for Chinese!"

Lindsey groaned and pulled the pillow tighter around her ears.

"What you want? *Meen bow*?" Pau Pau asked, offering to make toast. She added, "With strawberry jam? *Ho teem*!"

"No thanks," Lindsey replied.

Pau Pau desperately sought breakfast options that might please her finicky grandchild. "You want *gai-don*? You like scramble? How about Pepsi-Cola?"

Receiving no response, Pau Pau left the room but rapidly returned, advancing to rub a dollop of stinky Tiger Balm on the girl's chest and throat. Lindsey sprang up and covered her neck with her hands, yelling, "No, no, no!"

"Wha?" her grandmother stood back with the orangish-brown goo globbed onto her fingers. "Not sick?" Pau Pau looked bewildered.

"No, only tired. I'm O-KAY," Lindsey said loudly, assuming volume created clarity.

"*Ai-ya*, I make *doong-gwa* soup. Just in case." Pau Pau sputtered out of the room but left the door wide open.

Lindsey got up to shut the door and flopped back into bed. She couldn't explain her silly office romance to her mahjong-playing, soup-making grandmother. When Lindsey thought of Michael she used a totally different compartment of her brain, separate from any idea of Pau Pau and her old Chinese ways.

Lindsey forced her 128-pound self out of bed and into the shower. Afterwards, she tried phoning Mimi but only got her answering machine. Knowing she had to get out of the apartment before she drove herself crazy, she threw on jeans and a sweatshirt and decided to walk off her glum self-loathing.

Before she could dodge past the front door, Pau Pau approached, carrying a tiny plastic bottle. Lindsey was familiar with the green-and-yellow vial filled with dry, black powder consisting of mold particles scraped from decayed watermelon rind. It was used to heal canker sores and prevent scratchy throats.

"Open!" Pau Pau commanded, and Lindsey obeyed. Pau Pau squeezed the plastic walls and blew a small puff of black dust into the back of Lindsey's throat, then screwed back on the white cap. Lindsey tried not to taste the bitter remedy, and trudged down the stairs.

She ambled down to Polk Street and stopped by an empty taqueria for a lonely chicken burrito and a soda. She wanted a Coke, but the sight of the red-and-white logo reminded her of the cans at the office she had been stupidly picking up after Michael. She got the Orange Crush instead. Not that it mattered.

After eating, she still didn't feel like going home, and she didn't want to see anyone. Even having to put on her happy, well-adjusted face for other shoppers and store clerks was too much of an effort. She detoured off the main street and hiked up to the more residential area west of Van Ness Avenue. She walked farther up Washington Street until she came to a more secluded area with tall evergreen trees.

A bit out of breath, she stopped to admire a long, wide

brick driveway that wound around the hill and up toward a stately cream-colored mansion that resembled an ornate meringue. She studied the decorative plaster, the Corinthian columns, and the sparkling French doors lined with flouncy drapings.

This isolated house gave Lindsey a sense of déjà vu. She felt like she somehow knew this place but didn't know why or how exactly. She noted the elaborate baroque detailing and searched her brain for clues as to why she felt so strange. Perhaps she had seen an article about this house in a magazine. Oh, yes, now she knew. She vaguely recalled reading an article about a famous romance novelist who lived in the city, and this must have been the place. She remembered being impressed that a writer could afford such a sweet pile of bricks.

She took one last, wistful look at the palace, which gleamed as if it were speckled with sugar crystals, and headed back down Washington Street. She brushed her palm along the building's facade and took long strides down the sidewalk, being careful not to step on any cracks.

As her last fingertip lifted off the limestone wall, she had not one inkling that eighty-five years ago her Grandpa Samuel Gin and her Great Uncle Bill played on this very same spot.

On Sunday Lindsey's mom picked her up, and they headed to Fort Mason for an Asian antiques show. As the gold sedan pulled into the driveway, Lindsey ran outside and thought about how glad her mother was that she lived with Pau Pau. Her mom said she hoped Lindsey would learn to respect her cultural heritage more, now that she didn't live with strangers, especially foolish *bock-gwais*. As she jogged around to the passenger side and got into the car, she recalled the time her mom had visited her back in college. Her shared flat had been an embarrassing mess, and their conversation had gone something like this:

Mrs. Owyang: How can you live like this? This junky place is an insult to your father and me. If you respected your Chinese heritage, you'd clean up this rat's nest!

Lindsey: It's the Year of the Rat—good luck! Besides, I'm surrounded by Chinese culture. Just look at my fabulous chinoiserie drapes and place mats. I bought them at Pottery Barn.

Everything Lindsey knew about China she learned through shopping. And watching *Antiques Roadshow*, of course. The dynasties were all easier to remember in terms of porcelain narcissus bowls, Quan Yin statues, and bronze vessels.

Lindsey had asked her mother to attend the Fort Mason show because she figured it would be a good way to share quality time together while simultaneously demonstrating her interest in something Chinese. Although her mother had agreed to go, she didn't seem to notice Lindsey's effort toward cultural betterment. Her only comment to her daughter was, "Why do you want to buy *used* things?"

When they arrived, Mrs. Owyang almost ran over one of the valet parking attendants, insisting on parking herself. "Very Pau Pau," Lindsey noted to herself.

The admission price was twelve dollars, and once inside,

the place had a museum atmosphere with lots of revered whispering. About a hundred booths were lined up with all sorts of goods: pillows, rugs, ancient snuff bottles, cinnabar boxes, gold, jade, and pearl jewelry. Furniture and textiles were spread about the gigantic space, which had been arranged with glass cabinets filled with ceramic, stone, and metal treasures.

Lindsey and her mother strolled around alongside middle-aged whites. Several men wore tweed blazers with elbow patches, and a few women donned antique silk robes with horse-hoof sleeves. Lindsey wondered how, in the timespan of a hundred years, the elaborately stitched garments had gone from the backs of Mandarin officials to the backs of Tiburon housewives. She didn't think snooty American socialites should be cavorting in imperial Chinese robes.

Noticing the dearth of Asian shoppers, Lindsey wondered if other Chinese folks were uninterested in these furnishings because they had already inherited stuff from their families. Or perhaps they were attracted to more European styles or to sleek, modern decor. Even Mrs. Owyang preferred American Federal and Colonial-designed interiors. She disdained gaudy exportware and bought only Wedgwood or Villeroy & Boch from Neiman Marcus.

Mrs. Owyang clucked her tongue and made comments under her breath, criticizing the poor quality and outrageous prices. She picked up a candy dish and gawked at the price tag. "Four thousand five hundred," she said. "I don't think so!"

Admiring some Qing Dynasty porcelain serving dishes, Lindsey asked her mom about the designs on an oversized charger, but Mrs. Owyang shrugged and said, "I have no idea. Go ask the saleslady."

A woman resembling Dustin Hoffman dressed as Tootsie approached them. "Aren't those pieces wonderful?" she exclaimed. She fiddled with the sleeves of her brocaded jacket and boasted that she was an expert on feng shui and the *I Ching*. She described the symbols of the Eight Immortals that were painted in famille rose colors, and Lindsey scrutinized the pictures and followed along as the woman rambled, ". . . that one's a fan, and there's an umbrella, that one looks like a golf bag with clubs . . ."

Lindsey thanked the woman for her explanation and called over to her mother. "Hey Mom, did you hear that these designs symbolize good luck and long life?"

Mrs. Owyang glanced dismissively at the serving plate and pursed her dry, burgundy lips. "I suppose, but we're not paying a thousand dollars for that filthy old thing."

They passed ornate footstools, cylindrical hat stands, and long, sequined wedding skirts with yellow rhinestone dragons and red jeweled phoenixes. Lindsey stopped to inspect a porcelain cube also painted with the symbols of the Eight Immortal Golfers.

Lindsey and Mrs. Owyang continued down the aisles, passing trunks carved from camphor wood and a display of ceramic parrots and painted citrus fruits in the shape of Buddha's hand. By a lacquered altar table, Lindsey paused to observe several pairs of tiny embroidered slippers. She looked down to her boots and wiggled the toes of her left foot. As she lifted one of the miniature shoes, she wondered what physical pain and emotional anguish had been endured to tightly bind a normal foot into the space of a doll-size slipper.

A woman with a menacing smile stiffly stretched across a Katherine-Helmond-in-*Brazil* facelift swiftly descended upon Lindsey and whispered, "Don't soil them! The oil from your fingers is poison!"

Lindsey looked up, startled. She shuddered, then apologized as she placed the hooked heel back on the table.

She walked to a grouping of grotesque fu dogs, and nearby, a woman held up a rounded plate and turned to her design consultant. "Ooh, this says it's a *War Ming* dish. Isn't it a wonder that they made gorgeous porcelains even during the great war?"

The designer replied, "Mrs. Harris, that's a *warming* dish for reheating food."

Meanwhile, Mrs. Owyang was scrutinizing the jewelry cases. She worked as a sales manager at the Jewelry and Gift Mart downtown and was always keen on sizing up potential competitors.

Lindsey steered her mother toward one of the few stations manned by a Chinese vendor. She peered into a glass case filled with intricate jewelry made from brilliant turquoise kingfisher feathers and gold foil. On the next shelf, she was attracted to pieces made from delicate silver filigree.

"Oh, look at those earrings," she pointed.

"Silver is junk. Only 24-karat gold is worth wearing." Mrs. Owyang stated her opinion with authority.

"But I like those," Lindsey protested, pointing at silver hoops with small jade squares pressed into the woven design.

They inquired about the price of the earrings, but the

man didn't reply; he just turned over a price tag that said $99.99.

Lindsey asked her mother, "That's not such a bad price, is it?"

Mrs. Owyang stared at her daughter's face as if she'd just realized that she'd given birth to one of those suckers born every minute. She blinked a couple of times and nudged her daughter aside. Lucky for Lindsey, her mother was fluent in the most important Chinese dialect of all: bargaining.

As she dickered with the vendor in Cantonese, Mrs. Owyang punctuated her words with haggling gestures and grunts. She talked down the price to $40, and sealed the deal with a reverberating slap on the glass case that would have made Pau Pau proud. The man looked defeated as he placed the earrings in a silk pouch and somberly accepted the two twenty-dollar bills.

"No tax?" Lindsey whispered quizically.

Sounding bored, Mrs. Owyang replied, "Tax is for whites." She spoke as if exemption from sales tax between Chinese people was the most natural thing in the world. Swiveling her arm, she unsentimentally handed Lindsey her prize.

"Thanks, Mom!" Lindsey poked her finger inside the purse and lightly touched the delicate pieces of silver and jade.

"You're welcome. Your early Christmas present." Her mother spoke with stern reserve, but Lindsey noticed her tight but satisified smile.

Lindsey thanked her again, knowing her mother would forget by the time December rolled around.

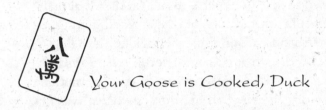

Your Goose is Cooked, Duck

Wednesday night Lindsey drove to her cousin Brandon's apartment. They were both go-betweens for their mothers, coordinating the delivery of Uncle Bill's next round of hypertension pills.

Her cousin answered the door wearing sweats and a faded Speed Racer T-shirt. She followed him inside and marveled at the collection of plastic Godzillas, Mothras, and Ultraman action figures that crowded the bookshelves and lined the perimeter of the carpeting.

She passed a room filled with Bruce Lee photos fastened neatly to the walls with map pins. Bruce was shown kicking Kareem Abdul-Jabbar, relaxing in gold sunglasses, defeating Chuck Norris, and winning a cha-cha dance contest.

"Wow, who knew Bruce was so versatile?" Lindsey said. She followed Brandon into the kitchen, where he reached atop the refrigerator and tossed her a vial of white-and-brown pills.

As a kid, Brandon was a scrawny little nothing. He was a braggart and a show-off who never knew when to shut up.

Many older kids considered beating the crap out of him, but they hesitated because they worried that all Chinese kids were natural kung fu experts. Brandon didn't actually possess any skills in martial arts, but he avoided getting his ass kicked by strutting around and mimicking the kung fu maneuvers he studied from Bruce Lee movies. Some impressionable classmates spread the rumor that he was one bad-ass mofo, and luckily, his fighting skills were never challenged. He considered Bruce Lee his personal savior.

"Remember when we saw all his movies at the Great Star Theater?" he asked, opening the fridge to retrieve a carton of Tropicana.

"Oh yeah," Lindsey replied. She reached out to accept a Bruce Lee mug filled with low-pulp juice.

"Yeah, those are the masterpieces of kung fu cinema. I own all those films now," he said proudly, gesturing to a stack of videos piled in the living room. He retrieved one of them and said, "Remember seeing this one? It's really hard to get. I got a bootleg copy from a friend in New York."

Lindsey really couldn't have cared less, but she nodded politely. She sat on a couch she recognized as a castoff from Auntie Vivien's house and surveyed the bachelor pad full of electronic equipment, Japanese animé videos, and, of course, more Bruce memorabilia. She was most impressed by a cubist painting of Bruce attacking Darth Vader with a flying kick to the neck, the light saber falling into a spiral galaxy.

Brandon noticed her admiring the painting. "Nice, huh?" he grunted.

"Yeah, what a postmodern pastiche," she replied.

Brandon scrunched up his face. He stared at her scornfully for a while, then finally blurted out, "So Kevin says you're a dairy queen."

"What?" she said, distracted by the sight of a Bruce doll riding piggyback on a storm-trooper model from *The Empire Strikes Back*.

"Yeah. Says you only like white guys. What's up with that?" He pulled a cigarette out of nowhere and lit it. He blew smoke in her face and waited for her to say something.

She thought about Michael for a second, and then said, "I don't like anyone right now." She sprung off the sofa and went to the kitchen to place her mug in the sink.

But Brandon didn't let her off that easily. He followed her to continue his questioning.

"Yeah, well, if you did like someone, he'd be white, huh?" He cornered her by the Fruit Loops.

"Um, I dunno. What do you care?" She crossed her arms.

"Hey, man, don't give away any Chinese secrets."

"What secrets? *Ancient Chinese secret, huh?*" she laughed.

Brandon scowled. "No man, it's real. Bruce Lee was teaching white guys the Chinese killing techniques, so the Chinese mafia had him assassinated."

She leaned against the tile counter. "How?"

"I dunno, poisoned him, man. He dropped dead, without any trace of evidence. The Chinese mafia really knows how to kill someone. Professional hit, y'know."

"So you're saying I'm gonna get snuffed by the Chinese mafia for dating a white guy?"

"I'm saying you better watch yourself. You don't know what those Big Noses want."

"Well, I'll be careful," she said. She picked her sweater

up off the couch and turned to leave, but Brandon grabbed her arm.

She yanked back her wrist. "This little one's not worth the effort," she said. "Come, let me get you something."

Brandon immediately recognized her words as dialogue from the *Star Wars* cantina scene. Any vague reference to the science fiction blockbuster usually had a pacifying effect on him.

"Okay," he said, appeased. "Drive carefully, k?" He lightly punched her on the shoulder and walked her to the door.

Back in her car, Lindsey reminded herself to generally avoid any future conversations with Brandon. As she drove, she recalled the days when they were kids.

About fifteen years earlier, Lindsey, Brandon, and Kevin had spent many afternoons together in a dark movie house in Chinatown, the Great Star Theater on Jackson Street. They were supposed to have been at St. Mary's Chinese School with their inkbrushes and string-bound paper booklets, practicing their calligraphy. Instead, they'd studied Bruce Lee.

Enter the Dragon. Fists of Fury. The Chinese Connection. Kevin and Brandon had been crazy over these martial arts movies. They begrudgingly allowed Lindsey to tag along because they couldn't have risked leaving her to purposely or accidentally rat them out.

Each weekday after regular grammar school, a handful of Chinese kids had all had exactly forty-five minutes to get from Franklin and Broadway to the corner of Stockton and Clay for classes in Chinese language, writing, and history. After sitting all day in a third-or fifth-grade classroom, the last thing they'd wanted to do was take the bus across town to sit and learn something else for another three hours.

They would arrive at the corner where St. Mary's stood with gothic black walls and a gulag gate. But instead of descending the cold, concrete steps to Chinese school, they would head across the street to the friendly cafe that sold thin-crust slices of cheese pizza and twenty-five-cent lime slushes.

The Great Star Theater was a short walking distance from the school. Once inside, the threesome would hunch down in a dark row of seats to avoid being quizzed about their truancy. Every once in a while, an old man who worked there would discover them and question them in Chinese. None of them had understood a word he'd said.

The boys had sat enthralled at the fantastic acrobatics and kung fu mastery. While Kevin and Brandon had studied each kick, each twirling of nunchuks, and the various types of blows that could be inflicted with a bamboo stick, Lindsey had eventually gotten bored. With lots of change in her school uniform pocket, she would wander through the lobby and peruse the vending machines.

She'd quickly become addicted to the cups of "chicken soup." She liked to watch the paper cup fall onto a platform behind a plastic, sliding window. A steady stream of hot water would dissolve a hefty bouillon cube, and the resulting broth had been filled with monosodium glutamate, which had made her see tiny white spots like pretty snowflakes. The salty liquid had tasted just like chicken.

But the vending machine with the tiny Hello Kitty toys had been the real attraction. Here in the private darkness of the movie house, where no white friends could see her, she had spent all her nickels and dimes in pursuit of plastic rings, sparkly necklaces, and puffy stickers. With the complete concentration of a veteran safecracker, eight-year-old Lindsey would carefully crank the silver handle with her sticky little hand and listened to the clicks. She'd watch as the plastic bubbles in the red case jiggled slightly with each turn, until one slid down the chute and stopped on the other side of the square hatch. When she'd flipped open the metal door, untold Kitty treasures had awaited her.

Between acquisitions, she'd fueled up with additional cups of the chicken-flavored drink of champions. She'd gulped the fluorescent yellow broth like an athlete chugging Gatorade.

Theater patrons would look out for her welfare but would occasionally startle her when they would speak to her. *"Leyeng neurr, gong tong wah?"* they would say, asking her if she spoke Chinese.

If she had actually been sitting in her Chinese language class, perhaps she would have known how to answer them, but instead she'd always run back to her seat and watched the rest of the kung fu action.

She had recently viewed some of the same martial arts movies on late-night cable and had been surprised to find that none of them contained snow scenes. She distinctly remembered seeing blizzards in those films, but eventually she realized all those white spots must have been MSG-induced delusions.

The next day after work Lindsey headed toward the On Lok senior center to drop off Uncle Bill's medication. Her mom had told her to give the pills to a woman named Barbara, so Lindsey asked for her and loitered in the foyer.

As Lindsey waited she flipped through some magazines and newspapers that were messily strewn atop a low table. She flipped over an *Asian Week* and the previous day's newspaper, and then her eyes settled on a free publication that highlighted trends in antiques collecting. She scanned the front page.

The cover story was about those trinkety little dolls with wobbly heads called "nodders." Lindsey had seen the ones in the likenesses of sports figures like Joe Montana and Barry Bonds and was surprised to read that the springy-headed tchotchkes originated in China. According to the article, they had first been made of a kind of papier-mâché and had depicted Chinese figures.

She looked up just as a woman in a floral smock approached.

"Are you Barbara?" Lindsey asked.

"Yes, I am. I'll take those."

Lindsey handed over the vial of pills, and as Barbara inspected the typing on the label, Lindsey rocked on her heels, trying to think of something to say.

Barbara looked up and smiled warmly. "You want to see him?"

Lindsey was thinking of the Bruce Lee nodder she had spied at Brandon's apartment. She was confused for a moment. "See who?" she asked.

The attendant smiled patiently and Lindsey said, "Oh, you mean . . . my uncle?"

Barbara nodded. "He doesn't have too many visitors. He would probably like to see a familiar face." She began to walk ahead of Lindsey, leading the way toward Bill's room. Lindsey stumbled as she ran to catch up. In protest she tried to explain, "Um, I'm not a familiar face. He's not even my real uncle, I mean, he probably won't know who I am . . ."

Barbara came to a door and opened it after a quick two-knuckled knock.

"Someone's here to see you, Mr. Gin," she said and soon disappeared, shutting the door behind her with Lindsey inside.

Lindsey stood by the upright scale in the corner and felt a sudden panic at being left alone with the elderly man. He sat on a vinyl armchair in his light blue pajamas and dark blue robe and stared at Lindsey. She hadn't even said hello to him weeks ago at the family association dinner, and she wondered if he recognized her at all. *Jeopardy* was playing on the television that was mounted over the mechanical mattress with stainless steel sidebars.

"Hi, Uncle Bill," she said, still ten feet away.

He smiled, but she could tell that he couldn't see her with his bad eyes.

"Come closer, closer," he said, stretching out his arm and moving his hand in an upside-down waving motion, like he was agitating bathwater.

Lindsey approached him and awkwardly squatted down by the side of his chair. She was a little put off by the smell of Vicks VapoRub, but she placed her hand on Uncle Bill's arm. "How are you?" she asked.

Uncle Bill reached over with his opposite hand and placed it atop hers. The scaly dryness of his palm pressed tightly against her younger skin, and he leaned his face close to hers.

"*Siu siu, tschow gerk?*" he said, and for a split second

Lindsey thought she saw a flash in his cloudy eyes. She smiled, realizing that yes, he did recognize her, but then it dawned on her that the first thought that came to his mind was her stinky malformed foot!

Despite her chagrin, she was pleased to suddenly hear the little nickname that she thought only Pau Pau knew. Even though it meant that someone else was privy to her midget secret, hearing the old man address her as such created an instant connection between them that soothed her uneasiness.

"I know you," he said. "You eat . . . lots of rice candy!" A bit of spittle sprayed Lindsey's face as Uncle Bill laughed jovially and patted her hand over and over.

"You know," he said, "your grandpa and me . . . long time ago we live in big house. My uncle who came over before us was cook there. We live in servant room and tiptoe on floors, genuine marble. We run outside and play tiddledywink." He pronounced this last word very carefully, then continued, "Your grandpa always dream of being president. 'How can you be president?' I say, but he learn Pledge Allegiance himself. This on top of regular lesson. Uncle Chang make us learn Chinese Five Classic, Confucius, and Tao Te Ching. Wrote essay and learn many dialect, too. He say learning Chinese will not rot our gut!" The old man laughed and laughed and continued to slap the top of Lindsey's hand.

"We have only two things left from China. One was old bowl like octagon shape. Other one was cricket in bamboo cage. When it die, your grandpa caught new American cricket to take place," he said. "Which you think smarter, Chinese cricket or U.S. cricket?"

Lindsey felt uncomfortable. "I don't know . . ." she said, trying to gently dislodge her fingers from underneath his, but he clasped her hand tighter.

"I remember when Chinese not safe outside Chinatown. Cross Broadway, you get beat up!" He gazed so intently at Lindsey now that she dared not wriggle away from his grasp. His shaky grip conveyed a sense of desperation that worried, almost frightened, her.

She nodded as he talked excitedly. "There were horse-drawn carriages . . . how you say? Cly-dale horses, and cars too, sure, sure." For no reason, he suddenly began to shout. "And whole table of food! Deliver right to your door, with tray and table, waiter carry on his head, no kidding! When done, just leave outside, *hai la* . . ."

Uncle Bill quieted down, patting Lindsey's fingers less vigorously. He lay his palm across her wrist and rested that way for a few seconds. Slowly she inched her hand off his forearm and slipped it into the pocket of her jean jacket.

"I have to go now, Uncle Bill," she said, slowly straightening out of her crouch and standing upright.

The old man nodded and stared up to the television although he probably couldn't even see it. "Okay, okay, things to do. I understand," he said.

Lindsey felt wrong just abandoning him there all alone. But she also could not imagine staying. She didn't think she had anything more to say and didn't have the nerve to stay longer. Besides, she was late to meet Mimi.

"Bye," she said, backing out of the room and quietly shutting the heavy door behind her. Her boots squeaked as she walked down the hall toward the exit. She waved to Barbara, then stepped out into the fresh air. She sighed and buttoned up her jacket, then walked to the corner to catch the bus.

That week at work Lindsey started to slowly drive herself insane with her imagined thoughts of Michael Cartier's life. When people called for him, she tried to glean information from the subtle nuances of the way they spoke. She tried to figure out if they were friends, or even—yipes—lovers. She began to think it was her responsibility to be his personal screener, and when a caller identified herself as a salesperson or telemarketer, she'd refuse to put the call through and felt that she had valiantly saved Michael from a terrible inconvenience. She had memorized his extension number, 979, and tried to decipher meaning in the digits. 2979 happened to be her street address, so wasn't that proof of some cosmic connection?

She particularly noticed if the people who called Michael were female. Anytime a Lisa, Julie, or Jennifer called, she practically fell into a panic. She was relieved when they identified themselves as a copy editor, an affiliate from the travel bureau, or any other mundane, work-related professional.

It was the unqualified female voices that started to drive her crazy. If someone said, "This is Mary calling for Michael," Lindsey turned into a three-headed dog guarding her crush with ferocity. She'd gently prod for a last name or ask, "Where are you calling from, please?" And sometimes she got the most exasperating answers, like, "Just Sarah," or "He'll know who I am."

Were these interlopers current love interests or romantic candidates who wanted to sink their talons into Lindsey's enigmatic litterbug of a non-boyfriend? She had no way of knowing for sure. When she buzzed these calls through to Michael and he said "Okay," she strained to hear any hint of affection, any wisp of emotion that might give her a clue to his life outside work.

Michael was oblivious. Maybe he would have been more revealing if he'd known Lindsey was actually interested in him. But she was often aloof, and her routine of systematically ignoring him confused even her. So she suffered silently, torturing herself with speculation about Michael's relationship to any and all female callers.

In the early evenings after work, Lindsey walked home, dropped her keys into the green, eight-sided bowl by the rotary dial telephone in the kitchen, and usually snapped open a Crystal Geyser soda. She waited for Pau Pau to come home, or sometimes went out for walks by herself.

Every now and then, thoughts of her cousin Stephanie popped into her head. Stephanie had been the perfect daughter from day one, and because they were close in age, Lindsey had always compared herself to her. Stephanie was slender and pretty, and as a kid, she'd actually enjoyed her piano and tap dancing lessons, which Lindsey had hated.

In high school Stephanie had been president of the Student Council and head of the Prom Committee while Lindsey had been a Goth outcast who'd gotten sent to the school psychologist for wearing black nail polish. While Lindsey had struggled to pass her remedial math classes at Berkeley, Stephanie had excelled at Stanford and had still found time to go home on the weekends to baby-sit Cammie, whom her parents had adopted from China. Now

Stephanie managed to have a high-powered career while Lindsey was still a wage slave. She made more than twice Lindsey's salary working as a talent coordinator for a local child-modeling agency. But that wasn't all. The thing that bothered Lindsey most about Stephanie was that she was already married. Stephanie and Mike had been hitched for two years now, and in a couple of months they were expecting their first baby.

Lindsey still remembered details from their distinctly un-Chinese wedding. The bride had worn a sleek Calvin Klein sheath instead of a red cheongsam, and in place of the usual Chinatown banquet, fat-free crudités had been served in a stark, whitewashed gallery. Cammie had been the flower girl, and she'd tossed white orchids with overabundant zeal. Lindsey remembered how she had hit several guests in the head, upsetting a few comb-over hairdos on some baldies.

She remembered that the Oakland relatives had all been quite somber at the wedding. Lindsey suspected the reason why—they were trapped in a repressed holding pattern that seemed common in Chinese families. Chinese parents never volunteered information about "the birds and the bees." Most figured girls didn't have to worry about physical particulars or amorous finesse until after they were married, and, supposedly, boys would work things out for themselves.

Lindsey remembered her mother recounting how Pau Pau had never told her about menstruation. When Lillian Gin was in the seventh grade, she ran bleeding to the bathroom while her girlfriends cried uncontrollably, certain she was going to die. None of the girls knew why she was mysteriously bleeding. They huddled together, sobbing, until a female teacher entered the bathroom to see what all the commotion was about. She, not their mothers, explained to them the facts about their developing bodies.

Such was the tyrannical modesty of old-school Chinese folks; parents reasoned that they had survived without any instruction, so why should their own kids need to know anything? No one ever mentioned the three-lettered s-word. Even Lindsey, her brother, and immediate cousins were still trapped to an extent, talking frequently about Disney movies and other sexless topics. God forbid they'd be watching a movie on HBO with their parents when jiggling boobies or thrusting buttocks appeared on-screen. Inevitably, either the parents or the kids would immediately have to excuse themselves from the room to avoid getting caught with their eyes popping out of their sockets. Even humping bullfrogs on the Discovery Channel would send someone scurrying to needlessly replenish their Cheetos.

So, it had been quite a shock when Stephanie had announced she was getting married. No one had even known she was dating, and now the family was forced to face the reality of one of their little peach blossoms indulging in sins of the flesh, which they referred to as "playing hanky-panky."

At first, the whole family had been extremely wary of Mike, Stephanie's white guy. That's what everyone called him, too, as if "that White Guy" were actually part of his name. No one ever referred to him without mentioning this phrase that identified him as a separate, white human. Every time someone spoke of him it was as though they meant to say, "Don't get too close to him, he's *That. White. Guy.*"

But after Stephanie and Mike had been married for a year

or so, most of the family seemed to like him well enough. Lindsey considered his eventual acceptance to be a genuine miracle, on par with the parting of the Red Sea. How had Stephanie accomplished such a feat? Lindsey would have to investigate.

But first, she was forced to participate in another "date" that Pau Pau had arranged. She assumed that these grand-sons of the mahjong cronies were also just humoring their grandmothers by agreeing to these meetings. But she wasn't always right.

BACHELOR # 2, COME ON DOWN!

Darren Gee hailed from the Outer Richmond dis-trict, where he survived on take-out chow fun and the occasional Kentucky Fried Chicken family bucket. He was an account representative for Pitney Bowes and was desperate to find a girlfriend who could cook au-thentic Sichuan-style dishes like his mother. He had high hopes for these arranged dates. He was forty-two years old.

Darren picked up Lindsey and took her to the House of Prime Rib. Strapped into the seat belt of his Acura, she quietly freaked out about his age and noted that, with his prickly hair and blocky head, he bore an uncanny resemblance to Sonic the cartoon hedgehog. She reminded herself that this wasn't a real date. Eventually, she managed to relax and settle into the upholstery. Fiddling with the radio, she was perturbed to find that all the pre-set buttons were fixed on easy listening stations.

Once inside the restaurant and seated at their table, Darren appeared jittery and sweaty, which caused Lindsey to worry that he was serious about this date.

"So, does your grandmother make you go out on a lot of these arranged dinners?" she asked, buttering a crust of bread.

He straightened his conservative tie and attempted to smile but instead managed to look as if he had a gas pain.

"Hopefully I won't need to meet anyone else after tonight," he replied, smiling to reveal yellowed, misshapen teeth like macadamia nuts.

Her eyes widened with panic, and she stared at the tabletop to avoid the desperate gaze behind his bifocals. He drummed his stubby fingers on the table excitedly.

When the waiter arrived, Darren took the liberty of ordering fish for her, even though he hadn't even asked what she wanted. His paternalistic presumption caused her to emit a nervous laugh, which garnered raised eyebrows from both Darren and the waiter.

After their entrées arrived, they ate in silence. Eventually, he tried to break the ice. "I don't think our age difference is a big deal, do you?"

She chewed her food, realizing she would have to throw dirt on this smoldering fire before it got out of control.

"Gee, Darren . . ." she said, trying to think of a way to let him know she was not interested.

"That's my name, get it? Darren Gee!"

Lindsey smiled weakly.

"So what do you think?" he asked again, his fingers now drumming on the table even faster.

"I think I need to go to the ladies' room," she said, excusing herself. He stood up and tried to help her out of her seat, but he fumbled clumsily. He missed the arm of the chair and accidentally grabbed her left butt-cheek instead. She shot him a dirty look and jerked away, appalled.

"Uh, sorry," he muttered, but she had already stormed out of hearing distance.

When she returned from the rest room, she offered to pay for her dinner, but Darren had already taken care of the bill. She tried again, but he refused. As he attempted to help her with her coat, she jumped back, afraid of another groping.

After driving her home, he insisted on escorting her up to the front door of the apartment.

"You really don't have to," she protested, fearing being alone with him in the elevator or, worse, walking up the stairs and having him goose her.

"What kind of gentleman would I be if I didn't see you safely to your door?"

In the elevator she backed herself into the corner furthest from him and then darted past him when they arrived on her floor. She swiftly opened the apartment door with her key and turned to say good-bye.

But Darren wasn't in the mood for talking. Puckered lips the color and consistency of monkfish liver were speeding toward her mouth to deliver a goodnight kiss. She had to think fast. She ducked just in time.

She actually felt bad when she heard his front tooth hit the door.

"Ow!" he yelped, grabbing his lip with his chunky paw.

"Um, sorry. Thanks for dinner," she said as she shut the door quickly behind her.

Simmering Below the Surface . . .

Who did Lindsey think she was kidding? She thought about Michael Cartier all the time. And not just every day but, like, every hour, and even every half hour. It was a problem.

She knew there were things she shouldn't be doing. Like looking up his address and driving by his apartment at night to see if his lights were on. She even went to work extra early one day to sneak a peek in the personnel files to check if his first name really was Miles. She didn't locate his folder immediately and was confused that the staff names were not sorted alphabetically. Her heart beat fast as she fumbled in a panic, worried about getting caught. A few seconds passed before she noticed the cardboard flags that separated the folders by astrological sign. In the Pisces section, she found his name and pulled out a health insurance application that confirmed the bitter reality of his Christian name. Nonetheless, this horrifying truth seemed somehow inconsequential when she imagined his hands on her thighs.

She decided to spy on Michael via the Internet. Knowing that she would be too conspicuous at work, she chose a cafe down the street from her apartment that had a couple of computer stations where she could surf the Web for free.

She purposely went late to the coffeehouse, about 11 P.M., which left only a half an hour before closing. She ordered a latte and sat at an uneven table pretending to sketch in her Badtz-Maru notepad while she eyed a nerd packing up his stuff at one of the terminals.

After the guy slinked out, she slipped into his chair. It was still warm from him sitting in it, and she felt slightly sickened when her rear squashed the imprint of his butt on the cushion. But she didn't have time for her ponderings on sanitation. She was on a mission.

She logged onto Google and typed in his name. She cringed as she typed the name Miles, but it had to be done. However, her initial search reaped nothing, so she tried Michael Cartier.

Et voilà!

She found eight items under this name, mostly short articles he had written for various publications. She found several pieces on travel, and she clicked open one essay about visiting distant relatives in the south of France. She read, "My Great Uncle Benoit ran the tabac in Berre Les Alpes. He allowed me to carefully flip through the imported *Sports Illustrated* magazines as he prepared a simple dish of lamb kidneys, which I forced myself to eat despite my semi-vegetarianism . . ." She continued to read about his trip to Marseilles and traveling to Cap D'Aille near Monaco to visit his Aunt Sabine, who kept canaries. Lindsey memorized these obscure details about his family life, in case someday it might be handy to know that his cousin Didier loved endive.

Meanwhile, in the cafe, the busboy began sweeping around the tables and flipped the Closed sign. She worried that he could tell she was spying on someone, so she quickly shut down the search engine, finished her beverage, and dashed out the door. The light from the streetlamp cast a cold flicker on the sidewalk, but she felt warm.

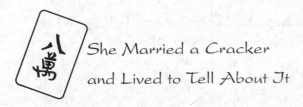

She Married a Cracker and Lived to Tell About It

Stephanie and Mike lived in a neighborhood that made Lindsey feel inadequate for not blocking the sidewalk with her own double stroller and multiple infants. Navigating through Noe Valley, she slipped past bulky ladies wearing balloony yoga pants and gardening clogs. They chatted obliviously as their hyperactive Jack Russell terriers ran in small circles, barking out of control as their leashes twisted into knots. Gray-ponytailed men wearing Guatemalan shirts and Teva sport sandals congregated by the coffeehouse and whistled as Lindsey passed. She jogged up a small hill and rang the doorbell on a glass-and-stainless-steel entryway.

When Stephanie opened the door, Lindsey noticed her cousin's pregnant belly, which looked like a soccer ball protruding from beneath her perfect Ann Taylor ensemble. It was a Saturday, and Lindsey wondered how her younger cousin managed to look so grown up and expertly styled even when she was just lounging at home. Lindsey, in her ratty jeans and sweatshirt, felt the twinge of inadequacy that always descended upon her in the presence of perfectly groomed people.

Lindsey walked in slowly, taking in her surroundings. She had never been to her cousin's home before, and she was immediately struck by its resemblance to a Crate & Barrel showroom. The place smelled like new leather and was filled with modern, expensive-looking furniture.

"Come sit down. I just took a pie out of the oven," Stephanie called over from the sunny kitchen nook.

Lindsey plopped down on a chrome chair and took in all the perfection, feeling like she herself was the only flawed thing in the whole place.

"What's that?" she asked, looking atop the stove and scrutinizing a small plaque showing a warrior with gold chains and a mohawk hairstyle.

Stephanie slipped off her oven mitts. "Don'tcha know? That's the kitchen god."

"Oh," Lindsey shrugged. "I thought it was Mr. T."

She asked where Mike was, and Stephanie said he was playing golf with her dad. Lindsey thought of Stephanie's father, her ex-uncle Donald, whom she hadn't seen since Auntie Vivien divorced him eighteen months ago. She wondered if his absence contributed to Brandon's being such a jerk and Cammie's being so hyperactive.

Lindsey glanced over at the sideboard and saw a silver-framed photo of Stephanie and her husband on the beach. Mike looked athletic and healthy, with a sun-bronzed complexion. How strange. He wasn't greige at all.

Stephanie brought over a cup of coffee, and then went back to the counter to check if the pie was cool enough to slice. Lindsey took a few sips of the hot liquid, then asked,

"So, how come you haven't been killed by the Chinese mafia yet?"

Stephanie slid a Henckels knife out of its block and rinsed it.

"What?" she said.

"Brandon says the mafia's got my number because I date white guys," Lindsey said. "So how about you? How did you get away with marrying the enemy?"

Stephanie wiped her hands on a striped tea towel and sat down. She sipped her coffee from a mug with the logo of a now-defunct dot-com.

"Well, what do you want to know?" she asked, kicking off her low heels and tucking her feet under her chair.

"Did Mike have any Asian girlfriends before you?"

Stephanie thought for a second. "Yeah, one. She was Japanese. But it was, like, four years before me."

Lindsey crinkled her nose. "Did you ever wonder if he only liked you because he had some Asian fetish?" She wondered if she should ask her cousin's opinion of the name Miles.

"I don't know. I can only assume he didn't keep the other girl's underwear or anything like that."

Lindsey leaned forward. "How did you get the whole family to like Mike so much?"

"Believe me, it wasn't easy. When he used to call the house, my dad would just hang up on him. For months, Dad gave me the cold shoulder, and when he wasn't ignoring me he'd scream about how I'd let him down. He'd say nonsensical stuff like, 'I knew I shouldn't have let you go to summer camp!' or 'You used to be so promising at your piano recitals!' Like that had anything to do with anything!

"Dad went crazy, saying I had no standards, even though he hadn't even met Mike yet. He asked me, 'How could you settle for a dirty *lo-fahn*?' We went weeks without talking to each other."

Lindsey was mesmerized. "So how come everyone likes him so much now?" she asked.

Stephanie smiled. "Well, let's see. First, Mike did his time in the chores category. He went over to my parents' house and cleared the thorn bushes, painted the whole house, and fixed some water damage in the garage. Then he and Dad started playing golf together. It's cool, because now I get to see my dad without my mom around, when he comes over to pick up Mike. Golf, I've decided, is a great bonding force."

Stephanie sighed, then perked up. "Oh, and there was the list! My dad gave Mike this list of Chinese stuff that he was supposed to give to my parents as an engagement gift."

"Why?"

"In China, the groom's parents give the bride's family a bunch of food and gifts to show their generosity. Of course, it kind of defeats the purpose when the bride's family forces the groom to do it and tells him exactly what to get."

"So, what was on the list?"

"Like, a whole roasted pig, a hunk of shark's fin, those dehydrated scallops that cost, like, forty dollars a pound . . . freaky tea with dried silkworms. Let's see, what else? I don't know, just weird Chinese stuff. Genitals of extinct animals, rhino horn, gallbladders from bears, reindeer antlers, tiger noogies—who knows? I guess my dad figured that if Mike was willing to go on this elaborate hunt, then maybe he was serious."

"Did you worry that people would be judgmental about your interracial marriage?"

"Yeah, but I figured that would happen no matter what. Besides, I had an ace in the hole. Right before we announced our engagement, I went to dim sum with Pau Pau."

"At the pink place?"

"Yeah. She'd met Mike that Christmas when I brought him to my parents' house. He knew that she couldn't chew very well with her dentures, so he brought Jell-O with baby marshmallows in it especially for her. Anyway, Pau Pau and I were sitting there in the dim sum place eating *wu tau goh* and all of a sudden she said to me, 'I like your boyfriend.' "

"Really?" Lindsey asked, amazed.

"Yeah! I said, 'You like him even though he's not Chinese?' " Stephanie paused, recalling the conversation fondly.

"What did she say?"

"Well, she chewed on a chicken's foot, spit out a bone, and said, 'You're in love, so it's okay.' " Stephanie punctuated this revelation with a simple shrug.

Lindsey shook her head, dumbfounded. "I never would have guessed Pau Pau would say something like that."

"Well, you live with her—you should talk to her."

Lindsey was defensive. "I do talk to her. But not about guys. That would be too bizarre. I don't think I could be anything except in 'granddaughter mode.' To her, I'm still only four years old."

"Yeah, I used to think that too, but you should try. She's had an amazing life, you know."

Lindsey didn't really know. Feeling envy creep onto her

cheeks like a light sunburn, she suddenly realized she didn't know her grandmother at all. As her roommate, she shared daily life with the woman—oatmeal in the morning and dinner almost every night. She knew what kind of Ovaltine Pau Pau liked and what kind of hair rollers she used. Didn't that mean she was closer to Pau Pau than anyone else?

"What kind of amazing life?" she asked.

"You should ask her yourself," Stephanie chirped as she cleared the dishes.

After she left her cousin, Lindsey stopped at Bell Market on 24th Street to pick up some green beans. As she stood in line clutching her baggie of Blue Lakes, the man behind her suddenly spoke. "For the restaurant, eh?" he asked.

She was unaware that he was addressing her, and she didn't turn around. A moment passed before he tapped her on the shoulder and repeated, "Need those for the restaurant, huh?"

Had this man mistaken her for someone he knew from his local take-out place? Or did he just assume that a Chinese person holding a large sack of string beans worked in a restaurant? She shot him an annoyed look and faced forward again.

The long line of customers came to a halt as the cashier stopped to change the register tape. Lindsey watched the other checkout lanes as customers moved along steadily, and she sighed. She should've listened to her mother, who'd once advised her to always choose the Asian cashier no matter how long the line. The Asian cashiers always went the fastest, she had insisted. Lindsey thought that was kind of racist, or supremacist, or something. So here she was now, in line at a standstill while two lanes away a middle-aged Asian man was moving his line along with stoic efficiency.

Her eyes glazed over as she spaced out at at the woman just ahead. The woman's checkbook design boasted Chinese symbols and a border that read, "Printed on 100% recycled paper with soy-based ink."

Everyone watched the cashier struggle until a female assistant manager finally helped him unjam the tape feeder. The checkbook lady smiled at Lindsey and said, "The Chinese say, 'Women hold up half the sky.' They are so right!"

For some reason, people often engaged Lindsey in conversation by quoting Chinese proverbs. More often than not, the speaker was a white lady with permed reddish hair, an animal-print blouse, and oversized pendant jewelry. Did these women feel compelled to educate Lindsey, or were they seeking her approval? Who knows. Perhaps they simply wished to share a bond with her as a sister in this global village.

Yeah, right. No Chinese person Lindsey knew ever talked like that. For instance, Pau Pau never quoted Lao-tzu. That would be absurd. She quoted episodes of *Bonanza*.

Out in the parking lot, a scrawny twentysomething guy flexed his arm and asked for spare change. Lindsey shook her head and tried to duck out of his way, but he walked alongside her, following her for half a block.

"Hey, Little Sister, wanna see my tattoo?" he asked, flexing his arm, which was decorated with the bold strokes of a graceful Chinese character.

"It means Loyalty. Pretty righteous, huh?" He bobbed his head up and down and waited for a smile.

"Actually, it doesn't say Loyalty," she countered.

"Whaddaya mean?" he asked.

She had no idea which character it was, but she was feeling irritable.

"It says Jackass."

As the guy gazed at her with a slack jaw, she nodded her head.

The guy grabbed his own elbow and wrestled with himself a bit, trying to wrap his mind around her words.

"No way! Liar!" he accused. Then he looked at her for a long second. "You Chinese?" he asked.

"Yeah," she said, and walked away as the guy performed a few shadow-boxing moves and hurried off in the other direction muttering, "Man, I'm gonna kill that guy . . ."

A Tale of Two Steves

That evening Pau Pau wasn't home by eight, so Lindsey called the mahjong parlor.

"Winning! Even missing *Gunsmoke!*" her grandmother
said.

Lindsey knew that if Pau Pau was willing to miss one of
her favorite shows, the winnings must be serious and her
grandmother would be home very late. Lindsey decided
that she, too, would go out.

She drove to the Orbit Room on Market and Octavia to
meet with Mimi and one of Mimi's former sorority sisters,
Andrea Wilson. Lindsey sipped grapefruit juice and vodka,
admiring the art deco interior and space-age lighting fix-
tures as she listened to Mimi and Andrea's conversation.
Having already drunk several concoctions of blue curaçao
and lemonade with multicolored sugar crystals around the
rim, Andrea was complaining that the fraternity boys she
desperately wanted to date had all recently been ensnared
by petite Asian women.

"They're stealing all of our men!" she said.

Lindsey frowned. Andrea smiled and patted her hand. "Oh, I don't mean you," she said. "You're white, anyway."

"What's that supposed to mean?" Lindsey asked.

"You know, you and Mimi are different from other Asian girls. You're normal like me," Andrea said.

Lindsey did not reply. What the hell did she mean by "normal"?

Lindsey felt the sting of this backhanded insult, but then, shamefully, realized she felt slightly complimented to be viewed as an equal by a blue-eyed blond. She had always seen herself as different from typical Asian-Americans; she hated hip-hop and sappy soul ballads but liked Abba and They Might Be Giants; she was terrible at math but preferred to bury herself in quasi-intellectual fare like Umberto Eco; instead of hanging out at the Asian food court in college, she had spent her days reading French fabliaux at Caffe Roma.

But despite these differences, Lindsey loathed herself for the small pride she derived from Andrea's opinion. She detested being called "white, anyway," as if the words were a consolation prize. She knew she loved Peking duck with *hoisin* sauce and rice porridge with bits of preserved egg; she had gladly eaten her life's share of wok-fried entrails, *nga choy*, and fishball soup. She loved her Chinese family and everything seedy, boisterous, and lively about Chinatown.

She wanted to rebuke Andrea in some way but could not think of the right approach. At times like these, she felt the urge to brag that China had invented porcelain, silk, gunpowder, and spaghetti. She was held back, however, by the embarrassment of her dark secret: during pre-kindergarten afternoons with Pau Pau at the travel agency, she had learned many Cantonese words and phrases, but she had abandoned all her Chinese vocabulary by the time she entered first grade. For all her academic education, Lindsey knew she had lost something important. She felt she couldn't defend herself against Andrea's half-compliment/ half-insult because she had let her own family's mother tongue slip beyond her grasp, and that somehow incriminated her or at least made her an accomplice in her own whitewashing.

Mimi wasn't paying attention to the conversation, especially when she spotted her ex-boyfriend.

Steve E. walked into the bar with his rock 'n' roll hair moussed into a windswept tangle. Lindsey glanced over at Mimi and knew she was a goner.

"He's got new highlights!" Mimi said breathlessly. Suddenly nervous, she started to twist the ends of her hair into spirals as she sat transfixed at the sight of Steve E.

Mimi was an Asian Hair Victim. Ever since junior high she had been captivated by her own beautiful straight hair, which she kept ultra-long, all one length past her waist. Despite having split ends that really needed to be snipped, Mimi saw long hair as the mark of supreme sexiness. She refused to trim it, even though she often awoke in the middle of the night to find her locks strangling her. Not to mention the fact that every time she got into a car a few strands got caught in the door by accident.

Her hair was her life. She collected hair accessories: barrettes, twisties, scrunchies, and hairbands. Oh, and she was also obsessed with hair bands from the Eighties, like Mötley Crüe and Poison (which, incidentally, was also the name of her favorite designer perfume).

Steve E. had once drunkenly admitted to Lindsey that the things he liked most about Mimi were her long hair and slim body. Of course, he liked her as a person, too. She had a great personality.

"Well, I gotta get going," Andrea announced. She scooped up her Kate Spade purse and exited quickly, sidestepping any need to backpedal from her previous statements.

As Lindsey quietly noticed the River Phoenix look-alike who accompanied Steve E., Mimi flipped her hair and pretended she did not see her former paramour. Lindsey finished her drink.

The two guys approached, and when they reached their table, Steve E. said, "Hey, Babe." He kissed Mimi on the lips, as if they had never broken up. She swooned like a backstage groupie, and the couple quickly retreated to a far corner of the bar, leaving Lindsey with the handsome stranger.

"You can call me Steve D.," he said, and Lindsey almost laughed. He offered to buy her a drink, and she nodded. Removing his jacket, he winked at her in a way that she found sleazy, but cute.

After a few minutes, he returned and set the beverages down.

"Here ya go. What was your name again?"

"It's Lindsey. Thanks a lot." Looking out the oversized window panes, she noted that tonight was one of those unusually warm and pink-skyed San Francisco evenings that made the building lights, even the fluorescent ones, glimmer. It was earthquake weather.

"So how do you know Steve E.?" she asked.

"You mean Sheila E.? He used to be my roommate in L.A."

Lindsey gave him points for the eighties reference. Demerits for being from Los Angeles.

"Where are you from?" he asked, sipping his Newcastle.

"I'm from here," she replied, expecting the surprise she usually got when people heard that.

"That's cool," he said. She waited for the inevitable "Wow, I've never met anyone who was actually *from* this city," but he never said it.

They conversed in a choppy way, interspersed with sipping and self-conscious gazes at the tabletop. He mentioned that Steve E. and the new Filipina had, in fact, just broken up. Lindsey glanced over at Mimi in the corner, missing it when Steve D. slyly checked her out. When she turned back around, his pupils were pinned on her as though he were a starving mutt and she a pork chop.

"Hold on a sec, don't move," he said, reaching toward her neck and lightly pinching an imaginary tuft of lint from her hair.

She glanced down at his hands. *Clean, short nails. Possible construction job during the summer, but generally well-kept. Small scar on right index finger. B+*

Mimi and Steve E. came over to retrieve her handbag.

"You don't have to drive me home," Mimi said, before dashing out the double doors.

Steve D. finished his beer, then put his hand on Lindsey's shoulder and asked, "Hey, do you want to go walk around?"

She slid off the bar stool and followed him outside. The light wind felt refreshing on her bare thighs.

On the corner of Haight and Laguna they approached a Victorian mansion, its gingerbread trimmings and finials highlighted by a nearby streetlamp. Behind the main house was a cottage with a wooden gate, slightly ajar.

"C'mon," he whispered, taking her hand and helping her through the gate.

They had been making out for a few exhilarating minutes before they heard the car crash. The sound of crunching metal, glass, and splitting wood startled her, but Steve D. muffled her squeal by pulling her close.

She breathed in the faint scent of fennel branches mixed with the musty smell of damp sawdust as they crouched down behind some unkempt shrubbery. They watched a man throw open the gate and storm into the backyard and up a flight of stairs. Lindsey wanted to get the hell out of there, but Steve held her hand tightly as they tiptoed into the carriage house through a sliding door that was open to the yard. It was completely dark inside except for illumination from the streetlight that was shining through a high window.

Old oak barrels leaned against the wall near an ancient-looking copper bathtub and an armoire with a cracked mirror. Steve climbed up a ladder and Lindsey followed, despite being worried about falling on her ass and ruining her platform knee-boots. From the top of the loft they heard muffled voices, running footsteps, and then the rattle of a van as it chugged away.

Lindsey sat back on an old crate as Steve mashed against her, his hands in her sweater. He was all over her like white on rice.

Slowly and cautiously, he slid his hand under her skirt. Kissing her neck, he said, "You're so pretty, Jinny."

How unfortunate. Lindsey couldn't possibly consider doing it with a guy who couldn't even get her name right.

"Steve?"

"Yeah," he mumbled, chewing on her necklace.

"My name's Lindsey, not Jinny."

He looked up, flashing her a boyish smile.

"Sorry," he said, reattaching his mouth to her neck. He didn't realize that, as far as she was concerned, Elvis had left the building.

"So, who's Jinny?" she asked, nudging his face off hers.

"No one . . . just . . . my . . . girlfriend . . . in Gardena . . ." he said. "But that doesn't mean you and I can't be friends, right?"

Lindsey had sobered up by now. "If we're only friends, could you please get your hands out of my underwear?"

They climbed back down the ladder and walked to her car on Buchanan, near the Mint.

"Hey, you're not mad, are you?" he asked.

For some reason, she wasn't, and she told him so.

"Good," he said. "I like you. I have a lot of Korean friends."

She nodded, amused. "Well, that's fascinating, Steve, but I'm not Korean—I'm Chinese." She leaned up against her car and awaited his brilliant reply.

"Well, I like you anyway," he said, suddenly kissing her on the cheek and turning to walk away. He broke into a short sprint, then, about twenty feet away, he looked back and blew her a kiss. "Bye!"

It was past midnight when she got home, and the apartment was dark except for the stove light. She stepped out of her clunky boots and padded over to her grandmother's bedroom to see if she was asleep yet.

Pau Pau was under the blankets, shaking. Her eyes closed, she thrashed around, mumbling in Chinese. Lindsey, still feeling the warm effects of her makeout session, snapped into a slight panic. She shook her grandmother lightly.

"Pau Pau, wake up!" She knelt by the bed, her knees still sore from crawling through the hayloft.

The elderly woman fluttered her eyelashes and slowly gained focus on her granddaughter.

"A ghost?" she asked.

Lindsey leaned over and switched on the bedside lamp.

"It's okay, Pau Pau. You were dreaming. Only a nightmare."

Her grandmother sat up, now fully awake.

"*Ai-ya!*" she shook her head, upset.

"What's wrong, bad dream?" Lindsey asked, relieved that Pau Pau had not had a seizure or something (in which case, she would have had no idea what to do).

"No, no dream!" she insisted. "Gung Gung need more money! We did not burn enough! He is so poor, so poor . . ." She rubbed her eyes and said, "Tomorrow we go back to cemetery! Must burn more money!"

She had dreamed that Gung Gung was a pauper in the afterlife, wearing tattered clothes and begging for coins. She was convinced that the paper money they had burned at the funeral two years ago was now all spent. She insisted they must return right away to the Chinese cemetery and honor the deceased with a feast, incense, and paper money.

Lindsey agreed to go to the cemetery the next day so Pau Pau would calm down. She turned off the light and went down the hall to wash up for bed.

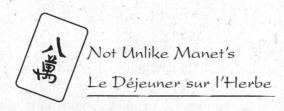

Not Unlike Manet's
Le Déjeuner sur l'Herbe

By the time Lindsey woke up at 9:00 A.M., Pau Pau had already gone to Chinatown and bought all the ingredients for the luncheon feast. She was slicing meats, chopping onions, seasoning chicken, and darting around the kitchen like the Tasmanian Devil.

While Lindsey showered (she took her time and used the expensive deep conditioner recommended in *Mademoiselle*), Pau Pau packed up several Tupperwares and wrapped food items in layers of aluminum foil, placing everything neatly into two cardboard crates.

"*Fai-dee*! Go get ready!" Pau Pau said, informing her that her aunts would be meeting them at the grave site.

"Is my mom coming?"

"Says too busy." Pau Pau muttered a few words in Chinese and then complained in English about Lindsey's mom, "Your ma never cook Chinese style. All she feed you is sandwich, hamburg, spaghett!" She said it like that, with no "er" or "i" at the end of the words.

Lindsey went down to the garage and loaded the boxes

of food into the car. She also transported blankets, bundles of paper tied with twine, and shopping bags filled with old framed photos in various sizes. Pau Pau came downstairs, and they headed off.

They drove through town and onto the highway, finally exiting at Colma. They proceeded through the maze of different cemeteries that held San Francisco's dead, and slowly searched for the Chinese section, where they would find Gung Gung's headstone.

Lindsey spotted Auntie Vivien's red BMW from afar. She and Auntie Shirley were unloading lawn chairs from the trunk.

Lindsey parked behind them and got out to help Pau Pau.

"Hi!" Vivien pressed against Lindsey in a light A-frame hug that ensured she would not muss her makeup and just-polished nails. Shirley hugged her niece, too, holding onto her for an uncomfortable length of time until Lindsey squirmed out of the tight embrace.

Vivien had been a disco-loving party girl in the seventies, and after raising her kids and divorcing her conservative husband, had returned to a life of glitz by wearing tons of cosmetics and too-tight clothes. Her sister Shirley was an aging flower child who took the whole Summer of Love thing way too seriously. They made an interesting contrast— one with dark red lipstick, inappropriately sexy stilettos, and a silver blouse tied at the waist like Daisy Duke, the other in a flowing shapeless dress of peach-colored crepe cotton and big quartz crystals dangling from a hemp choker. It was a sunny day.

"Hahng hoi, hahng hoi!" Pau Pau ordered everybody out of the way so she could spread down the big blanket that

smelled like mothballs. She laid it out over Gung Gung's grave and propped up the framed photos of deceased relatives whom Lindsey did not recognize. Pau Pau proceeded to empty out some waterlogged plastic urns, and several earwigs scattered, causing Vivien to jump back in disgust.

Shirley arranged the apricot-colored roses and white chrysanthemums she had brought. "Hi Daddy, how are you?" she said, like he was right there. She hugged the granite headstone and asked, "Have you been on any spaceships, Daddy?"

Pau Pau spread out the dishes she had carefully prepared that morning: salted chicken with scallion dipping sauce, scrambled egg and ground pork casserole, dried salted fish, bitter melon and seared beef strips with greens, and tender chunks of filet mignon, which Gung Gung had especially liked. Shirley had made a sugarless carrot cake.

They all sat down on the blanket, except for Vivien, who sat on a lawn chair to preserve her stockings and the line of her skirt. They ate with paper plates and plastic utensils, nonchalantly munching away as if they were at a regular picnic. In the distance, a hearse and a procession of cars were just arriving for a funeral service over in the German section.

They sat in silence for a while, and between bites Pau Pau got up and lit incense, placing the sticks right into the dirt. She stared at the picture of her deceased husband and stood alone for a long time. Lindsey found the combined odor of the mothballs and incense to be unappetizing, but she just nibbled quietly.

Vivien removed her dark, heart-shaped sunglasses with the rhinestone heart in the bottom corner of the left lens.

"Do you like my eyes?" she asked, batting her lashes coquettishly. She often asked her niece to keep her apprised of the latest trends in clothes, makeup, and slang.

"Yeah, what about them?" Lindsey asked, gnawing on a stray piece of cartilage.

"They're my new look!" Vivien screeched, flashing her green contact lenses. "Aren't they me?" She lifted her chin and widened her eyes like Gloria Swanson at the end of *Sunset Boulevard*.

"Um, yeah, I guess."

"You didn't even notice! What-ever!" Vivien elbowed her with exaggerated dismay. Lindsey winced at her aunt's painful efforts to sound like a cool kid.

"You know, with my green lenses, I bet I don't even look Chinese. Don't you think I look at least half-white anyway? Some men think I'm Italian or something," she said.

Yeah, *or something*, Lindsey thought. An image popped into her brain, that of the yellow contacts Lou Ferrigno wore as the Incredible Hulk. She also thought about Michael Jackson in the "Thriller" video.

Her aunt slapped her arm. "You know, you should get them, too. Your eyes aren't as big as mine, but you could look almost as good."

Meanwhile, Auntie Shirley called out to a small cloud drifting overhead. "Oh, the different planes of reality," she said. "This world is all maya, a web of maya . . ." From her tie-dyed cloth purse she pulled a strange device that emitted a low humming sound.

"What is that?" Lindsey asked.

"It's my portable negative ion generator. Really clears the energy." Shirley waved it around, inhaling and exhaling with exaggerated whoops.

Lindsey took a bite of carrot cake, but it tasted like potting soil. She buried her slice under a wad of napkins.

After they cleaned up from lunch, Pau Pau opened the car trunk and dragged out a gigantic cannister that had held huge quantities of caramel corn last Christmas.

They all huddled around the deep container as Pau Pau unwrapped the bundles of fake paper money and set them on fire, letting the cinders drift down into the tin. Some of the papers were newsprint squares with gold leaf characters and designs; others looked like fake Monopoly money in denominations of $500 and $1000 with pictures of Chinese gods and goddesses where Ulysses S. Grant or Alexander Hamilton might be. She lit only several "bills" at a time to make the fire catch properly, but once the flames grew, the papers ignited easily. The idea was that the more money they burned, the more Gung Gung would have in the afterlife.

Lindsey found a wooden stake from a floral display that had disintegrated nearby, and she stoked the small fire. As she poked down the cinders, she thought of how improbable it was that she might ever find someone to love as much as Pau Pau loved Gung Gung. She tried to imagine burning fake paper money for a future deceased husband, and the possibility seemed pretty far-fetched. Furthermore, she wondered if she'd be the one responsible for enacting this ritual when Pau Pau died. She certainly couldn't trust Vivien or Shirley to do it properly. Her own mother wasn't even here today.

Meanwhile, Pau Pau continued to drop a steady stream of papers into the container as Vivien checked her slender gold watch several times. Shirley resumed her conversation with the headstone.

They stayed this way for about a half an hour until Pau Pau said, *"Gow la, gow, la,"* meaning that they had burned enough papers and could leave. As they sidestepped around a newly filled grave, Lindsey noticed a headstone with a familiar face. She halted, transfixed, and her jaw dropped as she studied the colorized, oval-shaped photo of a Chinese husband and wife in sixties garb.

"Who is that?" she asked Pau Pau.

A cigarette dangled from her grandmother's lips. She flicked away some ashes and said nonchalantly, "Oh, that Uncle Bill when he was younger."

"But he's not dead!" Lindsey said, aghast.

Vivien and Shirley were already over by the car, and they yelled, "Hurry up!"

Pau Pau shrugged. "He buy plot twenty year ago, big enough for him and wife. He put this picture when she die." She pointed to the Chinese characters that ran vertically under each of their likenesses. The carvings under Bill's picture were rubbed with red ink, while his wife's name was white.

"See," Pau Pau explained, "there no year here because he still live, and letter is red. When die, is made white. This very hard to carve, so have to do all at once."

Lindsey was freaked out. She stared at the photo of the happy-looking couple and shivered. Even *she* thought it was bad luck to have your picture and name pre-engraved on a gravestone.

"Jow-la," Pau Pau said, herself anxious to leave. She said she wanted to make it down to the mahjong parlor by midafternoon.

A Fortnight in the Life of Our Favorite Receptionist

The next week at work was fairly terrible. Some girl named Cheryl kept calling for Michael. She called twice on Monday, three times on Tuesday, and then innumerable times on Wednesday. Lindsey noticed the way Cheryl said his name—fast and casually, like she had uttered the two syllables a million times. The nonchalant voice was sleepy in the morning, perky in the afternoon. Lindsey was in pain.

Making matters worse was the way Michael reacted when Lindsey announced, "Cheryl on line two." He'd say, "Oh, great," or "I'll be right there," and once, "Can you ask her to hold? I'll be there in a sec." Lindsey wanted to weep.

All Wednesday night Lindsey brooded. Cheryl was definitely not part of the plan. Did Lindsey even have a plan? No, but that didn't matter. The point was that no girlie named Cheryl was going to derail destiny. Lindsey knew she and Michael were meant to be together. As far as she was concerned, she and Michael had already begun a significant relationship. She'd ordered him a new pair of scissors and he had thanked her for it. Wasn't that proof of something?

Of course it meant something. Office supplies could be very intimate. For weeks now she had been going out of her way to make sure Michael's tape dispenser and stapler were always in tip-top working order, and when he was out she secretly replenished his paper clips and thumbtacks so that his supply never became inconveniently low.

Thursday morning she got to work early and retrieved a feather duster from the maintenance closet. She walked the deserted floor until she reached Michael's office, then she turned in and swooped the feathered stick atop his file cabinet and along the bookshelf. As she pretended to clean, she visually scoured his desk.

Everything was in place. She found no Post-it notes with girls' phone numbers, and there were no appointments marked on his wall calendar except for work-related meetings. She felt a little guilty for snooping, but not guilty enough to stop. With her arm midair, dusting nothing but empty space, she noticed a corner of the room where Michael had tossed a few of his personal belongings—a scarf, a sweater, and an umbrella. She knew she couldn't get away with swiping any of those things and couldn't believe she was actually considering doing it. She started to get nervous about getting caught in his office, and before she knew it she hastily scooped a felt tip marker from his pencil tray. On her way out, she quickly tucked the pen into her sleeve and sped-walked back to her desk.

Later that morning, Michael was in a meeting and Lindsey watched him through the glass conference room walls as she lightly ran the cap of the stolen marker across her neck. It was just a writing implement, but she treated it like it was a lock of his hair.

The jangling phone rang her from her stupor. Of course, it was Cheryl. When Lindsey offered her Michael's voice mail, Cheryl declined and said, "Just tell him I'll meet him at seven at his place."

Lindsey was all ready to hang up and plot the interloper's death, but right before they said good-bye, Cheryl apologized for calling so often and asked Lindsey how her day was going. She said, "It must be really exhausting to talk to so many people all morning." Then, "Have a great week, okay?"

Lindsey replaced the receiver quietly, then softly said to herself, "Don't play games with me, *Cheryl*." And that was when Lindsey decided that she, too, would be at Michael's at seven.

She was staked out in front of Michael's apartment building at 6:45 with a pair of binoculars just in case. It didn't occur to her that she had gone over the edge of decency. But it didn't matter now. Cheryl was walking up the street.

She had brown hair and a huge backpack. She was plainish but, unfortunately, not ugly. Lindsey slouched down in her car as she watched the young woman climb some stairs and knock on the door. It was one of those open stairways that ran up the center of an Edwardian fourplex, so luckily, Lindsey had a fair view. Michael opened the door and looked happy. He hugged Cheryl tight and said something. As Lindsey watched his strong hands on the other woman's shoulders, she felt her skin burning and a caving in of her stomach. She felt like someone had simultaneously slapped her face and slugged her in the gut, and as the door above closed, she started her car and drove away. The radio was playing "Tenderness," which was usually one of her favorite songs, but right now its peppy beat mocked her. There was only one thing left to do. She would have to go home and eat an entire chocolate cake.

Friday morning when she saw Michael she would have liked to say that he didn't look cute at all. She wanted him to have a big pimple or look miserable like he had been crying all night, perhaps from a horrible romantic breakup. When he said hello to her, she almost scowled. He seemed taken aback by this sudden shot of unfriendliness, which was chillier than anything he had ever gotten from her. He stood by the front desk looking unsure of what to do next, and Lindsey just wished he would go away. When he wouldn't leave, she looked up suddenly, and said, "What?"

Cautiously, Michael said, "Um, I know you're really busy . . . but will you let me know . . . if my sister calls?"

Lindsey's eyes rolled in her head, then came to a joyous halt like a row of sevens in a jackpot slot machine.

"You mean . . . Cheryl?" she said, jumping up like a jack-in-the-box.

She had forgotten her cool, and her excitement now showed more than she would have liked. Michael smiled and said, "Well, yeah."

"Oh," Lindsey said, sitting back down and composing herself. She quickly reverted back to her persona as a slightly aloof receptionist. "That's nice," she said.

Michael rubbed his chin and said, "Yeah, she goes back

to Chicago this weekend, but I haven't seen her in, like, a year. She's in town for a conference, so I'm showing her around."

Lindsey promised to find him if his sister called, and when he walked away, she felt relief wash over her.

She had it real bad and she knew it.

After work the following Monday, Lindsey and Stephanie met at the Williams-Sonoma flagship store. It was warm, and, feeling chronically frumpy in her cousin's presence, Lindsey was taking an enormous risk today. She had left her knee-highs at home and was wearing short, ped-like hosiery called not-socks. They were cut low, meant to be undetectable under the uppers of the shoes, but her flesh-colored ones were a bit thick and visible around the ankle. This was the first time Lindsey had ventured into this new stocking territory, hoping to prove that she was willing to infuse a modern fashion sense into her footwear repertoire, despite the dangers of possibly exposing the Midget.

She was checking out the crème brûlée mini-blowtorch when Stephanie noticed the unacceptable sock situation.

"Oh my God, look at your socks?" Her cousin spoke in that way, where statements sounded like questions.

"They're Donna Karan," Lindsey said, hoping for approval.

"Dang, how *fobbish* is that? You look like a tourist in Hong Kong!"

In Stephanie's world, Lindsey's blatant disregard for sock perfection made her look like a *fob*—a fresh-off-the-boat immigrant.

Lindsey leaned over and adjusted the offensive not-socks

that she had misguidedly hoped would inspire accolades instead of derision. For the rest of their shopping excursion she felt self-conscious and longed for the protection and familiarity of increased ankle coverage.

Meandering toward the baking stuff, Stephanie, despite her protruding belly, walked with a graceful gait toward the springform pans. A short distance away, an elegantly dressed Asian woman with shellacked hair and a Louis Vuitton purse tapped Lindsey on the shoulder and asked her a question in something that sounded like Mandarin.

Lindsey was more accustomed to hearing Cantonese because that's what most San Francisco Chinese spoke, the majority of immigration having been from southern China. There were hundreds of Chinese dialects that sounded completely different, and they all confused Lindsey. She knew Shanghainese had a few of the "sh" sounds of Mandarin, and Toisanese sounded slightly spitty in the back of the throat, but still she wasn't absolutely sure which dialect the woman was speaking. Just then, Stephanie stepped up and replied to the woman, exchanging pleasantries as Lindsey watched mutely, feeling like a child among adults.

When the woman walked away, Stephanie said, "She was looking for Gumps."

"Was that Mandarin?" Lindsey asked, stopping to adjust her footwear again. "How do you know how to speak it?"

"Oh, my dad used to speak it to me at home when I was younger," Stephanie explained, moving on to inspect the muffin trays.

"Hey, how did you get out of going to Chinese school?" Lindsey asked.

"I dunno. My mom finagled it with my dad somehow. Said she didn't want me growing up to be too *Chinafied*. She thought Brandon needed the discipline, though. It's funny, I think I actually learned more from my dad talking to me than Brandon ever got from St. Mary's.

"My mom hardly knows any Chinese herself, not like your mom. I guess because your mom's a little older and was the only sister actually born in China. That's how it works, I guess. The younger kids always learn less. Look at Cammie. Jeez, forget it, she doesn't know anything. Here, hold this."

Stephanie handed her a few stainless steel cooling trays, and they headed toward the cash register.

"What do you want to do now?" Lindsey asked.

"I should really go to the gym," Stephanie said, patting her abdomen.

"Even now?" Lindsey asked, pointing at her pregnancy bulge.

"Yeah, I do water aerobics. I don't want to be one of those moms who gets all fat and never loses it."

They exited the store, and Stephanie put on a pair of very large Gucci sunglasses that made her look like a glamorous fly. Lindsey looked forward to getting home and removing her not-socks immediately.

That evening, Lindsey watched *Antiques Roadshow*. Something about those appraisers, the Keno brothers, just made her happy. Maybe it was their snappy clothes, their polite demeanor, or just their nerdy, nifty magnetism. She appreciated a well-informed man, and as twins, they were just double-delightful in the most unoffensive way.

As she sank into the sofa, she watched the brothers appraise a piece of furniture called a "highboy." She listened intently as the owner proudly explained how years ago his father, knowing splendor when he saw it, traded a two-bedroom house for the chest of drawers. Leigh Keno was most gentle when he explained that the item's cracked veneer and its replaced dovetails significantly lowered the market price. In a matter of seconds, the owner's face distorted into blotchy, crestfallen agitation. He barked that he would never sell the piece because of its priceless sentimental value. Lindsey smiled. It relaxed her to watch people get wrecked on the *Roadshow*.

She had made it through half a bag of cheese puffs when the second segment of the show began. By now she had a bright ring of orange cheese dust around her mouth, but she couldn't stop eating until she emptied the bag. She chomped on the crusty, airy puffs as she watched the show's host, Hugh Scully, visit a museum in Salem, Massachusetts, where he inspected an intricate ivory bureau carved with the scenes of a Chinese tiger hunt.

"This is a most important piece of furniture. A true rarity from the Chinese imperial Summer Palace," he said, marveling at a miniature figure of the emperor.

Lindsey stopped crunching and scrutinized a misshapen cheese puff that looked remarkably like her midget toe, and the horrible resemblance made her immediately lose her appetite. She threw the puff at the television screen.

"If it's a Chinese national treasure, then why's it in Massachusetts?" she yelled out.

Hearing Lindsey, Pau Pau shuffled into the living room.

"Wha?" she said, thinking her granddaughter wanted something.

"Nothing," Lindsey replied and wiped her mouth with a paper napkin. "See that white chest? They say it came from China."

Pau Pau spit into the palm of her hand and rubbed the saliva into her arthritic elbow. She listened to Mr. Scully for a few seconds, then made a dour face. "All stolen!" she said. "Loot Summer Palace long time ago!" She squinted at the screen as the camera focused on the detailed relief of the ivory. Pau Pau raised her hand and swatted at the air as if trying to shoo away an annoying insect. "No matter," she said. "If foreign devil don't take, communist smash later."

Pau Pau hiked up the back of her stovepipe pants and sauntered down the hall. Lindsey returned her gaze to the television, and as the assessments of collectibles continued, she made a couple of her own appraisals. Ruminating on the vanilla complexions and side-parted, Mr.-Rogers-Neighborhood hair of those tidy blond Keno brothers, it suddenly occurred to her that their physical attributes landed them squarely in Hoarder territory. "Curiouser and curiouser," she wondered aloud like Alice in Hoarderland. Spontaneously, she decided to nominate "Leigh" and "Leslie" to her mental list of felonious names, then she quietly drifted into a cheese-puff-induced coma.

A couple of days later, Lindsey went to Pho House to meet her brother for dinner.

She spotted Kevin talking on his minuscule phone in front of the Vietnamese noodle soup restaurant. She was used to him acting like his time was more important than hers, so she parked and waited as he continued to talk in esoteric computer lingo.

Kevin's whole existence could be summed up in three words: Number One Son. Even as a toddler he was certain he could do no wrong. He was one of those little kids that already looked disturbingly good in a tuxedo, even though the size was only a 4T.

At age six, he was already an entrepreneur, digging through the neighbors' garbage in search of discarded items to resell for piggy bank money. Tapping into a natural gift for project management, he enlisted Lindsey and the neighborhood kids to run his makeshift tag sales, promising them a tiny share of the profits. He made future business contacts by hanging out with a pack of other Number One Sons at the Chinatown YMCA, and in Little League he learned about team dynamics and the importance of having psychological advantage over one's opponent. From then on, competition was his life: comparing baseball cards and playing kickball eventually evolved into comparing luxury cars and playing the stock market.

The summer after his eighteenth birthday, Kevin was determined to win a complicated radio contest. Listeners had to piece together song clues that would yield a mathematical formula, which somehow hinted at the identity of a certain baseball player. As the days passed, Mrs. Owyang would return from work and find her son lazing about on the sofa, listening to KFRC. She nagged him to forget about the silly contest, urging him to get a job somewhere, anywhere. But Kevin had set his mind to win. His ear glued to the radio, he whiled away precious hours he could have spent toiling as a theater usher or as an unpaid intern.

Lindsey was at the DMV, having just flunked her driving test, when she heard her brother's voice broadcast live on the transistor radio sitting atop a state employee's desk. Kevin was caller number eight, and he proceeded to name a slew of songs and their years of origin. He calculated math in his head and recited an impressive array of earned run averages, finally naming Vida Blue as the mystery answer. Lindsey couldn't believe her double-pierced ears when, over the din of congratulatory bells and whistles, the deejay announced that her brother had just won $25,000.

For months, KFRC replayed his winning moment as a promo between songs and commercials. It seemed to play every five minutes. The deejay screamed, "You could be a winner, just like Kevin Owyang!"

The phrase tormented Lindsey all summer long.

Kevin put the money toward his college tuition, which was the responsible Number One Son thing to do. He majored in business without a second thought. (When he was younger, Kevin had wanted to be an artist. He had shown great talent in drawing, but his parents had quickly convinced him that such endeavors could only lead to the poorhouse.)

A few months ago his Chinese boss told him he'd improve his sales if he affected a Chinese accent. "Don't say, 'This offer is the best price.' Instead, talk fast and choppy. Say, 'GET YOU BEST BUY!' Pretend you don't know good English. Clients feel better if they think you are not spoiled American-born. Also, you'll fit in better if you start smoking."

Kevin felt somewhat ridiculous practicing his fake broken English every day in the shower, but at least he was rich.

* * *

"I just made eight hundred bucks!" Kevin snapped his cell phone shut and pumped his fist in the air. He opened the restaurant door for Lindsey, and they went inside, choosing a table near the large fishtank.

"You're gonna love this—it's like *dai been lo*," he said.

"What's *dai been lo*?"

"You know, like on Chinese New Year when Gung Gung used to slice up all the seafood and stuff, and we'd make the soup in the hot pot. Like *shabu shabu* in Japanese restaurants."

Lindsey didn't know what *shabu shabu* was either, but she definitely remembered the special meal that Gung Gung used to prepare every Chinese New Year. It suddenly occurred to her that no one in her family had prepared the hot-pot dish since he had passed away.

"Just point to the meal you want," Kevin said, gesturing toward the laminated place mats, which had numbered photographs showing various meal combinations.

At a nearby table, a couple was debating whether or not the name of the restaurant was pronounced "Fuh House." Lindsey absentmindedly spaced out at them until she noticed that Kevin had ordered two tapioca drinks.

She liked the milky sweetness of the cold beverage. Pau Pau always expressed disgust at sugared teas, telling her granddaughter the only good *tcha* was the bitter Chinese kind. Lindsey, however, quite liked the trendy chai drinks, but was certainly alarmed when she noticed gelatinous balls that resembled gigantic brown salmon eggs sloshing around at the bottom of her glass.

"What the hell are those?" she asked, swirling the mixture.

"They're chewy, try it," Kevin said, inhaling the jelly beads through an extra-wide straw.

She took another sip of the drink, and one of the tapioca beads shot to the back of her mouth and made her gag. Coughing, she studied the pictures of the noodle soups and tried to figure out what kind of meats the squares were supposed to be.

The waitress came and took their order.

"Hey, I hear you're going to China," Kevin said.

Lindsey choked on another rogue tapioca bead. "I'm not going to China. Where'd you hear that?"

"Dad says Pau Pau wants to go back and visit Gung Gung's village. We all decided you're the only one without a real job so you're the one who should go with her."

This was the first time she had heard anything about Pau Pau wanting to go back to China.

"Well, I'm so glad you all have my life planned out for me. What if I don't wanna go?"

"Tough luck. You're going. Why are you complaining? It's a free trip."

"And when is this trip supposed to happen?"

"Oh, it's not for another few months or something."

"I'll have to see if I can get the time off from work," she said.

"Oh, gimme a break. If they won't let you go, then you can just quit. When you come back, you can get a real job." As he spoke, Kevin checked the calendar on his electronic day planner.

The waitress brought them bowls of rice noodle soup mixed with veggies, fish cakes, crab claws, and prawns.

They ate without talking for a while. When they were almost finished, Lindsey said, "They should sell impostor jewelry, steins of beer and schnitzel here, too. They could call the place Faux Häus."

She spelled out the words and giggled as Kevin rolled his eyes at her. He slapped down his American Express card.

The next night, Lindsey sat at the kitchen table while Pau Pau ladled *doong-gwa* soup into a fine, gold-rimmed bowl. Ribbons of steam swirled up and disappeared, revealing a clear broth that held delicate cubes of translucent winter melon and small chunks of ham.

Lindsey touched the bowl and immediately burned her fingertips.

"Ow, it's too hot," she complained.

"Must drink now. No good cold," Pau Pau snapped back, convinced that soup wasn't hot enough unless absolutely scalding.

Lindsey dipped a porcelain spoon into the broth and blew on it until she was light-headed. She sipped the salty, soothing liquid as her grandmother broke into a huge grin.

"See, you like it! It's Virginia ham. The best!"

Lindsey had no idea where Pau Pau had absorbed such information as the superiority of Virginia ham, but she nodded in agreement.

After she slurped some more, she asked, "Are you going to China?"

"Yeah, yeah," Pau Pau said, her eyes lighting up. "You coming, right?"

Pau Pau explained that they would go to Shanghai to see her cousin and then to Toisan to visit Gung Gung's old village.

"It sounds like fun," Lindsey said innocently. Pau Pau emitted a light scoff, then shuffled out of the kitchen to go smoke a cigarette on the roof.

Friday afternoon Lindsey was grappling with an undecipherable formula from her Excel spreadsheet when she detected the old-white-lady smell of fart-dusty talc.

"Hey Lindsey, do you know what this says?"

Yvonne, the public relations event planner, held up a travel guide to Tokyo and pointed to a page with illustrated captions.

Lindsey glanced at the characters and replied, "Nope, I don't. This is in Japanese."

"But aren't you Japanese?"

"No, my last name is Owyang. I'm Chinese."

By the look on Yvonne's face, Lindsey could tell that the woman didn't know the difference between Japanese and Chinese surnames.

She added, "As a matter of fact, I can't even read Chinese."

Yvonne shrugged and began to shuffle away. She turned around abruptly and said, "Oh, are you going to participate in the test today?"

Lindsey looked up. "What test?"

Yvonne rolled her eyes. She planted her hands on her hips and said, "Don't you know anything? Next issue we're having an article on how you can tell meat-eaters from vegetarians by the way they smell. We're starting the test in a few minutes. I'm trying to convince Howard that we should sniff out all the flesh-eaters and make them turn veggie if they want to keep working here."

As Lindsey listened, she kept her arms tucked tightly at her sides.

"Yeah, I'll be there in a jiffy," she said enthusiastically.

Yvonne smirked. "See you in the conference room," she said, and ambled away.

Lindsey exhaled with relief. She had successfully thrown Yvonne off her scent. For now. What exactly would they be doing in the conference room, smelling each other's armpits? Lindsey was suddenly grateful for her Asian sweat glands. She, like most Chinese, perspired very little, which allowed her to mingle undetected among her suspicious coworkers. What a happy coincidence, she thought, that here at *Vegan Warrior* her minimal body hair and underactive apocrine glands contributed to her job security.

Getting up from her seat, she pressed the answering machine switch so she could quickly run to the bathroom. Striding past the kitchen, out of the corner of her eye she spotted Michael. She paused near the doorjamb and poked her head out from behind the wall to spy on him for a moment. He didn't see her, but he peered around cautiously as if he could feel someone's presence. Not seeing anyone, he began to search through the cupboards and open all the drawers. Throwing open the refrigerator door, he took a gulp from someone else's carrot juice, then picked up the parcel of cat grass Yvonne had bought earlier that morning. He examined a clump and then tore out a few blades and started chewing on them. Lindsey covered her mouth with her hand to keep from laughing as she watched him then sift through the spice rack. He unscrewed the nutmeg and the cumin and began to inexplicably sprinkle his shirt and arms.

"What are you doing?" Lindsey whispered.

Michael looked up, startled. Seeing it was her, he smiled.

"Did you know today's the vegetarian Inquisition?" he whispered back. "I wouldn't have eaten a cheeseburger last night if I'd known." He rubbed his sleeves with oregano and shook off the excess by twisting his arms like a mambo dancer. He said, "I've got five minutes to smell like a hippie so I don't get fired."

"I think I saw some essential oils in the lost-and-found box in the mailroom," Lindsey suggested. Just then, Yvonne appeared out of nowhere, stepping from the hall toward the kitchen, holding a yam. She stopped and glared at Lindsey, who blocked the entryway while Michael replaced the spices in the rack and dusted off the countertop. Lindsey darted toward the bathroom, and as the door slowly glided shut behind her she heard Yvonne say to Michael, "Are you polluting the microwave again with your pork sprinkles?"

Holding her ear against the bathroom door, Lindsey heard him reply, "Those weren't real Bacos, I swear. They were Fake-O's."

Later, in the conference room, Lindsey waited in line to be sniffed. Ojna, the sullen and sallow HR troll, was running her nose along employees' sleeves, trying to hoover up any olfactory traces of top sirloin consumption. After her anteater impersonation, she held her cupped hand against her proboscis and told her victim, "Now come forward and breathe into my nose."

Lindsey considered how illegal, unscientific, and unsanitary this exercise was, but she awaited her turn quietly. She looked around for Michael but didn't spot him.

When Ojna was done with the mousy advertising coordinator with the weak chin and bleached blond hair frizz, she beckoned for Lindsey to step up. Lindsey blew a stream of air into Ojna's tunnel of fingers and noticed the grime embedded beneath the woman's chewed fingernails. She tried not to focus on Ojna's see-through blouse stained with sweat rings like circles on an old-growth redwood tree.

"Hmm . . ." The woman considered Lindsey's scent as if she were savoring the irresistible aroma of boiled tofu dogs. Although Lindsey had only eaten a fruit salad for lunch, she began to worry about the Virginia ham in last night's soup. Ojna squinted at her ever so slightly.

"I suppose you can go . . . for now," Ojna finally said.

Lindsey hightailed it back to her desk.

Before she left for the day, she e-mailed Michael:

If you ever invite me to dinner, I could read *Sports Illustrated* magazines while you prepare a simple dish of lamb kidneys. And we could have real Bacos.

Pau Pau Checks Her Look in the Mirror, Just Like Bruce Springsteen

Lindsey took a day off from work because of an afternoon dentist appointment, but first she was going to accompany her grandmother to Chinatown to buy groceries.

Pau Pau wasn't ready yet. She was standing in her high-waisted granny underwear and silken long johns, rummaging through two large shopping bags full of clothes.

"Vivien say she give me all these for gift, but I think don't fit her no more." She pulled on a pair of Jordache jeans that were meant to be worn tight, but instead sagged around her bony posterior. She grabbed Lindsey's shoulder with a viselike grip to maintain her balance as she pulled on a pair of rainbow toe socks. After struggling with them and then yanking them off, she exclaimed, "Sheesh! Too much trouble!"

Pau Pau then pulled a French-cut T-shirt over her low, loose-skinned breasts and admired the sparkly, iron-on decal that spelled Foxy Lady in puffy letters.

"*Ho leyeng*, eh?" She observed her outfit, delighted by

the crisp crease down the middle of the dark blue jeans. She zipped a polar fleece vest over the T-shirt and topped it all off with her favorite quilted jacket.

Lindsey sat back and admired her grandmother. She wore her salt-and-pepper hair in a bouffant style that, years ago, had been as large and poufy as Angela Davis's Afro, but now hovered about three inches from her scalp. With the added height from her hair, the old woman just cleared five feet.

Pau Pau's face was an even, golden pale tone with a pretty apple shape. Her fine features were accentuated by an elegant widow's peak that Lindsey was proud to have inherited.

"Bring here," Pau Pau said, pointing to her Famolares in the corner. She laced up her shoes, then sat up and reached into the pockets of her previous day's pants, which were folded on the bed. She pulled out handfuls of hundred-dollar bills and stuffed them into the pockets of her new designer jeans.

"You shouldn't carry that much cash with you," Lindsey said. "You should put it in a bank."

"Is just mahjong money! What's big deal?" Pau Pau glanced in the mirror one last time and said, "Ready to go!"

Parking was always terrible in Chinatown, so they decided to take the bus. Boarding, Pau Pau spotted two Chinese ladies she knew and chatted with them as Lindsey looked on. A few minutes later, Pau Pau grabbed Lindsey's arm, checking for bone density or flesh plumpness, and proudly announced to her acquaintances, "This is my granddaughter." The ladies exclaimed words in Cantonese that Lindsey recognized as "Pretty!" and "So fat!"

Saying that she was fat was meant as a compliment. It was supposed to mean, "How rich, well-fed, and healthy! Surely she will not starve during the winter!" But Lindsey just cringed. To her it only meant she had a big, Häagen-Dazs bootie.

The women continued to assess Lindsey as they would a suckling pig hanging upside down in a market. One of the ladies, wearing an ill-fitting wig, poked her in the ribs, testing her firmness.

"Ah," they noted appreciatively as Pau Pau beamed. They continued their gossip, and the bus lurched slowly down the steep incline. Lindsey glanced around at the other passengers, who were mostly Chinese folks mixed in with a few yuppies dressed in business attire or J.Crew ensembles.

The Chinese, with their unfashionable discount clothing and stoic faces, appeared to be more newly arrived in San Francisco than Lindsey's family. Many of them clasped multiple plastic sacks filled with various food items and Chinese newspapers. They looked straight ahead without smiling. The young professionals wore crisply ironed shirts and polished shoes. Some chatted on phones or listened to CD players.

Lindsey wondered where she fit into this scenario. Her posture and the smiling way she held her face was more akin to the other Americans on the bus, but her skin and features matched the Chinese. She admired the Fluevog shoes of a redheaded woman who sat near her.

A Chinese man a few rows behind was picking his teeth,

eating sunflower seeds, and loudly hacking the shells on the rubber floor. None of the other Asians took notice, but Lindsey turned around, mortified. She was silently grossed-out as she watched the man emit sprays of saliva with each chew, smack, and spit.

As she looked on, a white businessman in a pin-striped suit blurted out loudly, "Oh, that's disgusting!"

Lindsey was shocked and offended; it was as though he had insulted every Chinese person on the bus. At the same time, she worried that the businessman considered her equally capable of such an unsanitary act.

She felt obligated to explain cultural differences to the intolerant yuppie, but she also felt like commiserating with the old Chinese man about rude Westerners who didn't respect their elders. She said nothing. The suit exited at the next stop, and the Chinese man continued to obliviously spit out his shells.

Stockton Street was their stop. Pau Pau pushed toward the front, bulldozing against those who were trying to board the bus. Lindsey made her way to the back door, and when she finally jumped from the step, Pau Pau was waiting impatiently on the crowded sidewalk.

"Gee whiz! What take so long?"

Lindsey tried to explain how it's best to exit a bus from the back door, but Pau Pau just threw up her hands. She darted swiftly across Clay Street like a strong and determined quail as Lindsey tried in vain to keep up, bumbling as clumsily as a one-legged pigeon.

Passing the corner newsstand where Lindsey and Kevin used to buy fireworks and Wacky Packs, they neared the modest, maroon-tiled building where her family's travel agency had been. Now the office was occupied by an acupuncturist, and the sign with the neon airplane was gone.

Gung Gung had been big into neon. He'd loved anything flashy, shiny, and all-American, such as Cadillacs and taps on his wingtips.

He was always cracking jokes and making people feel at ease. Lindsey recalled how Gung Gung used to prepare raisin toast and Ghirardelli chocolate with hot milk. In the summer he would peel ripe nectarines for her and sprinkle sugar on the slices.

"Very nice! Very tasty!" he would always say.

She held on tightly to these memories. She wished she had talked to him more before he died, but it had never occurred to her that he wouldn't always be around. She felt guilty for having only childhood memories of him and for never having thanked him for anything.

"Fai-dee!" Pau Pau yelled, hurrying through the Washington Street crosswalk.

Before Lindsey knew it, Pau Pau had ducked into Orange Land and was tossing inadequate mangoes, inspecting *law bok,* and selecting tender *bok choy.* Old ladies were shoving Lindsey, stepping on her feet, and generally treating her like a nuisance because she wasn't moving quickly or decisively enough. Pau Pau handed her a twenty-dollar bill and several plastic bags filled with taro, *siew choy,* mustard greens, *dow gok,* and snow peas.

"Go pay over there," Pau Pau ordered, shoving her way out to the narrow, fishy-smelling sidewalk.

Lindsey stood in line at the cashier. People jostled each other even though there was nowhere to move. One after another, several old ladies cut in front of her and tossed their purchases on the scales as the cashier rang them up, unaware of Lindsey's presence. She tried to push her way up but was afraid of being rude, despite the fact that she herself was being bumped, squished, and elbowed. She waited, but the line didn't get any shorter.

"Ai-ya!" She heard a familiar voice behind her. Pau Pau grabbed the bags from her hands, hoisted the items above the heads of other shoppers, and in one swift motion, over-powered two ladies who were attempting to cut in front. She paid the cashier and thrust the packages back into her granddaughter's hands.

A few doors down, Pau Pau entered a store that sold mostly dry goods: rice-paper candies, various kinds of dried mushrooms, and stuff that looked like yellow shredded sponge for bird's nest soup. Lindsey glanced around at the other dried items: whole pressed ducks, flattened flounders, crystallized ginger, medicinal roots, dehydrated sea horses, and clumps of stringy brown seaweed.

Pau Pau purchased several packets of herbs folded indi-vidually in wax paper, a box of back plasters, and two cans of hairspray with black tint for covering gray hair.

"One more place," Pau Pau said, walking through crowds that parted effortlessly for her, like she was a Chi-nese lady Moses.

They stepped into a meat market, where Pau Pau cut several people in line and ordered two pounds of pork, trimmed and cut to her specifications.

"Sow yook," she said. "You have to get skinny kind of pork, not too much fat."

She pointed to two specific fish in a tank of a hundred

and made sure the butcher retrieved exactly the ones she wanted.

"Must buy swimming fish," she explained. "Fish in American store—Safeway, Cala Food—already dead. No good."

Leaving the bustling market, Lindsey organized the heavy bags of groceries and distributed their weight evenly so the handles didn't hurt her palms.

"Okay, you go home, I play mahjong," Pau Pau said before turning to depart.

Lindsey replied, "Okay, see you later tonight." After a brief moment of hesitation she quickly added, "I love you."

Pau Pau nodded in an unsentimental way, thrust her hands into her pockets, and walked off toward Spofford Alley.

On her own now, Lindsey strolled down Grant Avenue before heading home. She stopped at a store window with pretty silk lanterns and vintage advertisements depicting 1930s-style Shanghai girls. She was attracted to the sepia-toned nostalgia of the posters but suddenly felt uncomfortable when two white women approached and also stopped to admire the display.

They were tourists who had just traipsed up from North Beach, one wearing a floral tent and the other wearing a Property of Alcatraz sweatshirt stretched snugly over her tiramisu-stuffed paunch. Lindsey looked up and was amused to see an ancient, white-haired Chinese man zooming by on a zippy Razor scooter. He bounced against one of the tourist's ample posteriors and nearly fell. Deftly regaining his balance, he swore at the women in Chinese, then readjusted the bulging plastic sacks on his handlebars before pushing off and coasting away.

Lindsey eyed the tourists.

"Aren't Oriental girls beautiful!" Alcatraz exclaimed.

"Yes, they're so exotic! Maybe Dede would like that . . ."

Lindsey listened, feeling that somehow she, too, was being judged.

"So graceful," Alcatraz marveled again.

The women followed Lindsey into the curio shop, and the three browsed in close proximity for some time. A stationery section displayed notebooks and address books with close-ups of pretty Chinese faces. On a nearby shelf, Asian motifs adorned an assortment of pencil cases, jewelry boxes, and lipstick containers. Lindsey picked up a few items, but as soon as one of the tourists touched the same thing and remarked, "How darling!" she reconsidered her interest.

She didn't quite know why she was ambivalent about her own desire for the trinkets. Would she get any closer to her Chinese heritage by purchasing that embroidered coin purse, or would she disgrace her ancestors by writing a white guy's phone number in that brocaded filofax?

She decided to purchase a coin purse with a fan-pagoda motif.

"Thanks," she said to the woman behind the counter.

"ABC?" the woman asked.

"Yep," she replied, knowing that Mainland people derived great amusement and satisfaction from identifying American-born Chinese. Lindsey tucked away her change, and the woman nodded and swaggered off, seeming confident that she had Lindsey all figured out.

Lindsey suddenly remembered she was carrying raw meat. She needed to hurry home, but first she stopped in a corner store to buy a pack of gum.

She placed a pack of Wrigley's Doublemint on the counter and waited to pay as the old Chinese guy behind the register slowly stubbed out his cigarette. Pondering the illegality of smoking indoors in the state of California, she spotted a ripped calendar taped against the wall. At the bottom was a black-and-white group photo with a caption that read, "This 1988 calendar compliments of the Chinese Six Companies."

As the grocer talked lazily over his shoulder to a younger man unpacking cans of lychees, Lindsey focused on the photo of smiling Chinese men in suits and realized that her Gung Gung was standing third from the right. She recognized his big smile and the same posed stance from the picture with Jimmy Carter that hung above her bed.

She fished out two quarters, her eyes still glued to the tattered calendar. The man began speaking to her in Cantonese, but she only responded by blinking a couple of times.

"ABC, eh? What you looking at? Look at old picture?" he asked.

She nodded toward the photo. "That's my grandfather."

The man scooted closer to the calendar to get a better look.

"Oh yeah? Which? This one?" He pointed to the man on the far left, but she shook her head. He went down the row until finally she said, "Yes, that one. That's him."

The man furrowed his long eyebrows and looked up at some paint that was flaking off the wall. He seemed to be recalling a faraway time, and then, as though the name were magically written on the ceiling, he said, "Sam Gin?"

She couldn't believe it. "Yeah, that's him!"

"Ah," the old man nodded. "You daughter?"

"Granddaughter," Lindsey said, poking herself in the chest to illustrate the veracity of her claim.

"Oh!" the man exclaimed. Excited, he began to talk quickly in Cantonese but then waved his hand in front of his face and said, "Sorry, I forget." He thought for a second before restarting in English.

"Sam Gin, very good man. Gave me ride to airport once."

"Really?"

"Oh yes, yes, yes. Was president of Six Companies. And travel agency. Know everybody!" The man kept nodding for a few more seconds but said no more.

She smiled. "Did you know him well?"

"Oh, long time ago," he said, lighting a new cigarette.

She wanted to ask more questions, but the old man's mind shifted back into the present. He yelled something in Chinese to the guy who had been unpacking the cans.

She couldn't think of any other questions to ask. The man smiled and opened his cash register.

"You keep, you keep," he said, handing her two quarters. She took them, knowing it would be insulting to him if she refused.

"Okay, bye bye now," he said. With nothing else to do but leave, she thanked the man and left.

Chinese Water Torture

Lindsey awoke and could not get back to sleep. She felt restless and hyper-awake and sensed that she had been dreaming about something thrilling, but now she could not remember the shadowy images no matter how hard she tried to conjure them. She kicked out of her sheets, grabbed a notebook, and poised a pen above the page, trying to will herself to recall any vivid details. But the more she tried to put words down on paper, the more her ideas evaporated from her imagination and the only thing she could visualize was the ink drying up inside the pen's cartridge.

At times like these, when she couldn't sleep, she often fell into worry about a multitude of life's details: the coffee she spilled on Mimi's sweater, global warming, increased parking ticket fines, and what she would do with the rest of her life.

From her vanity she gazed out the window at the night sky, which glimmered like an intense sapphire. She wondered if anyone else in the city could see the financial district resting perfectly still, resembling a geometric pack of stars and galaxies floating against ultramarine blue glass. She slowly scanned the dark skyline of baby supernovas, as its imprint burned in her head like a silent film dissolving on a silver screen.

For forty minutes she sat wide awake, as her stream-of-consciousness worries drifted in and out of her mind like seafoam at low tide. She burrowed back under her comforter and eventually accepted the gentle gravity that drooped her eyelids like luxurious, plush curtains. She rested her head against the pillow and sank into a deep sleep. Her worries, like loose rocks in the caves of Ocean Beach, washed back into a crevice of her memory, where they would wait, dormant until the next wakeful night.

Every night that week Lindsey dreamed of the ocean, and Saturday she decided to go to Fort Point for a walk below the Golden Gate Bridge. She drove the winding road through the Presidio and descended into the cool stand of silver-green eucalyptus trees that swayed on the side of the road like a forest of tall, lanky boys.

The fog resembled bright white crystalline cotton reflecting off the liquid metal waves. She considered San Francisco Bay similar to a distant but protective ancestor, one who spoke no English yet communicated affection with the forceful motion of smooth, jade water.

Watching the swells crash against the wet, black rocks, she imagined the boat that had brought her grandfather here. How totally unsanitary it must have been, she thought as she pulled some Purell from her bag and rubbed her hands together until the alcohol gel evaporated.

She sat on the hood of her car and watched the surfers bobbing like puffins atop the waves. Roaring in her ears as loud as a roller coaster, speeding vehicles overhead rumbled between the red-orange girders of the bridge.

She walked closer to the fort and explored around the back, out of sight from the parking lot. Sand crunched under her boots as she kneeled down for a closer look at some pinkish pale specks fluttering in the water.

She heard a voice next to her.

"I was wondering what those were, too."

It took a second to register who he was because it was puzzling to see him so completely out of context. How strange it was to be standing here at Fort Point, standing next to Michael Cartier.

The logical question that she might have asked was, What are you doing here? but she didn't say that. In fact, she didn't say anything at all, and neither did he. In a moment of paused time, they stood and just looked at each other in the crisp November sunlight.

He wore jeans, a hooded sweatshirt, and dark brown suede shoes with crepe soles. She looked around and didn't see anyone who might be accompanying him here, but just as she was about to ask, he broke the silence and said, "Are you here by yourself?"

She nodded, forgetting that she knew how to talk.

"It's funny," he said. "I always noticed that clipping taped up on your desk, that scene from *Vertigo* where Jimmy Stewart is carrying Kim Novak out of the water. And it was on TV last night. I watched it and it gave me the idea to come here." He smiled, and Lindsey noticed a certain kindness in the crinkles around his eyes.

"And here you are, just like that," she said.

He nodded. "And you, y'just hang around here on a regular basis?"

She felt her feet sort of lift from the ground in the brief moment his hand touched her shoulder. They walked together along the concrete slabs near the edge, where the land dropped off and the Pacific Ocean began. An enormous, cracked, and rusted chain barrier separated sightseers from the ocean, but Lindsey and Michael stepped over it for a closer view of an old clipper ship that was cruising under the famous landmark. She figured it was a private charter for a wedding or some other special event, but with its billowed, wine-colored sail, it was nonetheless a spectacular sight, conjuring up romantic images of nineteenth-century adventurers sailing around Cape Horn.

"Let's go look in the fort," Lindsey said, finding her voice. She high-stepped back over the crusty cast-iron chain.

"Okay." Michael looked back for a final glimpse of the ghostlike ship, which was gliding gracefully out of view. As he raised his leg over the barrier, the sole of his right shoe suddenly slipped on the wet concrete and propelled him backward. Since his left leg was already hoisted in the air, poised for the small hop over the chain, the rest of his body had no choice but to swiftly fall back. He tumbled fifteen feet below, into the salty, shallow bay.

In the distance, a wave crashed against a large rock, sending up an impressive splatter of white spray, so no one noticed the relatively modest splash made by Michael's flailing body. Lindsey had been watching the surfers again, and when she turned to point out a particularly skilled boogie-boarder, she realized her companion was no longer on dry land.

Hopping back over the chain, she looked down and saw him, standing chest-high in the bay water, soaking wet. He did not appear hurt, but he seemed to have difficulty keeping his balance as the waves pushed against him and washed the sand out from under his legs.

"Are you okay?" she yelled.

He waded over to a more shallow area and stood to catch his breath, slightly bent over with his hands on his knees, like a quarterback in a football huddle.

"Yeah, I just came down here to see these starfish," he said, pointing to the pink and orange sea creatures that clung onto a phalanx of shiny black mussels.

A small crowd gathered to watch. Michael managed to hoist himself up and climb to safety. Dripping on the granite walkway, he ran his hands through his sopping hair and tried to pull off his sweatshirt, which was heavy with salt water.

A teenage boy in a Hard Rock Cafe T-shirt ran up and asked, "Hey, can I take your picture?" He handed Lindsey his camera and stood next to Michael. She clicked the camera and handed it back.

As the boy ran off, Michael yanked off his sweatshirt and twisted the water from it.

It would be an outright lie to say that Lindsey didn't check out Michael as best as she could. He was standing there in broad daylight with nothing on but wet blue jeans, socks, and shoes (and, presumably, underwear). He was somewhat pale, but that was fine with her, since no self-respecting San Franciscan actually went out of his way to tan, for heaven's sake.

She looked away, embarrassed by seeing so much of his flesh.

"Um, do you want a ride back to your house, or do you have a car?" she asked, trying to keep focused on practical matters to avoid picturing the rest of him unclothed. She noticed his skin had goose bumps and his Levi's were stuck to his legs and forming small puddles under his feet.

"Well, I walked here," he said, looking up. "But if this were *Vertigo*, shouldn't I be waking up in your bed?"

She just about fainted right there. She stood for a few seconds, not really knowing what to say.

He held up his clothes and said, "Seriously, though, the whole reason I'm walking around today is my apartment is being flea-bombed and I can't go back for another two hours. Is it okay if I take a shower at your place?"

Her mind raced a mile a minute. Flea-bombed? Who could make up something like that? If he wanted to come over to her place, then how great was that? But what about Pau Pau? Him naked in her bed. . . . Fleas are unsanitary. But he was getting rid of them. . . . He's standing there half-naked right now! He would drip all over the car, but so what? He had nice skin. He must be cold.

"Yeah, okay. Come on," she said.

Lindsey drove and Michael dripped.

"I liked your e-mail," he said. "I'll have you over for organ meats anytime."

Her heart leaped. Speaking of organ meats, she wondered how or if she should bring up the fact that she lived with her grandmother. He was bound to notice the old-person smells, in addition to the unavoidable Chinese smells. She hoped they would not be greeted by a pot of pig's feet simmering in vinegar on the stove.

"Hey, I'm sorry that lunch thing never worked out," he said. He launched into casual conversation about work and thanked her, explaining how the liberal application of arnica and tea tree oils had saved him from the vegan witchhunt. As he spoke, Lindsey unconsciously tuned him out, starting to panic about the state of her apartment.

What if Pau Pau was home for some reason? Would he gag at the overpowering stench of tiger balm? Was the bathroom clean and denture-free? Was her bedroom strewn with bras and undies?

She was barely stopping at Stop signs, but she forced herself to concentrate so he wouldn't think she was a bad Chinese driver.

She pulled the car into the driveway, and Michael got out quickly, seeming concerned about soaking the upholstery. Usually, the idea of anyone soiling the inside of her car sent Lindsey into a minor fit, but this was the guy whom she had been practically stalking. He was different. She managed to keep her cool, despite the big wet spot on the seat and puddles on the floor mat.

"Don't worry about it," she said nonchalantly.

Slamming the car door, she looked around to see if any neighbors or other tenants could see her coming home with a partially clothed man. In the stairwell on the first-floor landing, she stopped and said, "I have to tell you something."

"Yeah?"

"Okay, um, I live with my grandmother, so let me go in first and check if she's there, so she doesn't have a heart attack when she sees you with no clothes on, okay?"

He laughed and nodded. "Yeah, I guess this is kind of unusual. Are you sure this is okay with you?"

"You're more than okay to me," Lindsey said, and then immediately felt like a fool. She beckoned him to follow her up the stairs.

Once they reached her door, she asked him to wait a second. She turned her key and slipped quickly inside. Pau Pau, thank God, was not there. But that was not Lindsey's only concern. She grabbed some lavender-rosemary room freshener (an impulse purchase from two weeks ago—what luck!) and frantically sped around the apartment, madly spritzing the rooms to rid them of the faintly medicinal smell. She scooped up random socks off her bedroom floor and checked the bathroom for BENGAY, denture glue, and stray hairs in the bathtub. She grabbed Pau Pau's jars of stinky ointments, boxes of arthritis plasters, and anything with Chinese writing on it. Sprinting to the hall closet, she dumped everything messily onto the floor.

"Uh, come on in," she said, opening the door calmly.

Michael was barefoot, with his shoes and socks under one arm. He glanced around, unaware of the pains she had gone through to strip the environment of anything offensive.

"Shower's over there," she said, her eyes darting around. As they stood in the hallway, a framed photo of her parents watched her.

Michael wandered around the living room while she retrieved clean towels, making sure they bore no hotel logos that would betray her family's love of pilfering while on vacation.

"This picture of you is so cute," he said, inspecting a childhood photo of Lindsey taken at Candlestick Park.

"Oh, thanks," she replied distractedly. She was nervous and wanted him to get in the shower so she could continue her cultural scouring of the apartment.

Finally, he took the towels from her and headed to the bathroom. He shut the door, and Lindsey waited for the sound of water to begin. She relaxed. Things weren't that bad. The linoleum floor in the kitchen was clean, the Formica table had been wiped that morning, and Pau Pau's room was immaculate, as always.

She sat on the edge of her bed and waited for the shower to stop. She worried that he might open the medicine cabinet and find something unappealing, like a Chinese ear-scratching stick that had escaped her notice.

He soon emerged—clean, damp, and embarrassingly sexy. She blushed and stared down at a sizeable tumbleweed of fuzz on the carpet.

"Um, do you have any clothes I could borrow? You know, that might fit me?" He wore the towel around his waist and combed his hair with his fingers.

Words congealed in Lindsey's brain like sections of Mandarin oranges suspended in Jell-O. She hurried to her dresser and pulled out what she thought was a plain white T-shirt, but she quickly realized it had a Hello Kitty face on the pocket, so she shoved it back in the drawer. Searching around, she vaguely remembered having some of Kevin's clothes from months ago when he came over after playing volleyball. Behind her veil of bangs, she tried not to stare too hard at any part of Michael's anatomy as he stood nearly naked.

She handed him a pair of blue nylon shorts and a faded black T-shirt, and he returned to the bathroom.

When he emerged, she said, "I can throw your clothes in the dryer downstairs if you want. Do you need anything else?"

He tossed his towel on the armchair, then turned to face her. He stepped closer and placed his hands on her shoulders.

"Well, hmm, let's see . . . ," he said. He smiled at her, and she felt his hand lightly on her back.

Thinking he might kiss her, she tried to ignore the disturbing fact that he was wearing her brother's clothes. In her peripheral vision, Gung Gung and Jimmy Carter were smiling. "Go for it!" they both seemed to be cheering.

There was a click at the front door, followed by the sound of shuffling steps leading in the direction opposite Lindsey's bedroom.

Lindsey's eyes became as large as Nilla wafers, and she suddenly could not breathe. She began to hyperventilate. Although Pau Pau was a hallway and two rooms away, the romantic mist of lavender-rosemary had faded away, and the powerful odor of Tiger Balm seeped down the hall and wafted up Lindsey's nostrils immediately.

"Oh my God. Don't move!" she whispered between short, hopping breaths.

Her panic struck Michael's funny bone. He mussed her hair and tried to put his arms around her.

She stepped away from him, practically shoving him off. Her stomach turned over, and she didn't know if her urge to barf was caused by the excitement of him being so close or by the dread she felt, knowing she was caught red-handed "playing hanky-panky."

Pau Pau was sure to have an aneurysm if she discovered a white devil in her granddaughter's bedroom. There was only one thing Lindsey could think to do. She had to hide him.

"Don't move!" she whispered again.

"You're being silly. Let's just go say hi to her," he said.

She clapped her hand over Michael's mouth and told him to shut up.

From the framed photo above, the thirty-ninth president of the United States gazed down at her. He seemed to say, "You've blown it now. You're ruining everything."

Forgetting that she had dumped all the Chinese medicines and ointment jars in the hall closet, Lindsey now grabbed Michael's hand and shoved him inside. He tripped on a plastic jar of honeylike goo, which cracked into bits under the weight of his heel, releasing a peppery camphor smell into the stuffy air.

"I'm going to distract her. Meet me at the bottom of the stairwell," Lindsey said. Slamming the door, she left Michael in the dark.

Pau Pau called out, "Linsee-ah?"

Lindsey came running around the corner.

"Yeah, it's me," she replied, careening to an abrupt halt on the living room carpet.

"What smell?" her grandmother asked, sniffing the air.

"Room freshener," Lindsey answered, speaking softly so that Michael wouldn't hear.

Pau Pau headed toward the bathroom, but Lindsey jumped in front of her.

"*Ai-ya!* What wrong with you?"

"Where are you going?" Lindsey asked in a panic.

"Go to toilet!" Pau Pau screeched in Cantonese, pushing past her impatiently.

Now was her chance. Lindsey ran to the closet door, threw it open, and found Michael standing there with folded arms and goop on his bare foot. She grabbed him, cast him out the front door, and repeated, "Meet me at the bottom of the stairs!"

"But what about my shoes?" he whispered before the door whoofed shut.

Pau Pau came out and found the closet door flung open with her medicines strewn about and the broken jar oozing on the carpet.

"*Ai-ya!* What happen?"

"I was cleaning and I dropped that. I'll clean it up right now!" Lindsey made a feeble motion toward the spill, but Pau Pau was already gathering up her small jars and vials of herbs.

"Don't touch my things! You make too much trouble! Gee whiz!" Pau Pau lapsed into Chinese, muttering about Lindsey making more work for her.

Lindsey sneaked past her grandmother to retrieve Michael's wet clothes and shoes from her room. She crammed the stuff into a plastic bag and ran out the front door.

Michael was waiting at the bottom of the stairs, scraping the medicinal gunk off his foot.

"Hi there," she said, trying to sound apologetic. She handed him his clothes.

"Thanks," he said, pulling on his shoes. "So, what was that all about?" He looked at her with a grimace.

Uh-oh. Fifteen minutes ago he seemed like he might kiss her, and now he seemed put off.

"Do you want a ride home?" she asked. She could tell something had been lost between them but didn't know how to make things right again.

"No thanks, I'm all right. I guess I should go."

He stood for a second before walking out the door. Lindsey couldn't think of anything to say, so she watched him through the window as he disappeared out of sight.

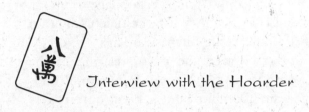

Interview with the Hoarder

Lindsey ordered a turkey sandwich at the deli and waited for her number to be called. She stood against the wall by the refrigerated case and wondered why Michael hadn't been at work for the past few days. She didn't flatter herself enough to think that he was ditching work to avoid her.

Maybe he was right and she should have introduced him to Pau Pau. She certainly shouldn't have trapped him in the closet with the stinky Chinese stuff.

Shaken from her reverie, she realized someone was talking to her. She glanced over her shoulder and saw Steve D., the River Phoenix–look-alike.

"Hey, don't I get a hug? We are friends, after all, right?" He put his arm around her shoulder and gave her a squeeze.

"Do you want to eat together?" he asked, following her as she made her way to the counter to collect her turkey on white.

"Um, okay. What are you gonna get?" she said.

"I can't decide between the California roll or the teriyaki bowl," he replied, studying the two prepackaged meals, which were each cocooned in layers of cellophane wrap. He chose the sushi and together they left the deli, ending up sitting on a bench in the Yerba Buena Gardens.

Downtown workers dotted the grass, relaxing in the dappled shade from various trees. A group of schoolchildren played by the water fountains, and a couple of teenagers tossed a Frisbee nearby. Seagulls with black-tipped wings circled overhead, and clumps of pigeons knocked about haphazardly.

Lindsey and Steve talked about their jobs and then gossiped a little about Steve E. and Mimi, but they quickly ran out of things to chat about.

Steve D. was busy scoping out each and every one of the Asian women in his line of vision. Lindsey watched him, fascinated by the consistent way his eyes swept the entire area, passing over completely attractive white women and stopping at each vaguely Asian-looking female no matter how attractive or not, age also not seeming to matter. It was like a game of connect the Asian dots.

"Wow, you're really something," she said.

"What?" He was unaware that he was being watched or even doing anything that could be detected by someone else.

"You're scoping out all the Asian women, aren't you?"

He smiled, totally busted. But he didn't seem embarrassed.

"Yeah, so I am. I think I know that girl over there." His discarded ball of plastic wrap got caught in a small gust of wind and blew a short distance away.

"Aren't you going to get that?" Lindsey asked, but he just shrugged.

She pushed herself up and chased after the plastic film, catching it and throwing it into a nearby wastebasket.

Steve D. continued to scan the area for Asian life. Lindsey plopped back down and said, "If we're going to be friends, you really can't go around littering like that."

He nodded and finished his sushi.

"So, what's up with your Asian fetish?"

He smiled. "Whoa, that's pretty direct of you, isn't it?"

"Yeah, it's a good thing we're only friends. I'm probably not demure enough for you."

"Definitely not!"

She outlined the details of her Hoarder theory to him, and, to illustrate her hypothesis, she pointed to his oatmeal-colored pants and his Pendleton shirt, which was a butter-scotch plaid. She knew she had him cornered when she asked if he loitered around Japantown, hitting on girls by pretending to be lost. As he listened, Steve's eyes bugged out of his head.

"Whoa," he said, nodding in dumbfounded awe. "It's like you've got a surveillance camera trained on me, 24/7."

Instead of being repulsed by his admission, she actually considered him amusing.

"So, the Siamese cat is out of the bag," he said. "I've got yellow fever, all right. I love rice, udon, and kimchee. If I'm at McDonald's, I always order the Chinese chicken salad. I love Asian women, especially Koreans. I love the idea of geishas, and I have fantasies about having sex with dim sum waitresses on top of those rolling carts!" He excitedly fished through his pants pocket. "Wanna see my personals ad?"

Flipping open his wallet, he poked his finger between two Kimono-brand condoms and slipped out a tiny square of newsprint. It read: "WANTED: Wanton wonton waitress. Sausage seeks steamy buns. I don't have a lot of dough but expert at making sweet dumplings sticky."

She couldn't believe it. She handed back the clipping and said, "You're disgusting." Then she began to laugh so hard that a couple of paper napkins went airborne and she didn't chase them. He laughed, too, enjoying cracking her up.

She caught her breath and said, "Let me guess. Your favorite bands are Shonen Knife and Pizzicato Five."

"YES!" he yelled out, amazed. "I hang out in Asian grocery stores waiting for unsuspecting chicks. I lay in wait and pretend I don't know the difference between the red mochi and the white-bean mochi. I get cute girls to explain them to me—"

"You're so heinous—"

"I've got a Korean phrasebook, a Japanese one, too. Sometimes when I'm on the bus, I—"

"Ohmigod, you're one of those guys on the bus—"

"Yeah, I am."

She was thoroughly pleased. She felt triumphant that a self-admitted Hoarder of All Things Asian had now confirmed her theory.

After they finished their lunch, they headed back toward their respective offices. At the corner of Third and Market they said good-bye.

"Maybe some night I could call you," he said. "You could bring over your opium pipe and we could watch reruns of *Kung Fu*."

She wasn't sure if he was joking or not. She turned to

walk away, but he surprised her with a big hug, saying, "I got your number from Miss Madlangbayan—I'll call ya." And off he went.

That evening she called Mimi.

"Why did you give Steve D. my phone number?"

"I thought you'd want me to. Didn't you?"

She could hear Mimi chuckling at a sitcom playing in the background, paying more attention to the TV show.

"I think he's pretty funny."

"Yeah, hella cute too. You kinda like him, huh?"

Just then Lindsey's phone beeped with another call on the line. Mimi heard the pause and said, "Go ahead and get that. I'll talk to you later."

"All right, call you tomorrow." Lindsey clicked over to the incoming call.

"Hello."

"Hey, it's me, Steve D."

"Oh, hi."

"So, what are you doing right now, Miss Lindsey Owyang?"

"Wow, at least you got my name right this time."

"Yeah. So what are you doing?"

"Um, nothing. I'm talking to you."

"Do you want to come over? We could watch cable and I'll make Top Ramen. Or Maruchan. Or Sapporo Ichiban. Or Bibim Mein. I'll make anything you want."

"I'm busy," she said, though actually impressed by his ramen repertoire.

"Oh, come on. I worship you, y'know," he urged playfully.

Lindsey thought for a moment. She knew he was just a liar, but she always fell for lines like that.

"Okay," she said, agreeing to be at his place in a half hour.

"Sexcellent!"

As Steve abruptly clicked off, Lindsey held the phone in her hand for a moment. She shook her head with amused dismay.

TONIGHT ON THE DISCOVERY CHANNEL: HOARDERS OF ALL THINGS ASIAN. OUR FEATURE WILL STUDY THE MATING HABITS OF THESE URBAN PREDATORS.

Like banana slugs clinging to the supple bark of tropical trees, this Caucasian male subspecies appears harmless but imperceptibly secretes a mollifying slime from his extremities, which he uses to glom onto a favorite variety of Asian female: Korean, Filipina, Chinese, Vietnamese, or other small-boned variations. Developing a specialized appetite, he stalks his prey by using cultural knowledge gleaned from previous victims to tempt another into his lair, which reeks of Drakkar Noir cologne.

The Hoarder speaks softly, hoping that a female might mistake his dull platitudes for sophisticated witticisms. His droning voice mesmerizes the victim, whose polite nature prevents her from immediately extracting her limbs from the sticky web of saliva. Eventually, the Hoarder collapses the delicate skeletal system of his demure captive, squelching her under his hulking Barney Rubble physique.

VIEWER DISCRETION ADVISED.

Steve D.'s apartment was the usual bachelor pad. The furnishings were all crappy dormitory leftovers, except for a huge-screen television. The floors weren't all that clean, but at least a Gauguin poster of Tahitian maidens was an attempt at decorating.

"Do you live here by yourself?" she asked, trying to guess the rent.

"No, but my stoner roommate's always at his girlfriend's. He gets high and passes out there, like, every night." He waited for the water to boil before he dropped in the dried noodle bricks. "You get Oriental Flavor because you're Oriental," he said.

"Yeah, but they don't have *Caucasian* Flavor," she replied.

"Did I hear a *cock* in that *Asian*?"

"You are out of control." Lindsey shook her head in exaggerated dismay. She took a sip of her beer.

Steve set the table with folded paper napkins and pulled three jars of different kimchees out of the fridge, explaining the difference between each of them.

He served the ramen and placed utensils on the table.

Lindsey picked up a spoon and inspected it for cleanliness before dipping it into the salty broth.

"Oriental Flavor, huh?" she asked. "I don't think I taste like this."

"We'll see about that later." He winked at her from across the table as he used a fork to pile kimchee into his bowl.

A jar of pickled cabbage and many beers later, they lounged on his sofa watching a video of *Apocalypse Now*.

"Don't you have any other tapes?" she asked. "Do you have *Clueless*?"

"Even if I did, I wouldn't admit to that. Guys don't have shit like that around."

"Oh."

She was drowsy from her carbo load. Steve pulled her legs across his lap and rested his hands on her knees as he adjusted the tracking with the remote control.

Right about the time when Robert Duvall and his platoon torched the Vietnamese village, Steve D. and Lindsey started making out. They kissed for a long time, pausing occasionally to watch more scenes of the movie.

In the long run, the flesh was weak. Clothing was removed and bad judgments were made.

By the light of the television set, Steve removed her underwear and she did not protest, although she did insist on leaving on her socks. As he kissed her between her thighs, Lindsey was distracted by Marlon Brando getting bludgeoned, but she tried to think of something else.

Neither of them heard the roommate come in.

"Oh, sorry!" the stoner yelped. Steve and Lindsey both jumped up and grabbed for clothes, a blanket, anything.

In a complete state of bewilderment and shock, the roommate dropped a box of assorted Hostess snacks, while a half-eaten Twinkie tumbled from his lips.

"Shit, man! What are you doing here?" Steve zipped up his pants, grabbed his slow roommate by the shoulders, and spun him out of the room and back out the front door. Lindsey fumbled around for her panties, which had been tossed like caution to the wind.

Steve came back in. "He's leaving. I mean, he left. I got rid of him." By now, she had most of her clothes back on and was ready to leave.

"I gotta go," she said.

"Want one for the road?" he asked, picking up one of the individually wrapped treats that had bounced onto the floor.

"No," she said, bolting for the exit. Watching her go, Steve unwrapped the flimsy cellophane from a Twinkie, split open the yellow snackcake, and licked the cream out of it.

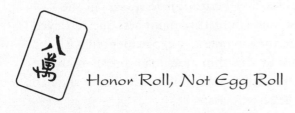

Honor Roll, Not Egg Roll

The next day at work, Lindsey checked her e-mail and found a message from Michael:

Dear Lindsey,

Hi. I'm in Hawaii. I won't be home until after Thanksgiving. Can we get together when I get back?

She felt irrational jealousy bubbling up inside her as she imagined the possibility of him vacationing with a girlfriend. She tried not to resent him for having a good time while she felt tortured by unrequited love. Why was he in Hawaii, anyway? Who could suntan at a time like this?

After work, she decided on a whim to quickly duck into the stationery store. She hadn't gone inside for years, and she hoped the old man did not recognize her face as the shoplifter from fifteen years ago. She skulked around the pastels and pen sets before quickly purchasing a tiny kit of watercolor paints, then scampered out the door like a hamster with a food pellet.

At home she locked her bedroom door, sat on the carpet, and studied her new miniature paint set. She retrieved a cup of water from the kitchen and experimented with the different colors, using the thin horsehair brush to make small lines of pigment across scraps of Arches paper she had saved from her college art class.

Back then, she had signed up for an Introduction to Painting course in the hopes of becoming the next Georgia O'Keeffe or Helen Frankenthaler. She'd wanted to paint gigantic, eerie paintings with shadows and light, liquidy drips, and thick, encaustic chunkiness. But the man who had taught the class had discouraged her from painting big or thinking big. Not that he hadn't liked her. In fact, he'd told her she possessed better drawing skills than most of his students. But she was so petite. He'd said he visualized her painting delicate, decorative pieces, and he'd suggested she sit cross-legged on a lotus meditation pillow or tatami mat. Action painting was not for the faint of heart, he'd told her, and a frail, Oriental girl like her would probably not be able to muster up the power to create monolithic or expressionist works. Those types of paintings, he'd said, were best left to masculine hands.

So he'd encouraged her to work small. He'd even urged her to get in touch with her roots. Due to his incomprehensible way of mumbling behind his bushy mustache, Lindsey had first misunderstood his suggestion. She'd thought he wanted her to *touch up* her roots (her auburn highlights had, in fact, grown out about an inch and could have benefitted from a trip to the salon).

Week after week she would ask his opinion about her Rothko-esque paintings, and time after time he would suggest, "Why don't you try calligraphy or small pen-and-ink landscapes?" Her abstract work had showed substantial talent, but he'd been fixated on the idea that Oriental girls should make classic Oriental paintings. He'd continued to give her average grades.

She'd loved the freedom of the large-sized canvases and the versatility of painting in oils, but she'd soon realized her dilemma. She wasn't getting A's. If she kept on her current path, this painting course was going to bring down her whole GPA for the semester. She'd cared desperately about her grades, so one week she'd tried switching to small watercolors and tiny floral studies to demonstrate that she was cooperative and open-minded.

Immediately her marks in the class had improved, despite the fact that she had felt little passion for the dainty still lifes. For her final project she had planned to return to large abstracts, but the instructor had kept urging her to "get really Oriental." Frustrated and exhausted by her finals and essays for other classes, she'd dusted off her calligraphy brush from her St. Mary's days. She'd traced symbols from a Chinese menu onto sheets of vellum paper and crafted a handmade book filled with a jumble of copied brushstrokes and Chinese characters. She'd passed off the whole booklet as a fourth-century Chinese poem describing the changing of seasons.

The teacher had been wholeheartedly pleased, feeling satisfied that he had inspired a young girl to embrace her culture. He'd had no idea that, in reality, her string of delicate calligraphy strokes had described the $3.99 lunch special at Kung Pao Express.

Lindsey got her A and learned that people see what they want to see about Chinese people and culture. However, she did feel deceitful and guilty. She never took another painting class again.

But painting now, here in her room, she felt excited to be making small swirls and doodles. After twenty minutes, she got up and tiptoed toward Pau Pau's room. Lindsey was alone in the apartment, but, nonetheless, she moved quietly as she selected a few of her grandmother's old cheongsams with colorful patterns. She snuck them back to her own room and began to copy the shapes and designs onto the stiff rag paper. She was having fun, enjoying the detail and precision the designs required. She worked quietly on the floor for quite a while, hidden behind the mattress and boxspring of her bed. When she heard Pau Pau come home, she quickly stashed the paints and papers under the metal bedframe and bounded out to the kitchen to help make dinner.

Pau Pau was chopping bumpy bitter melon with a cleaver bigger than her head, and Lindsey sat and watched.

"Pau Pau, tell me about your life in China before you came here. What was it like?"

Pau Pau guillotined several zucchini with swift confidence.

"Nothing to tell," she said, retrieving a slab of meat that had been marinating in soy sauce. She sliced the beef into cubes and fried a few chunks with bean sprouts, peppers, and minced ginger. She checked the temperature on her casserole of ground pork, shallots, and tofu, and as she lifted the lid, billows of white steam filled the kitchen.

"Nothing to tell," she repeated. "What you want to know?" She kept careful watch on the pots and pans and did not look up.

"I want to know about your life in China, how you met Gung Gung, and how you got here."

Pau Pau busily stirred the vegetables with her chopsticks, pulled pans from the fire, and scooped piping hot items off the stovetop and into serving dishes. She brought a plate to Lindsey and set it down on the table.

"China no good. Much better here." With those words, the two began to eat and did not say much else for the remainder of the meal.

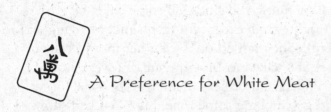

A Preference for White Meat

On Thanksgiving Day the soy imitation marshmallow topping just wouldn't fluff right. Auntie Shirley whisked the concoction, but it wouldn't stiffen into airy peaks like the picture in the *Hippie Wisdom Cookbook*. Lindsey peered into the bowl at the off-white liquid and felt sorry for the perfectly good yam slices that would soon be polluted by the drippy dollops.

Pau Pau was making a sticky rice stuffing with diced Chinese sausage and chestnuts. She liked to make it for herself, even though the turkey was already in the oven, packed with an American bread stuffing.

"Why do we always have the same thing?" Auntie Vivien complained, adjusting the rhinestone-studded straps on her black lace tank top. "We should have oyster stuffing. Oysters are an aphrodisiac, right, Lindsey?" Vivien elbowed her niece and gave her a knowing nod.

"Oysters, sheesh!" Pau Pau muttered, stirring the fatty, *lop-cheurng* sausage into the cooked sticky rice, which globbed stubbornly onto her spoon. "Chinese stuffing the best."

"Mom's old-fashioned. You gotta get used to it," Vivien said. "She doesn't understand your generation, but I do. You want to have fun, go to clubs, do some coke, be more like me, am I right? Well, except for Stephanie. My daughter is so boring!" She prattled on, saying her mom's values were obsolete. She talked as though Pau Pau were a child and couldn't understand or hear them from two feet away.

"We should go clubbing some time, huh? You can show me all the new moves. I bet all the guys will think I'm your sister, huh? Shoot, I look so young—I dress hipper than you! You know, you really should put your hair in an up-do like mine. And you shouldn't wear jeans all the time—gotta show it off, y'know?"

Lindsey wanted to crawl into the Magic Chef oven with the turkey. At least it would be quiet in there. Meanwhile, Shirley was gazing at the ceiling and asking the Universe to bond the soy molecules with pure rainbow light to create fluffiness for her marshmallow substitute.

The door buzzer rang.

"I'll get it!" Lindsey bolted to the front door.

Mrs. Owyang came in carrying a seventeen-pound honey-glazed ham decorated with cloves and pineapple rings. Lindsey took the heavy tray from her mother, who affectionately slapped her face to bring some color to her cheeks.

After putting the ham down on the kitchen counter, Lindsey went to hug her father, who patted her shoulder lightly and dismissively, saying, "Okay, okay, that's enough. Hi, hi." Mr. Owyang looked around, noted the presence of his wife's sisters, and retreated to the room with the largest television, where he would stay until his carving skills were needed.

Stephanie arrived with her sister Cammie, whom she had just retrieved from her gymnastics class. Mike was parking the car but soon entered carrying a red Jell-O mold with lychees. Lindsey planned to scrutinize his every move, but he floated out of the kitchen like a zombie in a trance, following a sixth sense that seemed to know ESPN could not be far. Like Mr. Owyang, he abandoned the females and parked himself in front of the television, falling into the abyss known as the Sports Channel.

Auntie Vivien and Lindsey's mom paired off to compare jewelry. Mrs. Owyang admired a new three-karat sapphire ring on her sister's finger but lost interest as soon as Vivien admitted it was artificial.

"Mommy," Cammie said, tugging at her shoulder.

"Later, Cammie," Vivien said, still captivated by her own glimmering faux gem.

"But Mommy, I forgot to tell you. Suzanne Somers called today."

"Why didn't you tell me?! I've got to call her back!"

Lindsey was across the room wiping down the silverware, but her ears perked up.

"Wow, does your mom really know her?" she asked Stephanie as they set the table.

"No," her cousin replied, rolling her eyes. "Suzanne Somers hosts a jewelry show on the QVC Channel. I think there's an automatic dial message that calls and reminds shoppers to watch the show." She smirked and shook her head.

There were not enough seats at the dinner table by the time everyone arrived, so the family ate in shifts. Kevin surprised everyone by bringing a girlfriend, named Karen.

Feeling proprietary, Lindsey forgot all about scrutinizing Mike the White Guy and instead focused her attentions on this new intruder. She watched her, noticing how *Chinesey* she was. Karen was so meek and deferential that Lindsey disliked her immediately, abhorring how she personifed such a stereotype of female servitude.

It wasn't just Karen's tortured, permed hair or the synthetic fabric of her Nordstrom Rack blouse. And it wasn't even the midcalf length of her polyester skirt or the rounded toes of her schoolmarmish pumps. What really disturbed Lindsey was the way she rushed to help each time Kevin reached for more stuffing or a slice of ham. Even though she was the guest, Karen constantly asked Kevin if he needed anything or if she could get him a beverage. And as if her actions weren't bad enough, Kevin simply sat back and let her pamper him, seeming proud of the way she jumped each time he yawned or looked at his watch.

Oh, please, Lindsey thought, sitting as far away from them as possible while still able to spy on them and disdain them from afar. After a few bites, she lost her appetite when she heard Karen speaking in Shanghainese, complimenting Pau Pau on the tastiness of her sticky rice stuffing. As they talked and Lindsey could no longer follow what they were saying, she leaned forward and shot her brother a dirty look. He caught her glaring at him and grinned. She got up and brought her plate into the kitchen.

Brandon came by himself, late. As he stacked his plate with food, he picked around the turkey carcass in search of some dark meat, which had mostly been eaten.

He called over to his cousin, "Hey, Lindsey, there's plenty of white meat here for ya!"

She stuck out her tongue at him as she scraped bones from her plate into the trash.

Mr. Owyang came into the kitchen during a commercial break. He asked his nephew, "Why are you the latest when you live the nearest?"

Brandon stabbed slabs of ham and a turkey leg with his fork.

"I don't live the nearest—she does!" he replied, gesturing toward Lindsey.

"Yeah, she does!" Mr. Owyang repeated. "Good rent, too. Pays nothing!" They erupted in hyena-like laughter as Lindsey finished rinsing a stack of plates. She didn't know why her cousin was hooting; Uncle Donald owned the apartment building where Brandon lived, and he didn't pay any rent, either.

Later on, the guys were still watching sports, Karen was massaging tiger balm into Pau Pau's stiff elbow, and Mrs. Owyang and Stephanie were discussing freshwater vs. saltwater pearls. No one was watching Cammie as she squirted an entire bottle of shampoo into the bathroom sink and overflowed the basin with soap bubbles.

"She's such a *Chinabug*." Vivien scowled as she, Shirley and Lindsey cleaned up the kitchen. "I bet she doesn't even know what Gucci is."

"Shh, Karen's still here, you know," Lindsey whispered.

"So what—she's in the other room." After a few moments, Vivien added, "She's fresh off the boat. Your brother can do way better than that."

"Her blouse isn't so bad," Shirley piped in. "Peach is such a high-vibration color."

Lindsey said nothing, but she sided with Vivien on this

one. She couldn't believe how swiftly and effortlessly Karen seemed to be ingratiating herself into the family. Fawning over her brother, soothing her grandmother. Lindsey would have to destroy her.

"Kevin is a good catch," Vivien mused. "He needs someone high-class, you know. More like me. Too bad for him I'm his auntie!" she laughed in her high-pitched wheeze, delighting only herself.

"How come nobody ate my soy marshmallow yams?" Shirley asked, realizing no one but her had touched the "candied" tubers. "Lindsey, honey, c'mon and try some."

"Oh, I'm so full. I just can't. Really."

"Maybe later then, okay? I'll save lots for you."

Lindsey tried to smile but merely showed her teeth.

Just then, Karen and Pau Pau entered the kitchen, both stinking of Chinese ointment. Karen's hunched shoulders and slightly bowed head struck Lindsey as a calculated, manipulative act. Kevin came in and kicked Lindsey's shoe to let her know that she had better be on her best behavior.

"Ready to go?" he asked, and Karen snapped to attention.

Pau Pau tried her darnedest to get them to stay for Jell-O, but she couldn't convince Kevin, who always seemed to have somewhere else to go. She made a big fuss about their taking leftovers and prepared a packet of loose herbs and tea for Karen.

Feeling envious and irritable in general, Lindsey said good-bye and spent the rest of the evening sulking in her bedroom, wondering when Michael Cartier might be returning from Hawaii.

*   *   *

Finally, after everyone left, she went into Gung Gung's old room to look for a coat she had transferred over the summer from her own overstuffed closet.

Pau Pau still kept the room tidy, and the chenille bedspread was always clean and cozy-looking. A large portrait of Gung Gung wearing what appeared to be a kind of army uniform leaned up against the wall on top of the dresser.

As Lindsey opened the closet door, she found a dozen of her grandfather's old suits and Arrow shirts neatly lined up. Pau Pau had had them cleaned two years ago, and now they hung there, still waiting for someone to wear them. Boxes of old blankets crowded the floorspace below the coats.

Lindsey recalled one day in the fourth grade when she was playing hooky from Chinese school. It was a day that, for some reason, she had not gone to the movies with Kevin and Brandon but instead had decided to stay and watch cartoons here at Pau Pau and Gung Gung's apartment. She had been dozing during a Pepé Le Pew vignette when she heard the front door swing open. Quickly jumping up, she'd turned off the television and darted into Gung Gung's room, where she'd scrunched herself deep inside the closet. She'd slouched her body into a cardboard box and flipped a quilt over her head.

As her luck would have it, Gung Gung had headed straight for his wardrobe. Between errands and meetings he would sometimes stop home to change into a different sportcoat. Lindsey had felt her heart pounding inside her school uniform. Through a crinkle of the blanket, she'd watched Gung Gung tapping his foot, wearing his trademark brown wingtips from Florsheim.

The coat sleeves had passed over her head, one by one,

back and forth, as he'd searched for just the right jacket. As each soft sleeve had brushed over her crown, she'd felt like she was in a car wash, with those fabric octopus arms swaying back and forth over the windshield that was her forehead.

She remembered that afternoon with fondness. Snapping back into the present, she found her red peacoat and pulled it off the hanger.

But she stayed in Gung Gung's room for a while longer. In a stack of papers on the dresser, she sifted through a few vintage copies of *Chinatown News* with Gung Gung's photo on the cover, and she scanned a newspaper article about a park cleanup he had helped organize. She found snapshots of her mom and dad's wedding, and one of Gung Gung and Pau Pau on a Christmas day about forty years ago. She discovered a faded photograph of Gung Gung posing in his Galileo High School football uniform, with a caption that read, "Sam Gin, a.k.a. Chinese Lightning." She also came across a diploma from George Washington University. Lindsey had had no idea that her grandfather had attended either of these schools.

Lindsey placed all the pictures and documents back as neatly as she found them. Closing Gung Gung's bedroom door, she took her coat to her room and trimmed the fuzzy, worn-out patches with her Brookstone sweater shaver.

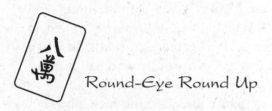

Round-Eye Round Up

M ichael returned to work the following Monday. He wasn't the least bit suntanned, and Lindsey noticed his chin was stubbly and his lips were slightly chapped. She had a way of unconsciously staring too long at his mouth.

"Hey," she said, standing up and resting her arm on the reception desk. He walked over and placed his hand on hers, and her heart leaped at this apparent sign of affection.

He took a deep breath and said, "My grandmother died."

His words swished around inside Lindsey's smallish head like brandy in a snifter. She tried to think of an appropriate reply, but just then several telephone lines began to ring.

"Are you free after work?" he asked.

She nodded and watched the red lights blinking urgently on her console.

"Okay, I'll see you later," he said, heading for his office.

After work, they walked down Kearny Street and tried to decide on a restaurant where they could have a bite and talk.

"How about Chinese?" he asked.

She broke into a slight panic. Her standard reply to non-Asians had always been, "I don't like Chinese food," and she usually suggested Italian instead. But she looked at Michael's somber face and dejected demeanor, and she didn't have the heart to argue with a guy who had just lost his granny. She nodded her head in agreement.

"Well, why don't you pick a place around here," he said. "I don't know a lot about Asian food. Well, except Top Ramen."

"Oh, you should talk to my friend Steve about ramen. He knows all there is to know . . ." She spoke without thinking and immediately regretted her words. Mimi had always advised her that it was bad date etiquette to mention other guys, especially in any positive way.

Michael hesitated for a moment, then asked, "Oh, is he your . . . boyfriend?"

An invisible mini-Mimi dressed in a devil costume sat on Lindsey's shoulder and poked her in the neck with a tiny pitchfork. "See! Now look what you've done!" said a small voice in her head, but she ignored the imaginary chidings.

"Umm, no," Lindsey said slowly. "I don't . . . have a boyfriend."

Good save.

"Oh, okay, um, just checking," he said with a small smile, his eyes crinkling in that way she especially liked.

She could not have been more delighted that Michael wanted her company, but as they passed from the financial district into Chinatown, she walked slightly ahead of him and looked at the pavement, worried that everyone could see her raging hormones shooting Fourth of July fireworks every which way. She tried her hardest to appear as though she were simply assisting a tourist in whom she had no romantic interest.

But she wasn't fooling anyone. As they navigated the narrow streets, the inhabitants and shopkeepers of Chinatown glowered at them. Michael was oblivious, but she was sensitive to the steely gazes that followed them down the alleys. On one corner a teenage boy even said, *"Diu nay, bock-gwai,"* under his breath, but she pretended not to hear and certainly did not point out to Michael that the teenager had just said, "Fuck you, white devil."

Even the waiter at the hole-in-the-wall restaurant scowled at Michael, and then eyed her disapprovingly because she should have known better than to flaunt herself in public with a non-Chinese. He tossed the menus onto the greasy table and sashayed back into the kitchen, where other Chinese heads soon poked out to look them over.

"What should we get?" Michael asked, scanning the menu.

She skimmed through the selections and said, "Darn, I don't think there's lamb kidneys at this restaurant."

Michael smiled, then stretched his arms wearily. "Hey, I feel kind of bad about that day, after Fort Point, you know."

The waiter clunked down a hot pot of tea and ambled off again. Lindsey poured a bit of tea in each cup, swirled it around, and dripped the liquid onto the restaurant's carpet.

"What are you doing?" Michael asked.

"Sanitizing the teacups," she replied, now ready to pour.

He looked at her with a puzzled expression, then studied the red, flocked wallpaper with gold double-happiness characters.

"You know, that smell in your grandmother's closet—"

"Sorry about that," Lindsey said, interrupting.

"No, it's okay. It's just that when I stepped in that stuff, I had this weird flashback . . . about *my* grandmother, the one who just passed away."

She sipped her tea and listened.

"I used to live in Honolulu, and she took care of me till I was about seven. But then we moved back to Metairie, in Louisiana, where I was born."

"On the lam?"

"No, nothing that exciting. After we left I hardly ever saw her, maybe three or four times after that. I'm such a jerk—I never even wrote to her. Well, she couldn't read English, but I guess that's not even the point. But, anyway, when I stepped in that goo in your closet, it suddenly reminded me of her. It was the exact smell of this same gunk she used to have."

He pulled a photo from his shirt pocket and handed it to Lindsey. The picture showed a woman with a polka-dotted apron, her face slightly in shadow, holding a small boy with chipmunk cheeks.

"What's this thing you're eating here?" she asked.

"It's a Spam sandwich, but that's not what you're supposed to notice," he said.

She looked up. "Oh?"

"Look again."

She inspected the picture some more, looking for any remarkable detail. She looked up at Michael, who had been attentively watching the expression on her face.

"What does Spam taste like?" she asked.

"You're supposed to notice that my grandmother is Chinese!" he said.

Lindsey looked at Michael closely. She searched his face for any Chinese detail: a slanted eye, a yellow undertone in his skin, or a certain shape of the nose. She saw nothing, but thought to herself, "Please, God, don't let us be second cousins or something."

"So, what are you thinking?" he asked.

She was thinking about how polite his table manners were, and how strange it felt to be actually getting to know him instead of just obsessing about the person she had imagined him to be. She was slowly absorbing the revelation that he was one-quarter Chinese.

"I'm thinking, where do I fit into the picture?" she said. She meant it to sound cute, but it came off sounding a bit accusatory.

He looked at her and thought for a moment. "Well, I don't know. Help me to understand better what it means to be Chinese, since I suppose I've avoided that part of myself. Maybe you can be my cultural guide."

At the words "cultural guide," she got agitated. She had been insecure that her last phrase sounded like she was too eager to take over his life, and now she interpreted his comment to mean that she was now responsible for leading him in a seminar on Chinese culture.

"Well, there's no guidebook or anything," she said, her ears feeling hot.

"Um, yeah, I realize that," he said, pulling back from the table. He had been leaning forward, closer to her, but now he leaned back into the chair as far as possible.

The waiter eyeballed them from the kitchen.

"I guess we should figure out what we want," Michael said, fumbling with the menu.

"Okay," she said. "Don't order anything with sweet-and-sour sauce, or egg rolls, or any of that tourist stuff."

"All right. What about this?" He pointed to a section that listed "chop suey."

She shrugged. "I don't even know what that is."

"You've never tried it? Isn't it supposed to be a famous dish?"

"I think in the gold rush days, Chinese cooks picked scraps out of the garbage and fed it to surly miners. They called it 'chop suey,' and foreigners have been ordering it ever since. I wouldn't trust it."

"Go ahead and order for us, then. I'll eat anything," he suggested agreeably.

She raised an eyebrow. "I thought you were a semi-vegetarian."

"It's just a cover so I don't get lambasted at work by the militant vegans," he replied, brushing her hand with his.

She smiled and relaxed. When the waiter returned, she ordered potstickers with meat, pork with pickled greens and smoked tofu skins, sauteed pea leaves with garlic, and steamed rice.

When the waiter brought the food to the table, he thrust a fork in Michael's face and dropped it on the table with a loud clank. As they ate their dinner, Lindsey noted with keen interest that Michael used the chopsticks instead. He didn't drop one sliver of tofu, poke feebly at rice grains, or stab clumsily at veggies. She was both surprised and re-lieved. Perhaps this manual dexterity was a small proof of his Chinese genetics.

After they finished their meal, Michael broke open his fortune cookie.

"Was this the favorite dessert of a Tang Dynasty emperor or something?" he asked.

She crunched the golden pieces. "No, these cookies were invented in Golden Gate Park by the Japanese gardener. They probably eat them in China now, though."

As they left the restaurant, Michael offered Lindsey a mint, and they walked through Chinatown, back toward the financial district. At one point, near a stoplight with no cars around, they jaywalked, and he took the opportunity to hold her hand, but she gently and ambivalently loosened her palm from his, worried about getting stares.

They passed the Buddha Bar and the Li Po, with its cave-like entrance and lantern hanging above the door.

"Do you want to get a drink?" he suggested.

Before she could answer, she happened to spot Pau Pau's friend with the lopsided wig who had called her fat on the bus. Although the old woman was lost in thought and unaware that she was being observed, Lindsey shifted her weight to obscure her face behind Michael's shoulder, just in case.

"Um, no thanks," she replied nervously, her eyes following the woman until she passed from sight.

Lindsey never drank in Chinatown because she believed spies lurked everywhere.

Once in the third grade, Lindsey had thought it would be funny to get back at Gilbert Soohoo for breaking the arm off her Superstar Barbie. After recess, she'd placed three sharp thumbtacks on his chair, and as the class had settled down and taken their seats, Gilbert had bounded down the aisle and plopped down hard on his fleshy rump.

"YOW!" he'd screamed as the sharp tacks had pierced through his uniform pants.

Gilbert's grandmother had picked him up early from school, and the Chinatown gossip switchboard had worked so fast that Pau Pau was screaming at Lindsey even before she'd gotten to the top of the stairs that afternoon. From that day on, she'd been convinced that all details of a Chinese kid's bad behavior were accurately and efficiently spread by a swift-acting Chinese rumor-mill. The appropriate elder was immediately notified of any wrongdoing, and the kid encountered hard-core smackdown so fast there was no time to revel in devious delight.

So now, as an adult, she still kept her eyes peeled. She couldn't risk going into a bar because anyone could be watching her at any given moment.

Lindsey and Michael kept walking. A few moments passed before they heard a loud jabbering voice behind them that directed Cantonese expletives at their backs and sent panicked shivers up Lindsey's spine. She turned and looked fearfully over her shoulder, half-expecting to get slapped by a Chinatown spy. Instead, an old woman in a peasant-style quilted jacket elbowed past them, yelling into a tiny cellphone mouthpiece attached to her ear. Lindsey sighed with relief.

Several blocks later, Michael and Lindsey were near the old Hotaling warehouse. One-story brick structures quietly nestled in the shadow of the skyscrapers above, and she relaxed now that they were no longer among Chinese eyes. No one was disdaining them or noticing them at all, since most of the businesspeople had already deserted the office high-rises. The sky was now cloaked in cobalt, and the air was crisp and smelled slightly of charcoal.

"These buildings are some of the only ones that survived

downtown after the earthquake," Michael said. He pointed out a few structures and elaborated on the details of their history.

As they meandered down a quiet alley, they exchanged furtive glances and were keenly aware of how their hands almost touched as they walked.

On one side of the street, a line of black hitching posts in the shape of horses' heads stood at attention. Near an antiques store with an old-fashioned gaslight, Michael stopped and put his arms around her. He kissed her, and she pressed against him, suddenly not caring at all if anyone was watching. Their mouths together, she took scant notice when her purse dropped into a slimy puddle.

Egg Fool Young

Lindsey drove out to her parents' house, which was one of the identical bungalows built in the Sunset District during the 1940s. After she parked and went inside, she walked into the living room and sat down in her dad's La-Z-Boy recliner and looked around, noticing the house was spic-and-span as always. Everything was pretty much the same as when Lindsey and Kevin were growing up, with just a few changes.

The house was a 1960s time capsule. There was gold-speckled linoleum, dinner plates with starlike atoms, and well-kept sofas with sparkly interwoven metallic threads. Everything that could be vinyl, was vinyl: the ottoman, sidechairs, tablecloth, and matching place mats. They still had one of those gigantic televisions with massive dials, fabric-covered speakers, and enormous antennae that resembled rabbit ears. The now-vintage hi-fi stereo was perched on a retro banquette near a rotary dial princess telephone.

Last Christmas, under the collapsible silver tinsel tree

they reused every year, Kevin had wrapped a new flat-screen television and set of cordless phones for their parents. The new contraptions were now propped nearby, but Mr. Owyang preferred his original appliances. He seemed to believe that design and civilization had reached its apex somewhere around 1968, and now the world was collapsing into an orgy of useless gadgetry that could never surpass what had peaked before.

Lindsey wandered into the kitchen and scrounged around in the refrigerator for something to snack on. She wasn't actually hungry, but being in her parents' house always made her feel like eating.

When she was small, her parents fed Lindsey and Kevin vats of egg noodles with bits of hot dogs, and the four main food groups were frozen, canned, store-bought, or pimento loaf. Fruit was either cling peaches or Del Monte fruit cocktail in heavy syrup. And aside from these "natural" foods, everything else was made better with ketchup: eggs, sandwiches, tacos, and fried chicken. For years Lindsey's standard school lunch had been two slices of any variety of luncheon loaf on white bread with ketchup and Miracle Whip. When her school tried to kick off Nutrition Week twice a year, she conceded to eating vegetables when her mom packed her a Ziploc of sweet pickles and cocktail gherkins.

She didn't see anything she liked in the fridge, so out of habit she opened the freezer. At an early age she had become a connoiseuse of Swanson's frozen entrées. She developed an addiction to salisbury steak and loved the apple pie portions bordered on five sides by the crenelated foil pan. She savored every compartment of the astronaut-like dinners and appreciated the aluminum partitions that prevented the lake of brown, all-purpose gravy from jumping its banks. Mmm . . . she could taste the freezer-burned mashed potatoes now. Closing the door, she sighed. She wished she had time to heat up a Hungry Man potpie.

She saw a pink box on the counter and wondered if her parents had recently had guests over. When people came to visit, Mrs. Owyang went to Chinatown or Clement Street and bought take-out dim sum and pastries. She'd get *gai-may-bows,* which translated literally as "cocktail buns," and she'd put them in the oven and pull them out at a perfectly timed moment as if she had baked them herself.

Lindsey snagged a *gai-don goh* egg cupcake from the pink box and plopped back down into the La-Z-Boy. She set the lumbar panel to "vibrate," and as she nibbled on the pastry she noticed the room was filled with plastic azaleas, polyester dendrobium orchids, plants with glass leaves, and an arrangement of fake jade fruits.

"What is it with Chinese people and artificial flowers?" she wondered aloud.

Her mom had just breezed in to dust the quartz crystal grapes and said, "They're easy to take care of. No trouble. Smells nice, too, don't you think?"

Mrs. Owyang had stuffed every nook and cranny of the house with hidden air fresheners, so everything always smelled like a spring bouquet. Lindsey wondered if her mom actually believed she was fooling anyone into thinking the fresh scent was caused by living flora rather than the adhesive discs manufactured by the Glade chemical corporation.

"We'll be late. Go call your father," her mom said.

Lindsey dragged her clogs across the wavy, plastic runner that protected the hall carpet. As she passed her old bedroom and the den, she noticed the furniture seemed more Lilliputian than she remembered, and she noted that every chair and sofa was perfectly fitted with plastic jacket coverings. She speculated that Chinese DNA predetermined an affinity for easy-wipe surfaces.

Lindsey approached the doorway of the master bedroom and watched from a short distance as her dad arranged the black suspenders that held up his gold-toe socks. She watched quietly as her dad fiddled with his silver shoehorn, cedar shoe trees, and his good shoes. Sometimes when she caught him alone like this she wanted to ask him about his childhood in Locke, near Sacramento. Once he mentioned how his parents had been fruitpickers and how hard their life had been back then. He said they'd worked ten-hour days sorting pears and asparagus, together making two dollars per day. He said he'd helped fold cardboard boxes after school and worked the orchards until he left for City College in San Francisco.

Lindsey watched her dad comb Brylcreem into his dyed-black hair, and she recalled the story he once told her about being a busboy at the famous Trader Vic's restaurant. The only meats he had ever eaten in Locke had been cow stomach, intestines, and other organs, so the food at the restaurant was very exotic to him. One evening he was clearing plates on the main floor when he stared too long at an uneaten, juicy New York Strip garnished with orange slices and teriyaki sauce. His dumbfounded face caught the eye of one of the dining room guests. He didn't know she was the movie star June

Allyson, but her complaint to the head waiter about his stupid expression promptly got him fired.

Her dad rarely talked about his younger days, and lately Lindsey thought more frequently about asking him, but she was unsure of how to bring up the topic casually.

"Hi, Dad," she said.

"Oh," he looked up. "Is Kevin here, too?"

"Yeah, I think I just heard his car," she said. Her dad searched for his cuff links, and Lindsey told him she'd wait outside.

On the sidewalk, looking up and down at the rows of identical stucco bungalows, Lindsey could guess which houses belonged to Chinese families. In front of the residences where plots of grass might be, there were paved squares of cement, painted green. A few places had "gardens" that consisted solely of wood chips or brick-colored bits of volcanic dog kibble. She studied some polyurethane stones that were slotted together like giant Lego toys, creating the illusion of a continuous border of river rocks.

Urban living had apparently curtailed the Chinese tradition of lovingly tended gardens, transforming landscaped greenery into a no-hassle zone made possible by the Home Depot. Lindsey stared at the plastic stones and the green plot of cement that connected the Owyangs' home and the adjacent house. Having just finished washing his car, the neighbor strolled over, noticing her admiring his handiwork.

He smiled proudly. "Don't have to mow!" he bragged. "Look classy, huh?"

She nodded, and just then her parents emerged. Kevin

transferred his car into the garage, and they all piled into the family sedan. They zoomed off toward the St. Francis Hotel.

They were on their way to the Miss Teenage Chinatown Beauty Contest.

When she was in high school, Lindsey's parents had tried to encourage her to participate in this pageant. The qualified contestants required a 3.5 grade point average and competed in Chinese language recitation, artistic talent, and evening gown and swimwear modeling. The winners received cash prizes, scholarship money, and the chance to wave from a motorized cable car at the next New Year's Parade.

Lindsey wondered why so many Chinese parents endorsed this community event. She had adamantly refused to participate, because she did not see what cultural or educational merit justified prancing onstage in a bikini. Her parents seemed to believe that the chance to win a college scholarship was worth the public humiliation of a packed audience scrutinizing her teenage stretch marks. While Lindsey was definitely grateful she hadn't been dropped down a well at birth, she certainly didn't feel obligated to demonstrate her family loyalty by sashaying around in a teeny maillot while singing a Mariah Carey ballad.

"Why are we going to this thing?" she asked from the backseat.

Her mom, digging through the glove compartment in search of some Certs, replied, "I ran into CiCi Toy, the gossip columnist. She tricked me into buying a table."

Once inside the St. Francis ballroom, they filled out raffle tickets and flipped through the program of events. The pages were filled with advertisements for Chinese-owned businesses, as well as parents' good wishes accompanied by glamour shots of the teenage girls posing with Little Bo Peep seduction.

From a nearby table, an old man shouted every five minutes, "Where's the food?" Lindsey could hear the old Chinese ladies at his table clucking their tongues, ruthlessly critiquing the contestants. They praised high foreheads and small mouths, and looked unfavorably on short hair, flat noses, or dark complexions.

Speeches by minor local politicians soon began. District supervisors attempted to encourage voting in the Chinese community, but hardly anyone in the audience listened. Lindsey turned her attention to a plump woman in a white fur stole and too-tight strappy sandals with golden coils that squeezed her ham-hock feet. She was making the rounds between tables with Wellbutrin-induced shakiness and high, arched eyebrows that seemed tattooed in place.

"There's CiCi," Mrs. Owyang said, and Lindsey craned her neck for a better look at the modern-day Chinese Hedda Hopper. Lindsey wondered why someone hadn't told CiCi that she was too old for white satin stretchpants. Even worse, the outline of her thong was showing.

Everyone enjoyed a roasted chicken dinner with julienned vegetables, and during dessert the "entertainment" began. A couple of girls wailed with canned emotion while lip-synching Celine Dion songs, but most contestants chose to sing the "I Will Never Be a Perfect Daughter" song from Disney's *Mulan*. As one after another got up to sing the same family-oriented song, Lindsey quietly begged for just one girl to have the guts to perform something unique, like a sweaty rendition of "Sugar Walls" by Sheena Easton, or maybe "Head" by Prince.

Between the evening gown humiliation and the swimwear and heels humiliation, so-called guest singers performed. Any fool who gave a five-hundred-dollar donation to the event could appear on the program. It didn't matter if a "guest star" had absolutely no talent whatsoever. As a result, the audience endured one "Greatest Love of All," one "When I Fall in Love" duet, and one rousing version of Barry Manilow's "Copacabana" sung with a heavy Cantonese accent.

Eventually, with great fanfare, last year's queen took the stage for her final royal duty and announced the names of the Third, Second, and First Princesses. The other twenty girls shifted their weight from foot to foot and stood helplessly with limp arms at their sides. A Friendship Princess blew exaggerated kisses from the stage as too-loud music blared from the speakers.

After the curtain dropped, the hotel manager cut off the pounding techno mix too abruptly, and an awkward silence descended upon the crowd. Following a few eardrum-piercing screeches from the sound system, the ballroom filled with a Muzak version of the "Macarena." As she and her family made their way toward the exit, Lindsey chewed her cheek to restrain herself from unleashing a litany of snide comments.

Having spent the night at her parents' house, the next morning Lindsey sifted through an old box of her baby pictures that her mom wanted her to organize. Spreading things out on the kitchen table, she came across a faded red envelope with her Chinese name written across the top and her American name below. It held a copy of her birth announcement.

Like most Chinese-Americans, she had a separate Chinese name. No one ever addressed her directly as such, not even Pau Pau. Nonetheless, she was at least supposed to know what the name was, how to say it, and how to write the characters.

Lindsey's name was Owyang Gum Lan, with the last name always first, so people could immediately identify the clan or family name. The rest of her name meant Golden Flower, or so she had been told.

Plucking a Post-it note and a pen from the kitchen counter, she wanted to see if she could remember how to write her Chinese name without copying the pictograph from the red envelope. As she touched the ballpoint onto the yellow paper, at first she faltered, stymied by the idea of how to create even the first stroke.

She was tempted to peek but then recalled her trick from Chinese school. She visualized the characters as pictures, starting with two lines that resembled the top of a fisherman's hat, followed by three horizontal strokes that she then bisected down the middle to look like a lamppost. When she came to the last part of the name, "Lan," she drew boxes like double doors with a square lantern below. Scrutinizing her attempt, she sensed she wasn't finished. Her eye thought the characters looked about right, but her wrist itched for something more. She stared at her unfinished name, and suddenly, what her brain couldn't remember her hand instantly recalled. With a dash to the left and then to the right, her wrist kicked out two strokes on either side of the lantern like matching ribbons. There. That felt better.

She compared her version to the characters on the red envelope and was pleased to see that she'd written everything correctly. Every little dot and dab was there. One missing stroke or swoop and she might have called herself a water buffalo.

"Hey Dad, how did you choose our Chinese names?" she hollered over into the living room.

Mr. Owyang looked up from his newspaper and thought for a long moment.

"Every family chooses the names a different way. But ours are predetermined," he replied.

"How?"

Her dad removed his reading glasses and rubbed his eyes. He scratched his head and frowned, like he was straining to remember a simple answer he once knew, as if she'd asked him to name the capital of Mississippi or something.

"Every eight generations the Chinese names are selected for the children ahead. The names are all words from an old Chinese poem, and every person born in the same generation has the same middle character."

"I don't get it," she said. "You mean Stephanie, Cammie, and I all have 'Gum' as a middle character, and it's part of a poem?"

Just then Kevin loped into the room and plopped down on the sofa.

"No, Dummy, not on the Gin side. It's only an Owyang thing. My middle character is 'Ming,' and in the poem it comes after Dad's name, which is 'Mun.' "

He continued, "But it doesn't matter with girls' names.

Only the boys' names are selected from the poem. Right, Dad? Girls don't count—right, Dad?"

Mr. Owyang was now engrossed in the sports section of the *Chronicle*. After a moment he said, "Shoot, the Forty-Niners don't look so good this year."

"Where's the poem, Dad?" Lindsey asked. She wanted to know if her name, "Gum Lan," was a part of the poem. She wanted to know if girls mattered or not.

"Oh, I don't know," her dad replied distractedly. "It's written on a scroll somewhere. I gave it to Uncle Bill to translate a long time ago. I think he has it." He removed a mechanical pencil from his chest pocket and scratched his stomach. "Hey, Kevin, who do you think's going to make it to the Superbowl?"

Lindsey was frustrated by her father's lackluster response regarding the poem, but she was used to being stonewalled by her parents' apathy. As much as they proclaimed that their children should know more about Chinese culture, they didn't seem very informed or excited about it themselves. Just as her mom knew nothing of the Eight Immortals at the antiques show, her dad never concerned himself with scrolls, poetry, or anything having to do with his own ancestors' history. He did, however, have encyclopedic knowledge of the Giants' lifetime batting averages and RBIs for the last twenty years.

Party Like a Rock Star

Lindsey saw little of Michael over the next week because he was feverishly fact-checking a piece about a spa that required guests to shave their nether regions. The hectic phones kept Lindsey occupied, but a few times a day she and Michael were able to catch sight of one another. They exchanged no words, but in small glances they shared the memory of their secret first kiss.

As luck would have it, each time one of them stole a moment away from their tasks, the other seemed to be busy. Lindsey would saunter by his office and he'd be meeting with a hairy intern in sackcloth; likewise, Michael would stop by for a chat when Lindsey was on the phone patiently explaining to a caller that the magazine was not a wholesaler of vegan S&M gear. The week passed quickly, and it was already Friday night when Michael phoned Lindsey late from the office.

She was at home in the bathroom bleaching her faint mustache and tweezing her eyebrows when she heard the ringing in the kitchen. Pau Pau was still out playing mahjong.

"Hello?"

"Hi, Do you know where I could buy a G-string made of tofu?"

Lindsey smiled to herself, the bleach on her upper lip sticking to the side of her nose a bit.

"I was hoping it was you," she said.

While Michael explained how tedious it was to research legal precedents for enforced crotch-shaving, Lindsey listened as she quietly wiped the white strip of foamy cream from her face and silently wondered if she should perform any hair maintenance "down there."

"Hey, do you want to go to a party with me tomorrow night?" Michael asked.

Lindsey felt a jolt of giddiness, but then paused to collect her cool before replying.

Michael added, "I mean, if you're free. If you want to go . . . with me." His slight stammering melted Lindsey's heart, and her undies.

"Yeah, sure," she said, quickly reassuring him that she was definitely free the following night.

When she hung up the phone she ran immediately to the bathroom mirror and checked her face for zits. She found one, but it was thankfully minor. Her mind raced with thoughts of the next night. The possibilities! Her eyes drifted downward, and she decided right then to trim her triangle.

The next morning Lindsey awoke with her stomach all aflutter. Pau Pau was gone again, with just a pork hash casserole with pickled duck eggs on the stove as evidence of her having been there. Lindsey knew the first thing she had to do was to call Auntie Shirley.

"Om Rama Shiva!" her aunt answered.

"Hi, Auntie Shirley. It's Lindsey."

"Don't you know it's my meditation hour?" she asked, and Lindsey could hear her aunt softly chanting under her breath, "Om Rama Shiva, Om Rama Shiva . . ."

"Sorry to interrupt, but I had to tell you I have to cancel tonight."

The chanting stopped, and her aunt's rhythmic incantations gave way to an exasperated whine. "But you're supposed to pose for your aura portrait! How can I paint your essence when you don't sit still long enough to let your colors speak to me?"

"I'm sorry. I have somewhere to go tonight."

"Guys, hmmm?" Auntie Shirley made a purring sound. "That sounds so delicious. Oh, I know how it is when that kundalini unwinds . . . well, it's been a while since a guy's blown my chakra wide open!"

Lindsey shuddered. Too much information.

She said good-bye and hung up the phone. She straightened up around the house, groomed her nails, and moisturized her skin from head to toe. She was daffy with anticipation of her evening, and she was too excited even to eat anything. Midafternoon, when the doorbell rang, she was so jumpy that she tripped over a chair as she ran to the window. Peering outside, she recognized Auntie Shirley's VW Beetle. A minute later the front door swung open, and any lingering notes of Pau Pau's medicinal smells were quickly overpowered by the signature fragrance of aging hippies everywhere. Her aunt's patchouli silently but fiercely announced, "Get out of my way, Tiger Balm, there's a new stench in town!"

"What're you doing here?" Lindsey asked, wondering if Auntie Shirley had been deeply stoned during their phone conversation and had maybe forgotten completely that Lindsey had canceled the aura portrait session.

"I'm here to feed you!" Auntie Shirley said. Lindsey noticed that her aunt was indeed carrying a large Crock-Pot.

"What is it?" Lindsey asked, fearing the worst.

Shirley set the stoneware pot on the kitchen counter and said, "For centuries the druids concocted delicious recipes mixed with love potions to be eaten before evening rituals of group copulation. I made this all for you, so eat up." Auntie Shirley lifted the lid of the crock and smiled with giant owl eyes that, frankly, scared the hell out of Lindsey.

"But . . . but I'm not hungry," Lindsey said.

She knew she was trapped. She had refused her aunt's cooking so many times, and now there was no way out. If she had eaten just one soy-dolloped yam at Thanksgiving, perhaps she could decline now, but today, it seemed, was payback for all the misshapen pakoras, chickpea cheesecakes, and bluecorn dirt waffles she had ever refused.

Lindsey looked at the steaming concoction and beheld the treasured recipe of the ancient druids. It was purple with chunks of brown. She saw something that looked like burned, mushy cherries, but with kidney beans, too. And baby marshmallows. Or were those human teeth?

Lindsey began to whimper as Auntie Shirley scooped a heaping portion into a bowl for her.

"Secret ingredients. Wiccan aphrodisiacs." her aunt whispered, scrunching up her face like one of those craft dolls made from a dehydrated apple.

Auntie Shirley wasn't moving an inch until she witnessed

her niece take several bites. Lindsey thought to herself, "The faster I eat these rat tails and warlock teeth, the faster she's outta here." Resigned to her fate, she held her breath and swallowed, nodding when Auntie Shirley asked, "Is it fabulous?" and "Are you feeling the power?"

Lindsey finished the bowl.

Delighted, Auntie Shirley performed a dance that looked like she was dog-paddling through pudding. When she finally left, Lindsey breathed a sigh of relief, then went back to her room to select an outfit for the evening.

Around nine o'clock Lindsey was waiting outside on the sidewalk in a lilac sweater set and slim white pants when Michael pulled up in a light blue Toyota circa 1975. She climbed in and he said, "I know she's old, but I just can't bear to let her go."

"I like it," she said, slamming the door. "It's cute. Kinda like you."

"Oh, c'mon," he said. "It's just dark in here."

Michael explained that the party was in the Western Addition, given by a friend of his brother, who actually wouldn't be there because he lived in Chicago. Lindsey remembered that Kevin's friends were having a party tonight, too, and when she mentioned it in passing, Michael suggested that maybe they could stop there later. Lindsey shrugged, not really caring either way as long as she and Michael would be together.

They found parking and walked up to a shabbily painted gray Victorian with rounded Queen Anne windows and Doric columns. Several old Vespa scooters were parked outside, and they could smell clove cigarettes as they climbed the tall staircase. Inside, there weren't too many people, or maybe it just looked that way because the room was so cavernous. The sixteen-foot ceilings swallowed everyone, and a big spooky chandelier sprouted from an overhead plaster rosette like an electric blooming dahlia.

Lindsey was glad to see that she had entered a sort of 1980s new wave, ska-inspired time warp. Everyone was wearing two-tone vintage cardigans, Creepers with thick soles, and skinny, black pegleg pants. The stereo was playing "I Confess" by the English Beat.

It was eighties heaven. Except that no one talked to her. Michael got led off somewhere in search of his brother's friend, and all the people slouching in the corners, leaning on the banister, and sinking into the couch with their wedge hairdos couldn't care less that Lindsey was there.

She made her way into the kitchen to find something to drink. Still nervous to be out on a real date with Michael, she poured herself a plain seltzer water to settle her stomach. That Hobbit stew Auntie Shirley had fed her was not sitting well. She sipped the soda and tried to appear like she was having a reasonably good time.

Whenever Lindsey was at a restaurant or party, she had a habit of scanning the crowd and taking a mental tally of how many other Asians were present. She was used to being in situations where she was the only Chinese person, and she wondered if she blended in almost as easily as any other brunette. Tonight, as she surveyed the partygoers, she saw no other Asians but counted seven black turtlenecks, two berets, and one cigarette holder that seemed at once sophisticated and ridiculous. She walked down the hall in search of a bathroom, and overheard conversations about beat poets and the record stores in Manchester, England. She felt she had actually stepped into a Smiths song.

She pushed open the bathroom door and saw two short blond girls wearing Chinese cheongsams with chopsticks stuck through their chignons. Lindsey suddenly had that sick feeling she sometimes got. Were they paying homage to Chinese culture or mocking it? She took a deep breath. Should she just lighten up and accept the dresses as a matter of fashion, or should she be bothered that Chinese clothes were considered campy costumes? The girls' backs were to Lindsey and they did not see her as she watched them tending to a white powder on the sink ledge. Their red lipstick against their sallow skin made them look a little like vampires.

Now Lindsey wasn't exactly naive, but she was a complete virgin when it came to drugs. She had never tried any of them and had never smoked anything, not even a cigarette. Hence, here in the bathroom, watching these two girls, drugs never occured to her. Instead, she wondered why they were bleaching their mustaches now instead of having performed this regimen in the privacy of their own domiciles.

"Don't forget to mix the activator crystals with the creme solution," Lindsey said, startling them. She was equally startled when she watched one of the girls take a bit of powder in her fingernail and snort it.

"Oh," she said, feeling like an idiot. "Sorry." She turned and practically ran down the hall. She really had to use the bathroom, but she was too embarrassed to go back.

Lindsey joined Michael in a gathering of guys in bowling

shoes and gals in sleeveless shifts. Michael introduced her, and they nodded at her with sullen mouths. After a while she excused herself to see if the bathroom was free yet, but the girls were still in there, now adjusting their chopsticks.

The party was more crowded now. It seemed that at least twenty people had shown up in the last five minutes. Lindsey made her way back under the chandelier, but Michael had moved and she had temporarily lost him. She didn't want to act pathetic and clingy, so she didn't run off immediately in pursuit of him. She gazed up at the ornate lights, which sparkled like flickering candles, and admired the old plasterwork of the wall cornices and picture molding.

As Lindsey scanned the decorative paneling, she could feel someone looking at her, and she turned to see a group of young women with slicked-back Elvis hair and mechanic jackets. One particularly short and childlike girl was staring at Lindsey with misty-eyed, Haley Joel Osment intensity.

Oh, yes. Hoarders of All Things Asian could also be lesbians.

The girl smiled, and Lindsey sort of smiled back and looked away. Lindsey knew she was considered a valuable commodity to lesbian Hoarders, especially because she was a total femme compared to most Asian dykes who, with their Patagonia shorts and polar fleece vests, rocked that pro-volleyball player look.

Being more Nancy Kwan than Charlie Chan, Lindsey attracted a lot of attention, and as a result, she'd been disappointing dykes for years. By now she had become fairly comfortable brushing off their advances. Lesbian Hoarders could be just as lumbering and clumsy as heterosexual male ones, but when they stared at her breasts just like gross guys did, Lindsey was more flattered than repulsed. Maybe because she felt a kinship with them as women, she likened the situation to someone driving a Mini Cooper pulling up alongside an Austin Mini to admire the mutually sleek headlights. However, despite their attraction to her, Lindsey knew in her heart that the only way she would ever beat off lesbians would be with a stick.

When the girl sauntered over, Lindsey noticed her jacket had an STP logo and a name badge that said Troy. Lindsey talked to Troy for a while and complimented her on her boots, which were more massive than Lindsey's. She knew lesbian Hoarders trawled for Asian flesh, too, but at least they did it with a modicum of style.

Spotting Michael across the room, Lindsey excused herself and caught up with him.

He put his arm around her and said, "I hardly know anyone here. You want to go to that other party you mentioned?"

Lindsey shrugged, and they made their way to the exit. They got held up in the hallway when Michael bumped into his brother's friend, who wanted them to stay a bit longer. They all three chatted a while as Lindsey scanned the ever-growing crowd of partygoers. There was now a line for the bathroom.

She was surprised when she spotted a little beatnik Asian girl with a mushroom cap hairdo and artsy glasses. Their eyes met, and the girl looked somewhat stunned to see another Asian face as well. The girl seemed suddenly embarrassed and kept looking Lindsey's way with more and more unease each time. She moved farther from Lindsey, who wondered to herself if the girl was deliberately putting distance between them. She wondered if the girl worried that any proximity might make their cumulative Chineseness unavoidably noticeable.

She understood if Mushroom Head was uncomfortable. When there was just one other Asian person around Lindsey, too, felt awkward. She felt obligated to talk to her simply because they had this obvious one thing in common. However, she dreaded an excruciating exchange such as, "So, you're Chinese," answered with, "Yeah, so are you." Complete silence would then be followed by, "Well, so long." End of conversation.

Just then someone over her shoulder recognized the mushroom-headed Asian and yelled, "Ellen! Hey, Ellen!" A guy made his way through the crowd toward her, and Lindsey watched the whole interaction very closely. Michael's friend suddenly turned to her and said, "Oh, Lindsey, do you know Ellen?"

"No, why?"

"Oh, I just thought you would," he said, taking a gulp from his drink.

"Really? How come?"

"Oh, because you're both . . . from around here." He seemed to hesitate, but Lindsey could have imagined it. A redhead behind them turned and said, "Dude, you know Ellen's from Tennessee. You went to high school with her, Moron."

Lindsey and Michael exchanged glances, and the friend changed the subject. As he and Michael debated the merits of the Specials, Lindsey kept her thoughts to herself. She wondered, if two obese people were at a party, would anyone assume they were friends just because they were both fat?

Of course, she had no proof, but she could have sworn the guy assumed she knew Ellen because they both happened to be Chinese. But even if she was brave enough to call him out on it, she was sure he'd deny it and she'd end up looking paranoid and confrontational. She told herself it didn't even matter, but these weird moments happened with enough frequency in her life, in various situations, that she knew she couldn't have imagined them every time.

A few moments later they were finally leaving, and Lindsey looked over and caught sight of the lesbian Hoarders huddling around Ellen like a butch Girl Scout troop welcoming a prospective recruit. She stepped down the stairs and followed Michael out the door.

Back in the car, Lindsey gave Michael the address of the other party, which was, luckily, not too far away. She still had to go to the bathroom.

"How 'bout that guy thinking you knew that girl from Tennessee, like there's some Asian pipeline," Michael said. "What a dope."

Lindsey thought Michael was quite perceptive to have noticed the very thing that she worried existed only in her own head. But still, she was embarrassed, as if the friend's assumption was partly her fault, and she tried to make a joke out of it. "Well, we do all look alike," she said.

This self-deprecating remark was a small defense, although in all probability she did not need to defend herself against Michael. Hers was an automatic comment, or maybe a test to see how Michael would react. Maybe she wanted to see if he had any self-loathing regarding his own Chinese blood. She was giving him the chance to air his true feelings in case a small part of him did think that all Chinese looked alike.

She was underestimating him, but her way of insulting herself was something she had learned through osmosis from thousands of other Chinese who had made an art form of not making trouble. Even her Gung Gung had sometimes referred to himself as "just a Chinaman," either to take the edge off a situation or to shrewdly get exactly what he wanted by letting his opponent assume a false sense of superiority.

"You don't look like that girl," Michael said. He placed his hand on hers and squeezed it tight. Hesitantly, he added, "You're stronger . . . than you might think." Looking over at her, he slid his hand above her wrist and forearm, then held his warm palm firmly against her shoulder.

Lindsey looked at him expectantly. She knew his next words would be something tender and sentimental, something she could savor for days to come, maybe even cherish forever.

Michael squeezed her bicep. He said, "You could totally kick that girl's ass."

With that, he let go and deftly whipped the car into a parking space. They both jumped out and made their way up the sidewalk.

Inside the newly constructed condo-loft, the crowd was a marked contrast to the group they had just left. This group was all Asian, and Michael stood out rather obviously. Lindsey wondered if he felt self-conscious.

She scanned the crowd for her brother, but Kevin was nowhere to be seen. As her eyes panned from one corner to the next she noticed segregated groups within the Asian whole. A large contingent of well-groomed business guys with silk shirts and shiny beltbuckles were comparing their various cell phones and handheld digital cameras. They drank shots of Blue Label Johnny Walker, and she assumed they all had MBAs, like Kevin.

The other main group was the Super Christians. They were less flashy, the guys all wearing high-buttoned shirts that left just enough space to prominently display their tastefully plain gold crosses. The girls wore non-designer jeans or long skirts, and little or no makeup. As Lindsey and Michael made their way through to the center of the room, Lindsey recognized Karen from Thanksgiving over by a lamp, and then she overheard a guy say, "I ask myself every morning, 'What would Jesus wear?' And then I put on my khakis."

Aside from the roaring laughter that periodically erupted from the Johnny Walker drinkers, the only excitement at this party surrounded a quintet of girls with bleached hair, tinted eyelashes and bare midriffs. They caught everyone's attention and provoked whispering, as well as stares of both admiration and scorn. Lindsey had seen their type before. In college she and Mimi had dubbed them the SLABS, short for Sleazy Asian Blonds.

The SLABS flirted with anything wearing pants. The Christian girls eyed them nervously, the MBAs stood up straighter, and the pious guys tried to concentrate on their nonalcoholic beverages while stealing glances at their cocoa-buttered skin.

Karen and a lanky friend walked over to Lindsey and Michael. The guys started talking about basketball as Karen barraged Lindsey with questions about her brother. Where's Kevin? He coming? Your brother so smart! And so on.

Lindsey peered around in search of the bathroom, but when she spotted it she could see two of the SLABS were already occupying the space. The door was half-open, and she could see them touching up their makeup, adjusting brastraps, and, she imagined, practicing come-hither looks.

Lindsey rocked on her heels and took in the scene. Some nerds by the sofa were kneeling and harmonizing a happy-clappy church hymn. One of the MBA's cellphones was ringing out an electronicized "America the Beautiful." The SLABS looked like Baywatch babes, but their coloring was all wrong, their sunny locks clashing with the yellow-orange undertone of their complexions. No one else seemed to notice their dark roots, because their bare underarms were sexy and their nipples like wasabi peas were peeping through their camisoles. The Christian boys sipped Squirt and sweated at the sight of temptation in the form of high heels and hairless gams.

Lindsey noticed some of the business guys unwrapping small, foil-encased pills and swallowing them. She drifted a short distance from Michael and Karen, and her curious stare caught the attention of a guy with amazingly smooth skin. She wondered if he used Bioré facial strips to achieve such poreless perfection, and she was even considering asking him when he spontaneously introduced himself as Harry Poon. What an unfortunate name, she thought.

"Want one?" he asked.

"What is it?"

He washed a pill down with a shot of Patrón tequila and said, "It's Pepcid AC."

Lindsey asked why everyone was taking it, and he explained that it helped prevent turning crimson while drinking.

"You know," he said, "Asians are missing some alcohol-processing enzyme. That's why we all get bright red when we drink. See those purple guys? They waited too long."

Lindsey was ignorant of this phenomenon. "Well, I don't turn red," she said.

Harry Poon didn't believe her, and they went back and forth arguing about it. All Asians turned red, he insisted. He had never seen anyone who didn't. She contradicted him until he finally said, "Wanna bet? Let's see you prove it, and if you're right I'll give you twenty bucks."

Lindsey looked across the room at Michael, and he was so damn handsome her stomach did a little flip.

"How 'bout it?" Harry said, slapping a twenty-dollar bill on the ledge.

He poured her a shot of Patrón, and Lindsey looked at it. Something in her suddenly wanted to prove her individuality, and although a drinking game wasn't the most mature way to disprove stereotypes, it suddenly seemed like a good enough way to do so. She knew for a fact that alcohol didn't make her red, so she downed the shot and placed the empty glass on the counter. With nothing to do except wait for the tequila to rush through her system, she downed another jigger, and then, eventually, another. The liquor at least made Harry's monologue about tax shelters a little less boring.

After a while she said, "See? I'm not red, am I?"

Across the room, she gazed dreamily at Michael, and the butterflies in her stomach fluttered their wings. She couldn't wait to kiss him later tonight.

As she reached for the twenty-dollar bill, Harry grabbed her hand and said, "Wait! Sometimes it's fine on an empty stomach, but as soon as you eat a little something you start getting red. Here, eat this." He spread some Cheez Whiz on a cracker and handed it to her.

Lindsey's stomach was a little queasy, since all she had eaten that day was Auntie Shirley's Hobbit stew, so she accepted the cracker, figuring it would be a good way to soak up the tequila and maybe settle her stomach. She chewed it and then had a few other nibbles from the picked-over snack table. She ate a pig in a blanket.

Harry Poon scrutinized every inch of Lindsey's face and finally admitted she was right. "I can't believe it," he said. "You got me!" He picked up the money and handed it to her. He walked away, and Lindsey looked over to a couple of the SLABS. The blonds were turning red, and even under their heavy makeup she could see that their faces were the color of raw steak.

Hmm. She was really starting to feel sick now. Where was the bathroom again? She stumbled over to where she remembered it was, and she saw a gaggle of girls waiting their turn.

Downstairs. Maybe there was an extra bathroom downstairs. Lindsey slowly made her way to the staircase, her feet floating above the carpet, it seemed. She heard a slurring voice asking for directions to a toilet. Who was that sloppy drunk? She soon realized it was her. She didn't see Michael

anywhere nearby, which was fine, since she didn't want him to see her like this.

Swaying down the stairs, both her legs turned to mochi, and she suddenly tripped. She lunged for the banister but missed it by a mile. Wham! She felt her spine compress as she slammed hard against the stair, landing on her tailbone. Ow! Yang!

She hurt like H-E-Double-Chopsticks. Her eyeballs spiraled in opposite directions, and she saw stars and tweeting birds circling her head. She sat there and waited for things to stop spinning. She tried to take a few deep breaths, but wait. What was that disgusting smell? What was that wet feeling down the back of her legs? Something was definitely not right.

She had pooped her pants.

Taking in the horror of her situation, a strange thought popped into Lindsey's head. She recalled once when she had been in the dressing room at Old Navy, and she'd overheard a guy in the next stall ask for jeans in a loose-cut style. The attendant had had a heavy Asian accent and had asked, "Do you want loose, or *hella* loose?" The guy had replied, "Definitely hella loose, Bro." As Lindsey sat drunk on the stairs, stinking like a baby's diaper, this sudden memory may have seemed out of place, but she thought of this now because she knew if a medical examiner were to ask her the condition of her bowels at this very moment, she would be compelled to answer, "Definitely *hella* loose stools, Bro."

She felt a light touch on her shoulder.

"You OK?" It was Karen.

"Oh, crap!" yelped one of the blonds, who came running over.

The girls lifted Lindsey up, and by their repulsed faces she could tell they had discovered her putrid mess. Lindsey prayed Michael was nowhere in sight.

"I'm sorry," was all she managed to say, over and over.

Another girl came over, and they all helped Lindsey down the stairs.

"I'm sorry," she said again.

Karen spoke to her in a soothing voice. "Don't be *solly*. Don't *wolly*. We clean you."

They carried her to the downstairs bathroom and helped her step into a tub that had a nozzle attachment. Someone turned on the shower as everyone held their noses. Throwing aside her sweater, they tried to strip off her pants but had to hose them down before they even dared to touch them. Lindsey wondered how she had gotten here, suddenly nearly naked.

"I'm sorry," she moaned again. She was too wasted to care that her pants and underwear had been peeled from her body and were now in a ball at the end of the tub. When she had trimmed her pubic hair the day before she hadn't imagined any moment like this being the grand unveiling.

She was crying now. Nothing could be as wretchedly embarrassing as this moment. The girls pointed the shower nozzle at her soiled bottom and fussed over her like bridesmaids fluffing a wedding gown. But Lindsey wasn't a bride, and she for sure was not decked out in Vera Wang. She was a total loser, and the only white she was now wearing was her socks.

Socks!

"Don't take off my socks!" she suddenly screamed.

"We have to, they're wet," the blond said, tugging one down just past her ankle.

"Noooo!" Lindsey screamed like the hysterical drunk she was, then she began to sob, "You can't . . . please . . . you . . .caaan't . . ."

Even in her lowly, vulnerable state, she knew the last shred of her self-esteem would be ripped away if her midget toe was suddenly, unceremoniously exposed.

"Don't hurt him . . . the poor elephant man," she sobbed.

The girls all exchanged baffled looks, then shrugged. "Okay," the blond said. "The socks stay on."

The girls continued to spray Lindsey's bare rump until she was relatively clean, and then one by one, each of them seemed to realize how awkward the situation was. One girl excused herself, and then another, until Lindsey and Karen were left alone. Karen turned off the water and helped Lindsey step out of the tub. She handed her a towel.

"Can you dry yourself?" Karen asked, and Lindsey nodded. As Karen stepped outside, she pointed to a hairdryer near the sink.

Alone now, Lindsey toweled off and tried to sober up. She gulped some tap water from the faucet and passed the hairdryer over her pants and undies for a long while until they were merely damp. She was glad her pants were lightweight cotton, but she was dismayed that they were also white. She pulled them on over her damp underwear and tried to hide the panty lines by yanking her sweater down over her butt so at least she looked decent. She dried her drenched socks as well as she could, then slipped her feet back into her shoes.

She had been in the bathroom for over an hour, and when she came upstairs she immediately saw Michael.

"I've been looking for you. Where've you been?" he asked.

"Oh . . ." She hesitated. "Just downstairs, with some girls."

Michael smiled. "I hope you didn't think I was neglecting you," he said. "Some guy over there just wouldn't stop talking. He had serious diarrhea of the mouth."

At the word "diarrhea" Lindsey felt another gurgling fissure trying to make its presence known.

"Um, I think we should go," she said, slightly panicked.

Michael seemed taken aback by her sudden insistence but said, "Uh, all right." He patted his pockets in search of his keys as they headed downstairs to the front door.

Lindsey was fairly certain she could make it home before she had another butt-tooting episode. Sitting in the car, she thought back to the day when Michael was wet in the passenger seat of her car, and she thought it ironic that the situation was now reversed. She was grateful that he was unaware of her current condition.

Glad to be in a sitting position, she tried yanking her sweater further down past her rump to keep the seat as dry as possible. As she pulled at the hem of her cardigan she was horrified to notice a tiny blop of poop that had gone undetected near the lower stitching of her sweater.

As Michael's eyes were concentrating on the road, she stared at the offending bean, which resembled one of those discontinued, light tan M&Ms. Aghast, she hoped to God that Michael couldn't smell it. She clenched the blop and the surrounding fabric in her fist and looked ahead, willing the streetlights to turn green so she could get home as swiftly as possible.

"You're awfully quiet," Michael said, breaking the sound of light pattering raindrops on the windshield. Watching the quivering drops of water on the glass made Lindsey nervous.

"Just tired," she said. Then she attempted merriment by adding, "But I'm just fine." She tried to sound like she was a happy little thing, instead of a damp-bottomed, midget-toed freak clenching a blob of poopie.

When Michael slowed the car to a stop in Lindsey's driveway, he set the brake and leaned over to kiss her. She felt the very tip of his tongue on hers and felt the butterflies in her stomach. Or was that her lower intestines? Her posture tightened, and she recoiled a bit. Michael pulled back and looked at her as if he worried that he'd done something wrong. He moved further away, and they smiled stiffly at one another.

After a tense moment and some lame, forgettable words, Lindsey bolted for the door. And that was the end to what was supposed to have been a terrific evening.

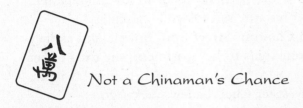

Not a Chinaman's Chance

The night had not been a complete disaster. The following week Michael stopped by Lindsey's desk to chat, and he smiled at her across the conference table during a staff meeting. Lindsey figured he wouldn't have wanted to get anywhere near her if he had actually smelled her Saturday night. She was in the clear.

Over the ensuing weeks, they each slowly and carefully released small bits of information about themselves and found things in common, such as their mutual admiration for Alfred Hitchcock movies and their disdain for Volvo drivers. They were surprised to find that they both followed the flocks of wild parrots that flew through the city, and they swapped information about the nesting sites they'd separately discovered.

One day after work Michael helped Lindsey carry some parcels down to the FedEx office, and she was pleased when he asked her over to his place. As they walked briskly down Montgomery Street, the December air was unusually balmy, prompting her to remove her coat.

"Want me to carry that for you?" he offered, his own shirtsleeves rolled to his elbows.

"Yeah, thanks," she said, swinging it toward him. He gathered it under his arm and folded it carefully.

They climbed Chestnut Street from Powell, and as they went up the rickety stairs to his apartment, she tried to act like she was in a place she'd never seen before, as if she hadn't stalked his sister Cheryl a few weeks ago.

"I've got *Rear Window* if you want to watch it," he said as they entered the door.

Inside, she quickly surveyed his living quarters. His furniture was somewhere between post-college and public library, with a Craftsman-style bureau, swivel oak chairs, and a makeshift table assembled from file cabinets and a wooden plank. A utilitarian sisal rug covered the hardwood floor.

"How come your apartment is so clean, but you leave candy wrappers all over the office?" Lindsey asked.

He smiled and lightly touched his index finger to the tip of her nose. "I just like getting you all riled up," he said.

As they toured his apartment, she peered into a small kitchen, and then they approached the bedroom. Numerous times she had imagined him late at night, snuggling alone in sanitary and tastefully decorated conditions. Now she did not want to see anything that might mar her image of him; she did not want to discover Playboy playmate posters, Star Trek sheets, weeks-old laundry, or anything else that might threaten to disqualify him as a mature and hygienic person.

Michael walked to the far corner of the room and adjusted the matchstick blinds to let in the last minutes of the early evening twilight. A television set and VCR supported a stack of books, and an unpainted pine dresser, a full-size bed, and an oak chair made up the remaining contents of the room. She was charmed to find that what appeared to be an overstuffed plush pillow was actually a full-figured Abyssinian cat snoozing blissfully in the center of the bed.

"Oh, that's Larry," he said, flopping down to pet the portly, declawed feline, which was the size of a small Butterball turkey. She sat on the edge of the bed and scratched under his chin.

"Watch out," Michael warned. "Unfortunately, he's basically a flea-transport system. He belongs to the downstairs neighbor, but he gets in through there." He pointed down the hall to a cat door, installed by the previous occupant, he explained.

"Are you hungry?" he asked, springing up and heading toward the kitchen. She followed and hovered in the doorway as he searched his refrigerator for snacks.

"How about this?" he asked, retrieving a pint of Cherry Garcia from the freezer. He pulled off the lid and searched for a spoon, but she began to worry about bits of cherry skin getting stuck between her teeth. "Oh, none for me, thanks," she said.

He tempted her, but she shook her head again. "Virtue untested isn't virtue at all, right?" he said.

She thought for a moment. "Are you quoting *Paradise Lost*?" she asked.

He shut the freezer. "Um, I don't know, maybe. Actually, I thought I was quoting a Billy Bragg song from 1988, but he was probably quoting Milton, so yeah."

She was enticed by his combined knowledge of eighties

pop music and seventeenth-century epic poetry. She followed him back to his bedroom.

A few minutes later, they lay on a cozy blue quilt as the credits for the Hitchcock thriller rolled on-screen. Larry spread out like a blob between them, making any subtle touching nearly impossible. Gentle nudges to the tomcat's thigh area elicited mere twitches of the whiskers.

"I don't have the heart to move him when he looks so comfy," Michael said, awkwardly trying to put his arm around Lindsey. As she tried to lean closer to him, her eyes wandered toward the open closet door. It was here where atrocities were spotted.

> **Exhibit A:** Tan jeans hanging next to beige corduroys. Yes, they were acceptable thin-wale cords, and perhaps the shadows could suggest a hint of olive or moss in the color of the trousers, but there was definitely something *greige* lurking there.
>
> **Exhibit B:** On the floor of the closet, were those *desert boots*??! *Wallabees*? The suede, sand-colored footwear of the seventies?
>
> **And the Kiss of Death:** She could have pretended not to see it. Behind a pair of gray running shoes, which were in themselves totally unacceptable, was a shoebox bearing the brand name of Satan himself, the footwear of Beelzebub: *Rockports*.

She sat upright and stared at Michael.

"What's wrong?" he asked.

"Nothing," she replied. She gazed slack-jawed into the depths of the closet.

"Did you see something?" he asked. "The tenants before had mice. And, as you can probably guess, Larry's not much of a mouser."

"Tube socks!" she yelped, jumping up. For some reason, despite her own dependence on knee highs, she considered tube socks with striped bands of color across the top to be really creepy, like something a child-molesting priest might wear with roller skates on the weekend. As she sprang off the bed, a blizzard of cat hair billowed up around her and she swatted the air with crazed, compulsive energy. She frantically slapped the Larry-fur away from her arms and legs.

"Where did you . . . where did you get that stuff?" she asked, wagging her finger toward the closet as if she had just discovered a severed human head.

"What? The socks?" he asked, confused.

"Everything—the socks, the seventies beige shoes . . ."

She smoothed down her Marimekko-patterned skirt and tried to get a grip on herself.

"You have *desert boots*," she said disdainfully.

He frowned. "Well, you have *Hello Kitty* stuff," he said.

Lindsey was mortified. "No I don't!" she yelled.

"Yeah, right. I was looking for a calculator one day and saw all that stuff in your drawer—the pink stapler, the scented erasers, and the teeny pencil sharpener. You've got a Hello Kitty *manually operated paper shredder*, and you think I'm weird because I have tube socks?"

She was both flattered and flabbergasted that he had noticed her personal belongings. "I don't even *like* . . . Hello Kitty," she said. "Besides, I can't believe you went through my desk without asking!"

She fumed for a second longer, then lied, "Besides, those were all gifts that other people gave me."

"You were at the dentist that day, and my brother gave me those socks. Who cares?"

"They were probably on sale at Ross. What a cheapskate."

"What's *wrong* with you?" he asked.

"You're a Hoarder!" she shot back, as if he'd know what that was.

She gathered up her backpack and coat. "I'm sorry, I have to go now."

She headed for the door, and left Michael standing in a cloud of cat fuzz, wondering what had just happened.

Scaling Filbert Street, she tried to calm down. She had to take inventory of a few things. Perhaps she had to revise her theory.

If someone was part-Chinese himself, was he automatically exempted from Hoarder status? Michael had dark hair and was not at all pasty, so could these attributes cancel out the dastardly implications of his Rockports and tan pants? Were tube socks really that bad, or merely a fact of life for the American heterosexual male? Could those desert boots be forgiven because his hands showed no trace of amphibian fingers?

She just didn't know.

The next day at work, her boss informed her that the magazine planned to host a special luncheon in attempt to solicit donations from left-leaning millionaires with a penchant for Tofutti.

"I want to serve really spectacular food," Howard proclaimed.

Lindsey listened as he flapped his arms, brainstorming out loud. He turned to her and said, "Could you research the yummiest ethnic restaurants? And make sure they can really deliver." He clapped his hands together, proud of the double meaning.

"I want the works. Vegetarian Pad Thai. Egg rolls, spring rolls, and sushi handrolls. Let's really put out a spread!"

She distributed a few phone calls before she could reply.

"Maybe PR has their own connections with caterers?" she suggested, not wanting to step on Yvonne's toes. (By the way, *Vegan Warrior* paid Yvonne triple Lindsey's salary to plan no more than five parties per year.)

"No, no! I want you to handle it," Howard insisted. "You are so much more . . ." He fumbled for the right words to express his assumption that she knew the tastiest locales for exotic foods.

"You've got your finger on the pulse of the Asian restaurant scene!" He held up his hand to high-five her.

She wrinkled her nose. She thought Thai and Japanese food never traveled well, and she anticipated problems keeping a hundred greasy egg rolls hot. Plus, she dreaded fielding questions from the staff about what foods were organic, or wheat-free, like she was some kind of nutrition expert.

She reluctantly agreed to help organize the menu.

The following morning, Yvonne bombarded Lindsey with questions. She paced the lobby and tried to interrupt Lindsey, whose other ear was glued to an irate subscriber who had called to complain about the magazine's recent direct mail campaign.

"How come you're in charge? You're only an admin!" Yvonne hissed.

In Lindsey's opposite ear, the caller fumed, "How dare you send advertisements saying your articles are 'meaty' and 'ballsy'! I don't pay good money to *Vegan Warrior* for meatball recipes!"

Yvonne continued, "Since when are you trying to move up to event planning? I have the *Waiters on Wheels* catalog memorized, y'know."

"Beef up your stories on hummus!" the caller growled and then hung up.

Lindsey sighed and put down the receiver. She turned to Yvonne and said, "If you have a problem, please just go talk to Howard."

"Men in power are threatened by groundbreaking feminists like me," Yvonne replied. "But I guess shallow receptionists with lipstick and miniskirts don't understand. Your mere existence is a willful slap in the face to true activists like me who paved the way for workplace pantsuits."

Yvonne stormed away, leaving only a lingering aroma of rosewater and baby powder. During her lunch hour, Lindsey ate a peanut-butter-and-jelly sandwich at her desk while she researched numerous restaurants for everything Howard had requested: dim sum, sag paneer, naan, lemongrass and green papaya salad, vegetable tempura, edamame, and udon noodles, for starters. She could tell this was going to be a bad workweek.

*   *   *

When the day of the luncheon arrived, all the visitors and staff had a grand time enjoying the variety of foods, while Yvonne eyeballed Lindsey from across the room and snapped her fingers to signal that the Sterno candles needed to be relit, or the napkins under the imperial rolls had become saturated with grease and required immediate blotting. As Lindsey swept up tempura crumbs, she looked up just as Yvonne tossed a piece of cucumber maki down the gullet of her wobbly turkey neck and laughed with an open mouth full of chewed food as people congratulated her on the delicious, well-organized meal.

"Don't forget to reheat the chow mein," Yvonne barked at Lindsey, beckoning to her with a soiled Chinet plate.

After the guests retreated to a back conference room for Howard's fund-raising presentation, Yvonne ducked out to buy some Nag Champa incense. Lindsey was left to do all the cleanup by herself.

"Need some help?" Michael asked, poking his head into the kitchen.

Having not yet reconciled her worries about his Hoarder-esque wardrobe, she regarded his presence with a blend of giddiness and dread. She knew she would eventually need to deliver an apology, but for now she just smiled and nodded, and together they finished wiping the folding tables. They cleared serving trays and wrapped up the un-eaten leftovers. While she loaded the dishwasher, Michael took the trash down to the back landing. She waited for him to return and tried to think of a way to tell him she was sorry for her previous behavior.

She finished cleaning the kitchen and moved on to straighten up the mailroom. She pinched away a mangled heap of staples strewn messily about the counter and un-jammed the heavy-duty Acco stapler that a coworker had abandoned for dead. Filling the copier trays with recycled paper, she made a mental note to order more #10 letter-head envelopes. She retrieved a Ziploc of rotting organic baby carrots from behind a bookcase and tossed the shriv-eled, toelike nubs into a nearby trash can.

Fishing the latest Office Depot catalog from her mail-box, she found a plain white envelope scrawled in ballpoint. Above the office's street and suite numbers, the letter was not addressed to her by name, but simply to *The Slant*.

Lindsey had found it under her own nameplate, so the envelope was obviously meant for her. Nonetheless, she was puzzled. It had been a long time since anyone had called her a slant, or any other racial epithet, for that matter. Could this slur even be applied to her, in this day and age? She was, after all, not an immigrant laborer, or even a fac-tory worker. She wasn't a *job-stealing slant*, but, rather, she was a flip-hairdo'd go-getter in Victoria's Secret undergar-ments who performed light clerical tasks born of white-collar, eco-friendly whims.

She leaned against the copy machine with a befuddled expression, her powdery lavender eyeshadow crinkling like crushed velvet. (Pau Pau had protested against this hue, saying, "*Ai-ya*, bad luck to wear color of zombies!")

Just then, from around the corner, Michael spotted her and approached. He brushed against her wrist as he leaned closer, reading over her shoulder. "What have you got there?"

"Isn't this outrageous?" she asked, feeling the warmth of his presence and anticipating the support of someone equally galled. Glancing again at the offensive word, she ripped open the letter, feeling a tingling mixture of anger and embarrassment.

Michael grasped the envelope and pulled it from her fingers. He replied, "What's outrageous? That you're reading my mail?"

She took a step back and looked him in the eye. "What are you talking about?" she asked.

"It's the magazine's new humor column. The name was my idea. I even won a gift certificate to Herbivore for coming up with the best title."

He smiled at her with vague pride, but she was appalled. "You have got to be joking," she said. He looked at her blankly, so she added, "You do know this is a racial slur, right?"

"What?" He paused for a moment to gather his thoughts and then collected himself. "Oh . . . ," he said, as the fact slowly dawned on him. "Hunh."

She waited for his eyes to register the realization of his wretched transgression. But several seconds elapsed, and he didn't seem half as disturbed as she felt he should be.

"Well?" she asked.

He bounced his head up and down and looked up, trying to think of something to say. "Well, 'Slant' is supposed to mean something like, a different point of view, or, you know, a different take on things . . ."

Lindsey clenched her teeth. "I know what it's *supposed* to mean," she said.

"Okay, then," he replied with a shrug. "It's no big deal."

"I think it is," she said, exiting the mailroom with a crimson burn spreading from her ears across her face.

*   *   *

For the next few weeks, Lindsey avoided Michael with the same stealth and precision she had previously devised to attract his attention. If she spotted him by the elevator as she was leaving, she would busy herself long enough to take the next lift down, and if she saw him standing in a doorway down the hall as she walked, she quickly detoured onto an alternate route.

First she had grappled with the possibility that Michael might be a Hoarder in sheep's clothing, and now his blasé attitude about racial slurs made her completely confused about who he was.

She was bothered by his lack of cultural knowledge and self-admitted distance from his partial Chinese identity. Although she was suspicious of Hoarders who delved too wholeheartedly into Asian customs, in contrast, she now took offense at Michael's ignorance.

She stewed over his insensitivity, but eventually she began to wonder if she could really blame him. After all, she had spent most of her own life disassociating herself from her Asian-ness. As a child she'd felt self-conscious as she'd watched the devilish Siamese cats in *Lady and the Tramp*, wondering if all slant-eyed creatures were supposedly evil. The Chinese feline in *The Aristocats* had frightened her as it had sung menacingly about egg foo young, and, later, Mickey Rooney's buck-toothed Japanese caricature in *Breakfast at Tiffany's* had made her young heart sink.

She had spent many hours, and then years, denying any relation to those stereotypes. When the world had routinely characterized Asians as unscrupulous, deceitful, and foolish, how could she criticize Michael for having the urge to downplay his Chinese background?

Despite having his grandmother's genes coursing through his veins, Michael did not appear of mixed-race heritage. With his tallish frame, straight nose, and easy-to-grow five o'clock shadow, what alienating incidences had he sidestepped by having a physical body that lacked Chinese features? Never having been called a "chink" to his face, alone in a parking lot or surrounded by friends at McDonald's, he had escaped discrimination and tears. Never having experienced subtle mistreatment or outright hostility due to race, how could Michael know the terrible loneliness, or feel the awful embarrassment, helplessness, and anger she felt when she heard a word like "slant" used so nonchalantly?

As for her, no matter how hard she tried, she could never escape being identifiably Asian; all her life she had had the same jet-black hair and eyes like skinny minnows, which remained unchanged whether she wore preppy Benetton cardigans, ruffled Betsey Johnson frocks, or thrift-store ensembles. When she was a youngster, she had been called names. She had not understood them then, but she'd known they were meant to be hurtful and had everything to do with her being Chinese. She remembered neighborhood teenagers pelting the house with mushy blackberries, and she recalled the glares from a boutique saleslady when she'd shopped for her junior prom dress. She had tried to ignore these humiliations, but each incident had stayed with her.

And what *good* Chinese things had Michael skipped? She supposed that he had never received a knowing glance from a Toisanese stranger passing on the street, or felt the sense of safety and belonging that she did in Chinatown. Perhaps he seldom heard the intonations of a familiar yet undecipherable language whose power flowed through the ears and had the ability to comfort the bones. He had not spent years tasting the flavors of ancient recipes that soaked from the taste buds into the heart; he had missed out on the fortifying crunch of every bamboo shoot, the soothing reassurance in each swallow of faintly tinted broth, and the surge of love in every pungent bite of ginger.

She knew that she gained a certain strength in not being able to hide who she was. And now that she reflected on her upbringing filled with Empress of China dinners, New Year's parades, and calligraphy lessons, she realized that each experience had formed an impression on her identity, augmenting her development layer by layer, like an intricate design carved over a thousand hours in soft cinnabar. Every experience, even the unpleasant ones, had helped to slowly build her character, creating a one-of-a-kind Chinese-American named Lindsey Owyang.

Given all these variables, she wondered if she was justified in holding Michael responsible for his lack of understanding. With romantic optimism, she wanted him to instantly know the depths of her heart and mind. She was disappointed that he clearly did not share her scope of experiences, and was saddened that he did not automatically know her feelings. She did not know if she had the strength to relive small hurts in order to teach him or love him.

Did she know enough of him to risk the opening of her heart? After an initial flirtation and the discovery of a common record collection, did True Love begin with a shy courage?

Chinese Chick & Salad

Lindsey knew that Chinese New Year had come around when she began noticing pomelos and tangerines multiplying atop the television. From her perch on the sofa she attempted to adjust the volume with the remote control, but its invisible electronic beam was intercepted by all the good luck from the cornucopia of citrus delights.

She held a sack of dried, cranberry-like fruits in her lap and was separating the meat from the pits. She was helping Pau Pau make *neen-goh*.

"Keep peeling!" her grandmother yelled from the kitchen.

She used her fingertips to mince the leathery *hoong jo* fruit into teeny scraps. Pau Pau would later mix the bits in with sugar, sweet red beans, and glutinous rice powder. She'd boil the whole mixture and spread it in a metal pan, steaming the whole thing until she announced that it was ready to eat.

Lindsey liked all the different types of *goh*, like the savory ones made from turnips and dried shrimp that were served in dim sum restaurants, and the white, dessert *goh* sold in triangles at Chinese bakeries. But *neen-goh* was a special dish made only during Chinese New Year. Once cooked, it would resemble a sticky gray quiche held together by bumpy fruit and beans. Its taste was sweet and its texture gummy. She loved the flavors, and ever since she was small, she had helped Pau Pau make it. It always meant Chinese New Year to her.

That night they went to China Garden for a big family dinner. Her family always had two Chinese New Year banquets: one to close out the old year and one to welcome the next. This evening was to celebrate the ending of the old year, and before the meal was served, the married couples distributed lucky money in red envelopes, called *lay-see*, to children and unmarried young adults.

When she accepted the *lay-see*, Lindsey made sure to say "*Dawh jeh, Goong Hay Faht Choy*," which meant, "Thank you, prosperity in the new year." This phrase was practically the only complete sentence she could say in Chinese. Incidentally, she always hated how non-Chinese people pronounced it, as if it rhymed with "flung may splat boy," but then again, she supposed that she had more incentive to say it right since, for her, it translated into free cash.

Kevin accepted a red envelope from Auntie Vivien and said, "*Sun neen fai lok*," which meant "Happy New Year."

"Show-off," Lindsey muttered under her breath.

"Hey, Steph," Brandon said, "it must be lousy that you don't get *lay-see* anymore, and now you've got to give it every year, huh?"

"Yeah, but I have a cutoff point. I don't give lucky envelopes to spinsters like Auntie Shirley. She's too old."

Kevin put in his two cents. "Damn, Stephanie. She baby-sat you and made Nehru jackets for your Barbies, and now you won't even give her two dollars every February? That's messed up."

It was polite to put away lucky envelopes right away. Nonetheless, Cammie ripped open her *lay-see* and counted up her fortune at the dinner table. She appeared somewhat dejected, and when Lindsey asked her what was wrong, she replied, "Dang, I got a lot more last year."

As they all snacked on dried cuttlefish, they heard a commotion at the entrance to the restaurant.

"Oh, there's going to be lion dancing," said one of her aunts.

Lindsey had misheard. "Line dancing, like in country and western bars?" she asked in disbelief.

"No, stupid," her brother said, jabbing her with an elbow. "You know, *li-on* dancing."

"Oh, right."

During this traditional performance, Lindsey felt undeniably Chinese. When the drums and cymbals started to clang, ringing in her ears and stopping her heart for a split second, something in her blood started to well up. The music was a cacophony of cultural noise, rhythmic and forceful. The strength of its distinctive beat made her think back to every past Chinese New Year celebration she had ever attended. And because she only experienced this music when surrounded by her extended clan of relatives, she enjoyed herself without worrying about having to explain this glorious, garish dance.

The members from the martial arts studio ranged from

eight-year-old kids to middle-aged adults, and in unison they banged on drums and knocked out the rhythm on large gongs and small brass cymbals. The festive excitement they created with their bodies and instruments was so intense and powerful that immediately the air changed. People sat up straight in their chairs, craning their necks to catch a first glimpse of the performers. Babies looked startled, but then began to clap their plump hands. Young kids, temporarily disengaging from their Game Boys, squirmed with zeal, and even the sullen teenagers snapped out of their deeply practiced apathy for a few minutes.

Costumed characters with pink-and-blue masks pranced about, teasing the lions, which were a creation of wire, papier-mâché, fabric, and feathers. Each creature was brought to life by two athletic performers—one who maneuvered the lion's head and shoulder area, while the other manipulated the midsection and rear.

They did not resemble real lions at all; rather, they appeared as pom-pom-festooned beasts that were part fu dog, part dragon or snake. The bodies consisted of alternating sections of gold and crimson satin, combined with pink, violet, and emerald quilted pieces in the shape of fish scales. The luxurious fabrics were all trimmed with white fur that zigzagged across the flowing, capelike midsections. Dressed in matching satin and fur pants, the performers twisted and kicked, creating wavelike motions as they brought life to the ferocious yet playful creatures.

The performers hoisted the lions' heads above their own, swinging the elaborately decorated headpieces side to side, then higher and lower. They waved their tireless arms to fan out the sequined fabric, creating the illusion of the lions'

bodies where there was only air. The beasts' flirtatious batting of glittery eyelids, the twitching of feather-lined ears,
and the flapping open and shut of their colorful mouths
captivated the audience.

"Where can I get some of those fabulous fur-trimmed
pants?" Lindsey wondered to herself.

The pounding, exuberant music continued its beat while
the masked characters tempted the lions with iceberg lettuce, dangling the crisp leaves from decorative fishing poles.
The lions moved aggressively yet gracefully, hypnotized and
temporarily tamed. They crouched down to eat the vegetable offering, and then suddenly, as the cymbals crashed
loudly, they tossed the lettuce into the air, startling the nearest viewers with a friendly spray of shredded lettuce.

In a joyous finale, the lion dancers were joined by other
members of the martial arts group, weaving together to
form a human scaffolding of legs and shoulders. The majestic lions, with the help of their human framework, grew
to a height of twelve feet and displayed red satin banners
with auspicious New Year's couplets written in Chinese calligraphy. A thick braid of firecrackers was set afire and
erupted in a series of ear-shattering mini-explosions.
Clouds of dark blue gunpowder smoke billowed up
through the air as bits of red paper flew every which way in
a celebratory fire hazard.

On the following Sunday, Lindsey and Mimi set out early
for the Alameda flea market. They were ready to pick up
some bargains, and maybe even some guys.

As they made their way toward the bridge on-ramp,
Lindsey noticed Mimi's pink patent leather slingbacks.

"Are you sure you can walk all morning in those?" she asked.

Mimi ignored the question. She was curling her eyelashes with the aid of the passenger-side mirror. As she squeezed the delicate, wispy hairs with the rubber-padded implement, she stuck her tongue out to one side of her mouth and contorted her face like a winking ghoul.

"Did you say something?" Mimi asked, now shaking up her mascara tube and plunging the small wand into the base as if she were churning butter. "Hey, you wanna stop off and go to confession?" She pointed with her lips toward a clump of folks who were gathered under a marquee that identified an unassuming stucco building as a Chinese Mennonite church.

Lindsey craned her neck for a better look. "Hmm, who knew? I guess that's like Vietnamese Amish people or something."

They drove in silence for a while, both of them still somewhat sleepy. Neither was accustomed to rising so early, but by the time they crossed the bridge, sped through the Alameda tube, and pulled into the stadium-sized parking lot, they were lively enough. The thought of shopping always perked them up.

Endless aisles of yesteryear's detritus loomed ahead of them. In addition to broken lamps and moth-eaten daybeds, they saw Bauer flowerpots, cradle telephones, rusted kitchen tools, stained muumuus, and fifties costume jewelry. While Mimi checked out a booth with vintage shoes and purses, Lindsey meandered toward a display of collectible lunchboxes depicting sixties and seventies TV shows.

She saw one with scenes from *Bonanza*, and one with Bruce Lee as Kato in *The Green Hornet*. She knew Pau Pau and Brandon would have gotten a kick out of those. Spotting one from *Kung Fu*, she wondered why David Carradine, a Caucasian actor, played the part of the Chinese lead. A thermos from *The Courtship of Eddie's Father* triggered her memories of the sitcom; even as a kid she'd thought it odd that the Japanese housekeeper was named Mrs. Livingston.

She noticed a lunchbox with *Hong Kong Phooey* and another showing a fat, mustached, Chinese man with his family members who resembled Shaggy and Velma from *Scooby Doo*, except with black hair and slanty eyes.

"That was a Hanna-Barbera cartoon about Charlie Chan solving crimes with his kids," the vendor said, snarfing scrambled eggs from a paper plate. "It's mint. One hundred fifty, if you're interested."

Lindsey traced her index finger over the embossed words *The Chan Clan*, and she tapped the surface lightly. Before sidling away to rejoin Mimi, she thanked the guy, who waved at her with his spork, which had a goober of egg-white dangling from its blunt tine.

"See anything good?" Mimi asked, slipping out of some too-wide clogs and back into her own pink sandals.

"Interesting, but no must-haves," Lindsey said as they continued down the midway.

Snaking through the maze of tables, it was apparent to Lindsey that Asian stuff was a hot item. She approached a selection of chalkware busts depicting Chinese children with cherry lips and elaborate hair ornaments. Some sucked their thumbs with sweet innocence, and others glanced coyly to the side with enchanting allure. The busts were lovingly crafted, yet mannequinnish, as if they knew they had been created to please the Western gaze and dared not express anything other than simpleminded charm. Lindsey herself was quite taken with the figures, and she contemplated whether it was inconsequential or deeply wrong that she found the objectifying sculptures to be pleasing to her own eye. She pressed a finger to the crumbling face of a girl's head, pockmarked with chips and dents that showed white, powdery plaster beneath the crackled paint.

As she and Mimi moved on, Lindsey couldn't stop thinking of the statuettes. She thought back to a book she'd seen a few months ago about San Francisco's Pan-Pacific International Exposition in 1915. She had read that one of the most popular exhibits had been called "Underground Chinatown," and it had portrayed subterranean hovels with tawdry dioramas of opium smoking and enslaved prostitutes. She had read that, after complaints from Chinese elders, the exposition's directors had changed the name of the attraction to "Underground Slumming," and replaced the Chinese slave girls with debauched white girls.

She ruminated on this bit of history and wondered why the concept of secretive, exotic Asians seemed to appeal to everybody. She realized that she, too, was strangely comfortable with motifs that reduced Chinese culture to only that which was entertainingly decorative.

The whole matter put Lindsey in a funk. She trailed Mimi and responded with lackluster comments as her friend fired questions at her regarding the multitude of halter tops, miniskirts, and fashion accessories she held up for opinion.

"Kind of tired?" Mimi asked. "There's a coffee stand over there. Get me one too, okay?"

Lindsey jogged over to the coffee cart to retrieve a couple of double lattes. When she reentered the area where she had left Mimi, she pivoted around but didn't spot her. Must have turned the corner, she figured.

Jostling through the throngs of shoppers, she could see Mimi sifting through Bakelite barrettes about halfway up the next section. Pausing to sip her coffee, she looked across the aisle to a table display of lotus slippers, the kind for bound feet. She approached the row of tiny shoes but stayed a couple of yards away. She didn't want to spill coffee on the silk, but also, she hesitated for a reason she wasn't sure of. As she studied the slippers from the short distance, she could see that some had heel reinforcements carefully sewn on, one arched dramatically into a pronounced point, and others were slightly ripped, with tattered padding peeking out from beneath the pinpricked embroidery.

Several weeks ago, similar slippers had been featured on the *Roadshow*. She had been watching it with Pau Pau, who'd explained that in the old days the ladies sewed their own designs all by hand, and the slippers themselves were never meant to be saved. "Once worn out, like saving underwear!" her grandmother had said, in a tone of voice that had expressed that she found the idea preposterous. And now Lindsey was seeing the slippers for sale, again. To no one in particular, she asked aloud, "If they can outlaw used panties on eBay, why are these slippers everywhere?"

She stood for several seconds, holding a latte in each hand, and stared at the display. From behind, a set of elegant, tapered fingers reached out and dislodged a paper cup from her loose grip.

"Are you talking to yourself again?" Mimi slurped some steamed milk. "I hope you remembered to get nonfat."

Lindsey nodded, and they continued on their way. They still had at least twenty rows left to peruse.

Over the next couple of weeks Michael made several attempts at reconciliation with Lindsey, but she would have none of it. She found little presents on her desk, like a chocolate-caramel Twix, a smoothie from the downstairs cafe, and an article about the city's cherry-headed conures that he had clipped from the newspaper. Lindsey was unfazed. She didn't eat the candy bar, gave away the fruit shake, and slammed the article in a dictionary without reading it.

It hurt Lindsey to like Michael as much as she did. She didn't completely allow herself to believe that he really liked her back. For real. She was afraid it was all some kind of bad joke, and she'd end up like Sissy Spacek in *Carrie*. Would Michael eventually rip out her heart while it was still beating, just like that insane shaman in *Indiana Jones and the Temple of Doom*? She had walked the plank as far as she could go for now, and she wasn't ready to jump.

Thoughts of Michael were temporarily stalled when Lindsey found out that Pau Pau had arranged another "date" for her. This one was with the grandnephew of Fanny Lee, Pau Pau's arch rival in the cutthroat mahjong world of Spofford Alley. The old ladies' hope was that maybe the two youngsters would hit it off and marry, and thus, the mahjong winnings would conveniently stay in the family no matter who won a set.

Lindsey was supposed to meet the guy at North Beach Pizza. As she waited for whatever his name was, she watched the delivery guys smoke cigarettes while leaning up against their double-parked cars. She studied the condiments on the table and rearranged her butt on the booth seat, unsticking the back of her legs from the vinyl.

A few minutes later, a Chinese guy strolled through the door. She recognized him immediately as a grammar school classmate.

"Hey, Franklin Ng, what are you doing here?"

"Oh hey, I haven't seen you in a while! What are you doing here?" He stood next to her booth and scanned the restaurant, but there were no other customers at this early hour, only the employees preparing for the evening ahead.

"I think I'm your date," she said as he sat down.

She had known Franklin since third grade. To other kids in the class he'd been most memorable as the boy who'd fallen asleep each day and earned the lowest marks of everyone, almost flunking every year. As a straight-A student, she had snubbed him initially, not wanting any association with a dumb kid to drag her down academically or socially. He'd been one of those kids who'd brought Chinese soup in a thermos for lunch and had tried to share his salty plum wafers or rice candies, when she'd only wanted Hershey's bars.

Sometime midyear she'd discovered that he attended the same Chinese school with her in the afternoons. When she hadn't been ditching out with Kevin and Brandon, she'd sat in the back of the class, fumbling with her *mok-but* ink and bamboo calligraphy brush. She had never understood what the teacher was saying, and she'd failed her memorizations. She'd had no friends at St. Mary's, so when she'd spotted Franklin a few rows away, she'd been glad to see a familiar face. Since he'd been a bad student too, she'd figured that maybe they could commiserate.

But at St. Mary's, Franklin had not been a bad student at all. In fact, he'd been one of the top students. He'd spoken Cantonese a mile a minute and had had the teacher praising his elegant touch in penmanship. On the playground, he'd been the most popular kid, with his Botan chewy candies, sesame crackers, and assorted flavors of Pocky sticks. Lindsey had stood friendless against the chain-link fence while other kids had played Chinese jumprope and *Chahng-Chahng-Doe*, which was the Chinese version of Rock-Paper-Scissors. As she'd watched Franklin from a distance, she'd been awestruck by his afternoon popularity. He'd seemed to be a totally different person than he had been in regular school. From 8:30 A.M. to 2:30 P.M. he'd been the dumb boy with bad grades and weird food, but here he'd been the life of the party. Strangely, here in Chinese school, Lindsey had been the dumb kid.

Among all the Chinese students, she'd been lonely for someone to talk to, so one afternoon she'd approached Franklin.

"Where do you get all that candy?" she'd asked. Since she'd usually ignored him, she'd wondered if he would even talk to her.

"Oh, my family has a grocery store, and I can have all the candy I want."

"Then why don't you have Lemonheads or Crunch bars?" she asked, feeling around in her own jumper pockets for any spare Jujubes.

"Sometimes I do, but I don't like them as much. They're too sweet."

She'd frowned. "How come you're always asleep in class?"

"I work in the store at night and weekends. I stock the cans and keep the inventory."

"What about your homework?"

"I don't have time," he'd shrugged.

"Where is this store, anyway?" she'd asked.

"It's on Franklin. I'm named after the store. My dad worked there before my brother and me got born. He looked up at that big sign all day and told my ma just to call me that name. So that's why I'm Franklin."

"Really? I thought you were named after Benjamin Franklin."

"Me?" He'd guffawed, not unlike Lindsey's Gung Gung.

Just then the class bell had rung.

"That's a good one," he'd said. "C'mon, let's go inside."

And that's how they'd become friends. Sort of. They'd been friends in Chinese school and during the summers, when Lindsey would sometimes poke her head into Franklin Market to see if he was there. He'd give her free Jolly Rancher Fire Stix and watermelon-flavored Now or Laters. But during regular school hours, during recess and at lunchtime in front of her white friends, she wouldn't talk to him very much, just from time to time when she thought no one was watching. She did stop making fun of him, however, and even made a point of "accidentally" stepping on Valerie Crinion's foot the time she called him a lazy, sleeping Chinky.

Now, here in the pizza place, Franklin looked very much the same as he did back then. He was skinnier than she would have expected, but he also looked very stylish in his black Dolce & Gabbana slacks.

"So, what are you up to now?" she asked.

"My dad and mom still have the store, but I'm a mortgage broker. How about you?"

"Oh, not much. I work downtown as a receptionist."

"That's cool," he said, looking at the menu for a minute. "Do you want to split something? I'm not too hungry."

They agreed on salads and garlic bread, and discussed how these set-up dates were mostly terrible but they both participated to please their family matriarchs. Talking for a while about the other kids in their classes, they traded gossip each had heard over the past few years. They stuck to light topics and skirted around anything uncomfortable about their past. Neither mentioned the awkward truth that, as classmates, they had both been alternately considered smart and dumb, depending on the time of day. They did not delve into how difficult it was for each of them to have split identities as American schoolkids and Chinese schoolkids, nor did they talk about how their self-esteem had risen and fallen several times per day back then, as they'd ridden a wobbly teeter-totter that had tried to balance Chinese and American expectations.

After dinner Franklin suggested getting gelato down the street. They strolled down upper Grant and browsed through the display windows. They looked in a record store and stopped in front of a vintage clothing boutique.

"Don has pants just like those," Franklin said absentmindedly as they passed one designer shop.

"Who's Don?" she asked, not recognizing that as a name of any of their former classmates.

"He's my boyfriend," Franklin said, giving her a quick nod. He looked at her for a second, and then added, "Yeah, we've been together more than a year now."

She was unfazed by his gayness, but she wondered if she should warn him that "Don" was in her pantheon of Asian Hoarder names.

They procured their frozen confections and stood on the steps of Saints Peter and Paul's Church to say their good-byes.

"Hey, I'm glad it was you tonight, Lindsey. At least we had stuff to talk about."

"Yeah, me too," she said, and with a friendly hug they went their separate ways.

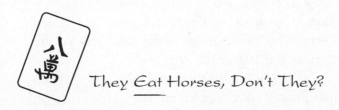

They Eat Horses, Don't They?

N either Mrs. Owyang nor her sisters ever wanted to go to China. None of them had any interest in experiencing China's pain and trauma firsthand, even though Pau Pau and Gung Gung had seldom revealed any details of their struggles. The idea that China was filled with suffering was an unspoken truth that floated like a mist in the air. It had settled and stiffened into a transparent mask on Pau Pau's face, like a sticky film that could never be washed off.

Everyone in the family made a big deal out of what a wealth of knowledge Lindsey would gain on this trip. It was not a cultural treasure trove any of them personally cared to attain for themselves, but somehow they were positive it would be a great road of discovery for her. The only person who had anything bad to say was Auntie Vivien. "Uncle Donald and I went to Guangzhou to get Cammie," she said. "They were so disorganized there, I had to wait three days to see her, and her blanket was filthy. So *backward* over there!"

Lindsey had done little traveling, and her own attitude

about the trip was nonchalant. She saw this journey as neither a vacation nor a chore, and her indifference was a
marked contrast to even her boss's enthusiasm.

"You'll have a wonderful time!" Howard exclaimed
when she went by his office to give him the name of the
temp who would be filling in for her.

"What a once-in-a-lifetime experience," he said. "When
you come back, you'll have to give me the inside story on
the *real* China, okay?"

She didn't know if there was a fake China, but she just
nodded her head.

Walking from Howard's office, she decided to stop by
Michael's desk. Her anger and doubts had dissipated, and
she wanted to make up with him before leaving the next
morning. She braced herself as she approached his door but
was disappointed to find the desk empty. He had already
left for the day. Now she wasn't sure what to do. She knew
she still liked him.

At home she distracted herself by jam-packing her suitcase with trendy outfits. She measured out small amounts
of all her toiletries into plastic, ounce-sized bottles and
packed them into her carry-on luggage. For the rest of the
evening she relaxed in front of the television, watching appraisers as they examined a Lalique decanter set, a Civil
War–era rifle, and a pair of Ch'ien Lung vases. She did
nothing else to prepare for her trip, figuring it would be
pretty much the same as when she'd gone to the Chinese
pavilion at Epcot Center in Walt Disney World.

About two hours into the flight, she realized that she
would be sitting in her plane seat for at least twelve more

hours. It slowly began to dawn on her that she was going really far away. Pau Pau was snoring softly.

After Lindsey fell asleep and woke up several times, she ate three meals and read four magazines, but the flight dragged on. The lights were dimmed now, so wherever they were flying above, it must have been nighttime. Pau Pau was now awake.

"We going to see my auntie's son," she said. Lindsey was groggy with airplane head, so she barely heard her grandmother.

"We go to Beijing to see her, and I show you some sightseeing." Pau Pau often mixed up "him" and "her," but Lindsey knew what she meant.

She sat up in her butt-numbing, matted-down foam airplane seat and pushed herself up by leaning against the aluminum armrests.

"Pau Pau?"

"Eh?"

"When did you leave China to come to the U.S.?"

Her grandmother feigned sleep. "During war," she answered, with her eyes still shut.

"World War II?" Lindsey asked.

She received merely an affirmative nod.

"Where were you born?" she asked, deciding to start from the beginning. She figured that Pau Pau was trapped on this plane with nothing to do except answer questions.

Pau Pau opened her eyes to find her granddaughter looking attentively at her. She, too, seemed to realize that now was as good a time as any to tell Lindsey what she had been angling for months to hear.

"I was born in Shanghai, but my father die when I was

very small. My grandfather had a tea factory, but we very poor. China very poor!"

Lindsey nodded and kept her mouth shut, hoping Pau Pau would keep talking.

"My mother remarry to old rich man who eat plum all day. He not know she marry before. I was secret, see? I live with grandparents, but my ma live in big house with old rich man. He own big store, like Emporium."

"So, did you ever see your mother?"

Pau Pau closed her eyes again. "After while, she told the old man she had friend who had daughter who need job as servant. So I went to live in big house, but she could not say I was daughter. So I was servant. "

Pau Pau spoke her sentences matter-of-factly.

"I go to school, come home and do chore. Old man say I have big feet, say, 'Like your ma, eh?' He laugh like, how you say, buff-oon? But he not know my ma is his wife, and her feet like lotus." Pau Pau held out her thumb and index finger a few inches apart to illustrate how small her mother's feet were.

Lindsey searched her mind for ways to keep the conversation going, but Pau Pau said, "No matter, no matter. When Japanese come, bomb everything! Kill so many people. Make me sick. Bomb everything."

Just then, the seat-belt light came on and an announcement about turbulence broke the mood of their conversation. Pau Pau closed her eyes and stopped talking.

They arrived in Beijing around 3 A.M. Lindsey was half-asleep as they disembarked from their plane and, although she should have been helping her grandmother, she reverted back to childhood and blindly followed Pau Pau through the baggage claim and customs.

She awoke in the hotel room the next morning, vaguely remembering the bus they'd taken in the middle of the night. Even though she had already slept in the twin bed, she did a quick scan now for mites or general lack of cleanliness. She decided it was all right, except the blankets felt thin and cheap.

Pau Pau's bed was already made, and she sat at a small table, pouring boiled water into a paper cup.

"I'm hungry," Lindsey complained. She knew she sounded whiny, but she was too cranky to reform her behavior just now.

"Don't drink from sink here," Pau Pau explained. "Brush teeth with this," she said as she handed Lindsey the cup of boiled water. Lindsey took the cup into the not-so-clean bathroom and washed up, annoyed further by a trickling shower that did not get hot enough and, even worse, blasted spurts of freezing water at random.

As she pulled her bra on, she tried to remember the things she had packed in her suitcase so she could figure out what she wanted to wear. She selected a blue sequined sweater with plaid pants. She pinched the midget toe in hasty greeting before thrusting it and its nine little friends into a pair of chartreuse socks.

Pau Pau went down to the hotel lobby and brought back breakfast, which consisted of a runny, dishwater-looking gruel with a stale, soggy bit of fried bread.

"What is that?" Lindsey asked, with a look of minor disgust.

"It's *jook*, eat."

Lindsey peered at the bowl. *Jook* as she knew it was a delicious, creamy, and thick rice porridge made with leftover chicken or turkey stock. At the least, it was a simple white-rice-and-water remedy to be eaten when one was ill. The concoction in front of her now, with its mysterious brown flecks, resembled something that would most definitely cause an upset stomach rather than relieve one.

"I'm not eating that. Don't they have scrambled eggs here?" Lindsey asked, already knowing that Pau Pau would have gotten her an American breakfast if one had been available.

"No scramble egg. Only *jook*," Pau Pau explained patiently. She pulled a plastic jar of malted Ovaltine out of her suitcase and mixed a heaping spoonful with boiled water. She handed it to Lindsey with a few Pepperidge Farm butter cookies she had stashed in her bag. "*Ho sik*, eh? I know you like."

Lindsey accepted the hot drink and nodded her head. She was grateful and was starting to have a slight inkling that this trip might not be so easy.

"We early one day. Sightsee today, go visit Auntie's son tomorrow." Pau Pau gestured for Lindsey to hurry up.

Down in the lobby, Lindsey looked through the glass door to her first daylight in Beijing. Her eyes were still tired due to the early hour, and she squinted at the cold yellow sunlight that was illuminating the concrete outside. A few hotel employees were watching her with expressionless faces. When she looked away and then back again several times, the men stood motionless, surveying her. She was too familiar with the fact that Chinese people never averted their eyes to be polite. For some reason she felt compelled to speak very loudly in English.

"Are you ready to go?" she yelled over to Pau Pau, who was conversing with a concierge.

Pau Pau came over and clutched her by the elbow in that decisive, grandma kind of way. She held her arm as they walked, and meanwhile, other Chinese men and women in bland outfits strained their necks to look at Lindsey like she was some sort of movie star.

They climbed onto one of the hotel's chartered buses and sat in silence for a few minutes, waiting for other tourists, mostly other Chinese, to fill up the seats so the coach could get going.

Pau Pau glanced over to her granddaughter.

"*Ai-ya*, why you wear this?" she asked, suddenly observing Lindsey's outfit for the first time. She slapped at the rhinestone and glitter fringe on her granddaughter's shoulder bag.

"Auntie Vivien gave it to me," Lindsey said, as if the fact that Pau Pau's own daughter had given it to her would somehow make it acceptable.

"Why you get dressed up here? No one know you, you don't know no one."

It hadn't occurred to Lindsey that she was dressed up at all. But as she looked out the bus window, she did notice that the people of Beijing looked rather dowdy.

The bus made the rounds to several other hotels before continuing on the route that would lead them to the Great Wall. In addition to the Chinese nationals and a handful of middle-aged Chinese-Americans, one German couple and one older French-Canadian couple joined the tour bus.

Lindsey definitely felt a part of the Chinese majority, with the two Anglo couples visually sticking out like sore thumbs. She did not understand the Mandarin chatter that was drifting down the aisle, but she easily translated the

French conversation a few rows back. She eavesdropped as the French-Canadians discussed how they were dissatisfied with their shower but were glad they'd remembered the extra film cannisters, which were good for holding travel-size amounts of Nivea hand lotion.

With twists and turns, and exhaust fumes permeating the coach's interior, the bus ride was fairly nauseating. Lindsey was glad she hadn't consumed that watery, gray *jook*. She listened to David Bowie's "China Girl" on her Sony Discman until she noticed that her grandmother was staring into space and might be interested in talking some more. Lindsey took off her headset and asked, "Pau Pau, how did you meet Gung Gung?"

The old woman shifted in her seat and fished a few Tootsie Rolls out of her purse. She handed the candy to Lindsey and thought for a long moment before saying anything.

"I have some girlfriend, very rich. Their family own business on Nanking Road, the best in Shanghai. We go to dance, I borrow nice dress from them, they very nice to me. We style our hair wavy, see? Very popular 1930 style."

Lindsey nodded.

"My friend say I prettiest of all, but how can? I poor. Just borrow dress, borrow nice purse, *hai-la* . . ." Pau Pau shrugged.

"One time we all stand there at dance, wait for someone to ask us. I see your Gung Gung. He walk like American, talk and laugh loud like American. I say, 'How can be Chinese?' He walk up to me and my three girlfriend, and guess who he ask to dance?"

Lindsey saw her grandmother's eyes light up and her lips spread into a proud smile.

"I see him lots time after that. We go to dance together, many time. But my ma . . ." Pau Pau shook her head. "My ma don't like Gung Gung. She say he too flashy. Call him white devil in Chinese clothing."

Lindsey couldn't wait to hear more, but just then the bus slowed down to pull into a rest area.

Pau Pau had signed them up for a package deal that included a luncheon before arriving at their final destination. The busload of passengers filed into the restaurant and crammed around three big round tables, drinking tea and warm Coca-Colas until the pre-ordered lunch arrived. Lindsey noticed that the tablecloth was stained. No one mingled much, and she and Pau Pau kept to themselves. She felt inclined to speak French to the couple she had overheard, but she figured Pau Pau might think she was making a spectacle of herself.

When the food arrived, she scanned the lazy Susan for dishes she might want. But the more she searched, the more she found that she didn't recognize anything. The mushy-looking brown goo bore no resemblance to the various dishes of mushy brown goo she was familiar with back home. A couple of selections looked vaguely like seafood but lacked discernible parts that could be verified as either animal or vegetable. A bowl of sautéed beef, upon closer inspection, was not beef at all but tiny severed duck tongues.

Lindsey was having another *Temple of Doom* moment. She didn't want to stick around and discover chilled monkey brains for dessert.

"What's wrong?" Pau Pau gestured with her chopsticks to the bowl of duck tongues and said, "Is delicacy!"

Lindsey nodded and ate some plain white rice.

The others at the table seemed to get along just fine, but she was almost convinced that this whole meal was a joke on tourists. She tasted small portions of certain dishes, but only after she watched Pau Pau eat them first. She noticed a platter with a whole fish, and that seemed safe to eat because it still maintained the shape of the original animal, but the "sauce" of oily sweet-and-sour red gelatin tasted slightly rancid, and the fried batter was spongy.

Once the bus arrived at the Great Wall, the passengers followed their guide, who held up a big orange megaphone and navigated the group through a maze of buses and tourists. As Lindsey jostled through the crowd, she felt like she was at Fisherman's Wharf in San Francisco.

On the plane she had read that the Great Wall of China was the only man-made thing visible from the moon. She had wondered if, upon first glance at the majestic monument, she'd be struck with instantaneous cultural enlightenment. Pushing through the tourists, she held the railing and climbed the steep steps and looked at the sweeping view of the enormous structure, which wound up through the dark green hills like a gargantuan serpent. She could barely believe that the Great Wall had been built over two thousand years ago, and she pondered the manpower it had required to build. Regarding any epiphanies about Chinese culture, however, no lightning bolts were going off in her head. She needed a Diet Coke.

They hiked up and down through crumbling walls and archways. Sightseers snapped through rolls of film as they oohed and aahed and captured perfect Kodak moments. Back near the buses, Lindsey perused the available sou-

venirs, impressed to find that one's portrait could be su-
perimposed on a porcelain plate with the image of the
Great Wall in the background. Plastic caps and Frisbees
with slashing, eighties-style letters read "Great Wau,
China." She spotted a bunch of bamboo sticks painted
with, "My godparents went to the Great Wau of China and
all I got was this lousy backscratcher."

That night she was so exhausted from the combination
jet lag, bus lag, and weird brown goo-lag that she took a
drippy, cold-spurt shower and went right to bed.

In the morning, Pau Pau went downstairs to the lobby
to figure out what local bus route would transport them to
her cousin's apartment. As Lindsey rubbed the sleep from
her eyes, she looked out at the concrete courtyard and
thought about the Russian stories she had read on prison-
ers of war. She thought briefly about Michael Cartier, and
wondered if maybe she should send him a postcard. She
wrote one to her parents instead.

She decided to skip wearing mascara and lipstick. She
supposed Pau Pau was right—she didn't know any of these
people, so who cared? Even with these makeup adjustments, she made sure to tease her hair up in the front.
Under no circumstances could she tolerate flat hair.

Pau Pau soon returned, and the two of them went out
wrapped in layers of clothing and jackets. The air was polluted with coal dust, and even the leaves of trees were
coated beneath layers of gray soot. They walked for a long
time through the chaotic city streets, dodging bicycles and
pedestrians rushing every which way, until they finally came
to a corner where they waited for a city bus. Despite the
downsized maquillage, Lindsey continued to attract intense

stares from the local Chinese as she stumbled along, trying to keep up with Pau Pau's fast pace.

The bus was dilapidated and had no cushioned seats, heat, or working windows. The side panels were scrawled with graffiti in Chinese characters. The passengers looked especially drab and crabby, their faces distorted by down-turned carp mouths and austere expressions. Lindsey looked around and thought that today, without her lipstick, she blended in a bit. Little did she know that every single person on this bus could instantly tell she was an American-born Chinese by her mannerisms, her posture, and the eager-to-please dopiness about her.

She felt good sitting there next to Pau Pau, and knew the two of them were sharing something special. She eagerly anticipated meeting Pau Pau's cousin and saw herself as an ambassador from the United States, representing the good life that Pau Pau had now.

"You know," Pau Pau said, suddenly breaking Lindsey's fantasy that she was an American icon, "your mommy almost died, long time ago . . ." She trailed off and left Lindsey hanging.

"What?" Lindsey jerked up at the same time the bus gave a lurch.

"My ma don't like Gung Gung but I marry anyway. Gung Gung work for newspaper that say bad things about Japan, so we have to leave for village so they don't catch him. Gung Gung tell my ma to leave Shanghai before too late. Japanese coming, he say. But no use. My ma have nice house, why leave? When Japanese bomb come, kill her, kill her husband. But Gung Gung and me already flee to village. We have your mommy, we on boat, but we have nothing to eat. We floating, pack like sardine. No wind to blow boat, see? We have no food, so I have no milk. I only have little bit of cookie to give her. She eat only cookie, like you."

At this last comment, Lindsey stopped stuffing her face with the rest of the Pepperidge Farm Mint Milanos. She decided to ration them for later.

"My father dead, and now my mother dead," Pau Pau said softly. Lindsey looked away.

After many more blocks, Pau Pau tugged at Lindsey's sleeve to signal that their stop was coming up. They were in a section of town that was dominated by concrete, institutional-looking structures. This place was not what Lindsey had thought it would be. Where were the enchanting pagodas, the beautiful courtyards with ruby-throated finches in bamboo birdcages? She had anticipated peaceful neighborhoods with lots of trees and ceramic tiled roofs, but these buildings looked like neglected government housing. She wondered if they might get mugged.

They climbed a littered, open-air stairwell, and Lindsey thought of the Ping Yuen projects back home in Chinatown. When they were kids, Franklin Ng briefly lived there and used to call it the Ping. He once told her he had seen ghosts dressed in old-style costumes floating through the walls. Now, here in Beijing, Lindsey remembered that story and got a little wigged out. As she and Pau Pau rang the buzzer on one of the doors, she didn't know what they might encounter.

A disheveled man in his late sixties wearing a very thin, short-sleeved shirt yanked open the security gate, shaking it on its shoddy hinges. He and Pau Pau greeted each other less warmly than one might expect. He was obviously the cousin, but if Lindsey was greeting her cousin after such a long absence, she probably would have at least hugged him. Maybe it was a Chinese thing.

He led them into the unkempt apartment. Junk was piled around everywhere—newspapers, cardboard boxes, and sacks full of plastic scraps. Lindsey wondered what kind of work he did, if any.

Pau Pau instructed her to hand over the shopping bag of stuff they had brought as gifts: See's candies, cartons of Marlboros, and clothing specifically labeled Made in the U.S.A. Pau Pau and the cousin talked in a serious kind of medium-level yelling, while Lindsey stood and looked at the ground. She had hoped for fragrant tea, perhaps offered on a sandalwood tray, but instead she sat on a ripped, dirty yellow couch as Pau Pau and the cousin retreated to another room, leaving her alone for what seemed like a long while.

Sitting there, she imagined hidden cockroaches watching her. In her head, she told God she wasn't psychologically equipped to deal with floating phantoms of any kind, and to further distract herself, she tried to think of happy things like marshmallow Peeps at Eastertime or her first pet guinea pig, Eddie Van Owyang.

She applied Purell on her hands and counted the Handi Wipes in her bag. She was relieved when Pau Pau came back into the room and gestured for her to get up and follow her out the door. Lindsey hauled herself up, which was no easy maneuver with her fourteen layers of clothing, and she barely said good-bye to the cousin, who nodded and casually stuffed a big wad of hundred-dollar bills into his pants pocket.

Out on the sidewalk, Pau Pau said, "Sheesh, all they want is money!"

Lindsey ran to keep up. She had anticipated a magical re-union with flowing tears, emotional embraces, and symbolic something or other, just like in a Steven Spielberg movie. But, instead, they were sitting on a grimy bus and Pau Pau was pissed off. Lindsey removed a moist towelette from her purse and disinfected her hands for the fifth time that morning.

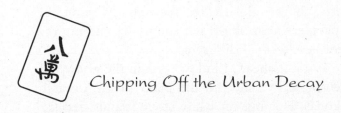

Chipping Off the Urban Decay

Located in the west suburbs of Beijing, the Summer Palace used to be the imperial garden of the Qing Dynasty. Lindsey hadn't planned on liking it much—it was another long and nauseating bus ride.

Out the bus window, she watched the tall, craggy cliffs that resembled Godzilla's shoulders, as if he were sleeping on the hillside. Fog and mist clung like skeins of white cotton candy to dark, rain-saturated bushes. She stared at the huge boulders jutting sharply like hatchets into the air from the valleys below, and she took in the serene beauty of the jade-colored rice paddies built in steps on the mountainside.

Once they arrived at the Summer Palace, Lindsey realized that here were the pagodas, gazebos, and gardens that she had recognized from all the export porcelains, chinoiserie cabinets, and toile de Jouy upholstery she had seen in decor magazines. But it wasn't just a showcase diorama at Walt Disney World, it was China. *Real* China, as her boss might say.

The palace and gardens occupied about seven hundred acres, most of which was water. Despite the throngs of other tourists, she could visualize the paths without the swarms of people. She took off her sunglasses and noticed that the light here seemed different.

With Pau Pau just ahead, Lindsey took in the glassy, still water, which perfectly reflected the many-tiered, ornately painted pagodas. Floating on white stone islands, red lacquered pavilions rose above black waters with lily pads that seemed to float atop like soft, lime-colored snowflakes.

Everywhere the colors were different from California. Milky transparent greens and periwinkle-saturated light contrasted against the metallic bronze beasts with horns and scales, sharp claws, and ferocious faces, guarding the palace gates.

She stepped into a mythical garden. Native foliage rose up in spires from the waters and hung from above like cascades of dry, green feathers. The tranquil sky blended effortlessly into the ancient waters. Bright grasses in the distance looked strangely new against the liquid dream lakes that were completely still. The water seemed determined not to ripple as long as any human gazed at it.

The rustling, round leaves and the swaying spears hanging down were so densely comingled that Lindsey could not tell where one type of tree ended and another began. She saw radiant branches but could not tell where they attached, like extended limbs reaching out in a bustling crowd. It was lightly raining now, and through these mysterious Chinese trees the wind seemed to move differently. It carried a foreign but familiar fragrance.

The scent was one of moisture on stone. It was a taste in

the mouth, like dirt and bone, fresh air and rare flowers that bloomed only once before dying; the flavor was like mud and bark mixed with fennel, eucalyptus mixed with paint made from milk. The aromas gave Lindsey a feeling from childhood, but also a feeling of growing older. She thought of glossy gardenia petals crushed between two blackened bricks, and she was suddenly aware of her skeleton.

As Pau Pau shuffled nearby, she observed the scenery silently. In the distance, layer upon layer of faintly lavender mountains became paler and paler until they dissolved into the high azure-gray sky. Temples of painted wood and stone were half-hidden within dark scrubby hills, decorated ornately with carved beams of dragon tails and faces wrapping around geometric balconies. The onyx bricks with white mortar looked charred and dusty compared with the shiny, smooth glaze of the curved rooftiles that jutted out like stacked firecrackers.

The Jade Belt Bridge rose out of the water as a pristine, gleaming white structure notched with die-cut precision. A majestic marble boat with a two-story balcony floated, resembling a Viking or Mayan vessel. The people inside, even in their plain peasant clothes, appeared too modern under the exquisite roof, which looked like tarnished, woven silver.

Pau Pau offered her granddaughter an Oreo cookie from her bag, and Lindsey took it. They gazed together at the turquoise and red boats on Kunming Lake.

"After we leave Shanghai, we try to go to village, because otherwise nothing to eat," Pau Pau said, continuing the story of her exodus with Gung Gung. "Many days we stay on Pearl River, no wind to carry. We have no shoes, Gung Gung and me, and Lillian so sick, almost dying. There were nine boats, and I saw with my own eye, all other boat get robbed one by one. I was so scare! But my boat is number nine and we very lucky. My boat has one woman, birth baby boy, right there, get born on boat and whoosh! Wind comes and blow our boat away. That boy was good luck lifesaver!"

Lindsey nodded and let Pau Pau continue.

"We arrive safe in Toisan, but you know you cannot eat too fast at first?"

Following Pau Pau's choppy, non-sequitur style of story-telling was a challenge, but Lindsey listened carefully.

"I have no milk for baby. We need medicine, but have no money. We very lucky Gung Gung have gold watchband. Sold it and buy medicine. Your mommy so weak! Not even moving. When we get medicine, I don't know what kind, she start to wiggle. Then I able feed her. We wash clothes, eat rice, just little bit meat, teeny-weeny bit. But then, *ai-ya*, I find out Gung Gung have other family in village!"

Lindsey's eyes got wider as Pau Pau continued her story, while they strolled down to the Cloud Dispelling Gate and the Pavilion of the Fragrance of Buddha.

"I say, 'How can?' but see, he agree to marry other girl only for false document. Old man in village come and say to Gung Gung, 'Not look good you come here with Shanghai city girl and new baby.' But Gung Gung say, 'I only marry your daughter so your grandson can go to U.S. with fake paper.' But still they don't like me, so I move with your ma to outskirt of village."

Lindsey hadn't known her grandfather had been married

before. She felt a displaced kind of anger and wasn't sure how to react, hearing these details all for the first time. She had only known Gung Gung and Pau Pau as her grandparents, and this story from the past was hard to superimpose onto the limited memories and images she had of them.

"Gung Gung went to Chungking to look for work, leave me outside village. He went to American embassy to ask for help as refugee, and he explain he went George Washington University, had degree in foreign service. At embassy, U.S. government decide to hire him. You know why? Because he know perfect English, and speak five Chinese dialect. He send me money to go Chungking and meet him, but I cannot leave village yet. I have so many illness! I get malaria. You know, from mosquito? Then I have one kind, what you call? Like snake. Body get hard and you cannot move. Gung Gung's friend's wife, she come to help me. She said to cure this kind of illness, then I must burn your hand, burn your middle, you see, like burn snake's head, middle, and tail. So I let her. She take stick on fire and burn me three times."

Lindsey had no idea what Pau Pau was talking about. She had never heard of any disease like that but knew better than to be contradictory.

After a while she asked, "So then what happened?"

"Finally I take boat to Chungking with your mommy. Boat has big holes, and I can see water underneath floor. I tie strip of cloth on Lillian so she not fall in. You can fall in and die! And I cannot swim, gee whiz!" She shook her head in exasperation. "I almost die so many times!"

That was all that Pau Pau said for the remainder of their time at the Summer Palace. They hiked around some more and eventually met the rest of the group back at the bus at the designated time. Pau Pau smoked a cigarette, and then they took their seats and settled in for the long ride back to their hotel.

They arrived in Guangzhou the next day around midafternoon. After navigating their way through the bustling airport, they took a shuttle to their hotel and ate a decent meal at a small nearby restaurant. Lindsey was relieved when the waiter brought over a plate of recognizable chicken with some kind of sour melon that she just picked around. As they ate, Pau Pau explained that they would rest that night, and the next morning they were going to take a bus to Toisan village. It was only about a hundred miles away, but the roads were reportedly so bad that it would take about four hours to get there.

They chewed in silence for a while. Lindsey hadn't figured that traveling was going to be so difficult. No one had told her there would be no Snickers bars in China. Every meal here was unlike the Chinese food at home. She hated squash, which was practically the only vegetable available, and the meat always had a too-hard or too-soft texture, like it had been cooked in wax or came from an animal she wouldn't want to imagine. And she was so tired, all the time. Thank God Pau Pau was here to wake her up and prepare her Ovaltine and cookie breakfasts.

Nonetheless, she was making adjustments. If anyone had told her a week before that she would be going completely without makeup after a few days in China, she would have balked. She loved her Lancôme lipstick, her Princess Marcella Borghese blush, and, of course, her Great Lash mascara. But now she wore nothing on her face except sun-screen. And her hair was flat. She didn't really care any-more, she just pulled it back in a ponytail because it was easier.

The next morning, not wanting to look too flashy in Toisan, Lindsey planned to wear a plain white long-sleeved shirt and jeans. She wanted to be respectful after hearing Pau Pau's stories. As she organized her toiletries, she wondered what was taking Pau Pau so long in the lobby.

She had just finished massaging moisturizer into her cuticles when Pau Pau came in. She sat down on one of the twin beds, looking troubled.

"Are you okay?" Lindsey asked, figuring that her grand-mother was fatigued.

"I call on telephone to your ma. She say Yee Sook pass away."

"Who?"

"Uncle Bill! He pass away." Pau Pau got up and paced the carpet. "Change of plans. We go Toisan today, but leave tomorrow."

Lindsey spent the first part of the bus ride chipping off her Urban Decay nail enamel. Metallic dark purple nail polish just didn't seem appropriate for a visit to an impoverished village. Pau Pau sifted through a giant Macy's bag stuffed with gifts, full of the same kind of things they had brought to the cousin in Beijing.

Outside, the bus passed brown dirt fields and a muddy river. Along the route every now and then they could see a peasant crouched down by the water, washing laundry. Skinny men with cigarettes dangling from their mouths tended to the long wooden boats that were huddled in small groups along the riverbanks. Some inhabitants rode carts pulled by decrepit horses, others tinkered with the saggy chains and dented fenders of their bicycles.

At a rest stop, dark-skinned country people sold clothing they had made, along with purses sewn of burlap and colored strips of cotton cloth. The bathroom consisted of four concrete walls. There were no doors on the stalls, no tissue, and no toilets, just holes in the ground. Lindsey held her breath and went in. She pinched her nose to avoid the stench but also tried to keep her mouth shut because of the numerous flies. Straddling the pit, she was glad she wasn't wearing the satin platforms she had had the good sense to leave in San Francisco. She finished peeing and wanted to sprint out as fast as she could, but she had to be careful because the dirt floor was wet and muddy with urine.

Back on the bus, Pau Pau pointed out the window to a sunburned woman carrying a big woven basket of hay. "See, I tell you not to go out in sun. Look like your ancestor work in fields." Lindsey nodded, having been told a hundred times of the importance of a refined, fair complexion.

When they arrived in Toisan, children ran up to the bus and hurled dirt clods. They laughed and ran away when the visitors gazed out the windows at them. While the bus parked, a few passengers waved as adult villagers stood and watched with curiosity.

In the village, the thick gray walls of dank, crumbling buildings were stained with moisture that penetrated cracks between the worn bricks. The paved pathways were interrupted periodically by a leafless tree with branches resembling shriveled, black hairs. Birds were nesting somewhere, but Lindsey could not see them. She heard periodic chirping that suggested that life was business as usual for the winged creatures: find a twig, eat a bug, fly over there.

The overcast sky held a high dome of clouds, as well as a low, eerie fog that compressed the bone-chilling air closer to the ground. Slabs of raw slate bordered a small sturdy bridge, which was partially obscured by the wispy fronds of a willow tree that hung listlessly above. The trees, water, dirt, and rocks seemed to purposely remain motionless to prevent the sensation of the frosty, frozen air rustling against their surfaces.

A shabby billboard displayed advertisements for drinks and cosmetics drawn with cartoonish, Communist stylings. Blocky, Russian-looking letters accompanied smiling Chinese androids who shook hands. Their faces seemed to say, "Comrade! Stop your bicycle and share a refreshing brown beverage! We look exactly alike, except my shorts are red and your scarf faces the other direction. Oh, how content we are!"

Clusters of concrete and brick structures were the standard. A dwelling made of mud with a thatched roof was interspersed here and there. Wooden beams stretched across a few of the pitched rooftops, and bamboo poles tied with twine held up drying laundry.

Despite the cold, children ran around giggling, as chickens and other fowl scratched about. Mothers held their babies, and no one seemed to do much of anything. Pau Pau asked a young woman for directions.

Lindsey followed Pau Pau around a few corners and past

a makeshift playground with a slide made of stone. They passed a concrete slab where, unbeknownst to them, the modest dwelling where Gung Gung had been born once stood years ago. Also gone were the flimsy wooden structures that had housed Uncle Bill's family decades ago. Now the area was used as a public space. Someone had laid out rounded forms of woven straw that would later be bent into large baskets.

They came to a doorway, and Pau Pau called inside. A teenage girl replied, running out and speaking so rapidly in Toisanese that even Pau Pau had trouble understanding. Another girl came out to join them, and soon everyone was chatting excitedly except Lindsey. Pau Pau gestured to her granddaughter, and the two teenagers hugged her and patted her arm with affection. Lindsey handed them the gifts from the bag one by one, and with each box of candy or piece of American clothing, they brought their hands to their cheeks with genuine surprise.

She liked both girls immediately for their unaffected ways. Pau Pau explained to Lindsey that they were the granddaughters of the woman who had taken care of her when she'd had malaria. Knowing who they were made Lindsey feel grateful.

Although their grandmother had passed away, they said that their mother would be back soon. Pau Pau asked after any person she could think of who might remember Uncle Bill, but the girls did not seem to know any of the Chinese names.

As Pau Pau and the girls chatted, Lindsey looked around. The place was made of whitewashed bricks, and the kitchen was equipped with wooden bowls and some enamel and aluminum dishes. Heating up water for tea, one of the girls used fistfuls of straw to kindle a fire beneath the stovetop.

After a while, the girls' parents rushed in, having heard that their visitors had arrived. They all talked fast, loudly, and jovially. Lindsey stood and smiled, happy that Pau Pau seemed happy.

Just then she saw something she did not expect. Her eyes drifted toward the wall behind the older girl, and something familiar caught her eye. She blinked several times to make sure she was seeing correctly. On the ledge next to a small bundle of joss sticks was a snapshot of Lindsey from the fourth grade. She was wearing her soccer uniform and was standing outside Winchell's Donut House on Van Ness Avenue.

The older girl noticed her squinting over her shoulder. Plucking the picture from the ledge, she stepped back and gestured for Lindsey to follow. She chatted in Toisanese as she proceeded toward an adjacent wall.

Lindsey was dumbfounded. She stood there on the dirt floor and just stared. On the crumbling cement wall she saw a collage made of many Scotch-taped, grade-school photographs. And every single one was a photo of her.

She recognized her kindergarten snapshot with her hair sticking up in the back, her first-grade photo with the missing front tooth, and every school picture all the way through high school. There was a Polaroid of her dressed for Halloween as the Chicken of the Sea mermaid, and a snapshot of her and Kevin as kids in front of the old Hippo's hamburger restaurant. She realized that Pau Pau must have been sending these pictures to Toisan during all these years.

Everyone came over to look at the pictures. They talked excitedly, and Pau Pau said in English, "See! They all know who you are! I write them everything!" Lindsey was so overwhelmed that she felt like bursting into tears, but everyone else was so happy that she forced a smile. She gave her eyes a rough swipe with her sleeve when she thought no one was looking.

She felt a sense of awe around these sincere, openhearted people, who seemed oblivious to the fact that they had nothing. She followed out the doorway as they all traipsed through the village in search of Uncle Bill's grandniece.

Behind a separate cluster of low, crude buildings, they found the grandniece scrubbing pots by the common washing area. After initial explanations, everyone retreated back to the first house, where they had more tea. Pau Pau, her Toisanese a little rusty, talked slowly and listened carefully to decipher the thick village accents.

Lindsey sat quietly, remembering Pau Pau's stories of the last few days. She looked at her now, sitting on a stool in this village where she had so much history, and she thought of the malaria, and the mysterious "snake" illness, and how these girls' grandmother had helped Pau Pau survive. She thought of her mother as a baby almost dying in this same village, so many years ago.

When it came time to leave, she gave each person a hug and felt, for the first time, exasperated that she could not speak Chinese. She felt cheated that she was not able to express her feelings to these people, to say how happy she was to have met them. When she'd left the hotel that morning, she'd had no idea that she would be meeting people who had watched her progress since she was a baby. Why hadn't

Pau Pau told her anything before? Her good-byes seemed feeble.

Pau Pau delivered the bad news about Uncle Bill. She distributed some money, and soon after, she and Lindsey were alone, walking the short distance back to the bus.

"Your Gung Gung was born here," she said as they strolled along. "So different now, not so many mud house," she added, making casual observations. Lindsey wondered what else Pau Pau might be remembering, but she let her grandmother keep her private memories to herself.

When they arrived at the bus, Lindsey climbed inside right away. Pau Pau stood outside smoking until all the other passengers trickled back and mounted the steps. She stubbed out her cigarette and was the last to board the bus before it revved its engine and carried them away from the past.

Early the next morning, after packing up her suitcase in the hotel, Lindsey prepared her own Ovaltine and fixed Pau Pau's tea. She had just gotten used to her travel routine, and now it seemed a shame that they were leaving so abruptly. She still hadn't completely absorbed all the things she had seen and heard (and smelled) in only one week. She felt as though she had read just the first page of a thousand-page history book, and even this single page was difficult to translate and digest.

After checking out of the hotel and riding the shuttle to the airport, they finally settled into their airplane seats. She had become accustomed to drinking warm sodas, so when she ordered a 7 UP from the flight attendant, she was shocked to find it refrigerated, and with ice. A week ago she never would have noticed such a detail, having expected all her life to receive a cold drink upon demand.

"You getting sick?" Pau Pau asked from her adjacent seat.

"No, I'm okay," Lindsey replied.

Pau Pau touched her cheek and said, "When we get home I make you *doong-gwa* soup again. Make you better." Satisfied, she turned around and closed her own eyes, intent on napping.

A few hours later Lindsey and Pau Pau were both awake, with ten more hours of flight time left. Lindsey asked, "What was Chungking like?"

Pau Pau sighed, then tried to eat a peanut but couldn't chew it, so she spit it out.

"In Chungking, life very good. Gung Gung getting paid good U.S. money, and we live on mountaintop surround by cloud. On other side mountain is Chiang Kai-shek Kuomintang headquarter. He move there from Nanking after Japan destroy, see?"

Lindsey nodded.

"Gung Gung move to U.S. army base in Kunming, but send money every month. I finally have time enjoy myself. I have one servant help take care of baby, and in evening, sedan chair come for me, take me to Nationalist government party. Thousand of step, up and down the Sichuan mountain, but I insist walk myself. Night breeze very nice, and four man carry sedan chair behind me. Dance every night in Chungking. Was best time."

Lindsey smiled, but then noticed Pau Pau's expression darken. Her grandmother's voice dropped down to a whisper. "One night was eclipse of moon. That night I wish I am anywhere but Chungking. I was asleep when I hear bomb begin. I wake up and grab Lillian. We crawl down beneath kitchen table, and I pull chair around us. Japanese bomb so loud! Chunk of wall break apart above my head and slam on top of table, smash rosewood chair. The ceiling shake, building next door complete destroy!

"Your ma still baby, and crying, crying. I don't know what to do, so loud. Bomb falling, I can hear wood and bamboo burning outside. I rock Lillian back and forth. I try to sing song to her Gung Gung teach me. I sing, 'Oh, Susanna, oh don't you cry for me . . .' I sing over and over, all night. Then I heard gong. It was early morning, but moon still like shadow. Chungking all gone, destroy. But your mommy and me, we alive."

Pau Pau tapped her fingernails on the plastic tray and poured herself some more 7 UP. Her face brightened and she said, "Finally we reunite Gung Gung in Kunming. I learn English from GIs, little by little, *siu siu*. I learn 'gee whiz,' and 'mess hall.' I play pink-ponk, and GI give me color cigarette and big heart fill with American chocolate. *Ho teem*! One day Gung Gung say we take boat to United State. Too dangerous stay, he say. My ma die in China so I know Gung Gung telling truth. We board great big boat! Nice one, American one. We eat very tasty food from can. That was first time I have best Virginia ham!"

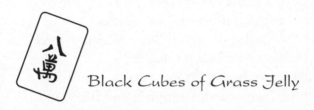

Black Cubes of Grass Jelly

indsey had missed the comfort of her own snuggly bed. She was just becoming aware of the cozy flannel pillowcase against her skin when she was roused by the voices of her mother and Pau Pau in the living room discussing Uncle Bill's passing and the logistics of his funeral arrangements. Apparently, in his room at On Lok, he had had a stroke in his sleep and slipped into a coma. He had quietly passed away at St. Francis Hospital.

Pau Pau and Mrs. Owyang then moved on to describe the cemetery plots the family had purchased years ago.

"We lucky," Lindsey heard Pau Pau say. "No place left to buy in Chinese section. I hear some have to bury in Russian cemetery. *Ai-ya!*"

Lindsey listened as the two older women described how Uncle Bill would be buried next to his wife, and how several other plots had been reserved for Pau Pau, Lillian, Lindsey's dad, Vivien, and Uncle Donald. From her bed, Lindsey heard these morbidly matter-of-fact details and felt sick. She wondered if, when the time came,

Auntie Shirley would have to fend for her own burial site.

Just then, she overheard her mother. "Shirley wants to be cremated and sprinkled in the Marin Headlands."

Pau Pau said, "Cremate no good! Since Vivien divorce, put Shirley there. No more Donald, *hai la*."

Lindsey rolled out of bed and took a quick shower. The convenience of her own soaps, shampoo, and hair conditioner struck her as extremely decadent after her week of skimping with travel-size toiletries. She appreciated the even-temperatured water and the softness of her own towels.

When she emerged, she helped herself to the pink box of assorted dim sum items that Pau Pau had bought earlier that morning in Chinatown. The greasy *hom gok* dumplings were familiar and comforting. In addition, her mother had brought over an assortment of Noah's bagels and spreads, and Lindsey helped herself to those as well. As she stuffed her face with a big gob of lowfat lox shmear, Pau Pau said, "Cold food no good! Gee whiz!"

Mrs. Owyang and Pau Pau continued to discuss the details of paying for the funeral service and organizing the meal afterward. The telephone rang several times, and Mrs. Owyang made many outgoing calls as well, to florists, her sisters, and other relatives.

"Lindsey, everyone else says they're too busy, so you're going to have to run errands," her mother said. "You still have time off from work, right? Here's a list of things and the addresses where you should go." She handed her daughter a scrap of paper with notes in the margins.

Lindsey was jet-lagged and hadn't even had coffee, but soon she found herself walking through Chinatown on a random weekday, as if she had never traveled to China at all. She passed all the same markets and stores she had visited a hundred times before, but she saw them slightly differently now.

She went to a florist on Waverly Place and purchased a black ribbon wreath to hang on the apartment door to signal that they had a death in the family. Next, she stopped at the bank to get crisp twenty- and fifty-dollar bills, which would be given as *lay-see* gifts to friends and relatives who sent condolences. She exchanged some bills for coins that she and her cousins would later place inside tiny red envelopes to dispense at the funeral.

Doubling back down Grant Avenue, she looked up Clay Street toward the window where she used to spend her days as a toddler. Her mom used to drop her off at the travel agency every morning before heading off to work. Clients came in and out, booking flights to Hong Kong, Vancouver, and other destinations. When Pau Pau or Gung Gung met with customers, she stayed in the back room, playing with the rotary-dial telephones or typing nonsensical words on the manual Underwood typewriter.

She recalled a Chinese funeral procession from those pre-kindergarten days. She had heard the dolorous horn section of the Green Street Mortuary band, and had run to the window to see the slow stream of uniformed musicians strolling at a mournful pace, playing dirges in their bright white hats.

"*Ai-ya!*" Pau Pau had screamed, whisking her away from the Levolor blinds before she could get a good look at the

Cadillac hearse topped with a large portrait of the deceased. Lindsey had wanted to see all the flowers draped on the big black car, but Pau Pau shooed her into a coat closet and locked her in there until the procession moved out of sight. Pau Pau said that the hovering ghost would see the lively girl, so full of life, and might snatch her away. After the funerary music could no longer be heard, Pau Pau let her out and took her across the street to Uncle's Cafe for grass-flavored gelatin and vanilla ice cream.

Lindsey now headed toward Pacific Street to a store called Supernatural Exquisite, where they sold the fake paper money. She walked through the aisles, past incense and a variety of portable altars with small statuettes of various gods. Lindsey read the words in the margins of her mother's note: cigarettes, cell phone, watch, shirts, and Nikes.

"What you need?" a young girl asked. Lindsey showed her the slip, and the girl rushed around the cramped shop, selecting different items and finally bringing them over to the counter.

"Here you go. Anything else?" the girl asked. Lindsey looked at the plastic packages. Each individually wrapped bundle contained a three-dimensional, colored-paper version of an item on the list: a cardboard cell phone, neatly creased fake shirts, cartons of phony cigarettes, a wrist-watch with digital numbers printed on the face, and a puffy pair of paper shoes with a big Nike swoosh. The cashier explained that all these items, in addition to the fake money, were to be burned so that the deceased would have these necessities in the afterlife. Lindsey wondered why Uncle

Bill would need Nikes and a cell phone, seeing as how, while still among the living, he'd had no concept of what these things were at all.

Last of her errands, she needed to buy tiny red envelopes for the coins and white envelopes to hold small pieces of candy. She stopped at several places before finding the items at the same store where Gung Gung's picture peeked out from under the calendar. She paused and gazed at her grandfather's image, and wondered whatever had happened to that dapper hat he always used to wear.

When Lindsey arrived home, Pau Pau was sitting at the kitchen table eating a bologna sandwich on Wonder bread. Between small bites she said, "I meet your boyfriend today. He very nice."

Lindsey was washing her hands at the sink, and, with the water running, she wasn't sure she had heard her grandmother right.

"What?" she asked, drying her hands on an apron.

"Your boyfriend very handsome. He bring this—not your birthday, so must be Valentine sweetheart." Pau Pau stood up and retrieved a largish red box, carefully wrapped and tied with a grosgrain ribbon.

"Who's it from? Franklin Ng?" Lindsey stared at the package, picked it up, and shook it.

"No, not Fanny Lee nephew!" Pau Pau said. "Your American boyfriend bring this one hour ago." She squirted some French's yellow mustard on her sandwich.

Lindsey whisked the package away to her bedroom. She unfolded the layers of crimson paper and found a note:

Dearest Girl Goddess,

Happy Belated Valentine's Day.
I've corrected the mess at work, and hope you like the
gift. Maybe we can use it together some Saturday
morning.
Please talk to me!

Michael

Digging through the bubble wrap, Lindsey clapped her hand to her mouth in disbelief.

It was something she had always wanted. She had gone to the specialized store many times to admire the pink plastic device, but she'd always been too embarrassed to ask a salesperson to show it to her. She had wondered if its electrical cord was long enough or if it was difficult to clean. How had Michael known she had secretly coveted it?

As she fingered the knob that offered various settings, she could not wait to use it with her favorite sourdough bread. Dropping a piece into the slot of electric coils, she'd watch the device as it imprinted Hello Kitty's face onto the bread with crispy perfection. The slice, with Kitty's head lightly toasted onto it like a holy image on the Shroud of Turin, would no doubt add scrumptious flair to her morning breakfast routine.

Gleefully, she placed the appliance back in its box and stashed it under her bed. She jogged back out to the kitchen to interrogate her grandmother.

She wondered if Pau Pau had offered Michael stinky soup or picked her teeth in front of him. Lindsey hoped

Pau Pau hadn't asked him to fix the garbage disposal or the leaky toilet.

"Were you nice to him?" she asked, worried.

Pau Pau responded with a low, rumbling fart. "I always nice! You think I country bum-kin?"

Lindsey chewed a fingernail. "So what did you think of him?"

"I told you! He ring bell and come in. Very polite, and nice face."

"You don't mind that he's not a grandson of your mahjong friends?" Lindsey sat at the table and fidgeted with the loaf of Wonder bread, nervously squeezing it until it was misshapen and squashed with her handprints.

"Gee whiz, be glad not Fanny Lee nephew. She big cheater," Pau Pau said, working a toothpick between her incisors.

"So . . . is it okay with you if Michael comes here, or I go out with him?" By now Lindsey had mangled the loaf into a piece of modern sculpture. She anxiously awaited Pau Pau's reply.

"Why ask me?" Pau Pau said, lighting a cigarette and blowing the smoke out a crack in the window. "Your life, not mine. My ma, she no like Gung Gung, but I am like you, no listen. Good *think*. Gung Gung bring me here, and I have nice life. Don't ask me."

Pau Pau shimmied the leftover bologna into a Ziploc bag and placed it in the refrigerator.

"We watch *Gunsmoke*, then we go, okay?"

She shuffled to the living room and left Lindsey alone in dumbfounded silence.

The Chinese Must Go

At the mortuary, Uncle Bill's body looked waxy, with over-rouged cheeks. White and yellow chrysanthemums were festooned with red ribbons painted with Chinese characters in silver ink, bearing the names of those who sent sympathies: the On Lok senior center, the Lions Club, various benevolent associations, and the Chinese Chamber of Commerce. One arrangement of stargazer lilies and carnations ingeniously displayed rows of fake mahjong tiles with the message, "In heaven you win every match."

Lindsey's mom poked her in the shoulder and asked, "Did someone remember to put a coin in his mouth?"

"What's that for?" Lindsey whispered.

"So he can pay his way to cross into the afterlife."

Lindsey shrugged and watched her cousins and aunties as they somberly filed between the pews. Pau Pau smoked a menthol in the corner behind a floral display and pretended she didn't understand English when the funeral director told her smoking wasn't allowed. When she was done, she stubbed her cigarette out on the carpet and sat in the aisle near Lindsey.

Soon after, an officiant from the mortuary stepped to the podium and made a wooden speech about salvation and the Holy Trinity. Lindsey picked the lint balls off her black sweater and pretended to care. Not that she wasn't sad about Uncle Bill. She was. It's just that she knew Uncle Bill had been Buddhist, and this talk about the Holy Trinity was about as relevant to his life as cell phones and Nikes.

Pau Pau had brought along the same giant Christmas tin she'd used at Gung Gung's grave, and when it came time to burn the paper items, she unceremoniously clunked the container on top of the coffin and dumped everything inside. An old Chinese man set the whole lot on fire with his Zippo lighter.

Mourners approached the casket and tossed wads of fake dollar bills into the smoldering pile. Since Pau Pau hadn't bothered to remove the plastic wrap from the paper Rolex and cardboard cell phone, an awful burned chemical smell filled the mortuary as the flames leaped three feet above the deceased's head. Lindsey and her cousins watched at first with curiosity, amusement, and then panic as an overhead banner caught fire and lifted through the air. It floated up to the rafters as people gasped, but then it spiraled down in wispy, crumpled cinders and disappeared into translucent spirals of smoke.

After the commotion died down, mourners made a single line down the aisle to pay their last respects. The older Chinese stopped in front of the body, and each bowed three times slowly before moving aside.

"Lindsey, go help pass out the envelopes with coins," her

mother instructed. "And make sure people know they have to spend it right away or it's bad luck."

She did as she was told.

Afterward, a stretch limousine led a circuitous route through various parts of the city as a caravan of family members and other mourners followed behind in their own cars.

"Why are we driving in such a roundabout way?" Lindsey asked.

"We go through Chinatown, then past the On Lok senior home, then past his old house in the Avenues where he used to live," her dad explained. "So his spirit will know the way to come back if he needs to."

When they finally made it out to Colma, it was cold and overcast at the cemetery. Auntie Vivien wore her black-cat-eye sunglasses, and Auntie Shirley chanted "Om" with her arms outstretched and palms facing up. Kevin and Brandon wore the white gloves of pallbearers, and Cammie sat on the grass and played with pale roses she had picked out of the flower arrangements. Stephanie and Mike were not there, since their baby was due any day now, and it was bad luck for them to be around death. Lindsey stood near her parents and Pau Pau, whose face was plain and unreadable.

Lindsey and her cousins had hardly known Uncle Bill. Over the years, they'd seen him only occasionally at family gatherings and had never made any effort to talk to him. They knew nothing of his life. Now everyone seemed spaced out, anxious for the service to end so they could get on with their weekend.

Except for Lindsey. As she stood and watched the

seatbelt-like straps lower the coffin into the rectangular pit, she felt guilty. Why hadn't she stayed and talked more with Uncle Bill that day at On Lok? She remembered the touch of his dry, fragile hand on hers and tried to recall what they'd talked about. She remembered how Uncle Bill had always given her rice candies as a child. He would slip the small squares into her hand and bring his index finger to his lips and say, "Shhhh . . ." When she'd grabbed the candy greedily, he'd always laughed.

Lindsey ruminated about how she had never expected Gung Gung to die either, and now Uncle Bill was gone too, and all their stories were gone with them.

Auntie Shirley distributed single flowers among the group, and everyone took turns throwing stems and fistfuls of dirt onto the casket. They threw in the black wreath that Lindsey had bought, and heaped in an arrangement of white chrysanthemums for good measure.

Finally Vivien said, "Well, I've got an open house in the Marina, see you all later."

They all mumbled appropriately serious good-byes, and everyone dispersed into their respective cars. Pau Pau paired up with Shirley for a ride back home, and as Lindsey and her immediate family climbed into their own vehicle, Kevin and Mr. Owyang talked about the upcoming March Madness basketball games.

In the car, Lindsey's eyes and nose were leaking, and she soon ran out of tissues. Mrs. Owyang fished a small packet of Kleenex from her purse, then tossed it in the backseat to her daughter, hitting her in the forehead by accident.

Never one to divulge much emotion herself, her mom seemed somewhat irritated by Lindsey's inability to suck up her tears. She sighed and looked at her kid in the reflection of the visor mirror. In a scolding manner, she asked, "What's wrong with you, eh?"

Lindsey didn't reply. She dealt with her face, then feigned sleep for the duration of the ride back to the city.

When she bobbed awake, Lindsey found that they were parked in front of the On Lok senior center. Her dad said they were there to retrieve the remainder of Uncle Bill's belongings. They all got out of the car and went inside.

Loitering in the lobby, the fluorescent light panels and smell of rubbing alcohol were so familiar to Lindsey that it seemed only a week ago that she had been here to drop off Uncle Bill's medicine. She got a Coke and some Twizzlers out of the vending machine and stood eating in the hallway until her mom beckoned to her from the doorway of Bill's old room.

"Help carry some things," her mom said, gesturing to a large moving box filled with various items. As Mrs. Owyang talked with the attendant, Lindsey put down her soda and rifled through the box's contents. She found several asthma inhalers, recent copies of *TV Guide*, a few mismatched socks, and a brittle, woven cup made of bamboo, with a tiny, latched lid.

"Hey, Mom, what is this?" she said, holding up the dusty trinket.

Mrs. Owyang waved her hand and frowned. "Not now," she said, speed-reading a stack of paperwork. Kevin and Mr. Owyang came in and hoisted away several heavy boxes of clothes and bedding.

Lindsey chewed on a red licorice rope and held it dangling between her lips as she reached deep into the box and pulled out a cylindrical item wrapped in limp tissue paper. She unraveled it and found a small ream of white silk, damaged with water stains and mildew. An embroidered border of elaborate stitches showed frolicking children with tiger booties and topknot hairstyles. With symmetric uniformity, Chinese calligraphy characters spread eight-deep in a horizontal expanse across the fabric. As Lindsey took in the graphic beauty of black brushtrokes upon the supple silk threads, she gazed at the jumble of pictographs resembling candle wicks, bridges, and rooftops. They all just looked like lines and squiggles to her, but then, unexpectedly, a few characters jumped out with immediate clarity. She suddenly noticed, in the fifth to left row, several words that her brain immediately translated into a series of familiar pictures. She recognized the top of a fisherman's hat. As her eyes scanned downward, she was both surprised and relieved to then find three strokes bisected into the form of a lamppost. She squinted and held her breath when she then discovered two rectangles like double doors, followed by a boxy lantern with a ribbon to each side. She traced her finger over the brushtrokes and looked again to make sure she was seeing correctly. She wasn't hallucinating. It was her Chinese name.

Holding the silk in her hands, she felt the lightness of the fabric as she regarded the full weight of her discovery. This was her family's scroll, and her name was written on it. While this fact was sinking into her thick head, her dad popped back into the room.

"Hurry up," he said. "The game's on TV pretty soon."

Lindsey stood motionless, the scroll still suspended loosely in her grip. Mrs. Owyang took her stack of forms and manila folders out to the car, and Kevin carried out the remaining suitcases.

"Don't be such a snoop," her brother said, cocking his head toward the door. "Let's get out of here."

Lindsey rewrapped the silk in its disintegrating paper cover and placed it in the last cardboard box. She lifted the cumbersome load and waddled out to the car, where they crammed the last of Uncle Bill's possessions into the trunk and then headed home.

One Thousand Saturdays

Several nights after Uncle Bill's funeral, Lindsey drove to Mimi's, desperate for some boy advice. Mr. Madlangbayan answered the door, poking his head out mischievously.

"Oh, hi," Lindsey said, startled. "Is Mimi here?"

He looked to the left and then to the right with a big grin. "Saint Bernard tonight, tastiest meat of all!"

"Dad!" Mimi yelled and swung open the door.

"Ah haha!" he whooped and headed upstairs.

"You're just in time," Mimi said. "How does it look?" She swung her tresses, and Lindsey noticed that at least three full inches were missing from the length.

"What's gotten into you?" she asked as Mimi led her into the bathroom with a basin full of her hair trimmings.

"It's the new me. I'm through with Steve E., and this is the amount of hair I grew when we were together. I've cut it off to prove I'm done with him." She snipped some stray strands, and as they detached from her head, she scooped the cuttings into the trash.

"I forgot to tell you." Mimi whipped around and flashed her eyes at Lindsey. "Monday night at El Rio I met this *Asian* guy named Duan, and he's the most amazing rocker. He looks *exactly* like David Lee Roth!"

Lindsey kicked off her sneakers. "How's that work? Are you kidding?"

"He's got bleached-blond hair and it's all huge like how I love it, and he's so cute. He's in a Van Halen cover band."

"So are you gonna go out with him?"

"I want to, but I've never dated an Asian guy before."

Mimi began to reshuffle some records in her collection. She said, "Usually, Asian guys smoke too much, and I hear they have small dicks."

"Oh, come on, that's just a cliché," Lindsey said. "For instance, not all Chinese girls are bowlegged and flat-chested. Actually, I wish mine were smaller so I could fit into my grandmother's cheongsams."

Lindsey inspected some new high-heeled Candies that sat in a box at the edge of the bed. She slipped her toes into the red leather mules and decided they weren't her style. "Besides," she said, "my brother doesn't smoke, and . . . well, I've never seen his, uh, *wang*, so I can't verify."

Mimi was flipping through her old LPs but looked up excitedly. "Does *wang* mean 'penis' in Chinese?"

"No!" Lindsey yelled, even though she didn't know for sure.

Mimi placed *Diver Down* on the turntable and stood for a second, soaking in the first sublime notes of the "Cathedral" guitar solo.

Lindsey snapped on the television and channel-surfed until she found *Fast Times at Ridgemont High* playing on cable in Spanish. She turned the volume down since they both knew all the dialogue by heart anyway, and while she rifled through various moisturizers and perfumes and tested their fragrances, Mimi experimented with a curling iron, singeing her newly cut layers into thick rolls like two cannoli on each side of her head. Their conversation veered off onto several different tangents, and eventually Lindsey gave her friend the lowdown on her China trip, the funeral, and the toaster.

Mimi sprayed her whole head with Aqua Net, then said, "Oh, God, you need to snag that sweetie if he actually went into the Sanrio store and got that for you."

The next day, after taking a shower and handwashing a couple of bras in the bathroom sink, Lindsey called Michael.

"Hello," he answered after one ring.

"Hi, it's me. I just wanted to say hi."

In the background, she could hear him lower the volume on his stereo.

"I'm glad it's you. How are you?" he asked.

She felt her lower intestines flutter with nerves. "I'm fine. I love my toaster. Thanks a lot."

They talked for a while, exchanging pleasantries, and tried their best to regain the sense of familiarity they once had. He asked if she wanted to go for a drive on Saturday afternoon and she agreed. After she hung up, she screamed into her pillow for no apparent reason, except that she was anxious, had low blood sugar, and perhaps was just a little happy.

He picked her up at about four o'clock in the afternoon, and they headed over the Bay Bridge.

"So, what was China like?" he asked.

She talked about the crowds of bicyclists pouring over the Shanghai streets like a huge swarm of wheeled bees, and described the no-nonsense ways of the city people who clothed their children in bright, bottomless pants for convenient defecation. She mentioned the industrial diesel smells, the choking soot, and the stiff legs that resulted from riding in a tour bus for hours. She told him about the amazing Buddhas carved into the mountainsides, and talked about the breathtaking marble boat at the Summer Palace.

She did not mention the snapshots on the wall of the modest Toisanese dwelling, nor did she describe how she finally extracted Pau Pau's life story by gathering slow drips of information like golden droplets of sap through tough, unyielding bark.

They passed El Cerrito, Hercules, and several other towns. After a while, they exited off Highway 80, and soon there were no billboards advertising Jack in the Box, Marie Callender's, or casinos.

Gazing at the sky mottled with thin, opaque clouds, she said, "Tell me about growing up in Hawaii."

"Hmm . . ." Michael thought for a second. "My parents were sort of bohemian types. They meditated and made bad sculptures, and they dumped me off at my grandmother's grocery store for her to baby-sit me."

Lindsey listened, and Michael went on, "I've been thinking a lot about back then, trying to remember things. She took me to the beach a lot, and I learned to swim when I was pretty small. I vaguely remember, she used to make this sweet, sticky dessert. I think it was only for special occasions. It had beans or something in it, and she'd make me peel this dried fruit . . ."

Lindsey felt a small jolt inside her. "Was it for Chinese New Year?" she asked.

Michael thought for a moment. "I can't really remember," he said. "All I know is that it looked weird, but I really liked it . . ."

She was certain that Michael was talking about *neen-goh*, and she wanted to tell him all about how she loved it too, and how she still made it with her grandmother. But she hesitated for a moment. She had never talked about Chinese food with someone who wasn't in her family. She stared straight ahead and screwed up her courage.

"It's got red beans and rice flour, right?" she said.

Michael furrowed his brow and said, "Yeah, I think so."

"Did it look all fatty and gray, like some kind of melted human brain after an alien abduction?"

He swiveled his head with sudden surprise. "Yeah, it did. How do you know?"

"That's *neen-goh*! It's a special Chinese New Year treat," Lindsey said. She found herself rambling on about the ingredients and how Pau Pau mixed everything together and boiled it. She described the other kinds of *goh* and was surprised by how easy it was to talk about Chinese food after all. Michael listened attentively and interjected enthusiastically when any details triggered his memory. As she mentioned the ingredients of certain dim sum items, he remembered things like the bitter taste of turnip squares, the dusty purple hue of taro, and the bright yellow centers of tiny, glistening custards.

Lindsey couldn't stop talking. She hadn't realized she

had such extensive knowledge of gelatinous dumplings in their various forms, but now she was thrilled to be divulging such details to Michael's receptive ears.

"This is so wild," he said. "It's just like in *Spellbound*, and you're Ingrid Bergman trying to help me with my amnesia." He glanced over at her and smiled. He veered the car slightly to the right to give a wide berth to two great blue herons who were taking flight from a culvert, spreading their capelike wings and straining for a gust of wind to help them get airborne. Lindsey watched the giant birds aloft over the wetlands, their reedy legs tucked beneath their taut, feather-lined bellies. Soon after, Michael turned the car onto a grass field in the Antioch fairgrounds.

"Where are we?" she asked.

He jumped out and opened the passenger side door for her. They walked toward a building usually reserved for auctioning livestock, and they entered a room where an antique glass show was in progress. The large hall was lined with elaborate displays of shimmering aquamarine, amber, and violet pieces that included Mason jars, candlesticks, Pyrex pipettes, and bell-shaped cloches for miniature Victorian greenhouses.

They approached the tables and discovered one-hundred-year-old bottles that had been dug from the trash dumps of California. Some had once contained medicines, sarsaparilla, or elixirs; others had intriguing names embossed into their glass panels: Balm of One Thousand Flowers, Indian Cholagogue, Dr. Kilmer's Kidney Cure, and Ocean Weed Heart Remedy. There was bear's grease, macassar oil, and mustache dye for the men, and complexion powders, vegetable compounds, and magnolia cream for the ladies.

They handled the bottles, drawn in by the beauty of thick, heavy milk glass; iridescent, paper-thin vials of opium powder; hand-turned, crude-necked pints of lemon extracts; and dazzling, lopsided eyewash cups. Onion bulbs of dark-green glass pockmarked with seed bubbles sparked their imaginations, and they touched the glob tops of old rum bottles found off the coast of Florida, discarded, perhaps, by real pirates. They ran their fingers gently across cracked lips which held corks that smelled of licorice and crystallized honey.

"There's a lot of old S.F. stuff here," Michael said. "I figured you'd like it."

Lindsey approached a display and touched a few items. Like brittle bones dug from sandy soil beneath San Francisco's rotted piers, most of the soda and bitters bottles she held were corroded and flaking, but some were as perfect as the day they were first sold. She came to a table of embossed drugstore bottles and found a slope-shouldered vial from 24th Street and Mission, toothpowder from LeFevre's pharmacie Francaise on the old Barbary Coast, and an eye salve from Lucky Baldwin's chemist shop.

Most of the items were high-priced, but Lindsey looked for a souvenir she could afford. They came to a display of Owl Drugstore items, and she chose a pocket-size bottle of clear flint-glass, embossed with a one-winged grandfather owl clutching a mortar and pestle in its talon.

Walking to the car, Michael reached for her hand, and she gladly held his. The sun was already setting, showing its age by its readiness to retire so early in the evening. As they sped out of the Antioch area, rose-gold light backlit the lush, leafy trees while they headed northeast up the Garden Highway. Along the lazy Sacramento River, fishing boats churned through the still waters. Salmon occasionally flipped, creating concentric rings of bubbles that rippled out like pebble-size planets encircling specks of liquid sun.

As they made their way through the overgrowth of berry bushes, Mother Nature's flowering foliage was disheveled and tangled, rustling in the wind like wild curls that had lost their tidy bonnet during an active day of romping through garden paths. Edwardian farmhouses peeked out from behind canary palms and weeping willows, cloaked behind slightly opened shutters. The porches and out-buildings were strewn with shovels and pitchforks that could have been laying there for days, or perhaps years.

"This reminds me of Louisiana, on the river road between New Orleans and Baton Rouge," Michael said.

For this time of year, the region was enjoying an unusual warm spell, and Lindsey watched barefoot teens skipping rocks over the silty water. Smaller children on the opposite bank played in the mud, and some ate potato chips as their parents rinsed out plastic pails and toys.

Michael slowed down as they passed a boarded-up Chinese market. It was painted a faded pink, with its black lettering giving the impression of having been charred onto the wood, beaten down by sun and rain. They continued past the old store, past fruit trees, and rows of planted soil, rich with peat from the decayed vegetation of last autumn's harvest. The landscape suggested that people here still lived off the land, but there was no one in sight.

From her passenger side window, Lindsey saw a metal green sign that said they were passing the town of Locke, but there were no numbers indicating any population.

"Can we stop here?" she asked. "My dad is from this town."

No other cars were on the road, so Michael easily slowed down onto the dirt shoulder as overgrown branches bent against the sideview mirror. They crossed the deserted blacktop and quietly walked toward the main street, which was lined with unpainted shacks that barely supported weary balconies.

As light extinguished itself behind the horizon, the plank sidewalks sank into blue darkness. Cowbells, withered flowers, and abandoned chairs, buckets, and brooms cluttered the doorways of deserted residences. A bar at the end of the block showed the only sign of life, and even the anemic string of lights on the window barely managed to flicker.

They crossed the street to a makeshift museum, where the bluish glow of an overhead bug-zapper provided dim illumination. They wandered slowly in the direction of an old Chinese school, but it was empty as well. Lindsey could sense that the stairs where they stood had once been a lively spot, and she sniffed the air, straining to detect the last whiffs of crayons, or kids' smelly, well-worn sneakers. She placed her ear against the banana-yellow clapboard siding and imagined hearing the last faint notes of an old man's piano lessons from when he was a boy.

She knew that the Owyangs had lived here in this old town that had once been bustling with farmhands, share-croppers, and laborers—all Chinese. She wanted to find the places where her father's family had lived and worked, and

KIM WONG KELTNER

she had a sudden desire to grasp the tattered threads of this town and run her fingers along the fibers that were all but worn away. She quickly promised herself that she'd return to this place with her parents and brother, because now that Pau Pau had shown her that it was possible to mend un-raveled stories, she was determined to gather the loose ends of her dad's history, knit together the discarded pieces of yarn, and fasten up the ripped stitches before any valuable memories slipped through the moth-eaten holes and ne-glected tears.

Alongside her, Michael gazed into the alleys, which served as pass-throughs to the residential street behind the storefronts. He didn't ask questions or make small talk, seeming comfortable enough with her silence.

When they returned to the car, the night was upon them. In the pitch blackness of the unlit country road, Michael turned on the high beams, and they resumed their drive along the levee.

They sat quietly as the rustle of night air blustered through the partially open windows and into their ears. The impact of one bug, then two, three, and four flitted onto the windshield as the polished glass bore the remains of their delicate, silk-threaded wings. In this strange, warm darkness, they both stared straight ahead, intoxicated by the romance of an old California that still existed, right here on this hidden, dreamlike highway.

The remaining heat from the afternoon billowed up the scents of magnolia, burnt alfalfa, and the ripe fruit of old-growth orchards. Yellow-bronze pears shone occasionally in the headlights, and animals on the side of the road periodically darted between the tall thickets, flashing like fast-prancing apparitions. Cottontail rabbits gazed at the car's speeding brightness, and couples parked on the side of the road kindled small orange fires. In the river water just beyond, lanterns attached to bobbing rowboats outlined fishermen's silhouettes. Every beast was in its private wonderland.

A white barn owl opened its wings and clumsily flapped across the road to land on a fencepost. Lindsey had never seen a real one before, and they stopped the car to watch as it surveyed the land in anticipation of its night of hunting. In silence she wondered, Do animals think or dream?

They passed a sign pointing toward Rio Vista. The night played tricks on them as suddenly the river appeared on the left where just a mile or so ago they had followed it on the right. They turned the headlights to where they expected to see water, but they illuminated only fields, scaring up two more caramel-cream owls, which took flight like secret-keepers who had come to study them with curiosity.

She wondered how many owls had left their nests every dusk and explored the star-speckled night, while city occupants passed their evenings under artificial light, swept up only in themselves and dilemmas of their own invention. Along the banks of the still river, she imagined the hundreds of residents past. Had they asked themselves, "Who will love me?" And had they fled toward the city lights, restless for an answer?

Lindsey saw constellations she had not seen since childhood; she had forgotten about Cassiopeia and Andromeda, but they had been here all along, in the bright shadow of Ursa Minor.

The night held heat in its air, like moisture in a buoyant droplet of rainwater that would not burst. With her wits keenly about her, Lindsey felt something in her cells awaken, like protons in an oscillator, or night-blooming jasmine opening its fragile petals. Up until this day, she had kept Michael at arm's length from her heart as if he were a stranger, and now, unconsciously, she decided to trust him. Light rain blew through the windows, and as the temperature outside broke, something inside her dissolved invisibly. Heavy splashes of water trembled on her arm and melted, slowly penetrating her skin.

They crossed the bridge to Isleton, Antioch, and the city beyond. She spotted bright lights in the distance, but she knew even before seeing them that she and Michael were not lost. As they made their way closer into the clusters of civilization, they cruised past cottagelike resorts with merry inhabitants drinking cocktails on the patios. They sped toward home, and she felt strong.

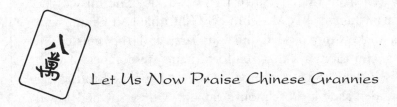

Let Us Now Praise Chinese Grannies

Lindsey made her way to the video store, taking her time in the afternoon to amble through the blocks where North Beach and Chinatown melted into each other. Wanting some exercise, she took a long, scenic route, and approached the intersection at Kearny and Columbus, where the gigantic Marine World mural once overlooked the Financial District. She could still clearly envision the lion's mane that had fanned out like a bright, satsuma-colored sea anemone, and she recalled how the animal's human face with red lipstick had stirred her imagination. Gazing up to the Transamerica Pyramid in the evening light, she remembered the time when someone had strung a massive web of rope across the building, and an enormous Spiderman had hovered over the city streets and traffic below. Now from the foot of Columbus Avenue, she looked up toward the black dragon design embedded in the tiles above the Broadway Tunnel. She hardly ever bothered to look up and see it anymore, but now that she did, she was glad it was still there.

As she crisscrossed through Chinatown and passed Commercial Alley, she thought of all the things that had disappeared from the city since she was a kid. She missed the scary Chinese Wax Museum on California and Grant, with its snakes and pickled mice in jars, and the sinister Fu Manchu dioramas that reinforced the stereotypes of Chinese villains. She wondered what had happened to the big wooden slide in Portsmouth Square, where she and Kevin used to burn their legs on the sunlight-heated metal. And when did they replace the old mustard-colored honeycomb play structure in the Chinese Playground? She used to like hiding in the hexagonal cubes, and she recalled the gravelly sound of the coarse, pebbly sand crunching under her Mary Janes.

Did they still have the yearly carnival at the foot of the Empress of China? She had won a souvenir there once by shooting a stream of water into a plastic clown's mouth. But this was all back when kids could wander aimlessly and safely through San Francisco. Now the city seemed so different. Not only had these physical pieces of Chinatown and San Francisco been demolished but their disappearance left an emotional emptiness in the gaping sinkholes destined for new construction.

As she continued down toward the water, she thought about the fact that San Francisco had been destroyed and rebuilt many times before she ever came along. She knew that Montgomery Street used to be the shoreline, and that the landfill that extended the city into the Bay was packed with the remains of gold-seekers' clipper ships.

Years ago, the construction workers who dug the underground tunnels for BART stumbled onto the burned remains of a mid-19th-century Chinatown. She knew that Chinatown and San Francisco had always been in a constant state of flux and, despite her sentimental tendencies, she probably should take a hint from Pau Pau and not look to the past so much. After all, Pau Pau often said, "Now is the best time in my life," and Lindsey wanted to feel that way, too.

When she returned home, Lindsey's grandmother proclaimed that enough time had passed since the funeral, and the family could now have their dinner to welcome the New Year.

"I want to cook the dinner that Gung Gung used to make," Lindsey said.

"*Dai been lo*, eh?" Pau Pau asked with big eyes. Lindsey nodded vigorously.

"All right. You and me make," Pau Pau said.

They spent all week planning the ingredients for the special hot-pot dinner. Lindsey and Pau Pau made many trips on the bus into Chinatown and purchased fresh clams, mussels, scallops, and tiger prawns. Lindsey sliced thin strips of chicken and made iceberg lettuce leaf cups, and Pau Pau minced black mushrooms and meat for the filling.

Saturday night finally came, and some relatives began to arrive early to help with the preparations.

"Wow, Linds, I can't believe you organized this," Kevin said. He had busted up with Karen and was alone tonight, drinking his Tsingtao beer and watching his female relatives do all the cooking as they tried to work around him.

Kevin jumped out of Vivien's way as she brought a heavy

serving tray into the kitchen. Jerking his bottle of beer to safety, his elbow knocked over the green bowl that held Lindsey's keys.

"*Ai-ya!*" Pau Pau yelled.

Lindsey picked up the porcelain pieces, which had broken cleanly into three parts.

"Throw those away before someone cuts themselves," Auntie Shirley fussed.

"Oh, I can glue it," Lindsey said. "It'll be easy."

She pressed the pieces together and showed how the bowl fit neatly back into its octagonal shape.

"Suit yourself. Seems like too much trouble for that old thing," Auntie Shirley shrugged.

Vivien interrupted, "Daddy used to get liver. Did you get liver, Lindsey?"

"Oh, I'm making gluten liver!" Shirley piped up.

Everyone exploded in excitement when Stephanie and Mike arrived with their baby.

"Armani Huang-Wilkinson has arrived!" Stephanie announced gleefully. As the infant boy stirred, Vivien rushed over and gently lifted him from his mother's arms. He immediately began to wail as she bounced him vigorously.

"Look at my grandson! I think he looks like me, and he's even got an Italian name!"

Stephanie beamed, looking just a pinch less perfect than usual with slightly droopy hair and yellow-gray circles under her eyes. As everyone hugged her and Mike, she explained, "The name was going to be Prada for a girl, but I'm glad he's a boy 'cause 'Armani' is so classic."

Kevin called over as he untangled Cammie from a set of wires behind the television. "Hey, Mike, help me set up the karaoke machine!"

As everyone settled down, Lindsey rinsed the gold mesh ladles they would use to lower the seafood and meats into the bubbling hot broth from the electric chafing dish. After she dried all the utensils, she set the table. She made sure everything was ready for the dinner, and then she slyly looked around to see if the coast was clear before dialing Michael's number. After several rings there was no answer, but on the ninth ring he picked up, and Lindsey felt relieved.

"Hi, it's me," she said. "Do you want to do something after work on Monday?"

"Yeah, what do you have in mind?"

"I could bring over *Dial M for Murder,* and we could watch it at your place."

Just then, Brandon bounded into the kitchen. "Is that a white guy you're talking to?" he yelled in her face. He didn't know he had guessed correctly—he was just teasing her as usual. Lindsey kicked him lightly on the shin.

"Who was that?" Michael asked.

"Oh, that's my cousin Brandon. He's gonna clobber you with his nunchuks."

"Great. I look forward to it."

"So how about the video?"

"Yeah, sounds good," he replied. "I could make red beans and rice. Or maybe I'll fry you up some Spam."

"Maybe we could just have Hello Kitty toast." Lindsey had a spontaneous idea. "Hey, do you want to come over for dinner?" She blurted it out before she had a chance to feel nervous or worried what her family might think. She was feeling peppy and confident.

"Right now?"

"Yeah, sure. My grandmother and I made this big meal, and everybody's over. Just come by."

Michael said he'd be over in fifteen minutes. Lindsey set another place at the table and whistled to herself as she finished rinsing a few extra spoons.

As Mike and Kevin put the finishing touches on the karaoke system, everyone nibbled on cold meat appetizers, pickled baby octopus, and long strips of marinated jellyfish.

When the doorbell rang, Lindsey dried her hands and ran over to the door to let Michael in. She introduced him to her family.

Mr. Owyang looked at Michael and then turned to Stephanie's husband and said, "What's this? I guess all white guys are named Mike now?" He chuckled and went into the kitchen to retrieve Tsingtaos for all the guys, including both Mikes. He was in a good mood because the Giants had some good hitters this year.

Brandon eyed Michael with suspicion but seemed too cowardly to actually say anything insulting. He stood in the corner and glared at him. After everyone at the table introduced themselves, Michael unzipped his jacket, and Brandon's eyes suddenly lit up. Michael was wearing a silkscreened T-shirt that showed Bruce Lee mixing records on a turntable.

Lindsey looked at Michael's shirt, then at him, then over to Brandon. She smiled to herself without saying anything. Looking at her, Michael stood a little confused for a moment, then said, "Oh, whoops. Sorry I didn't dress nicer. I was washing the car when you called, and I just rushed over."

"It's fine," she said. She glanced at Brandon, who stared

at Michael's shirt in awe as he hesitantly handed him a beer. Just then Auntie Shirley swooped over to them and said, "Hey everybody, look out the window! Mother Moon is shining down on us!"

Lindsey, Brandon, and Michael peered out the window and saw a bright crescent in the sky. Auntie Shirley held her arms around the trio for a moment and inhaled deeply. When she pranced away, Brandon shuddered and shook his shoulders as if their aunt had cooties.

Michael squinted at nature's toenail in the sky. With mock disbelief he said, "That's no moon . . . it's a space station."

Brandon's icy demeanor spontaneously melted. Little did Michael know that his single line of dialogue from *Star Wars* had just completely disarmed his potential adversary. An immediate admiration visibly swelled in Brandon's puny chest, and suddenly he transformed into a friendlier person.

"Hey Lindsey, go get us some more beers." He nudged her aside and started to question Michael about the origins of his Bruce Lee T-shirt.

Meanwhile, everyone made their way toward the dining room table and began to find seats.

"Hey Michael, try these spicy noodles," someone said, handing him an appetizer plate jiggling with strands of jellyfish. Pau Pau shuffled over and said, "Nice to see you again." She pinched his cheek with enthusiastic force, and then used tongs to pop a shriveled, gray chicken foot onto his plate. Lindsey got a little nervous, but Michael amiably ate anything anyone put in front of him. Chewing on some sliced beef tongue, he whispered to Lindsey, "I thought you said there'd be weird food. Where is it?" Then much to Pau Pau's delight, he picked up the chicken's foot and started gnawing on it.

Everyone dipped mesh ladles into the boiling water, which held mounds of clear, thin vermicelli noodles. After a few minutes, they lifted out the handles, and the small baskets were filled with cooked shellfish and meats. As they kept dipping, the broth became infused with the seafood flavors, and the leafy greens eventually cooked to a tender texture. Lindsey's chilled lettuce cups held dollops of finely chopped squab, water chestnuts, and mushrooms, which the family devoured hungrily. Shirley's gluten liver remained uneaten.

Lindsey asked, "Mom, did you know that Gung Gung sold his gold watch to save your life?"

Mrs. Owyang elbowed Vivien and said, "Yeah, I'm glad Dad's watchband was gold. If that thing had been a fake QVC number, I wouldn't even be here now." She pursed her lips and jabbed her sister's arm, causing her flashy faux bangles to jangle down her wrist.

As Auntie Shirley rocked Armani in her caftan-draped arms, she welcomed him to Earth and gently asked him how many incarnations he remembered.

Leisurely, everyone finished up their food, and Lindsey left Michael with Kevin and Brandon as they argued about which Bruce movie was the best. Lindsey cleared some plates, and Stephanie followed her into the kitchen.

Rinsing the dishes, Lindsey and Stephanie talked about Chinese superstitions about babies. "When you were pregnant did Pau Pau tell you not to eat orange foods because they'd turn the baby too yellow?" Lindsey asked. She added, "Are you going to shave his head? Pau Pau says they used to do that in the old days to make the hair grow in thicker."

Her cousin looked at her like she was crazy.

"Did I miss your shower?" Lindsey asked.

"No, I only had one with my work girlfriends, but we're trying to pick a date for Armani's red-egg-and-ginger party."

Stephanie looked out through the doorway to make sure someone was watching Armani. Satisfied to see her mother rocking him, she turned her attention back to Lindsey.

"Yeah, it's really important to choose a lucky day for the red-egg-and-ginger party. Like, Pau Pau says the fourteenth is bad because in Chinese, the numbers sound like the words for 'sudden death,' or something like that. She wants the party on the twenty-eighth. She says the number two sounds like 'easy,' and eight is always lucky."

From the next room, Kevin bellowed, "Hey, we're ready!"

Brandon, Mike, and Cammie crowded around the karaoke machine as Kevin programmed the machine with pop songs they had selected. Even Mr. Owyang emerged from the back den to see what all the commotion was about. Meanwhile, Lindsey's mother and aunts squabbled over which local newspapers had the best horoscopes.

Getting up to retrieve her baby, Stephanie walked into the living room as Michael walked into the kitchen to find Lindsey. She was sitting at the table and gluing the porcelain bowl. He helped her hold two of the broken pieces together as she applied the fixative.

"What eighties songs do you have?" Lindsey yelled out. Through the doorway she could see Cammie dancing The Robot.

Several songs later, Lindsey and Michael eventually

joined her family on the sofa. Lindsey noticed Pau Pau standing alone by the window, gazing at the blue fog churning and tumbling through the dark sky. She called over, "Pau Pau, do you want to sing something?"

The elderly woman turned, her face brightening. She smiled at her granddaughter.

"I don't know any these songs!" she protested. She shuffled over and eagerly took the microphone from Kevin.

"Sing anything!" he said.

"Yeah, Mom, sing anything!" Vivien encouraged.

Pau Pau looked up for a moment and tried to think of any song in English she might know. She nodded to herself, slowly recalling the words to one song she had learned long ago. She looked out to the faces of her children and grandchildren, and was pleased to feel their eyes on her.

She began, tentatively at first, and then stronger,

> "It rained all night the day I left
> The weather it was dry
> The sun so hot, I froze to death
> Susanna, don't you cry
> Oh, Susanna, oh don't you cry for me . . ."

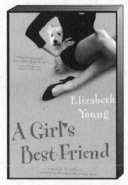